SONS OF THE DEVIL

TRAVIS CROWE is a blue-collar mechanic whose rough childhood was spent in foster care. He struggles with fear of abandonment and has anger issues until a "chance meeting" leads him to his half sister, JENNIFER, and the realization that he has eight siblings...

... all fathered by an '80s cult leader named DAVID DALY.

Travis doesn't know it, but David made a deal with the devil to sacrifice his children. And not only is he still alive, but he is determined to finish the devil's work that he started 25 years ago.

And unbeknownst to Travis, Jennifer is covertly working with David to assemble all of the siblings for sacrifice.

At the end of Book One, Travis learns that his live-in girlfriend, MELISSA, is pregnant and was keeping that information from him. With his relationship in jeopardy and a commitment to help Jennifer unite their family, Book Two begins with Travis at a crossroads...

IMAGE COMICS, INC.

Robert Kirkman – Chief Operating Officer
Erik Larsen – Chief Financial Officer
Todd McFarlane – President
Marc Silvestri – Chief Executive Officer
Jim Valentino – Vice-President

Eric Stephenson – Publisher
Corey Murphy – Director of Sales
Jeff Boison – Director of Publishing Planning & Book Trade Sales
Jeremy Sullivan – Director of Digital Sales
Kat Salazar – Director of PR & Marketing
Branwyn Bigglestone – Controller
Drew Gill – Art Director
Jonathan Chan – Production Manager
Meredith Wallace – Print Manager
Briah Skelly – Publicist
Sasha Head – Sales & Marketing Production Designer
Randy Okamura – Digital Production Designer
David Brothers – Branding Manager
Olivia Ngai – Content Manager
Addison Duke – Production Artist
Vincent Kukua – Production Artist
Tricia Ramos – Production Artist
Jeff Stang – Direct Market Sales Representative
Emilio Bautista – Digital Sales Associate
Leanna Caunter – Accounting Assistant
Chloe Ramos-Peterson – Library Market Sales Representative
IMAGECOMICS.COM

SONS OF THE DEVIL ™
Volume 2
OCTOBER 2016.
FIRST PRINTING. Published by Image Comics, Inc. Office of Publication: 2001 Center Street, Sixth Floor, Berkeley, CA 94704. Copyright © 2016 Brian Buccellato. All Rights Reserved. Contains material originally published in single magazine form as Sons of the Devil #6-10. Sons of the Devil™ and the Sons of the Devil logo, are the copyright and trademarks of Brian Buccellato. The entire contents of this book, all artwork, characters and their likenesses of all characters herein are ©2016 Brian Buccellato. Image Comics® is a trademark of Image Comics, Inc. All Rights Reserved. Any similarities between names, characters, events, persons, and/or institutions in this magazine with persons living or dead or institutions is unintended and is purely coincidental. With the exception of artwork used for review purposes, none of the contents of this book may be reprinted, reproduced or transmitted by any means or in any form without the express written consent of Brian Buccellato. Printed in the USA. For information regarding the CPSIA on this printed material call: 203-595-3636 and provide reference #RICH - 707698. ISBN: 978-1-63215-721-8.
For international rights, please contact: foreignlicensing@imagecomics.com

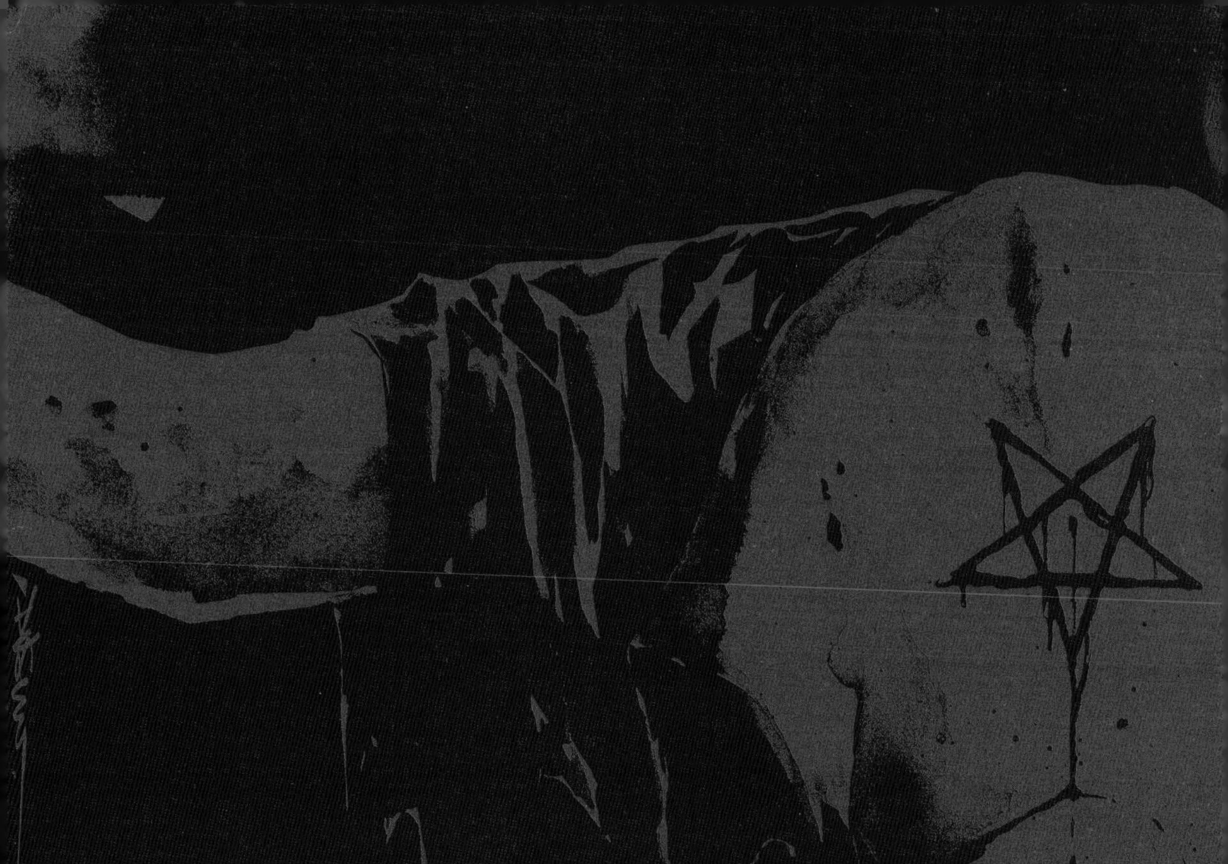

BRIAN BUCCELLATO
STORY

TONI INFANTE
ART

JENNIFER YOUNG
EDITOR

A LARGER WORLD STUDIOS & TROY PETERI
DESIGN & LETTERS

PRODUCED BY OMAR SPAHI &

CREATED BY BRIAN BUCCELLATO

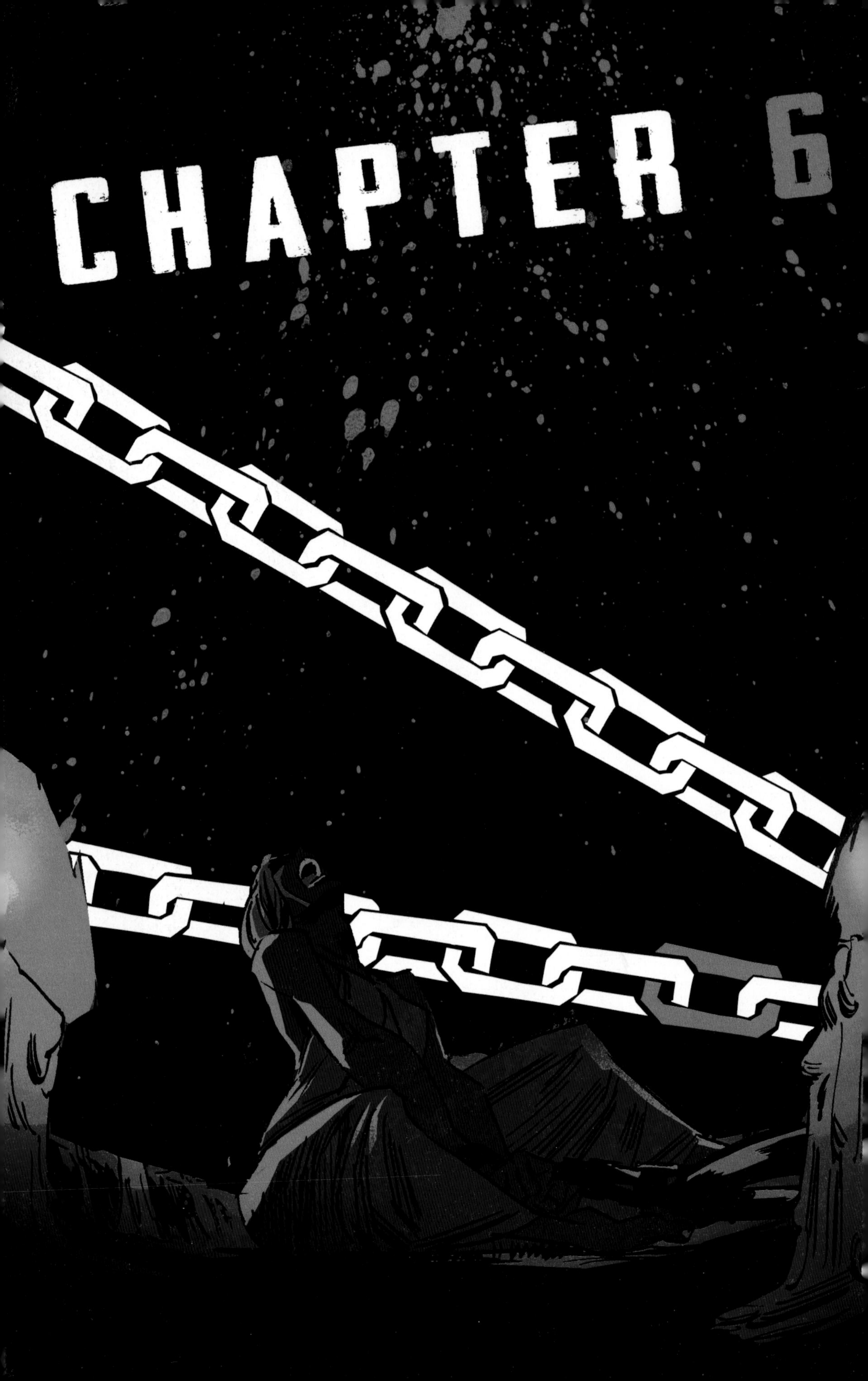
CHAPTER 6

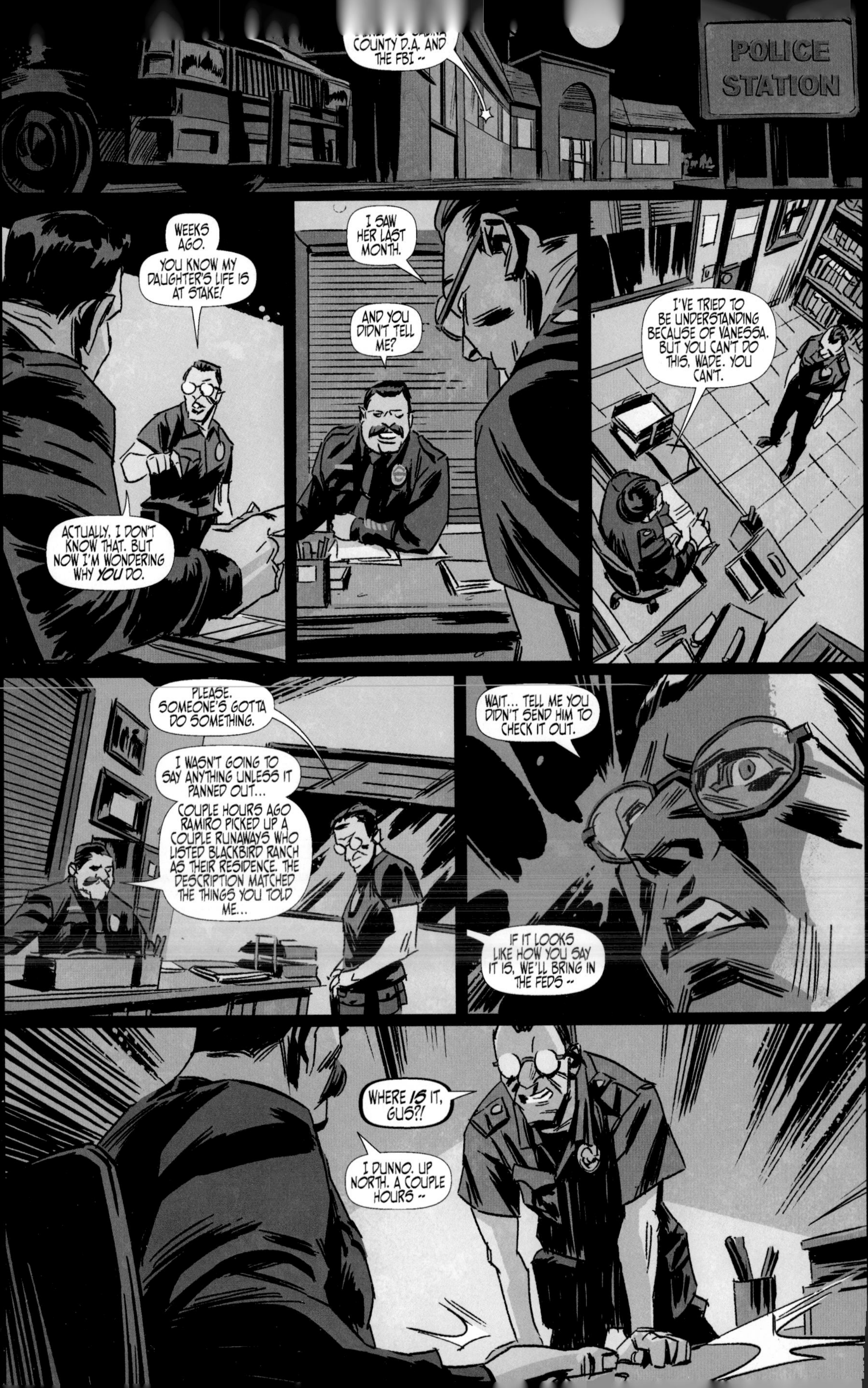
COUNTY D.A. AND THE FBI --
POLICE STATION
WEEKS AGO. YOU KNOW MY DAUGHTER'S LIFE IS AT STAKE!
ACTUALLY, I DON'T KNOW THAT. BUT NOW I'M WONDERING WHY *YOU* DO.
I SAW HER LAST MONTH.
AND YOU DIDN'T TELL ME?
I'VE TRIED TO BE UNDERSTANDING BECAUSE OF VANESSA. BUT YOU CAN'T DO THIS, WADE. YOU CAN'T.
PLEASE. SOMEONE'S GOTTA DO SOMETHING.
I WASN'T GOING TO SAY ANYTHING UNLESS IT PANNED OUT...
COUPLE HOURS AGO RAMIRO PICKED UP A COUPLE RUNAWAYS WHO LISTED BLACKBIRD RANCH AS THEIR RESIDENCE. THE DESCRIPTION MATCHED THE THINGS YOU TOLD ME...
WAIT... TELL ME YOU DIDN'T SEND HIM TO CHECK IT OUT.
IF IT LOOKS LIKE HOW YOU SAY IT IS, WE'LL BRING IN THE FEDS --
WHERE *IS* IT, GUS?!
I DUNNO. UP NORTH. A COUPLE HOURS --

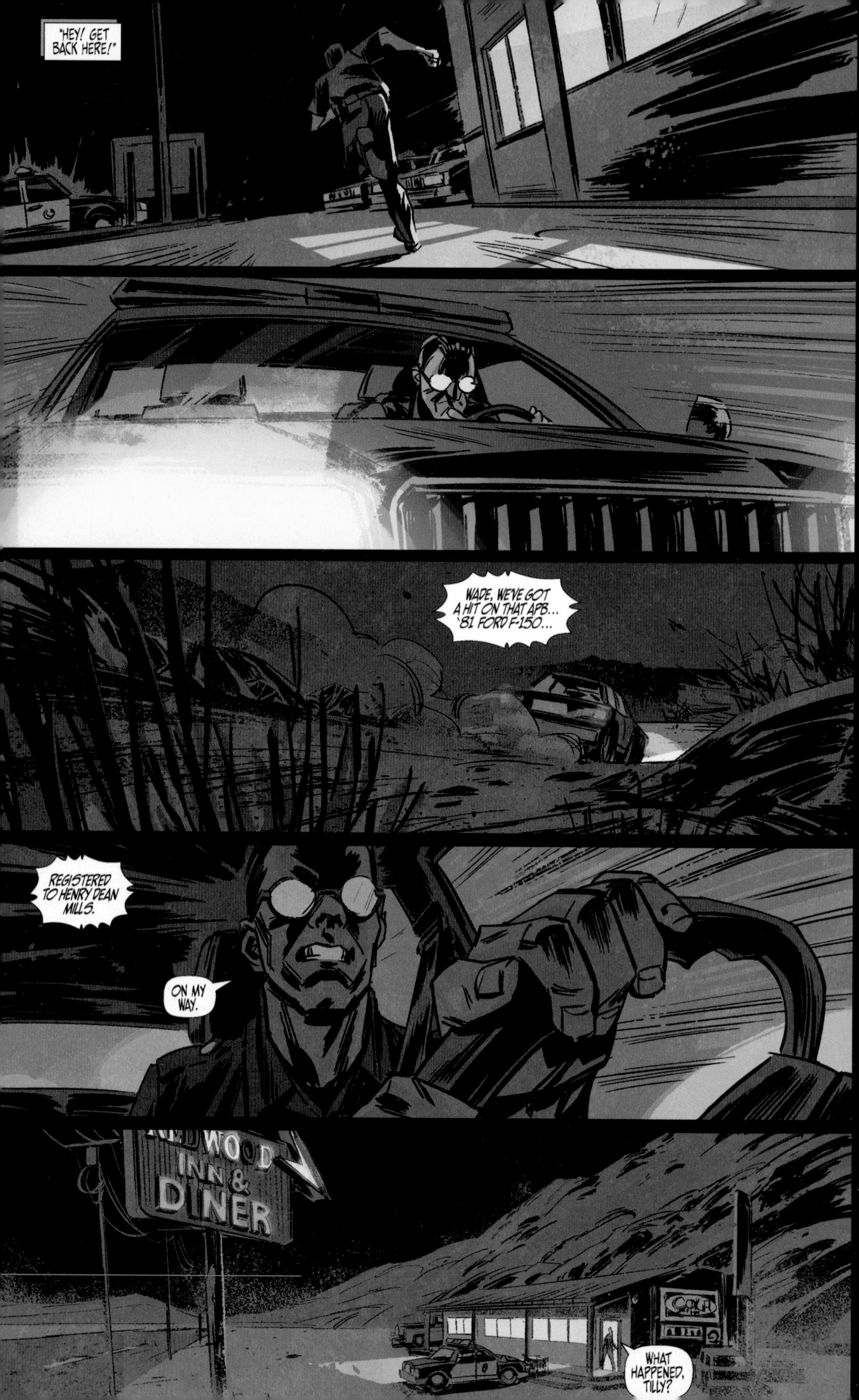
"HEY! GET BACK HERE!"
WADE, WE'VE GOT A HIT ON THAT APB... '81 FORD F-150...
REGISTERED TO HENRY DEAN MILLS.
ON MY WAY.
INN & DINER
WHAT HAPPENED, TILLY?

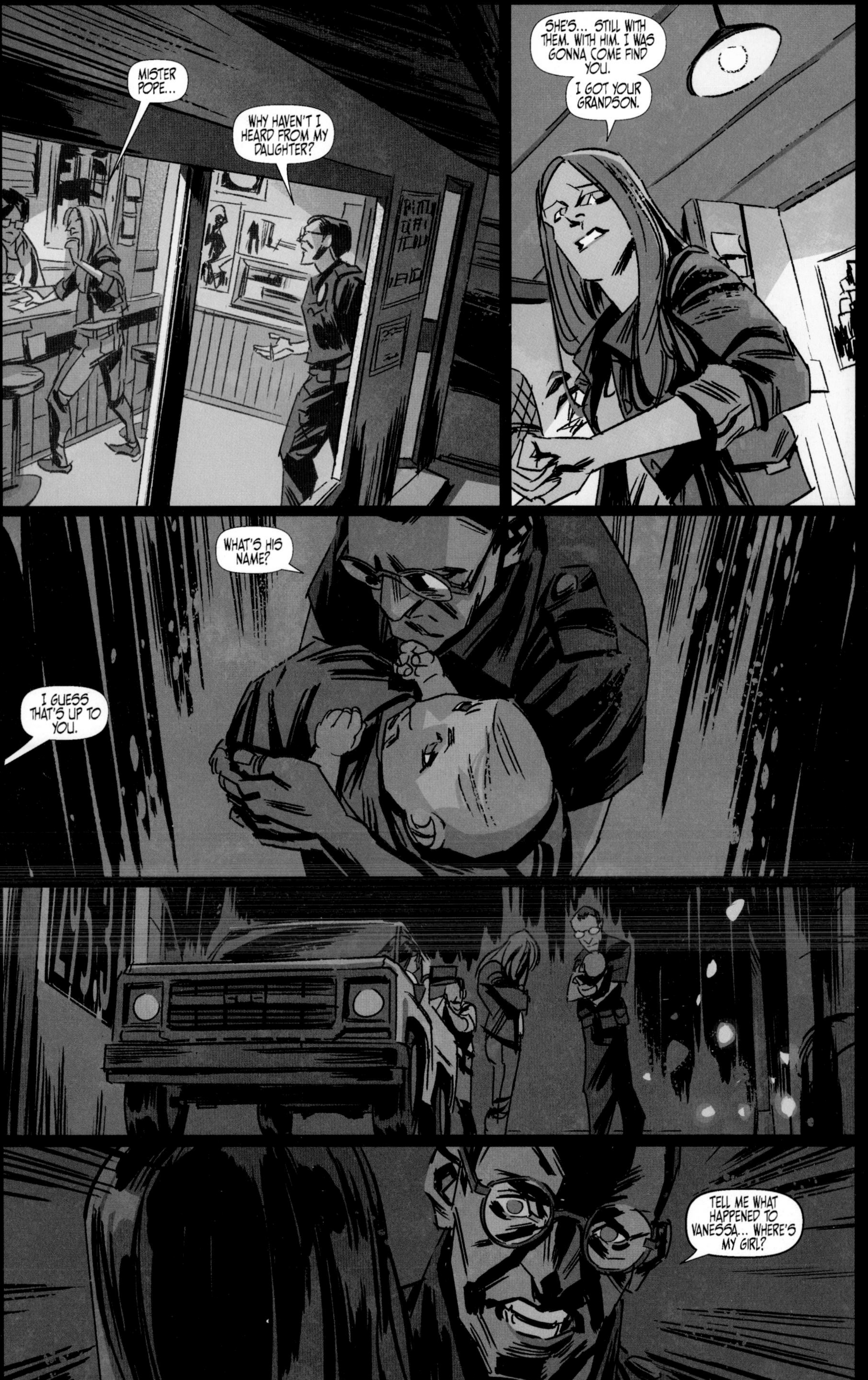
MISTER POPE...
WHY HAVEN'T I HEARD FROM MY DAUGHTER?
SHE'S... STILL WITH THEM. WITH HIM. I WAS GONNA COME FIND YOU.
I GOT YOUR GRANDSON.
WHAT'S HIS NAME?
I GUESS THAT'S UP TO YOU.
TELL ME WHAT HAPPENED TO VANESSA... WHERE'S MY GIRL?

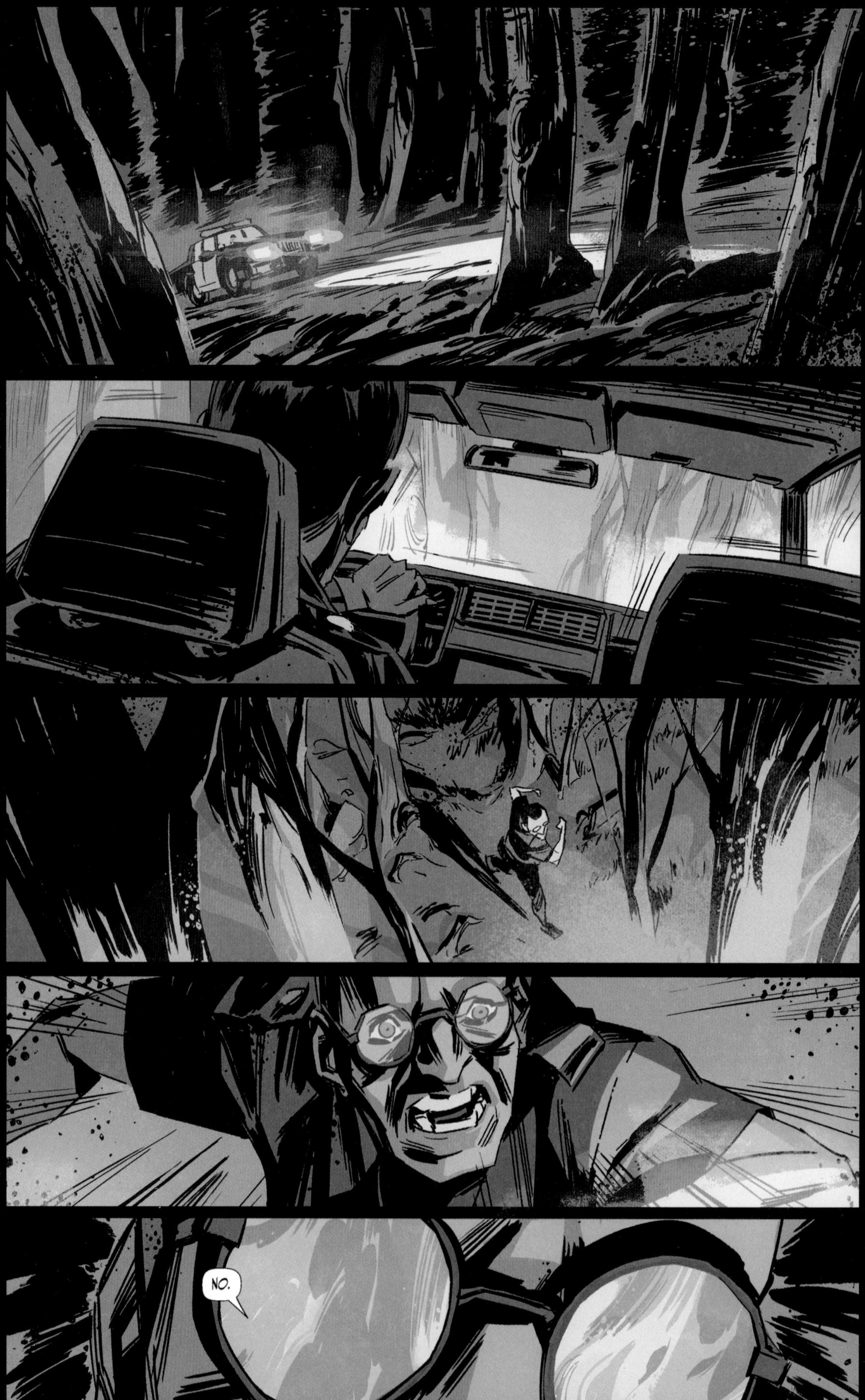
NO.

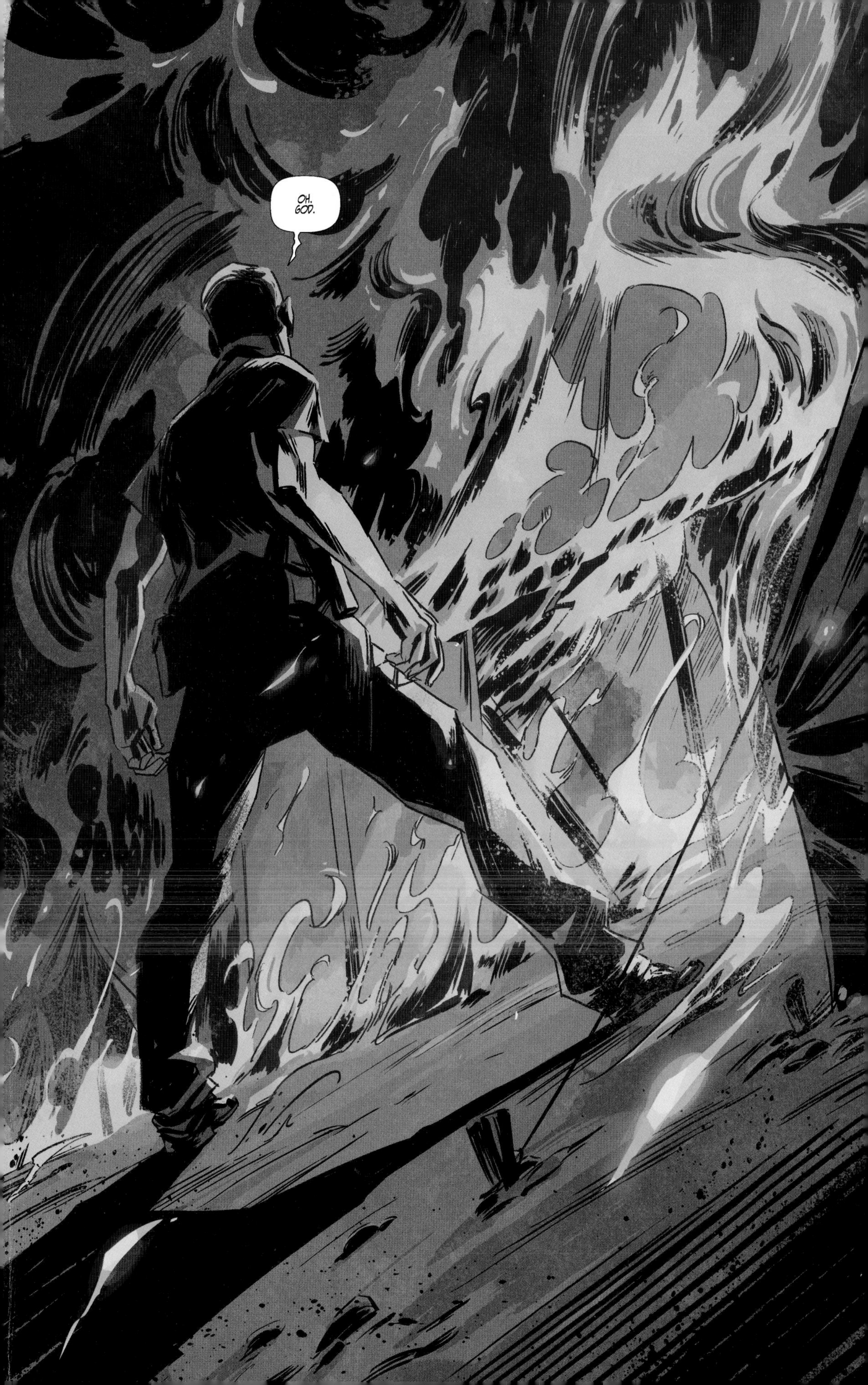
OH. GOD.

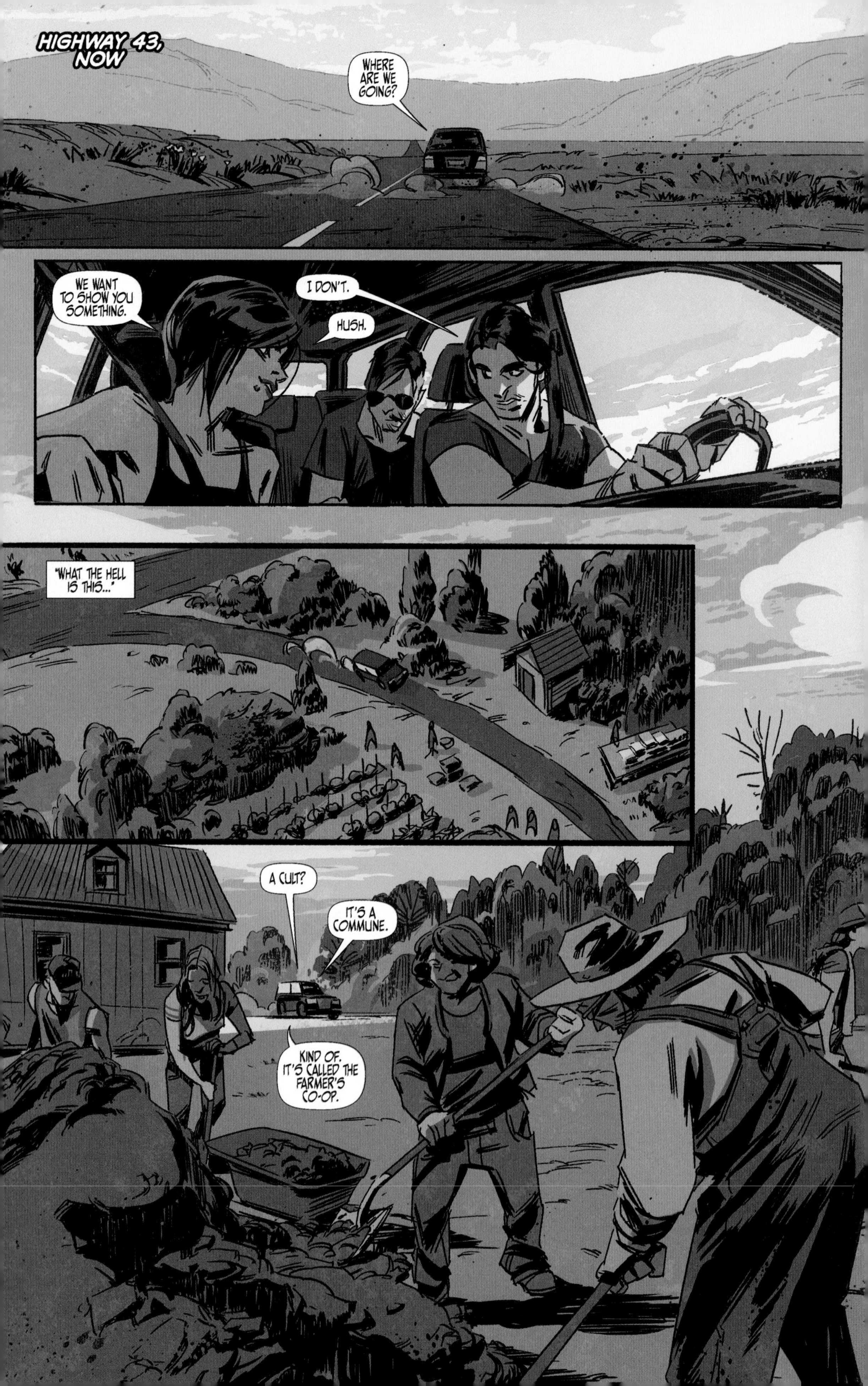
HIGHWAY 43, NOW
WHERE ARE WE GOING?
WE WANT TO SHOW YOU SOMETHING.
I DON'T.
HUSH.
"WHAT THE HELL IS THIS..."
A CULT?
IT'S A COMMUNE.
KIND OF. IT'S CALLED THE FARMER'S CO-OP.

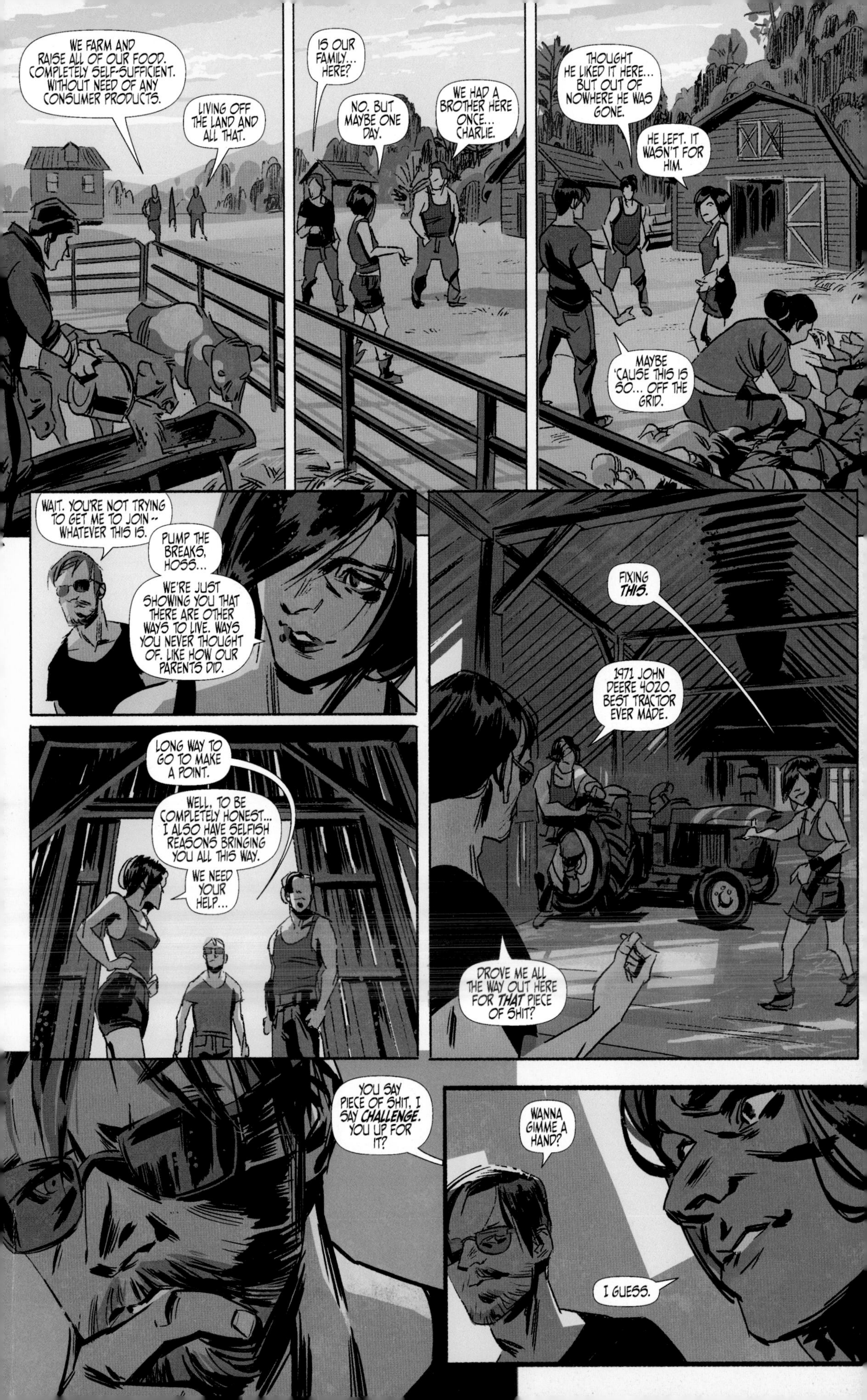
WE FARM AND RAISE ALL OF OUR FOOD. COMPLETELY SELF-SUFFICIENT. WITHOUT NEED OF ANY CONSUMER PRODUCTS.
LIVING OFF THE LAND AND ALL THAT.
IS OUR FAMILY... HERE?
NO. BUT MAYBE ONE DAY.
WE HAD A BROTHER HERE ONCE... CHARLIE.
THOUGHT HE LIKED IT HERE... BUT OUT OF NOWHERE HE WAS GONE.
HE LEFT. IT WASN'T FOR HIM.
MAYBE 'CAUSE THIS IS SO... OFF THE GRID.
WAIT. YOU'RE NOT TRYING TO GET ME TO JOIN -- WHATEVER THIS IS.
PUMP THE BREAKS, HOSS...
WE'RE JUST SHOWING YOU THAT THERE ARE OTHER WAYS TO LIVE. WAYS YOU NEVER THOUGHT OF. LIKE HOW OUR PARENTS DID.
LONG WAY TO GO TO MAKE A POINT.
WELL, TO BE COMPLETELY HONEST... I ALSO HAVE SELFISH REASONS BRINGING YOU ALL THIS WAY.
WE NEED YOUR HELP...
FIXING *THIS*.
1971 JOHN DEERE 4020. BEST TRACTOR EVER MADE.
DROVE ME ALL THE WAY OUT HERE FOR *THAT* PIECE OF SHIT?
YOU SAY PIECE OF SHIT, I SAY *CHALLENGE*. YOU UP FOR IT?
WANNA GIMME A HAND?
I GUESS.

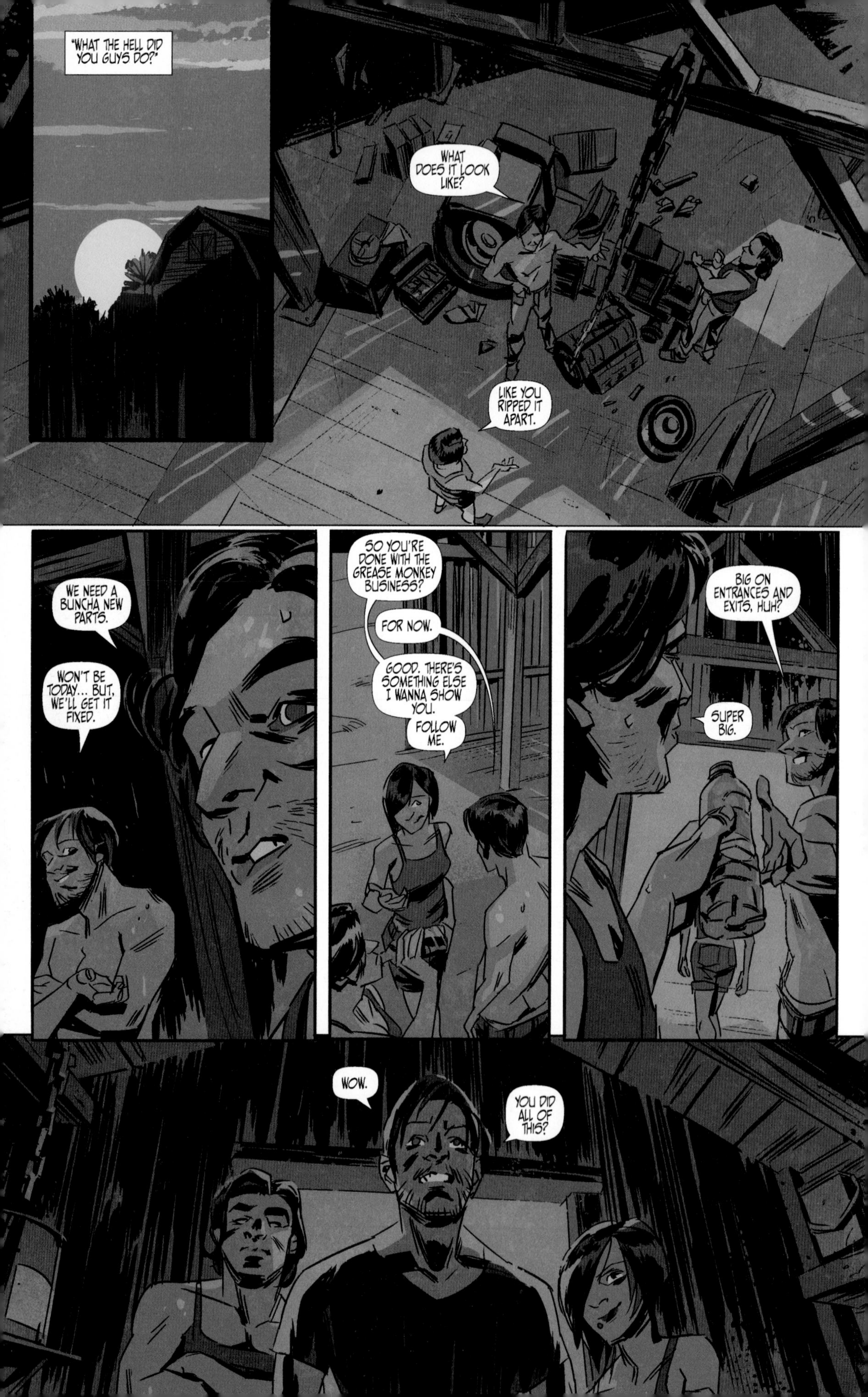
"WHAT THE HELL DID YOU GUYS DO?"
WHAT DOES IT LOOK LIKE?
LIKE YOU RIPPED IT APART.
WE NEED A BUNCHA NEW PARTS.
WON'T BE TODAY... BUT, WE'LL GET IT FIXED.
SO YOU'RE DONE WITH THE GREASE MONKEY BUSINESS?
FOR NOW.
GOOD. THERE'S SOMETHING ELSE I WANNA SHOW YOU.
FOLLOW ME.
BIG ON ENTRANCES AND EXITS, HUH?
SUPER BIG.
WOW.
YOU DID ALL OF THIS?

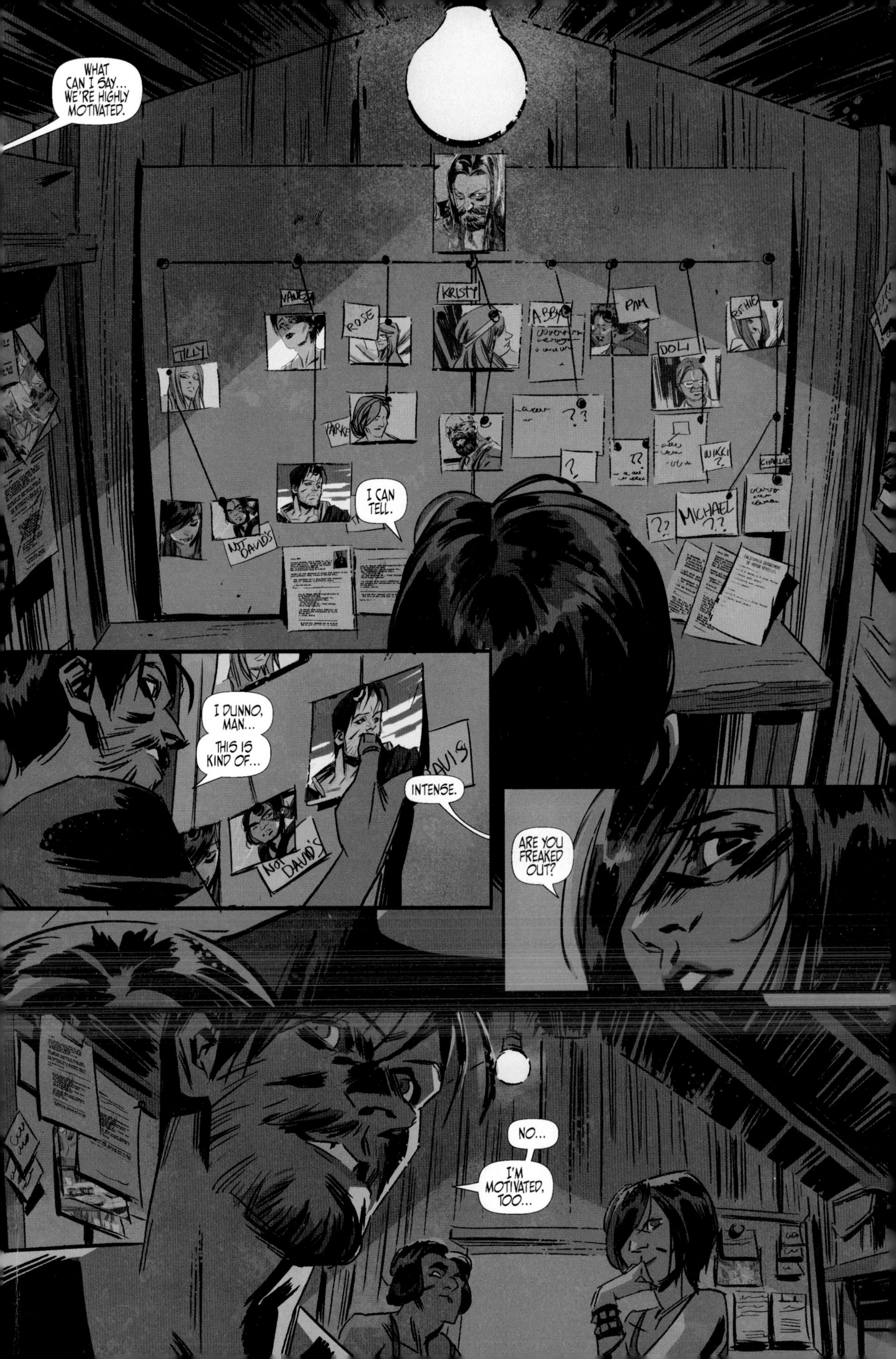
WHAT CAN I SAY... WE'RE HIGHLY MOTIVATED.
TILLY
ROSE
KRISTY
PAM
DOLI
NOT DAVID'S
MICHAEL ??
I CAN TELL.
I DUNNO, MAN...
THIS IS KIND OF...
INTENSE.
ARE YOU FREAKED OUT?
NO...
I'M MOTIVATED, TOO...

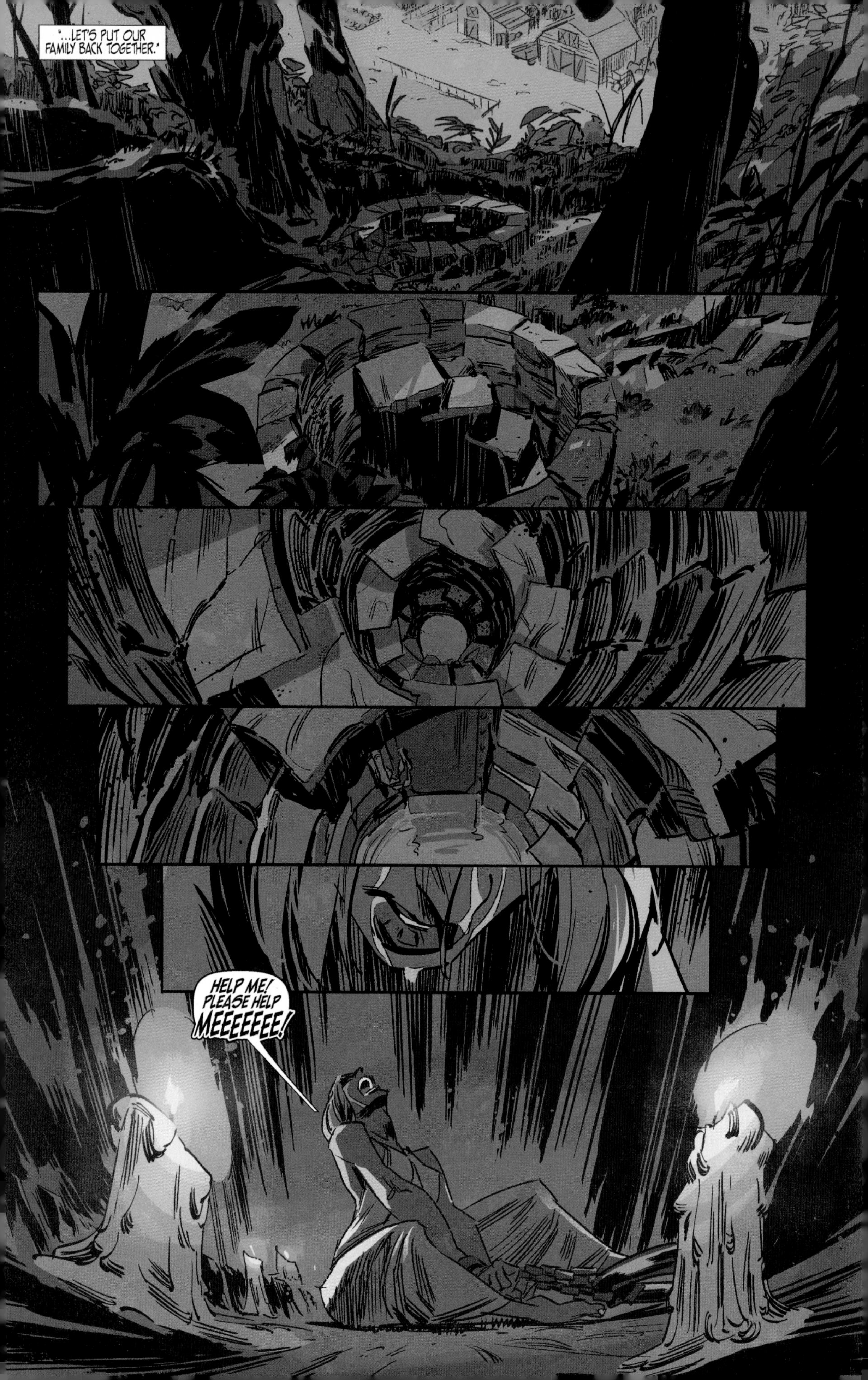
"...LET'S PUT OUR FAMILY BACK TOGETHER."
HELP ME! PLEASE HELP MEEEEEEE!

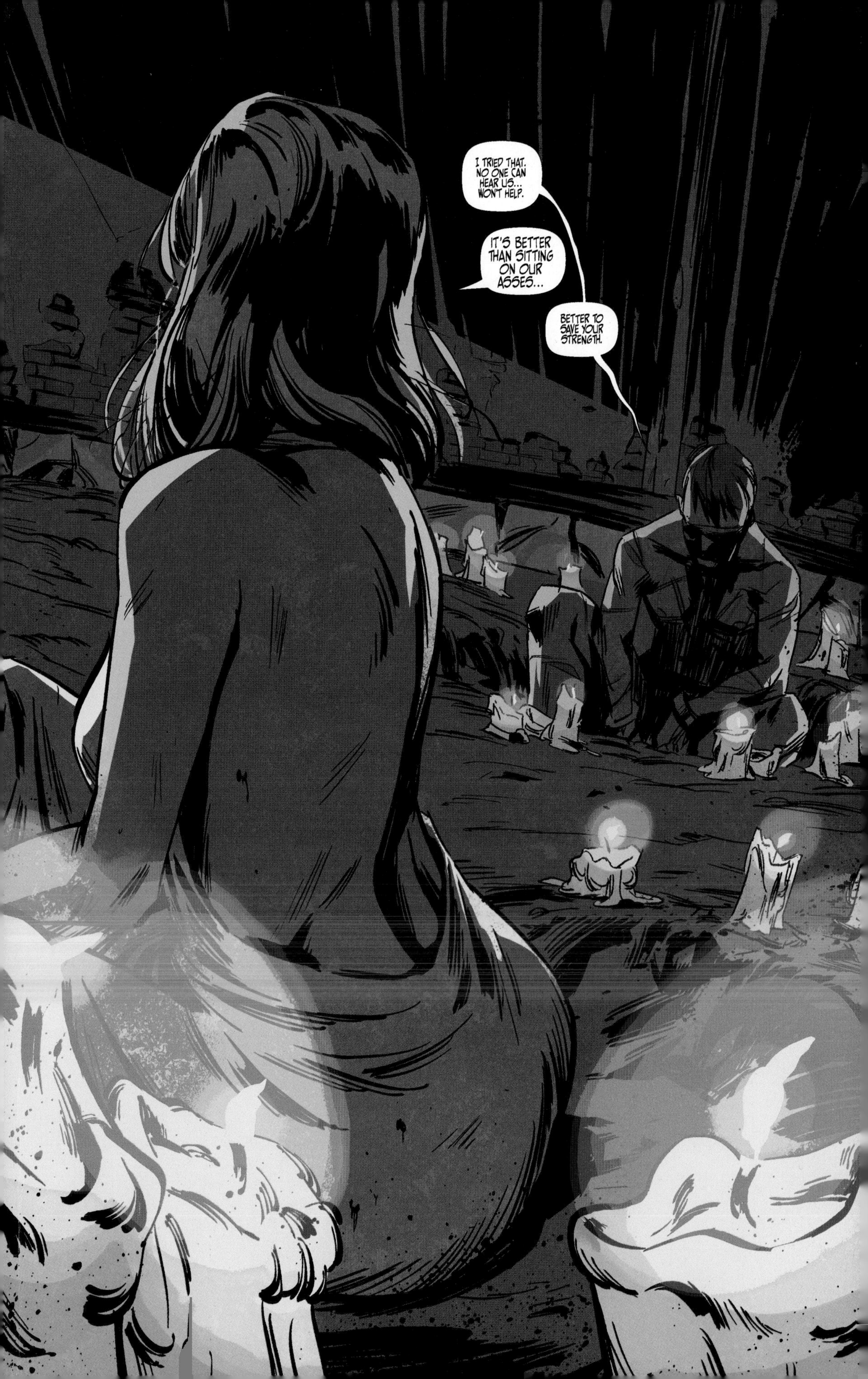
I TRIED THAT. NO ONE CAN HEAR US... WON'T HELP.
IT'S BETTER THAN SITTING ON OUR ASSES...
BETTER TO SAVE YOUR STRENGTH.

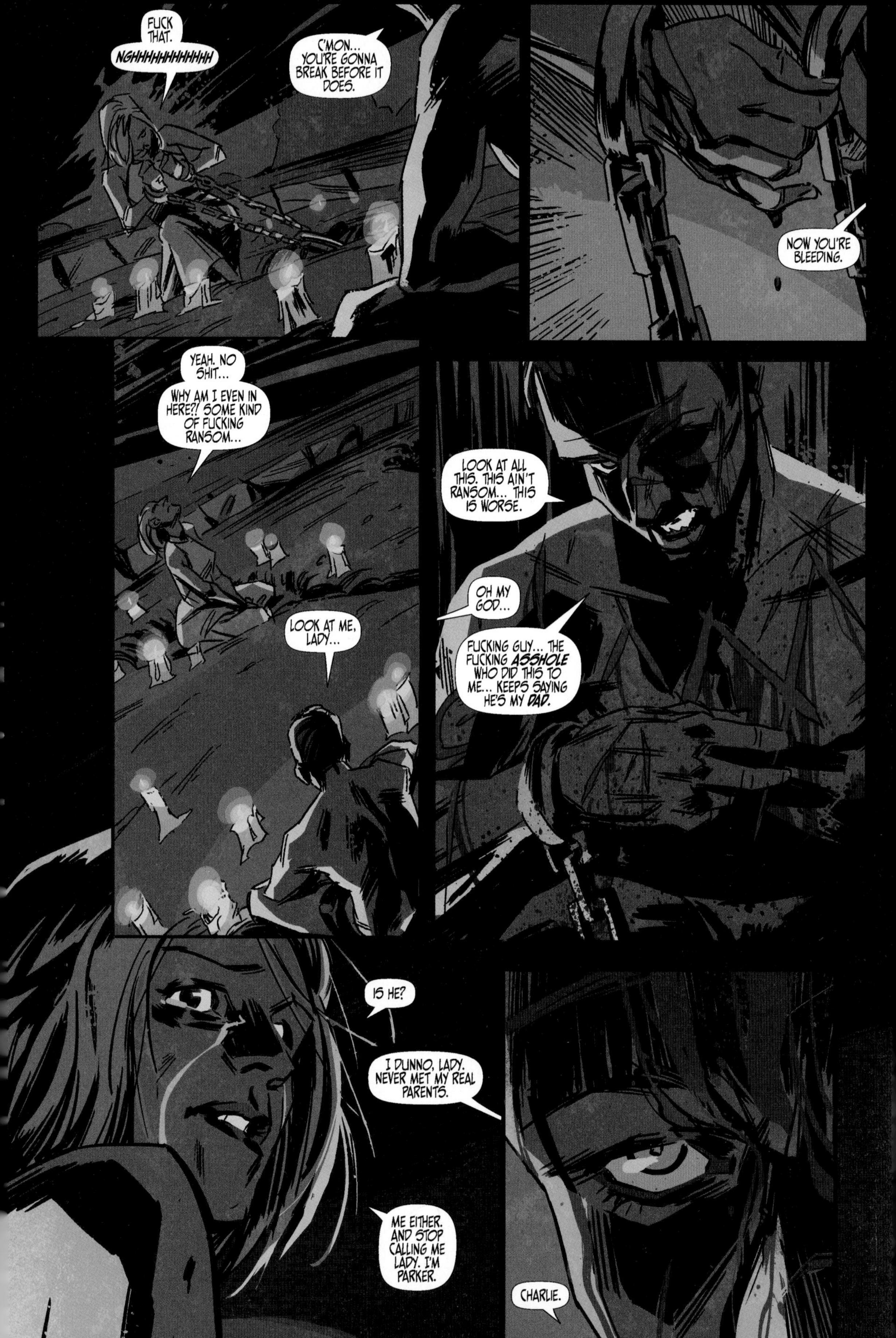
FUCK THAT.
NGHHHHHHHHHHHH
C'MON... YOU'RE GONNA BREAK BEFORE IT DOES.
NOW YOU'RE BLEEDING.
YEAH. NO SHIT...
WHY AM I EVEN IN HERE?! SOME KIND OF FUCKING RANSOM...
LOOK AT ME, LADY...
LOOK AT ALL THIS. THIS AIN'T RANSOM... THIS IS WORSE.
OH MY GOD...
FUCKING GUY... THE FUCKING ASSHOLE WHO DID THIS TO ME... KEEPS SAYING HE'S MY DAD.
IS HE?
I DUNNO, LADY. NEVER MET MY REAL PARENTS.
ME EITHER. AND STOP CALLING ME LADY. I'M PARKER.
CHARLIE.

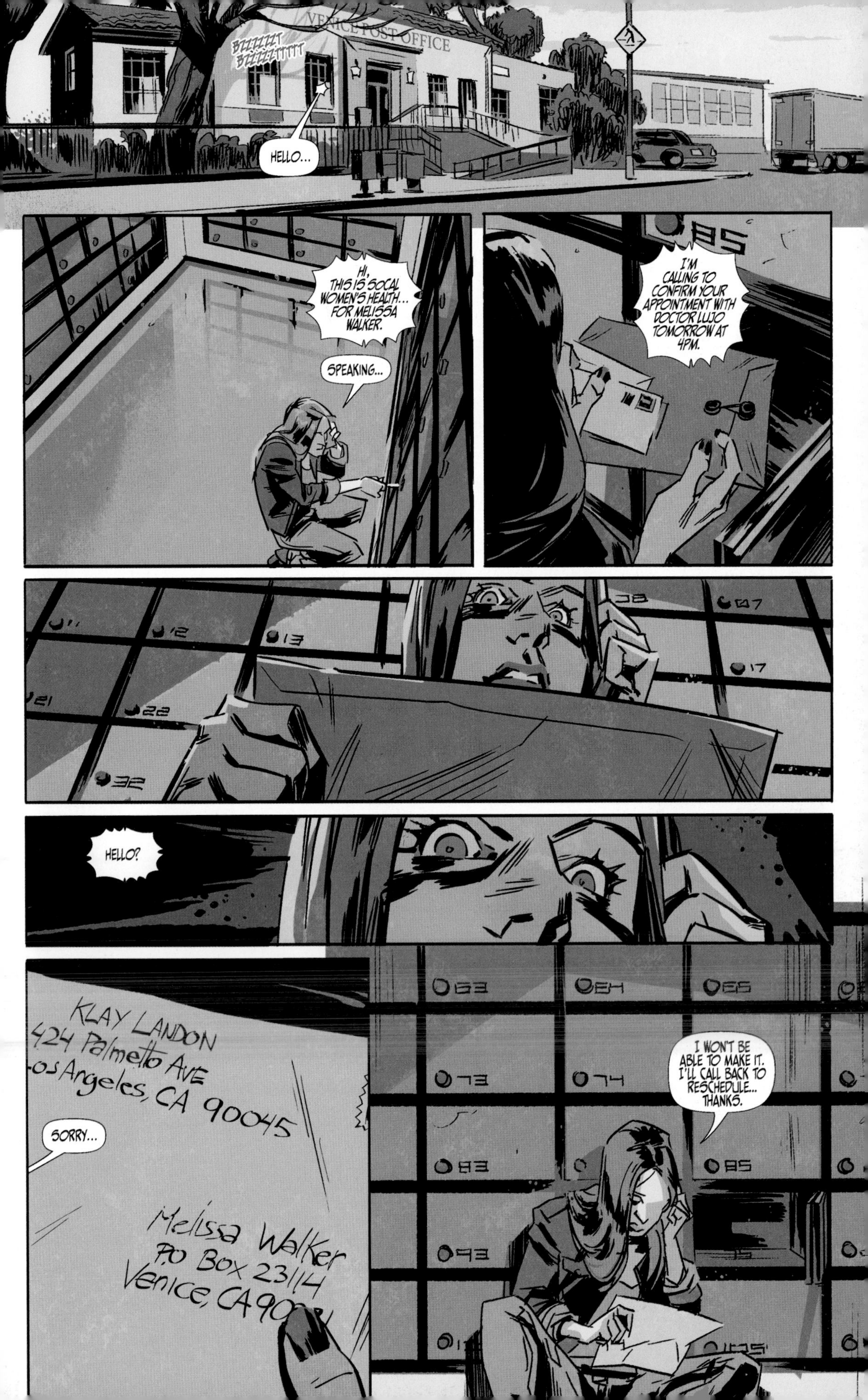
VENICE POST OFFICE
BZZZZZZT BZZZZZTTTTT
HELLO...
HI, THIS IS SOCAL WOMEN'S HEALTH... FOR MELISSA WALKER.
SPEAKING...
I'M CALLING TO CONFIRM YOUR APPOINTMENT WITH DOCTOR LUJO TOMORROW AT 4PM.
HELLO?
KLAY LANDON
424 Palmetto AVE
Los Angeles, CA 90045
SORRY...
Melissa Walker
P.O Box 23114
I WON'T BE ABLE TO MAKE IT. I'LL CALL BACK TO RESCHEDULE... THANKS.

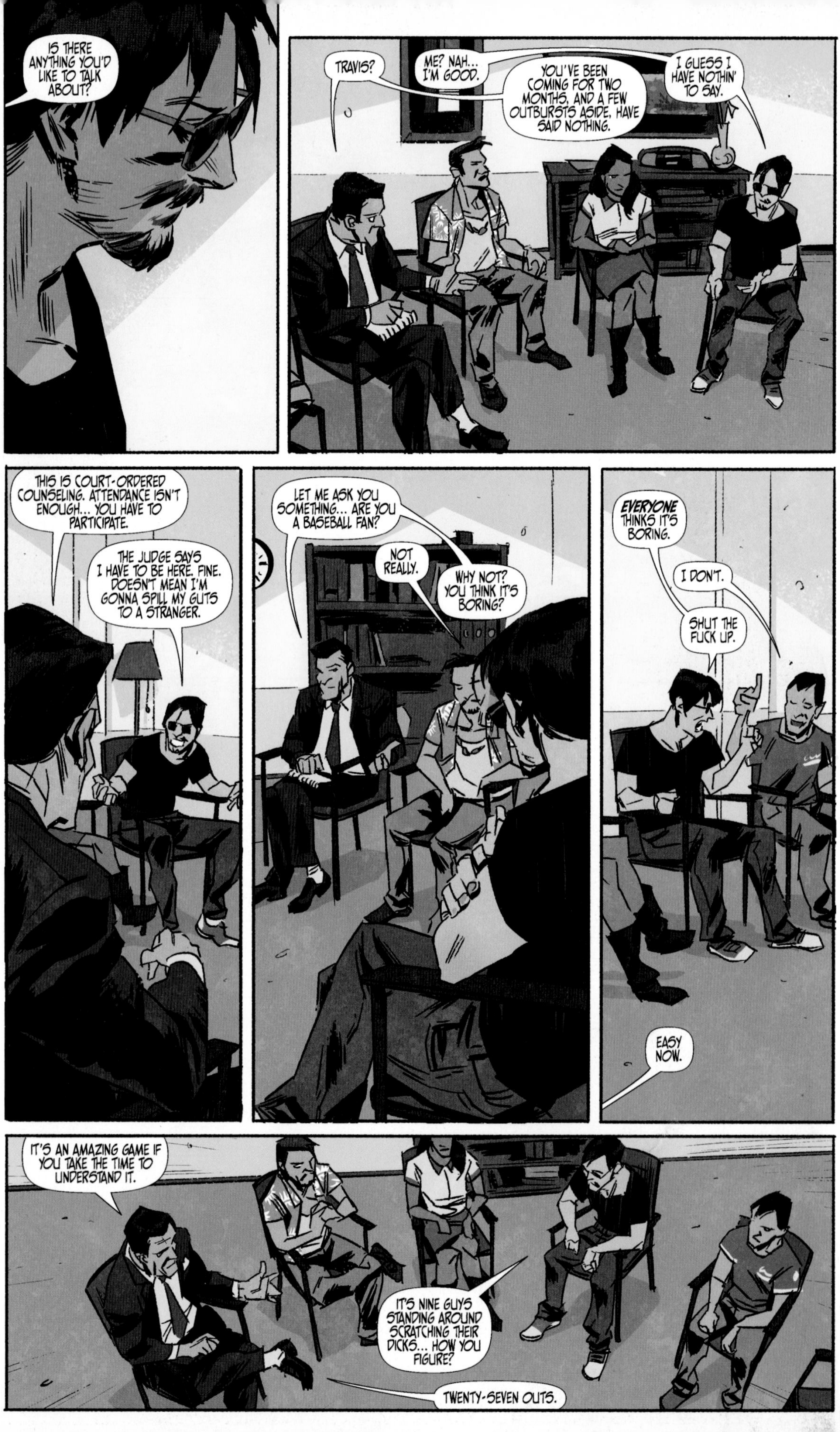
IS THERE ANYTHING YOU'D LIKE TO TALK ABOUT?
TRAVIS?
ME? NAH... I'M GOOD.
YOU'VE BEEN COMING FOR TWO MONTHS, AND A FEW OUTBURSTS ASIDE, HAVE SAID NOTHING.
I GUESS I HAVE NOTHIN' TO SAY.
THIS IS COURT-ORDERED COUNSELING. ATTENDANCE ISN'T ENOUGH... YOU HAVE TO PARTICIPATE.
THE JUDGE SAYS I HAVE TO BE HERE. FINE. DOESN'T MEAN I'M GONNA SPILL MY GUTS TO A STRANGER.
LET ME ASK YOU SOMETHING... ARE YOU A BASEBALL FAN?
NOT REALLY.
WHY NOT? YOU THINK IT'S BORING?
EVERYONE THINKS IT'S BORING.
I DON'T.
SHUT THE FUCK UP.
EASY NOW.
IT'S AN AMAZING GAME IF YOU TAKE THE TIME TO UNDERSTAND IT.
IT'S NINE GUYS STANDING AROUND SCRATCHING THEIR DICKS... HOW YOU FIGURE?
TWENTY-SEVEN OUTS.

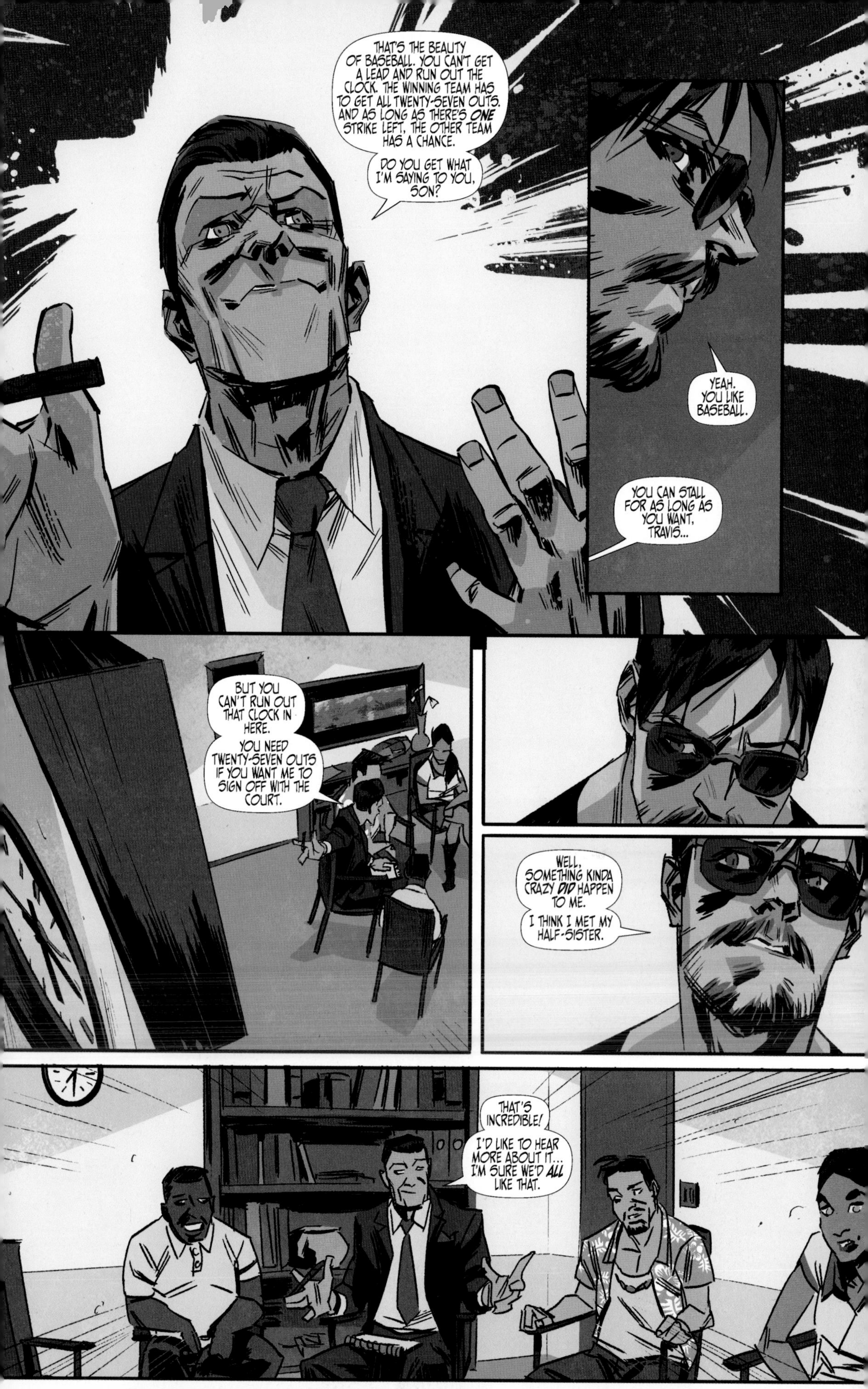
THAT'S THE BEAUTY OF BASEBALL. YOU CAN'T GET A LEAD AND RUN OUT THE CLOCK. THE WINNING TEAM HAS TO GET ALL TWENTY-SEVEN OUTS. AND AS LONG AS THERE'S *ONE* STRIKE LEFT, THE OTHER TEAM HAS A CHANCE.
DO YOU GET WHAT I'M SAYING TO YOU, SON?
YEAH. YOU LIKE BASEBALL.
YOU CAN STALL FOR AS LONG AS YOU WANT, TRAVIS...
BUT YOU CAN'T RUN OUT THAT CLOCK IN HERE.
YOU NEED TWENTY-SEVEN OUTS IF YOU WANT ME TO SIGN OFF WITH THE COURT.
WELL, SOMETHING KINDA CRAZY *DID* HAPPEN TO ME.
I THINK I MET MY HALF-SISTER.
THAT'S INCREDIBLE!
I'D LIKE TO HEAR MORE ABOUT IT... I'M SURE WE'D *ALL* LIKE THAT.

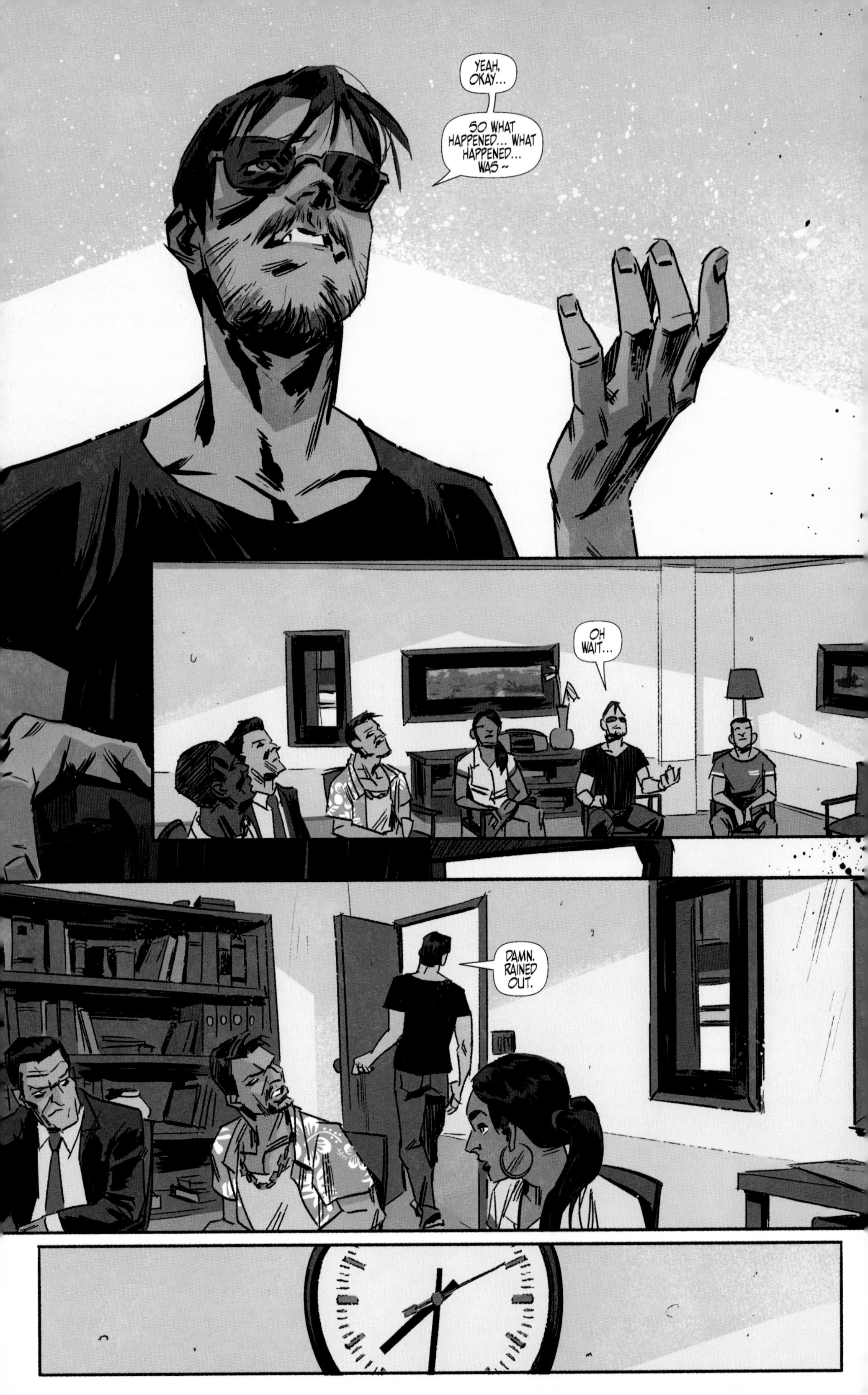
YEAH, OKAY...
SO WHAT HAPPENED... WHAT HAPPENED... WAS --
OH WAIT...
DAMN. RAINED OUT.

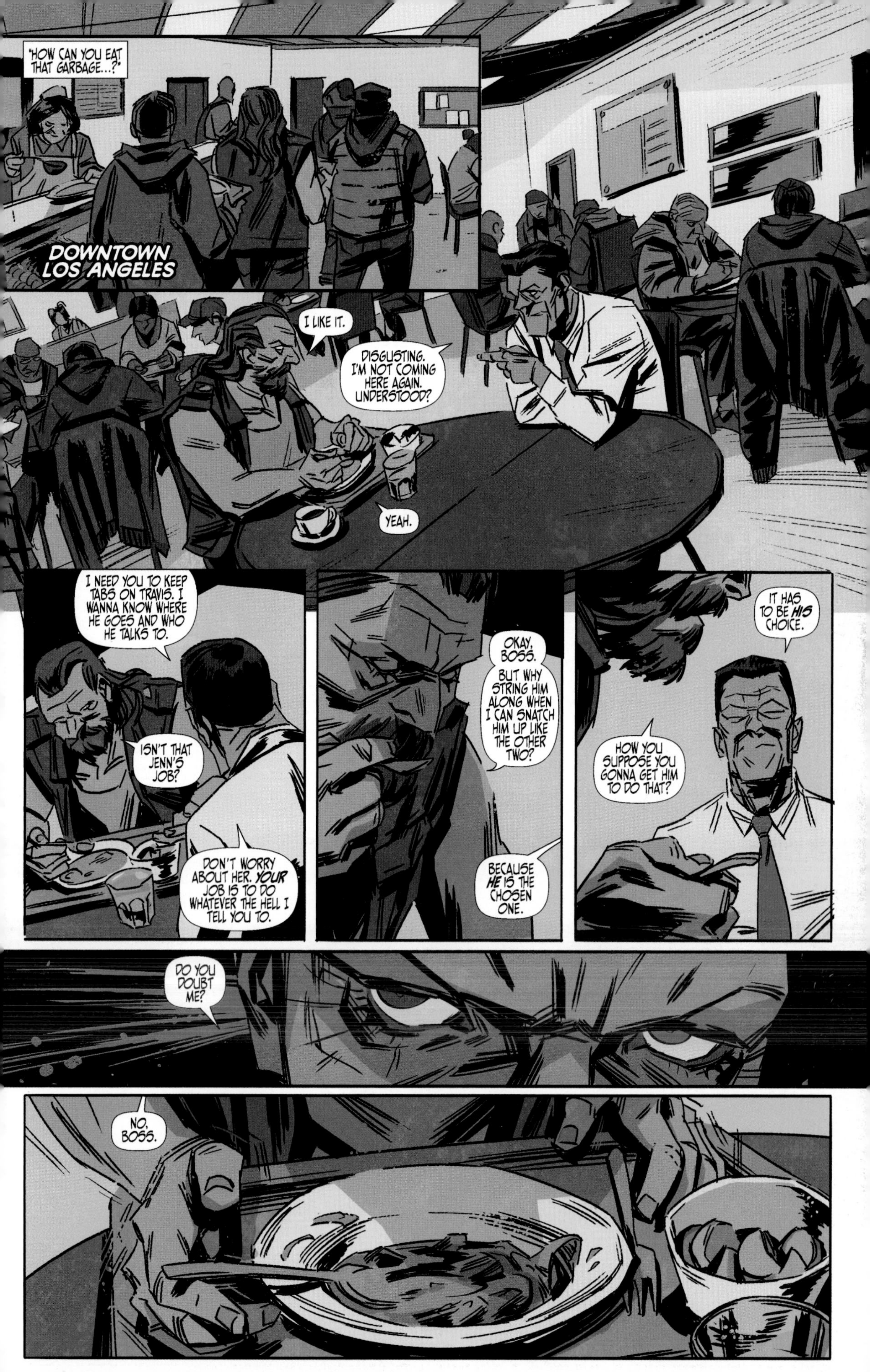
"HOW CAN YOU EAT THAT GARBAGE...?"
DOWNTOWN LOS ANGELES
I LIKE IT.
DISGUSTING. I'M NOT COMING HERE AGAIN. UNDERSTOOD?
YEAH.
I NEED YOU TO KEEP TABS ON TRAVIS. I WANNA KNOW WHERE HE GOES AND WHO HE TALKS TO.
ISN'T THAT JENN'S JOB?
DON'T WORRY ABOUT HER. YOUR JOB IS TO DO WHATEVER THE HELL I TELL YOU TO.
OKAY, BOSS.
BUT WHY STRING HIM ALONG WHEN I CAN SNATCH HIM UP LIKE THE OTHER TWO?
BECAUSE HE IS THE CHOSEN ONE.
IT HAS TO BE HIS CHOICE.
HOW YOU SUPPOSE YOU GONNA GET HIM TO DO THAT?
DO YOU DOUBT ME?
NO, BOSS.

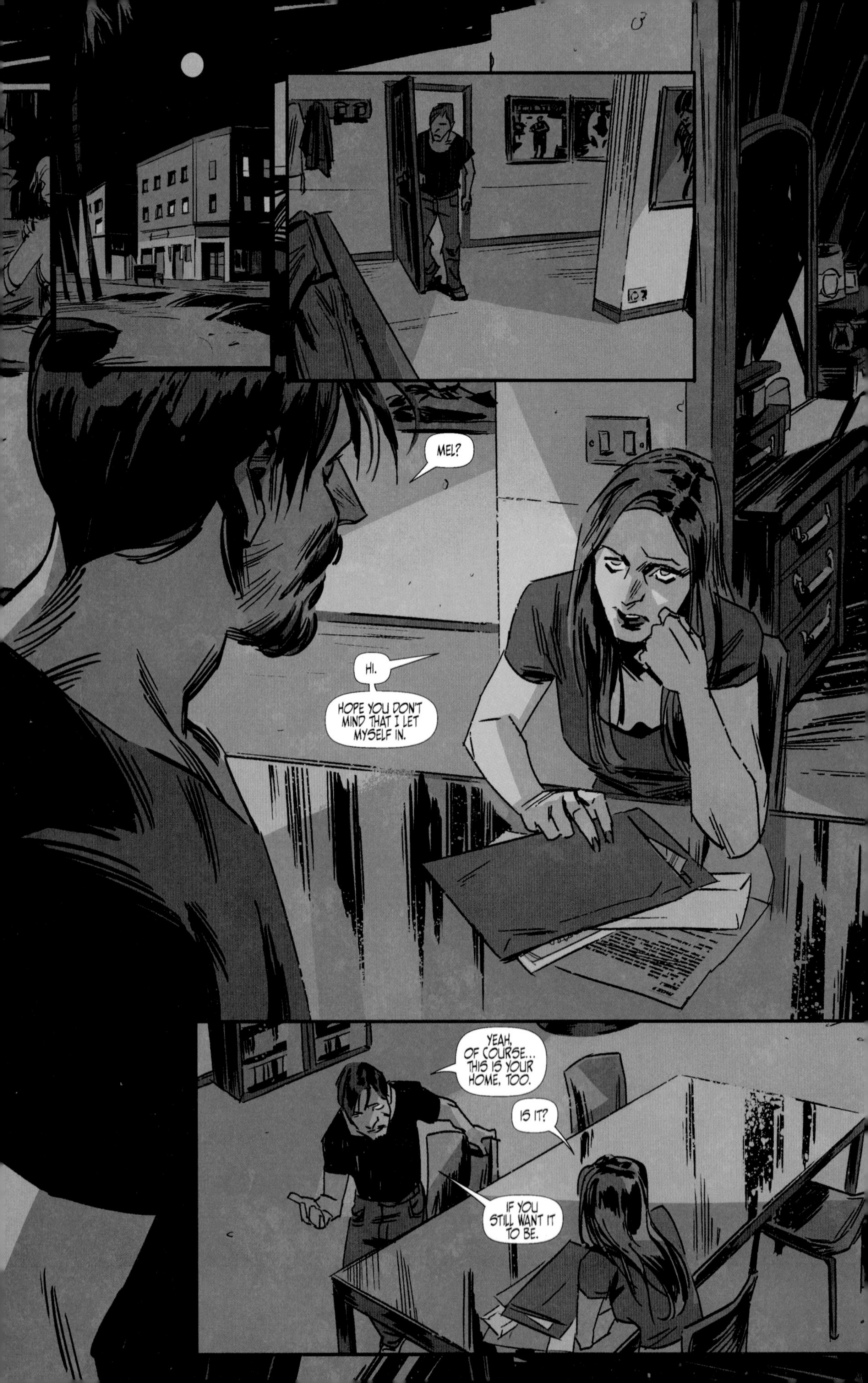
MEL?
HI.
HOPE YOU DON'T MIND THAT I LET MYSELF IN.
YEAH, OF COURSE... THIS IS YOUR HOME, TOO.
IS IT?
IF YOU STILL WANT IT TO BE.

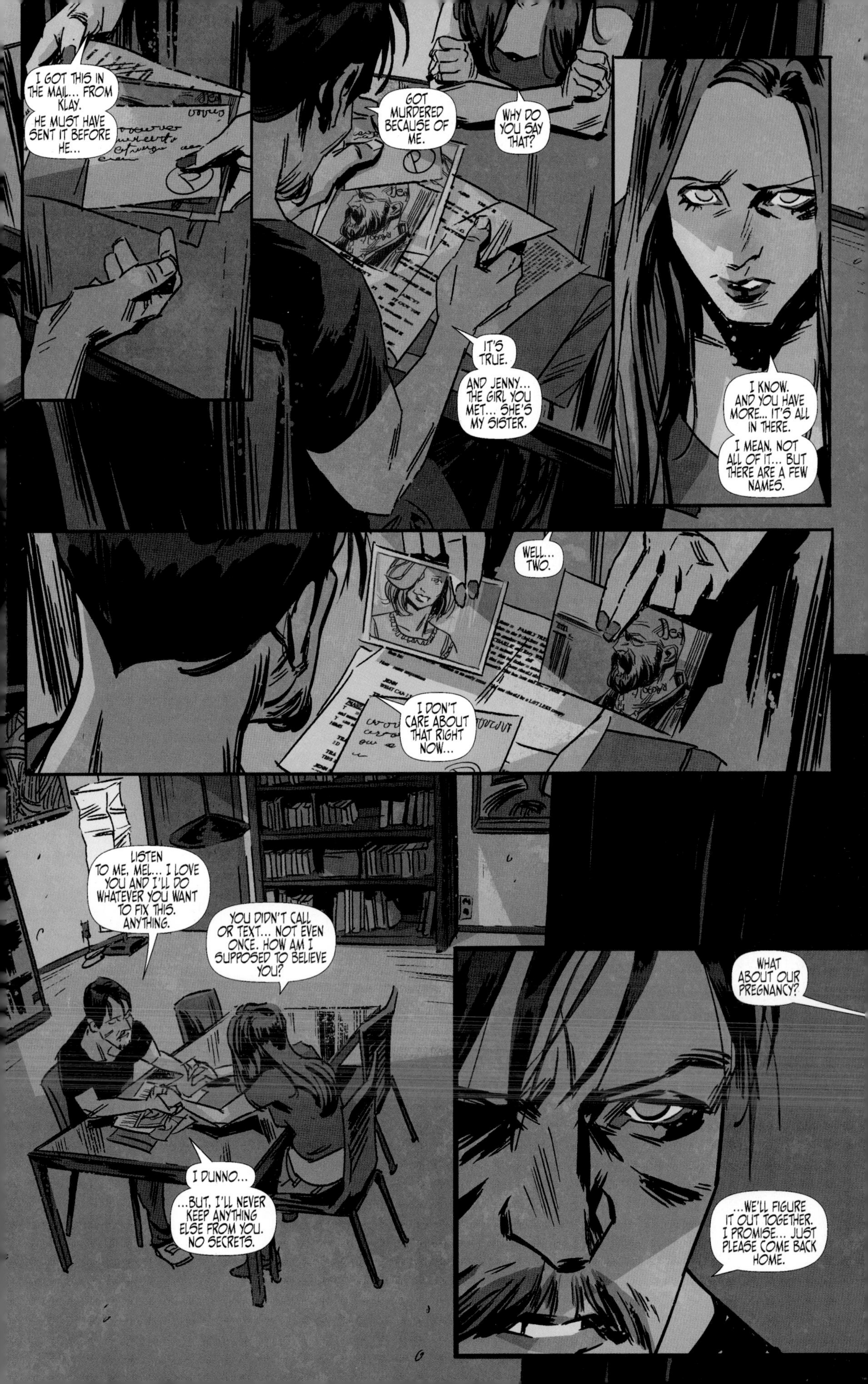

I GOT THIS IN THE MAIL... FROM KLAY.
HE MUST HAVE SENT IT BEFORE HE...
GOT MURDERED BECAUSE OF ME.
WHY DO YOU SAY THAT?
IT'S TRUE.
AND JENNY... THE GIRL YOU MET... SHE'S MY SISTER.
I KNOW. AND YOU HAVE MORE... IT'S ALL IN THERE.
I MEAN, NOT ALL OF IT... BUT THERE ARE A FEW NAMES.
WELL... TWO.
I DON'T CARE ABOUT THAT RIGHT NOW...
LISTEN TO ME, MEL... I LOVE YOU AND I'LL DO WHATEVER YOU WANT TO FIX THIS. ANYTHING.
YOU DIDN'T CALL OR TEXT... NOT EVEN ONCE. HOW AM I SUPPOSED TO BELIEVE YOU?
I DUNNO...
...BUT, I'LL NEVER KEEP ANYTHING ELSE FROM YOU. NO SECRETS.
WHAT ABOUT OUR PREGNANCY?
...WE'LL FIGURE IT OUT TOGETHER. I PROMISE... JUST PLEASE COME BACK HOME.

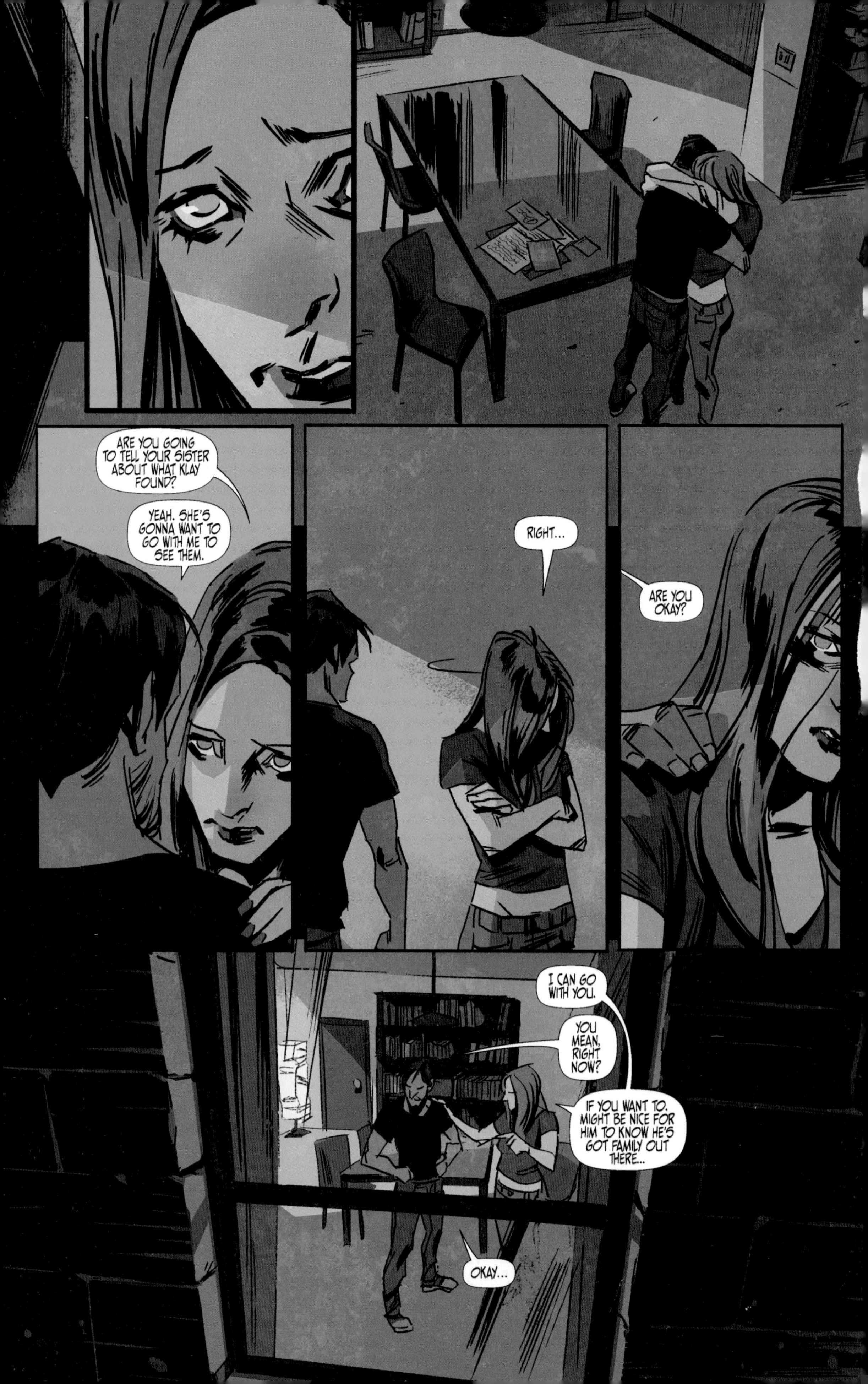
ARE YOU GOING TO TELL YOUR SISTER ABOUT WHAT KLAY FOUND?
YEAH. SHE'S GONNA WANT TO GO WITH ME TO SEE THEM.
RIGHT...
ARE YOU OKAY?
I CAN GO WITH YOU.
YOU MEAN, RIGHT NOW?
IF YOU WANT TO. MIGHT BE NICE FOR HIM TO KNOW HE'S GOT FAMILY OUT THERE...
OKAY...

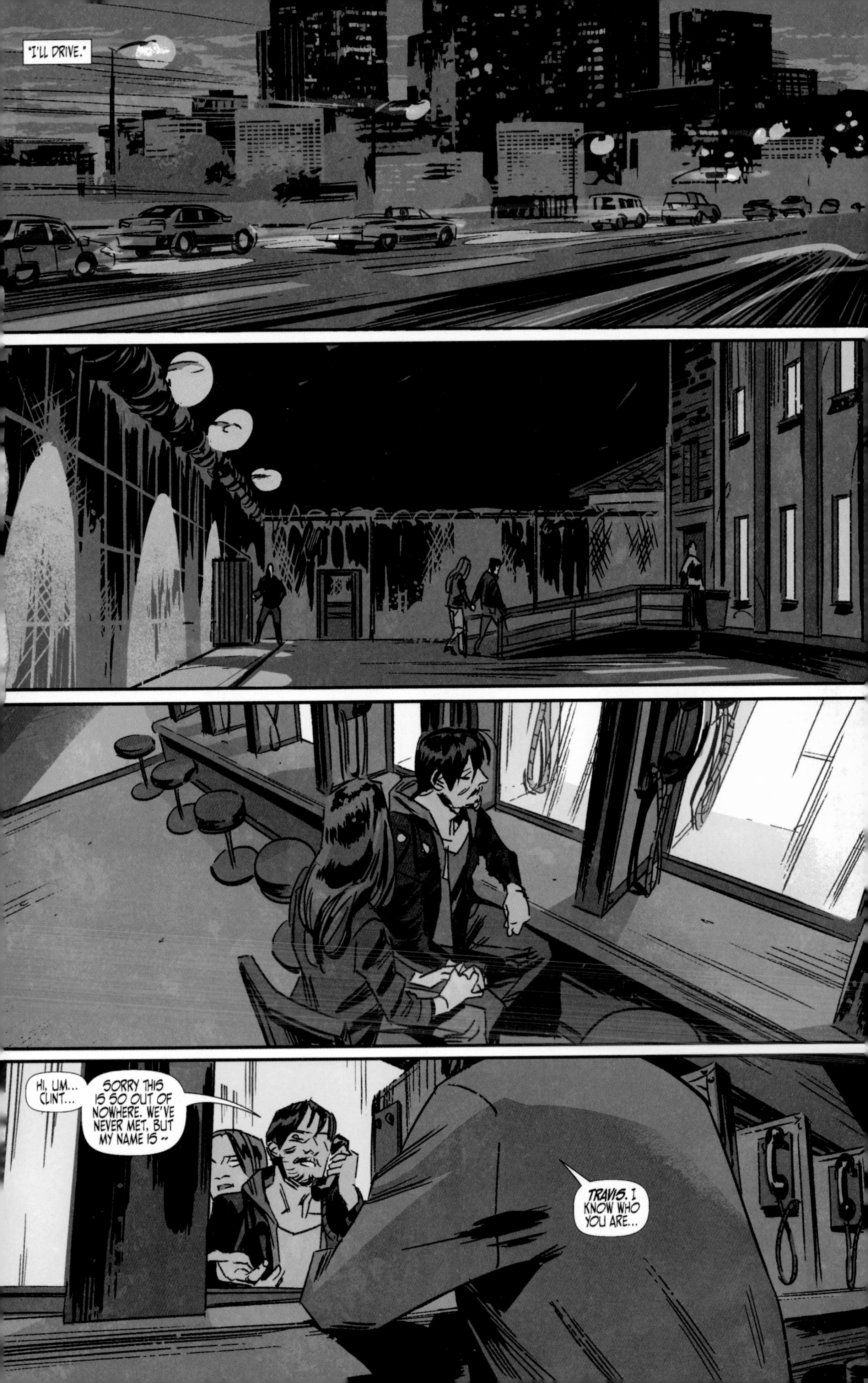
"I'LL DRIVE."
HI, UM... CLINT...
SORRY THIS IS SO OUT OF NOWHERE. WE'VE NEVER MET, BUT MY NAME IS --
TRAVIS. I KNOW WHO YOU ARE...

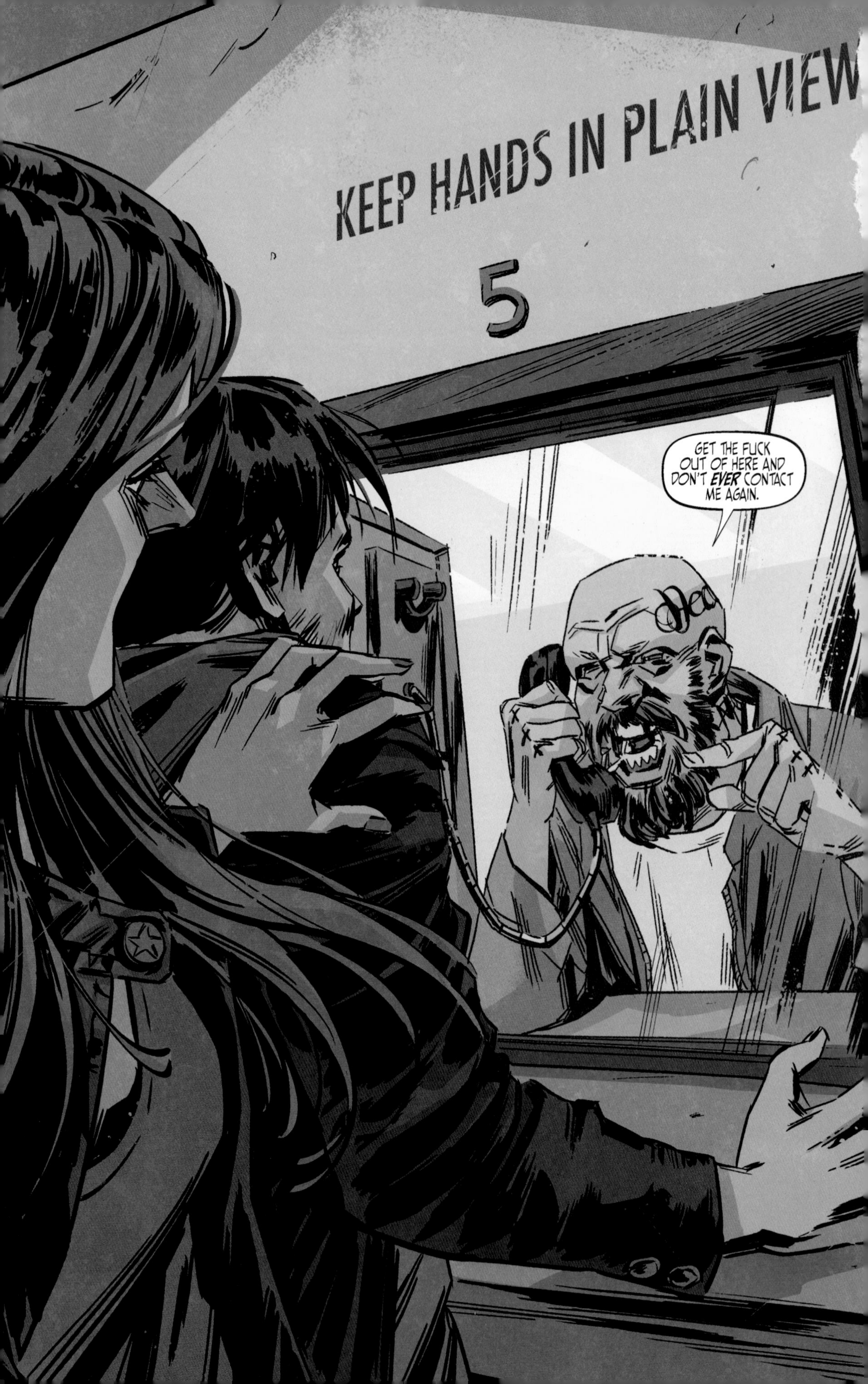
KEEP HANDS IN PLAIN VIEW
5
GET THE FUCK OUT OF HERE AND DON'T **EVER** CONTACT ME AGAIN.

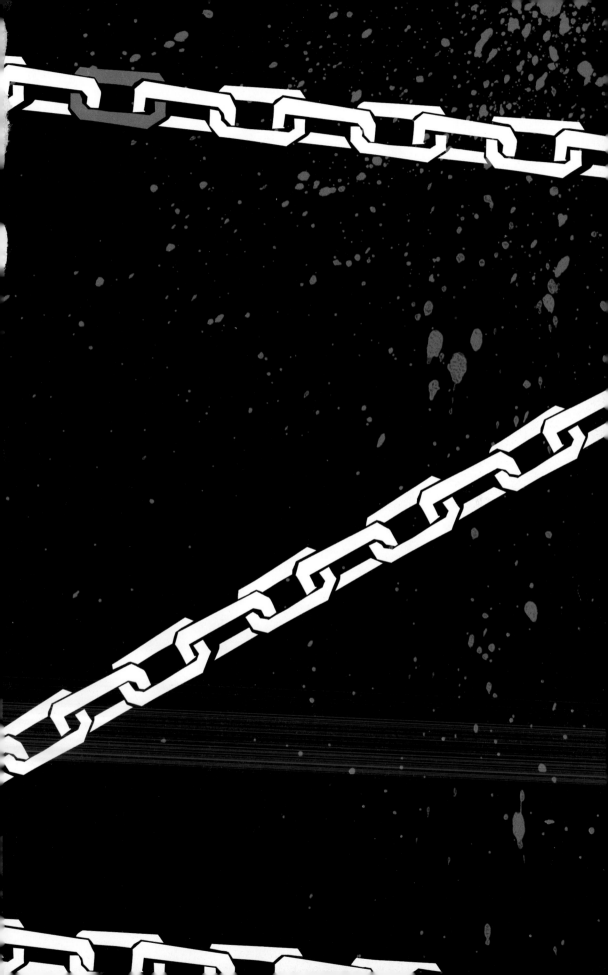

CHAPTER 7

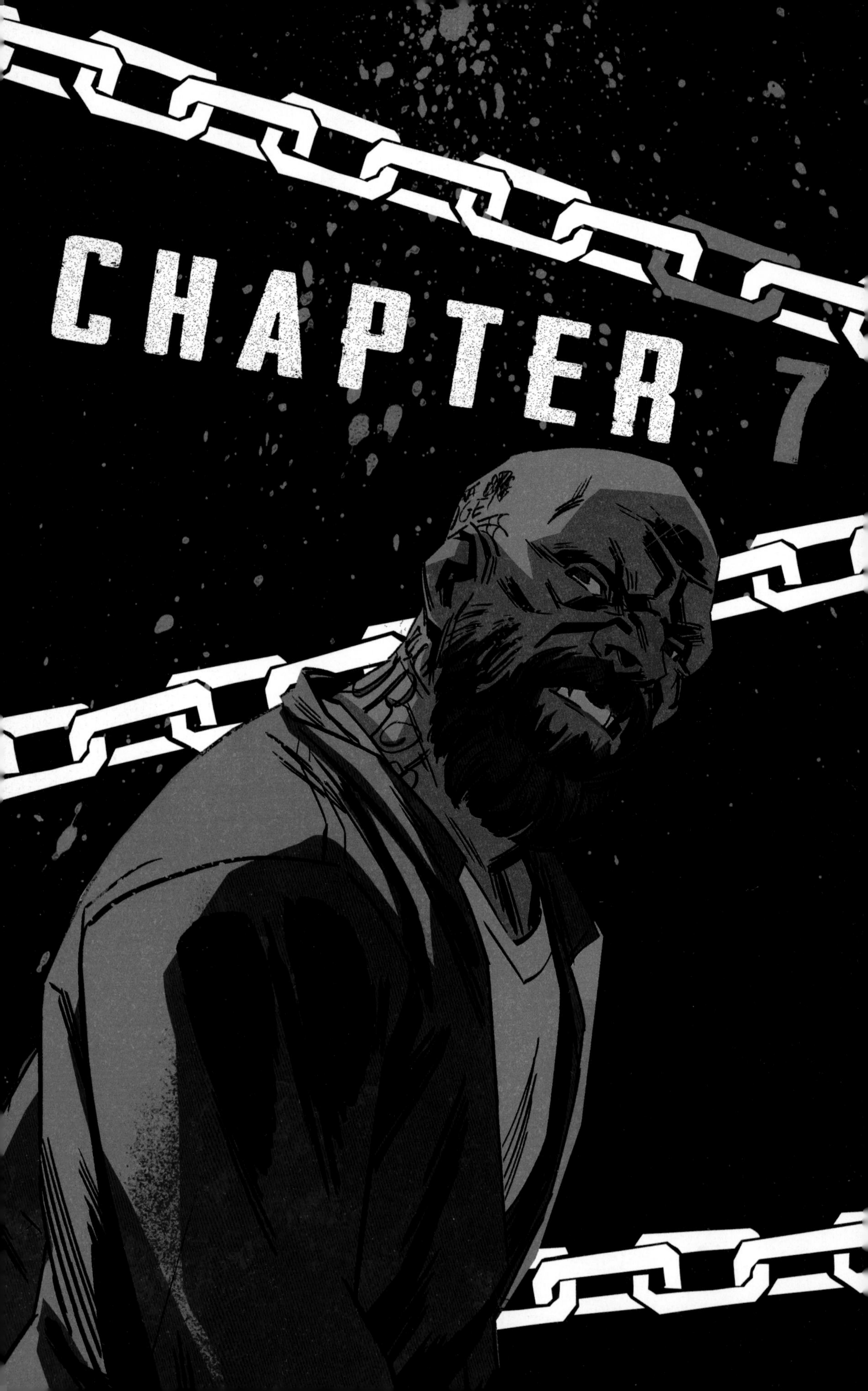

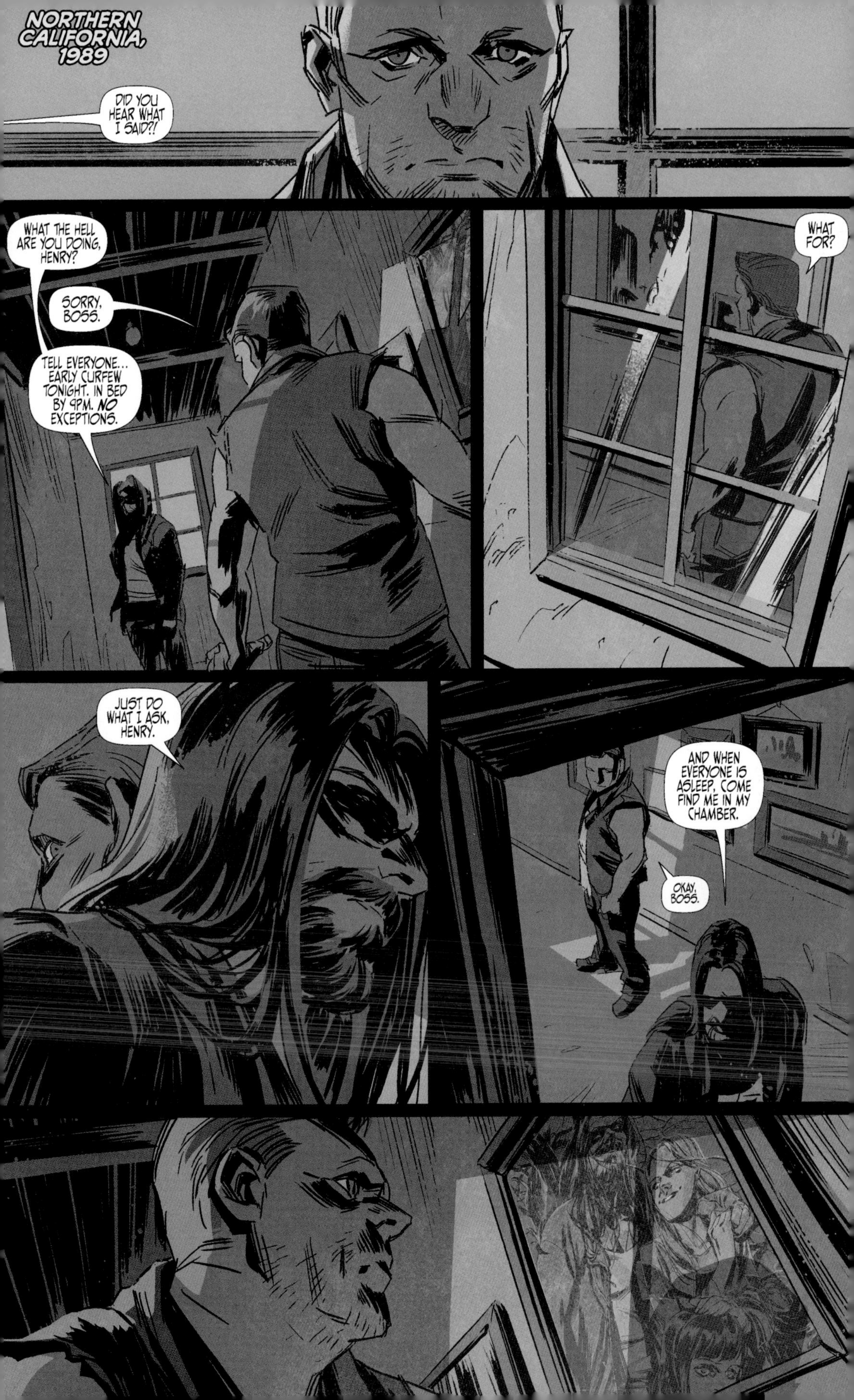
NORTHERN CALIFORNIA, 1989
DID YOU HEAR WHAT I SAID?!
WHAT THE HELL ARE YOU DOING, HENRY?
SORRY, BOSS.
TELL EVERYONE... EARLY CURFEW TONIGHT. IN BED BY 9PM. NO EXCEPTIONS.
WHAT FOR?
JUST DO WHAT I ASK, HENRY.
AND WHEN EVERYONE IS ASLEEP, COME FIND ME IN MY CHAMBER.
OKAY, BOSS.

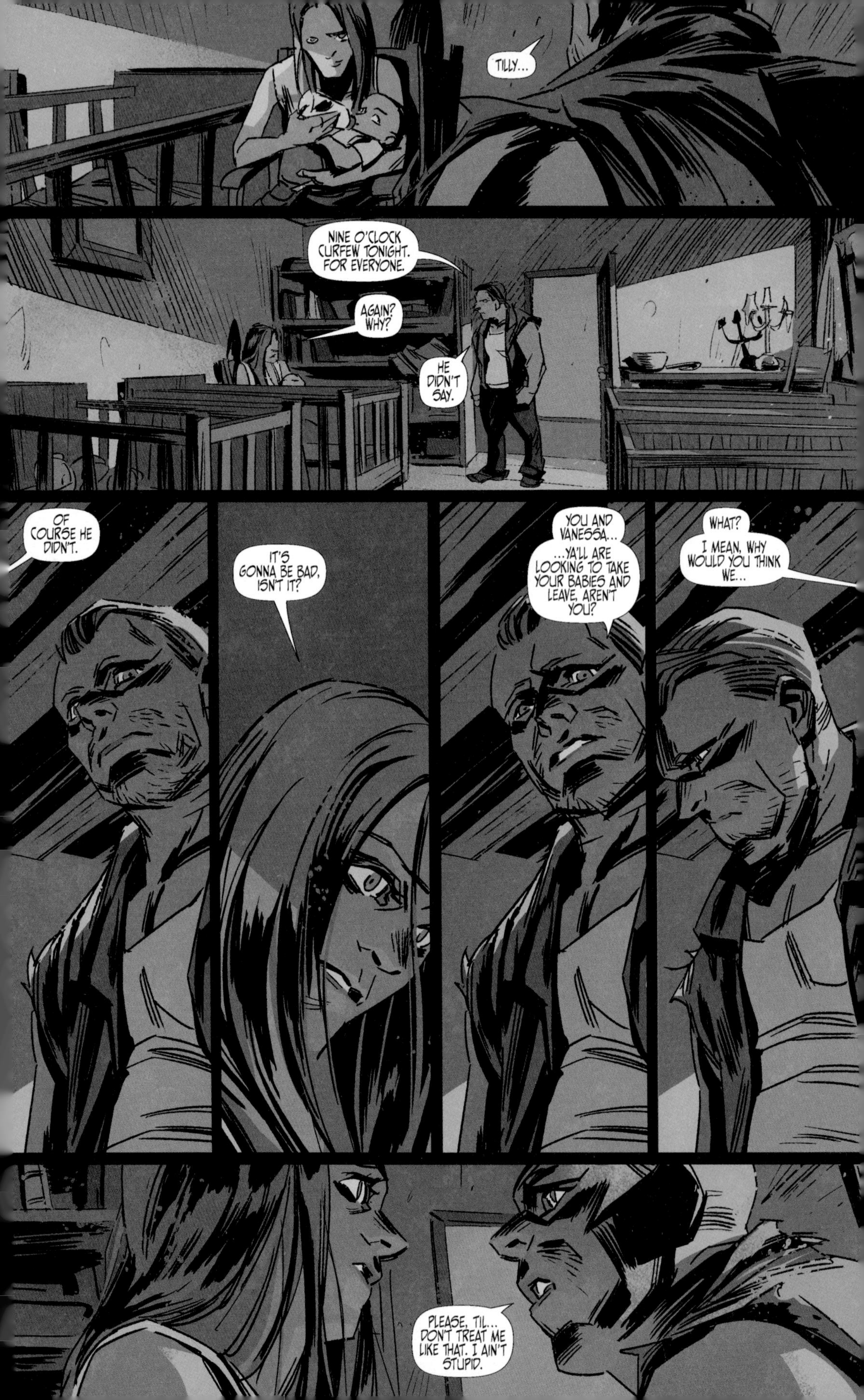
TILLY...
NINE O'CLOCK CURFEW TONIGHT. FOR EVERYONE.
AGAIN? WHY?
HE DIDN'T SAY.
OF COURSE HE DIDN'T.
IT'S GONNA BE BAD, ISN'T IT?
YOU AND VANESSA... ...YA'LL ARE LOOKING TO TAKE YOUR BABIES AND LEAVE, AREN'T YOU?
WHAT?
I MEAN, WHY WOULD YOU THINK WE...
PLEASE, TIL... DON'T TREAT ME LIKE THAT. I AIN'T STUPID.

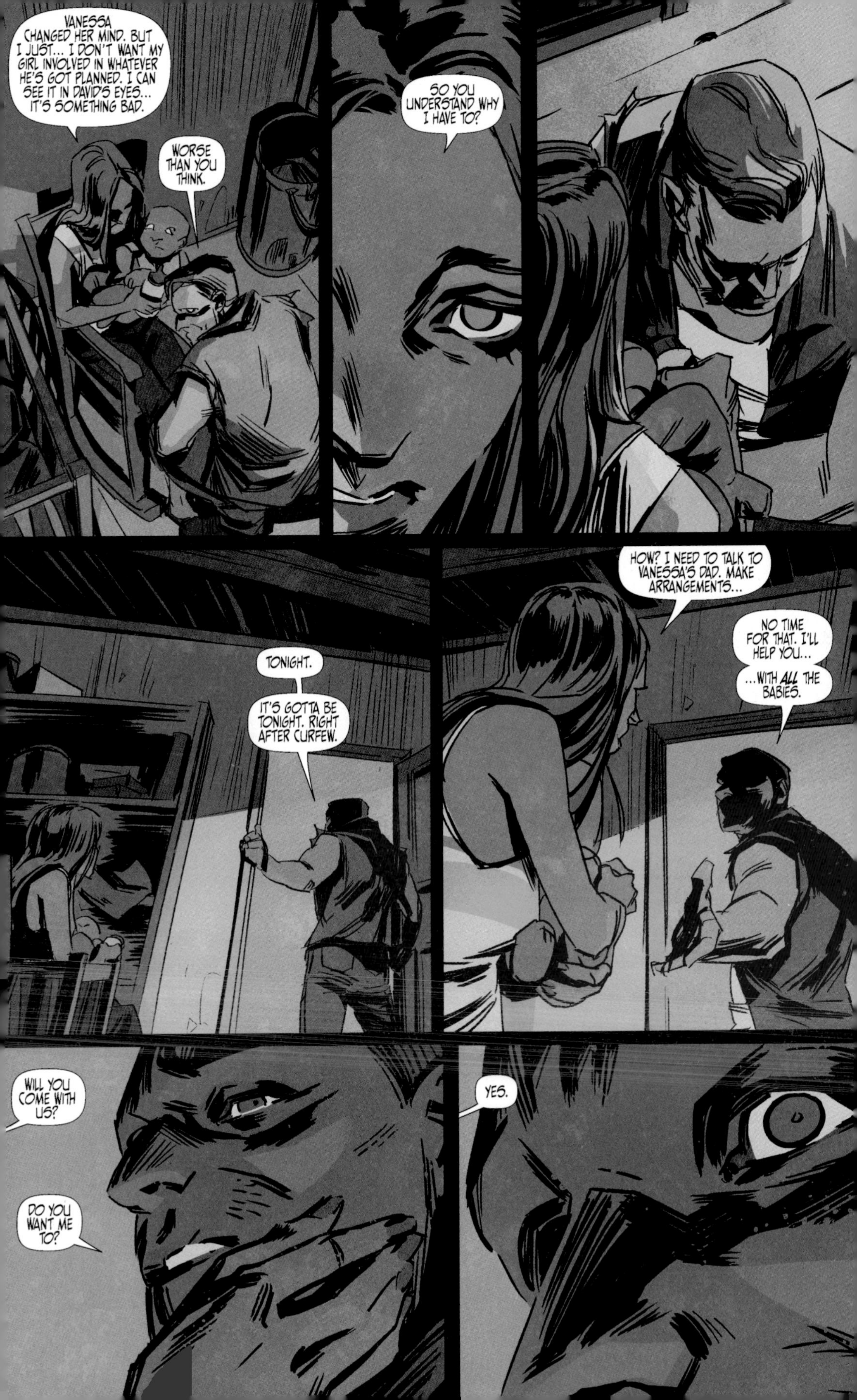
VANESSA CHANGED HER MIND. BUT I JUST... I DON'T WANT MY GIRL INVOLVED IN WHATEVER HE'S GOT PLANNED. I CAN SEE IT IN DAVID'S EYES... IT'S SOMETHING BAD.
WORSE THAN YOU THINK.
SO YOU UNDERSTAND WHY I HAVE TO?
TONIGHT.
IT'S GOTTA BE TONIGHT. RIGHT AFTER CURFEW.
HOW? I NEED TO TALK TO VANESSA'S DAD. MAKE ARRANGEMENTS...
NO TIME FOR THAT. I'LL HELP YOU...
...WITH ALL THE BABIES.
WILL YOU COME WITH US?
DO YOU WANT ME TO?
YES.

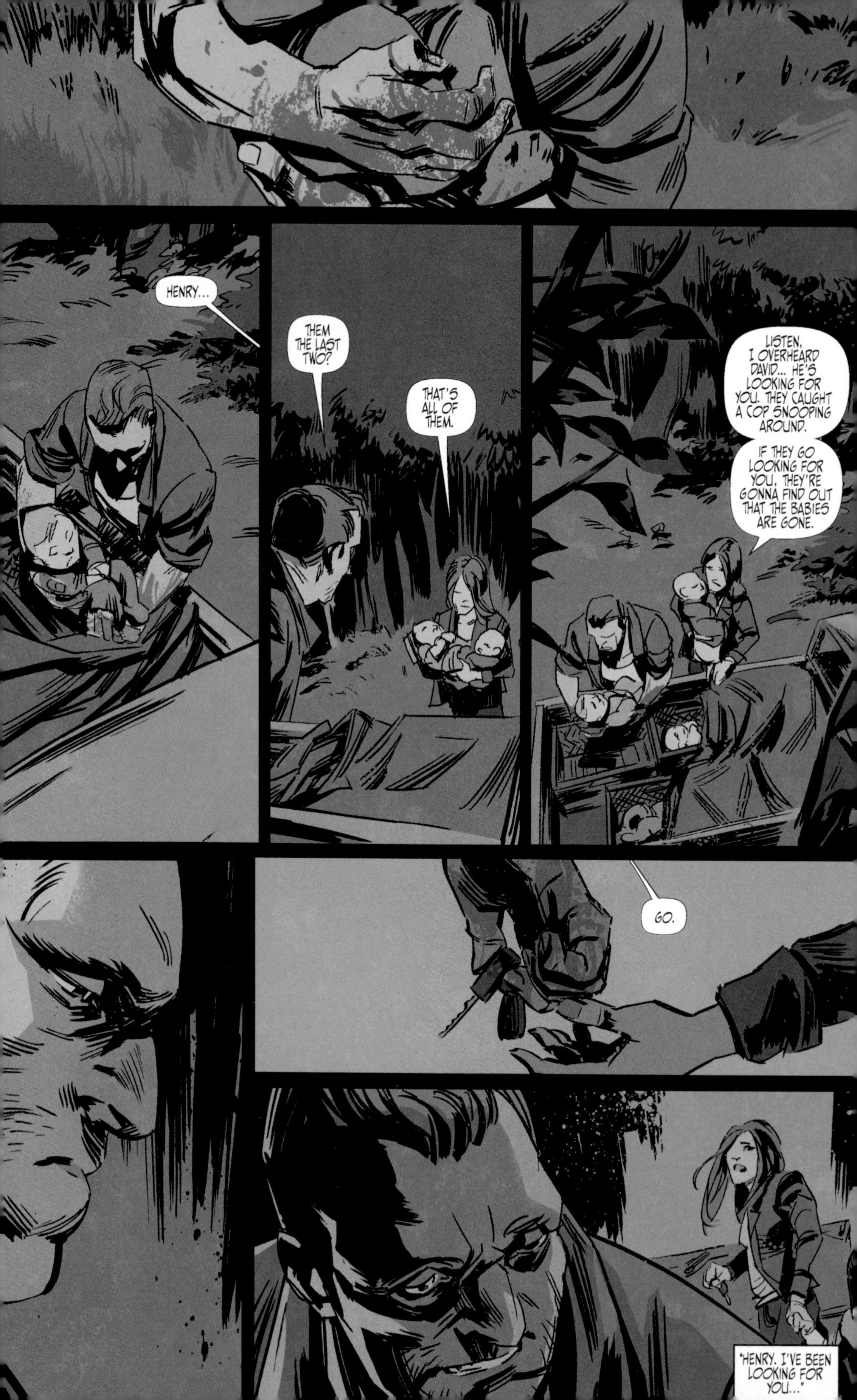
HENRY...
THEM THE LAST TWO?
THAT'S ALL OF THEM.
LISTEN, I OVERHEARD DAVID... HE'S LOOKING FOR YOU. THEY CAUGHT A COP SNOOPING AROUND.
IF THEY GO LOOKING FOR YOU, THEY'RE GONNA FIND OUT THAT THE BABIES ARE GONE.
GO.
"HENRY. I'VE BEEN LOOKING FOR YOU..."

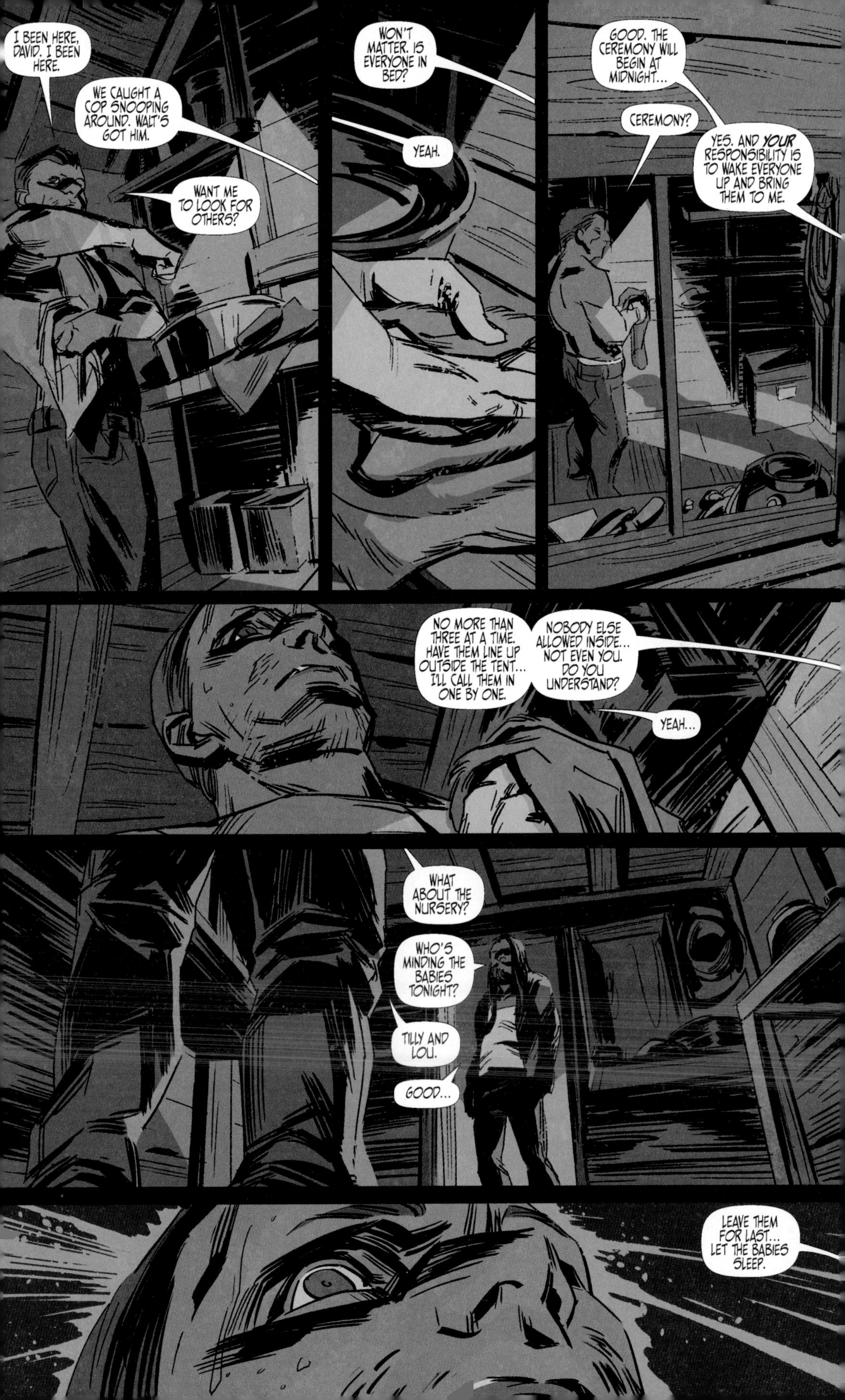
I BEEN HERE, DAVID. I BEEN HERE.
WE CAUGHT A COP SNOOPING AROUND. WALT'S GOT HIM.
WANT ME TO LOOK FOR OTHERS?
WON'T MATTER. IS EVERYONE IN BED?
YEAH.
GOOD. THE CEREMONY WILL BEGIN AT MIDNIGHT...
CEREMONY?
YES. AND ***YOUR*** RESPONSIBILITY IS TO WAKE EVERYONE UP AND BRING THEM TO ME.
NO MORE THAN THREE AT A TIME. HAVE THEM LINE UP OUTSIDE THE TENT... I'LL CALL THEM IN ONE BY ONE.
NOBODY ELSE ALLOWED INSIDE... NOT EVEN YOU. DO YOU UNDERSTAND?
YEAH...
WHAT ABOUT THE NURSERY?
WHO'S MINDING THE BABIES TONIGHT?
TILLY AND LOU.
GOOD...
LEAVE THEM FOR LAST... LET THE BABIES SLEEP.

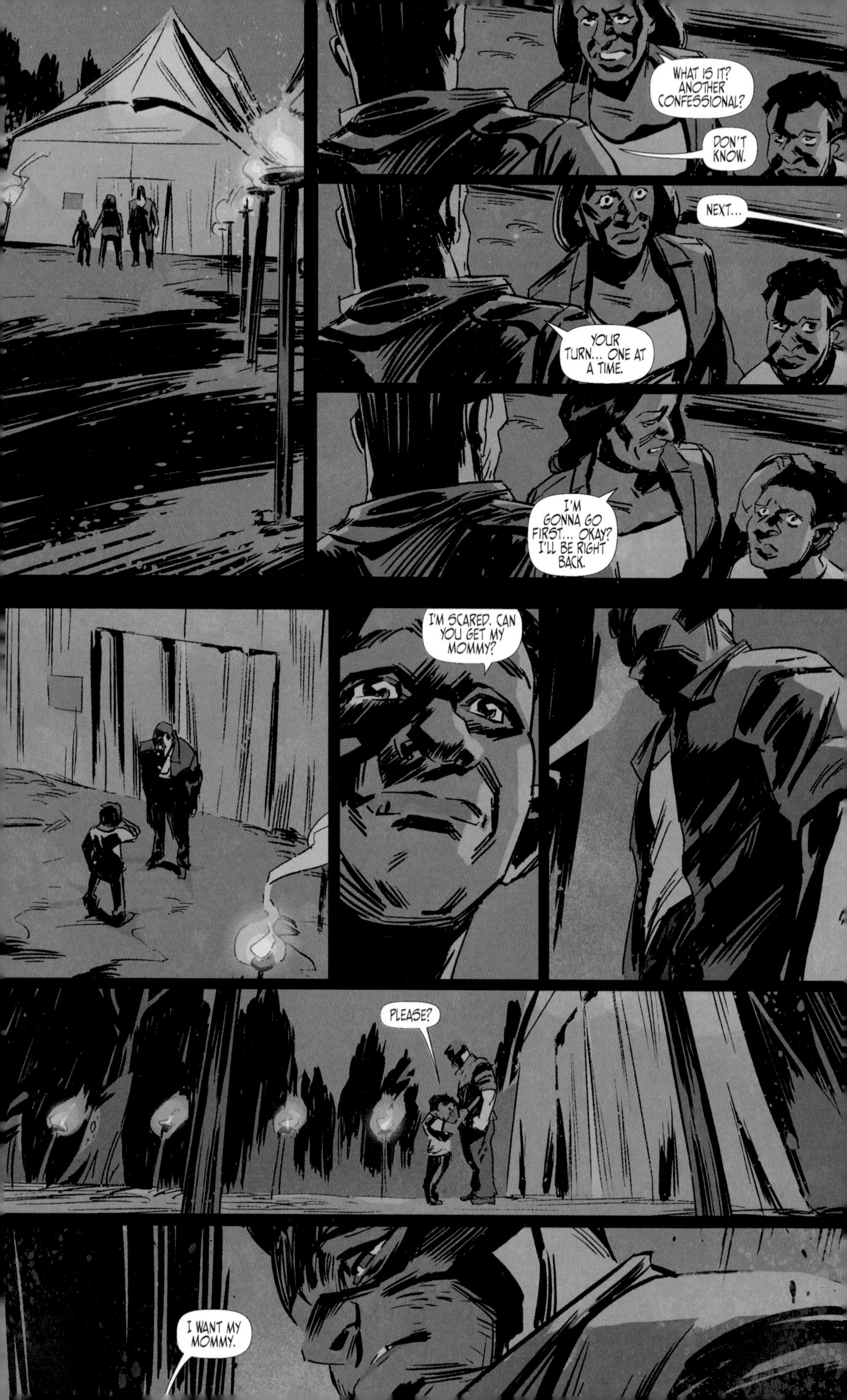
WHAT IS IT? ANOTHER CONFESSIONAL?
DON'T KNOW.
NEXT...
YOUR TURN... ONE AT A TIME.
I'M GONNA GO FIRST... OKAY? I'LL BE RIGHT BACK.
I'M SCARED. CAN YOU GET MY MOMMY?
PLEASE?
I WANT MY MOMMY.

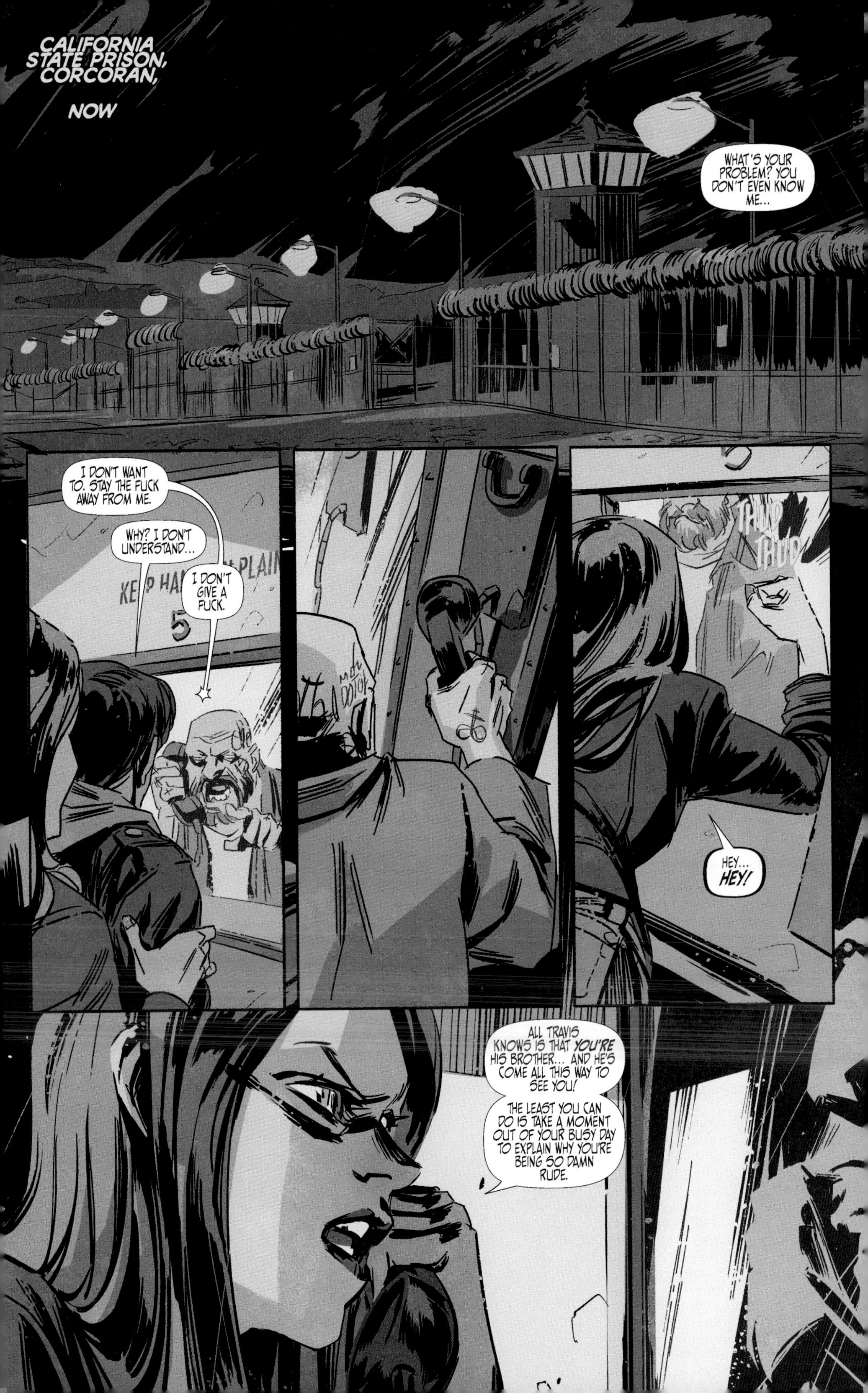
CALIFORNIA STATE PRISON, CORCORAN,
NOW
WHAT'S YOUR PROBLEM? YOU DON'T EVEN KNOW ME...
I DON'T WANT TO. STAY THE FUCK AWAY FROM ME.
WHY? I DON'T UNDERSTAND...
I DON'T GIVE A FUCK.
THUD
THUD
HEY... HEY!
ALL TRAVIS KNOWS IS THAT YOU'RE HIS BROTHER... AND HE'S COME ALL THIS WAY TO SEE YOU!
THE LEAST YOU CAN DO IS TAKE A MOMENT OUT OF YOUR BUSY DAY TO EXPLAIN WHY YOU'RE BEING SO DAMN RUDE.

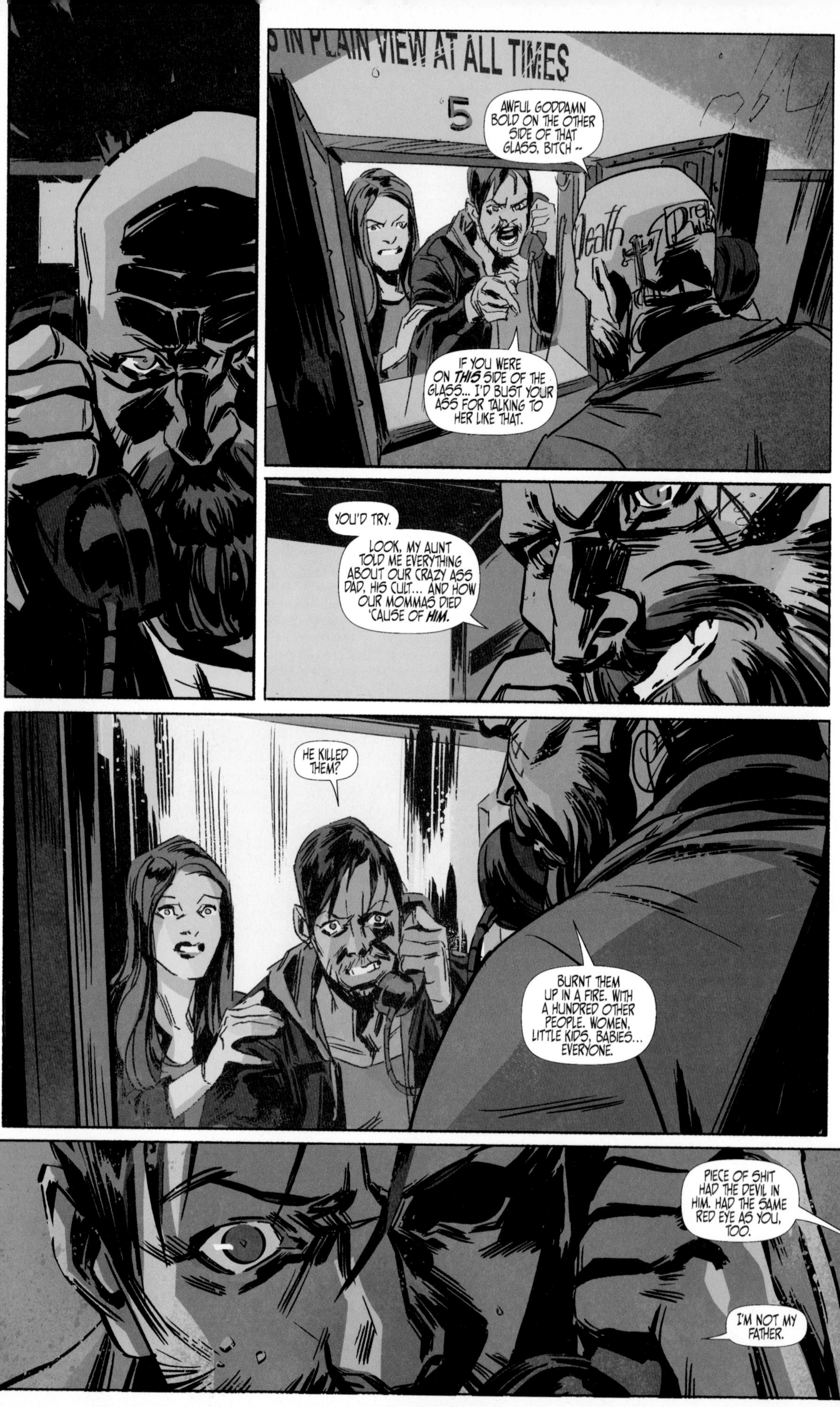
S IN PLAIN VIEW AT ALL TIMES
5
AWFUL GODDAMN BOLD ON THE OTHER SIDE OF THAT GLASS, BITCH --
IF YOU WERE ON THIS SIDE OF THE GLASS... I'D BUST YOUR ASS FOR TALKING TO HER LIKE THAT.
YOU'D TRY.
LOOK, MY AUNT TOLD ME EVERYTHING ABOUT OUR CRAZY ASS DAD, HIS CULT... AND HOW OUR MOMMAS DIED 'CAUSE OF HIM.
HE KILLED THEM?
BURNT THEM UP IN A FIRE. WITH A HUNDRED OTHER PEOPLE. WOMEN, LITTLE KIDS, BABIES... EVERYONE.
PIECE OF SHIT HAD THE DEVIL IN HIM. HAD THE SAME RED EYE AS YOU, TOO.
I'M NOT MY FATHER.

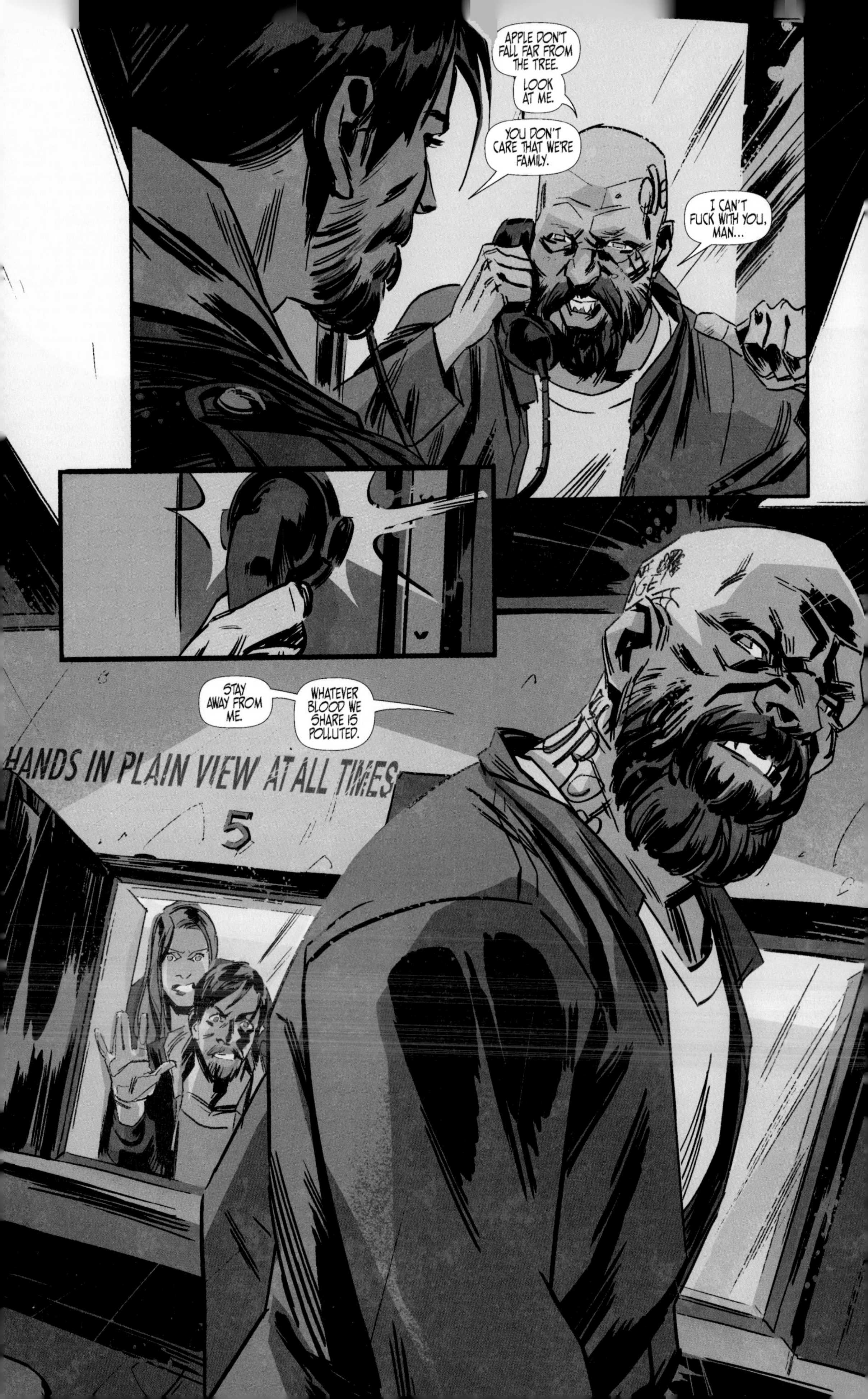
APPLE DON'T FALL FAR FROM THE TREE.
LOOK AT ME.
YOU DON'T CARE THAT WE'RE FAMILY.
I CAN'T FUCK WITH YOU, MAN...
STAY AWAY FROM ME.
WHATEVER BLOOD WE SHARE IS POLLUTED.
HANDS IN PLAIN VIEW AT ALL TIMES
5

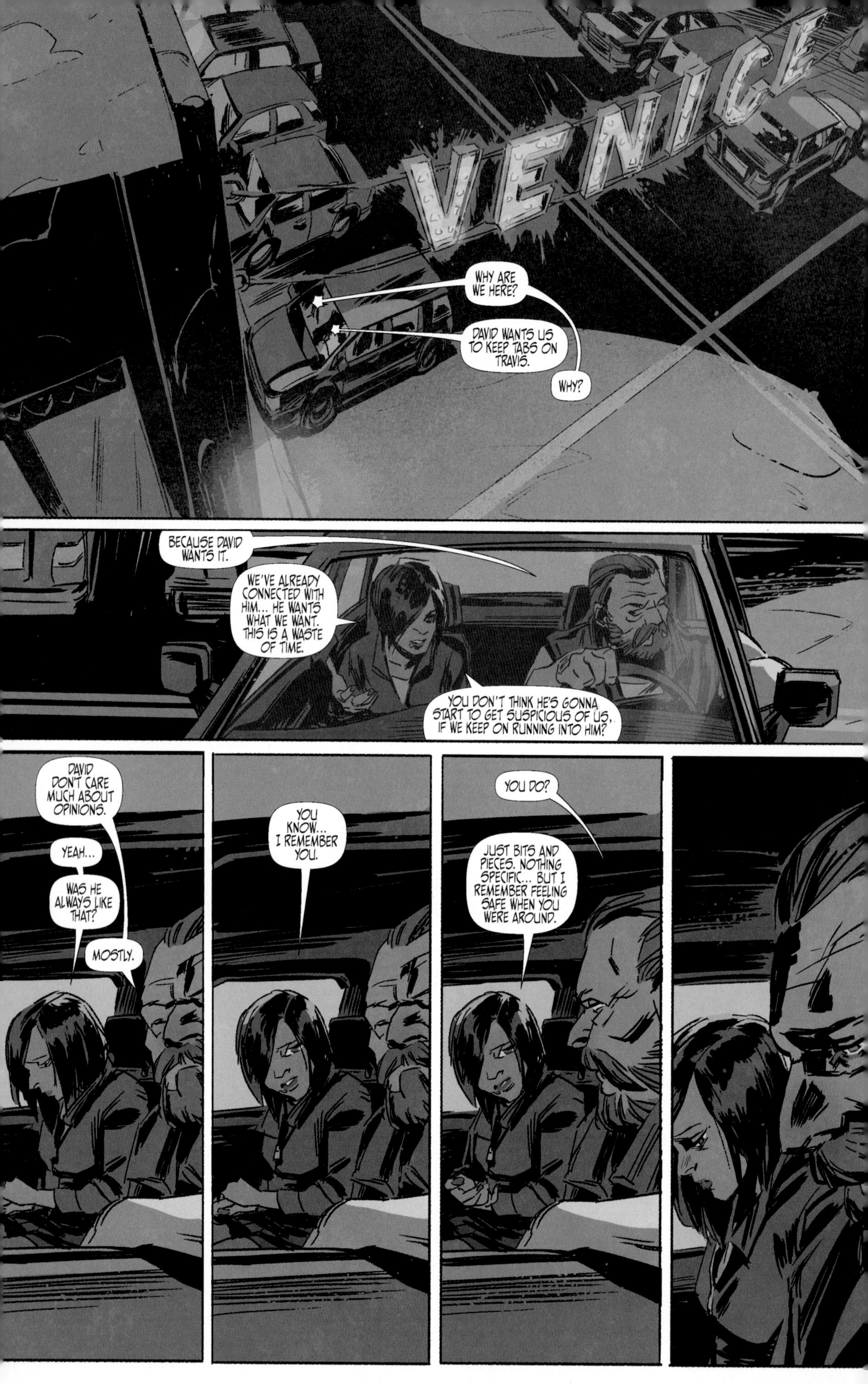
VENICE
WHY ARE WE HERE?
DAVID WANTS US TO KEEP TABS ON TRAVIS.
WHY?
BECAUSE DAVID WANTS IT.
WE'VE ALREADY CONNECTED WITH HIM... HE WANTS WHAT WE WANT. THIS IS A WASTE OF TIME.
YOU DON'T THINK HE'S GONNA START TO GET SUSPICIOUS OF US IF WE KEEP ON RUNNING INTO HIM?
DAVID DON'T CARE MUCH ABOUT OPINIONS.
YEAH...
WAS HE ALWAYS LIKE THAT?
MOSTLY.
YOU KNOW... I REMEMBER YOU.
YOU DO?
JUST BITS AND PIECES. NOTHING SPECIFIC... BUT I REMEMBER FEELING SAFE WHEN YOU WERE AROUND.

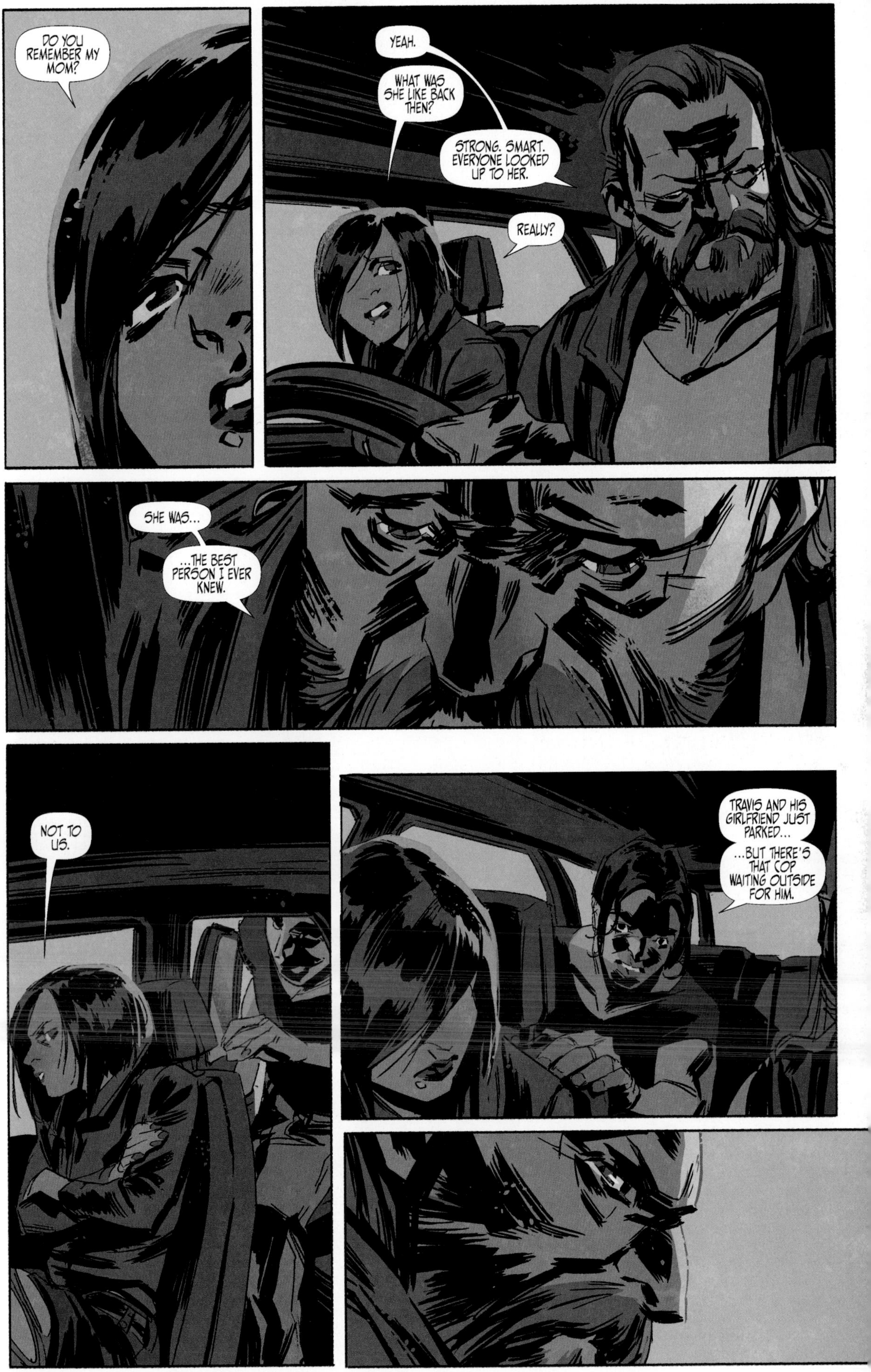
DO YOU REMEMBER MY MOM?
YEAH.
WHAT WAS SHE LIKE BACK THEN?
STRONG. SMART. EVERYONE LOOKED UP TO HER.
REALLY?
SHE WAS...
...THE BEST PERSON I EVER KNEW.
NOT TO US.
TRAVIS AND HIS GIRLFRIEND JUST PARKED...
...BUT THERE'S THAT COP WAITING OUTSIDE FOR HIM.

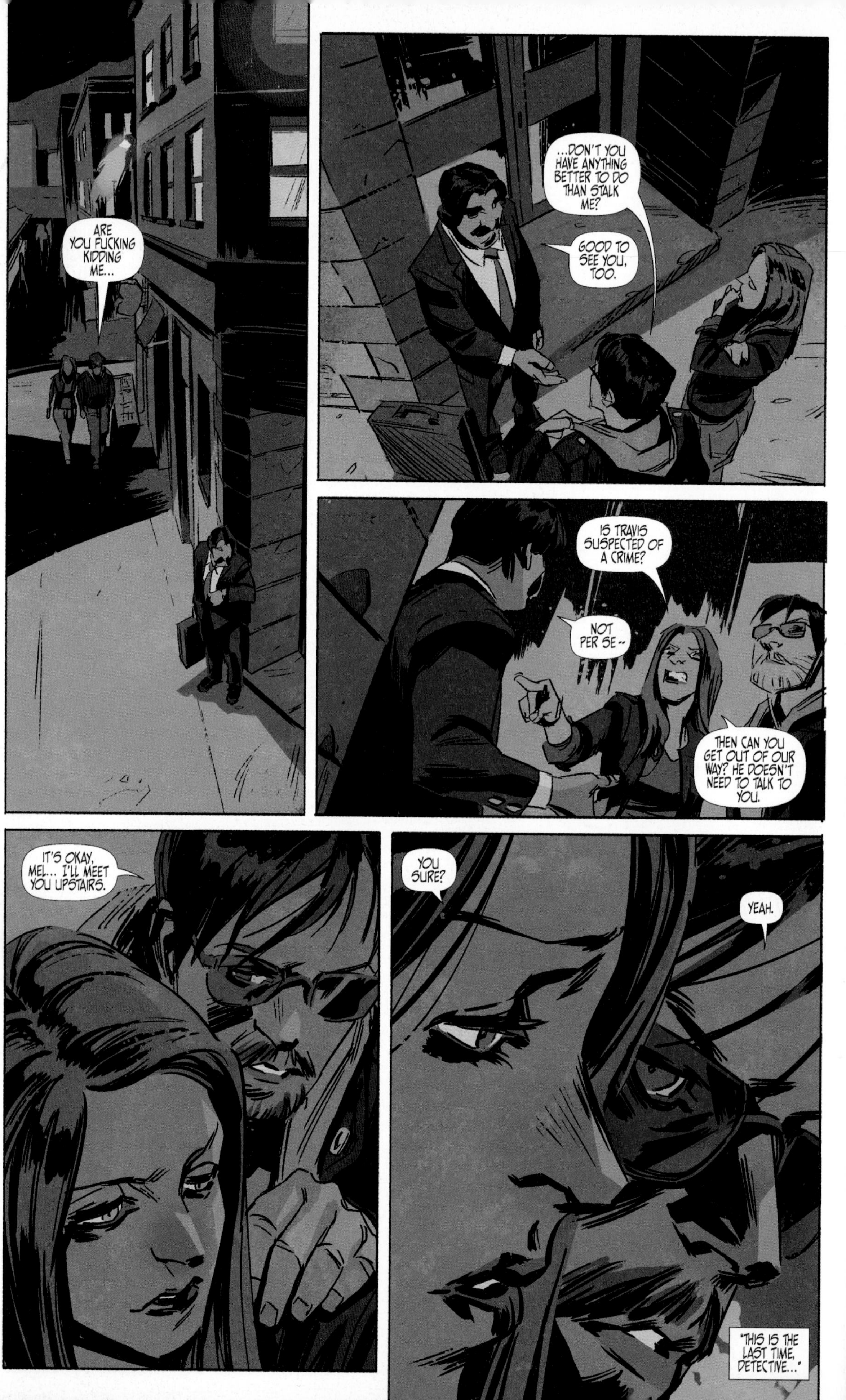
ARE YOU FUCKING KIDDING ME...
...DON'T YOU HAVE ANYTHING BETTER TO DO THAN STALK ME?
GOOD TO SEE YOU, TOO.
IS TRAVIS SUSPECTED OF A CRIME?
NOT PER SE--
THEN CAN YOU GET OUT OF OUR WAY? HE DOESN'T NEED TO TALK TO YOU.
IT'S OKAY, MEL... I'LL MEET YOU UPSTAIRS.
YOU SURE?
YEAH.
"THIS IS THE LAST TIME, DETECTIVE..."

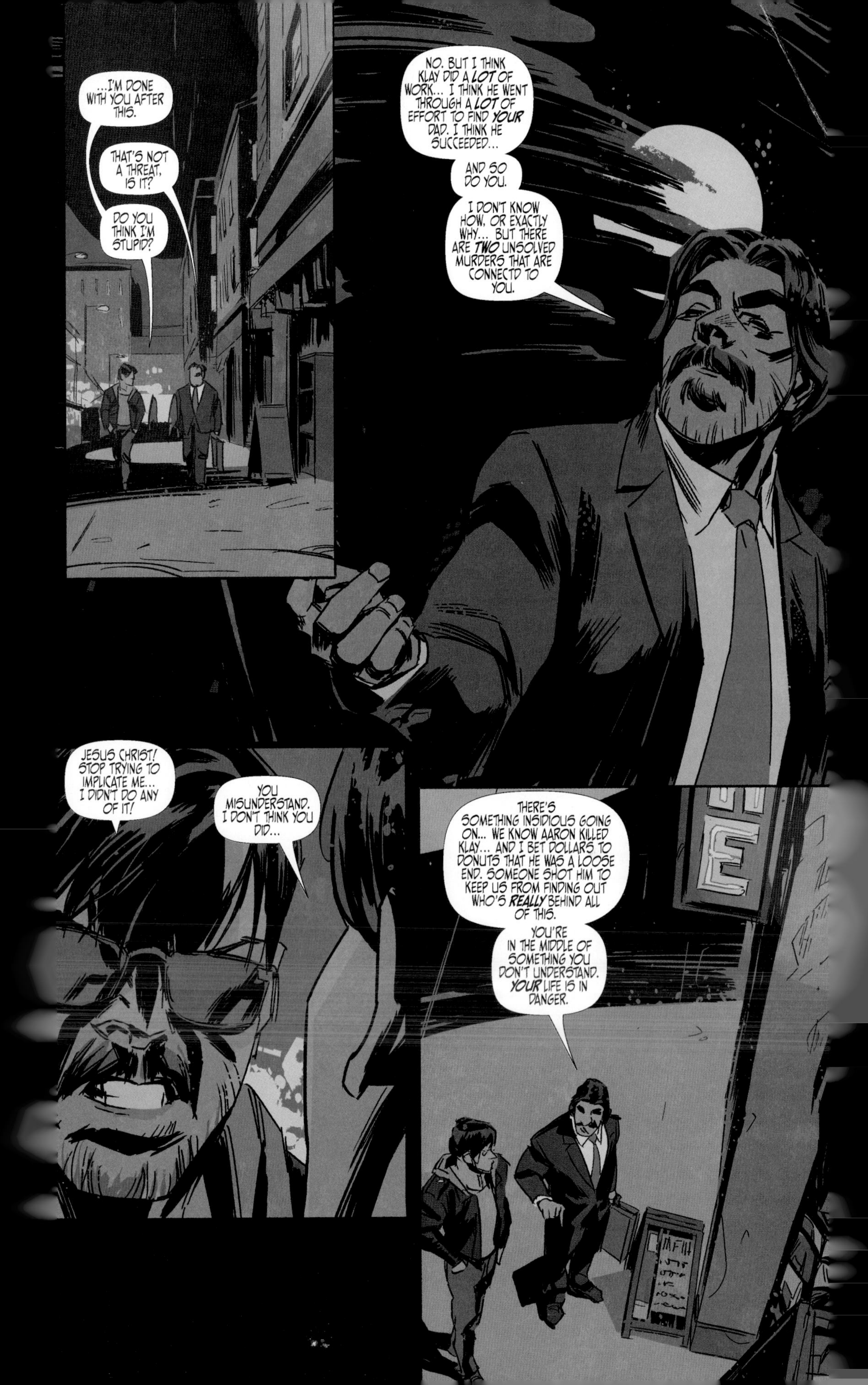
...I'M DONE WITH YOU AFTER THIS.
THAT'S NOT A THREAT, IS IT?
DO YOU THINK I'M STUPID?
NO. BUT I THINK KLAY DID A *LOT* OF WORK... I THINK HE WENT THROUGH A *LOT* OF EFFORT TO FIND *YOUR* DAD. I THINK HE SUCCEEDED...
AND SO DO YOU.
I DON'T KNOW HOW, OR EXACTLY WHY... BUT THERE ARE *TWO* UNSOLVED MURDERS THAT ARE CONNECTD TO YOU.
JESUS CHRIST! STOP TRYING TO IMPLICATE ME... I DIDN'T DO ANY OF IT!
YOU MISUNDERSTAND. I DON'T THINK YOU DID...
THERE'S SOMETHING INSIDIOUS GOING ON... WE KNOW AARON KILLED KLAY... AND I BET DOLLARS TO DONUTS THAT HE WAS A LOOSE END. SOMEONE SHOT HIM TO KEEP US FROM FINDING OUT WHO'S *REALLY* BEHIND ALL OF THIS.
YOU'RE IN THE MIDDLE OF SOMETHING YOU DON'T UNDERSTAND. *YOUR* LIFE IS IN DANGER.

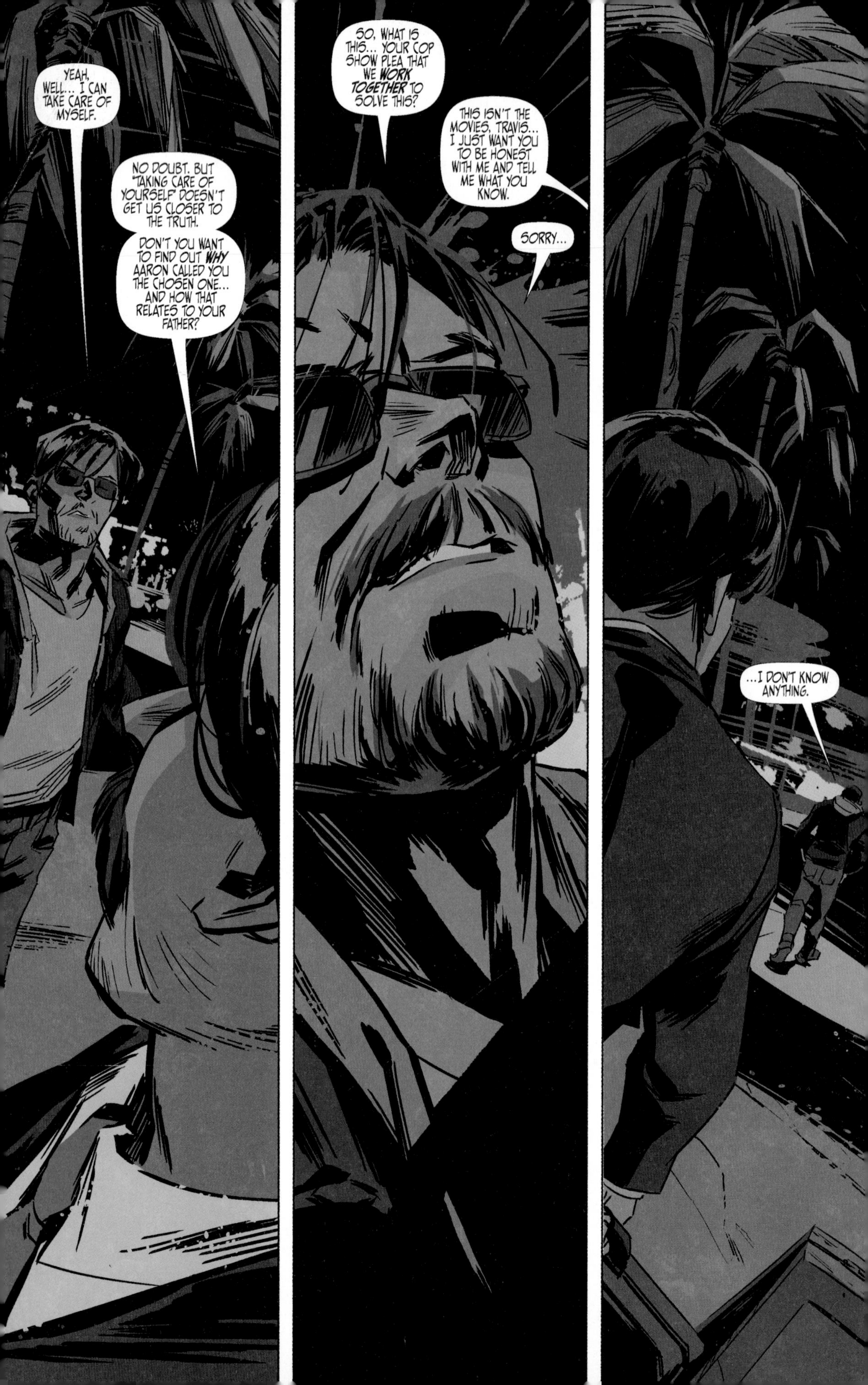
YEAH, WELL... I CAN TAKE CARE OF MYSELF.
NO DOUBT. BUT "TAKING CARE OF YOURSELF" DOESN'T GET US CLOSER TO THE TRUTH.
DON'T YOU WANT TO FIND OUT WHY AARON CALLED YOU THE CHOSEN ONE... AND HOW THAT RELATES TO YOUR FATHER?
SO, WHAT IS THIS... YOUR COP SHOW PLEA THAT WE WORK TOGETHER TO SOLVE THIS?
THIS ISN'T THE MOVIES, TRAVIS... I JUST WANT YOU TO BE HONEST WITH ME AND TELL ME WHAT YOU KNOW.
SORRY...
...I DON'T KNOW ANYTHING.

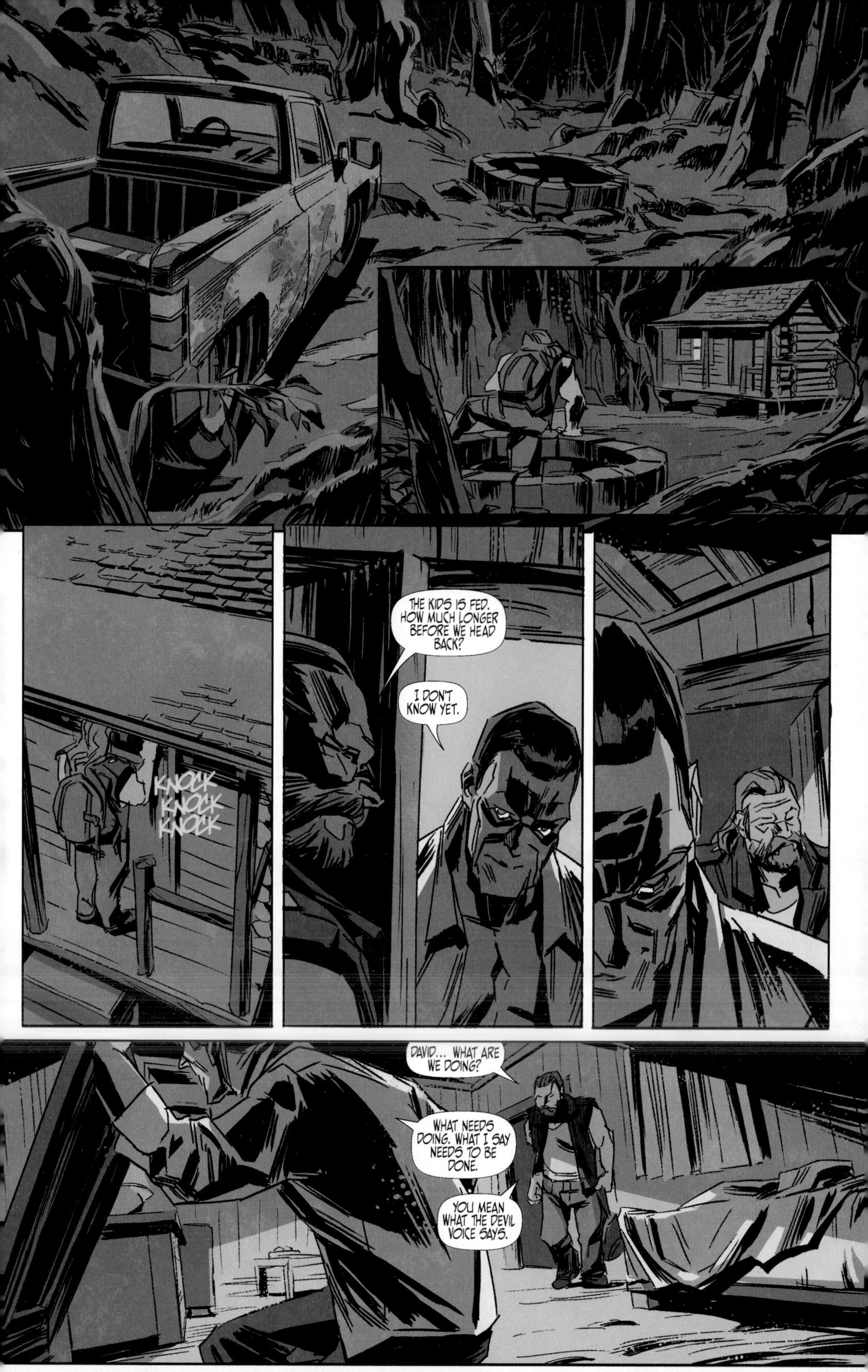
KNOCK KNOCK KNOCK
THE KIDS IS FED. HOW MUCH LONGER BEFORE WE HEAD BACK?
I DON'T KNOW YET.
DAVID... WHAT ARE WE DOING?
WHAT NEEDS DOING. WHAT I SAY NEEDS TO BE DONE.
YOU MEAN WHAT THE DEVIL VOICE SAYS.

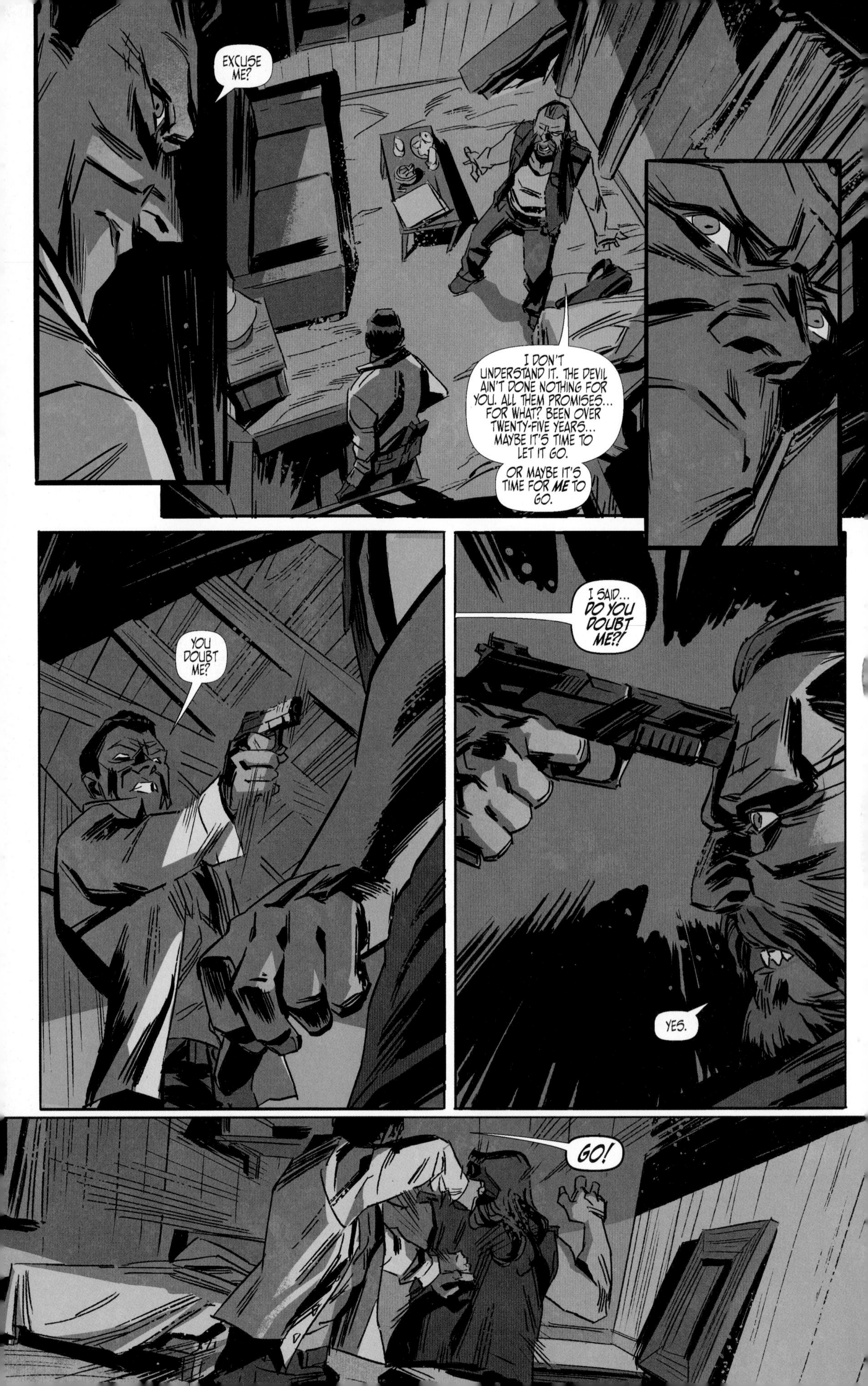
EXCUSE ME?
I DON'T UNDERSTAND IT. THE DEVIL AIN'T DONE NOTHING FOR YOU. ALL THEM PROMISES... FOR WHAT? BEEN OVER TWENTY-FIVE YEARS... MAYBE IT'S TIME TO LET IT GO.
OR MAYBE IT'S TIME FOR ME TO GO.
YOU DOUBT ME?
I SAID... DO YOU DOUBT ME?!
YES.
GO!

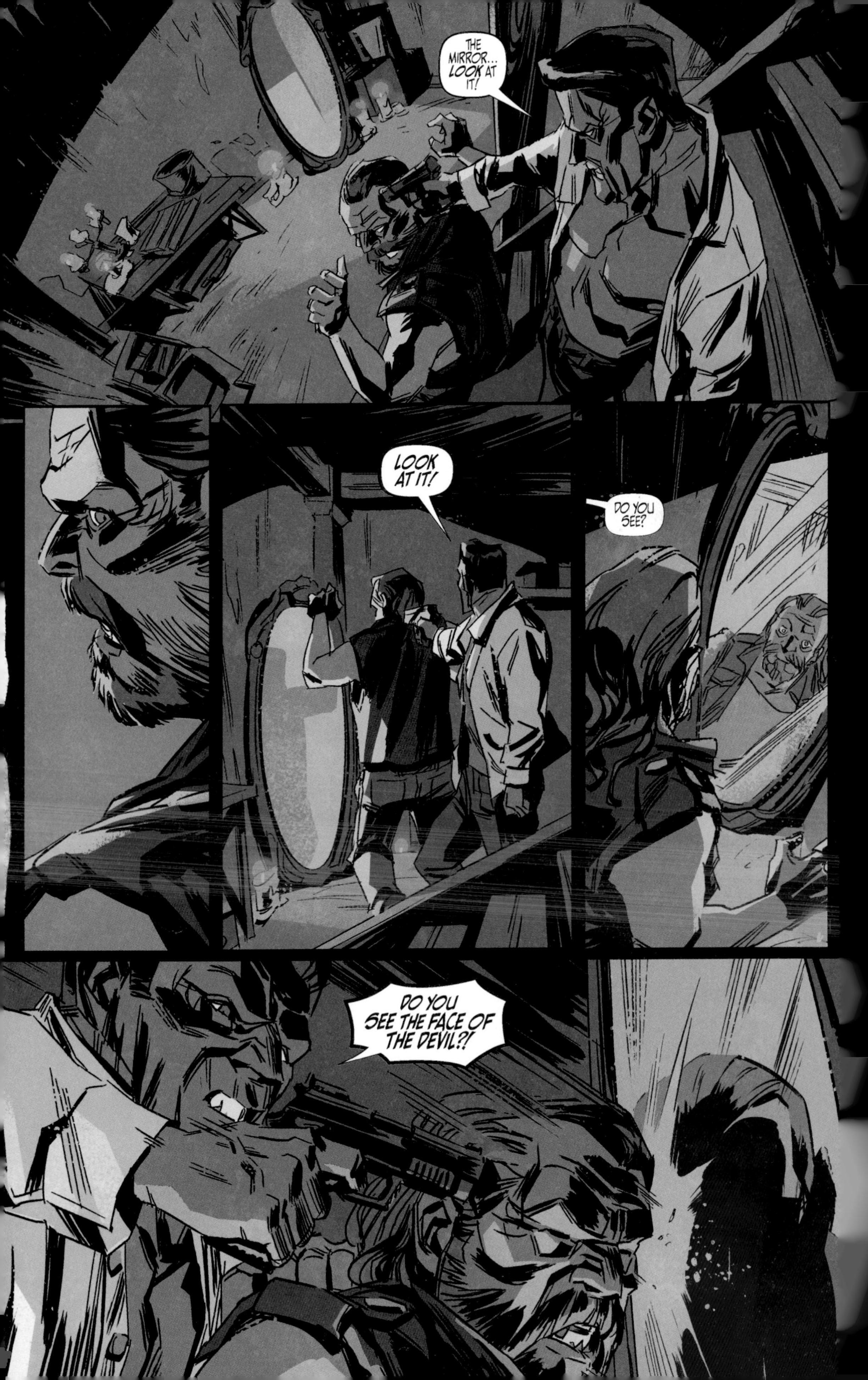
THE MIRROR... LOOK AT IT!
LOOK AT IT!
DO YOU SEE?
DO YOU SEE THE FACE OF THE DEVIL?!

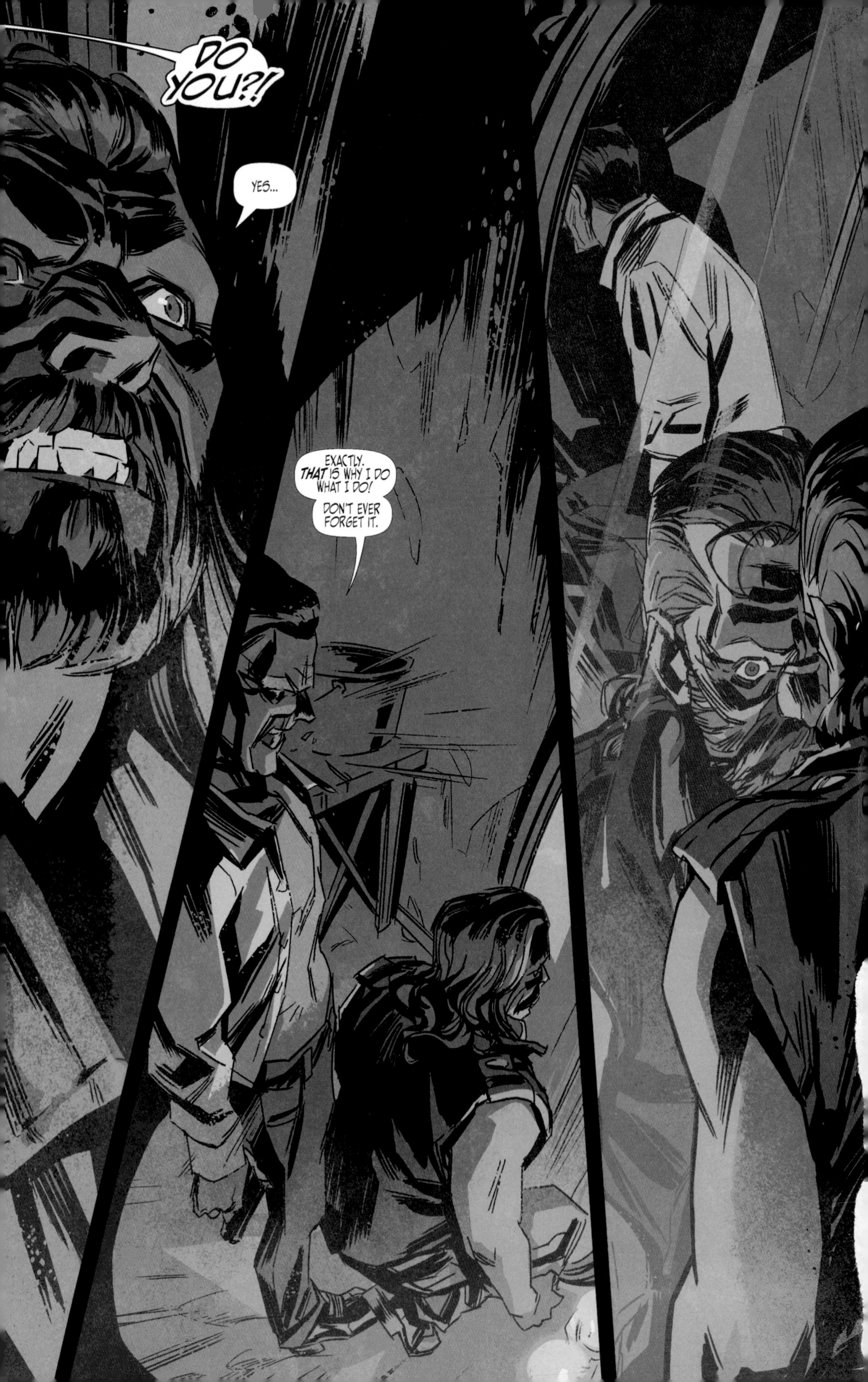
DO YOU?!
YES...
EXACTLY. THAT IS WHY I DO WHAT I DO!
DON'T EVER FORGET IT.

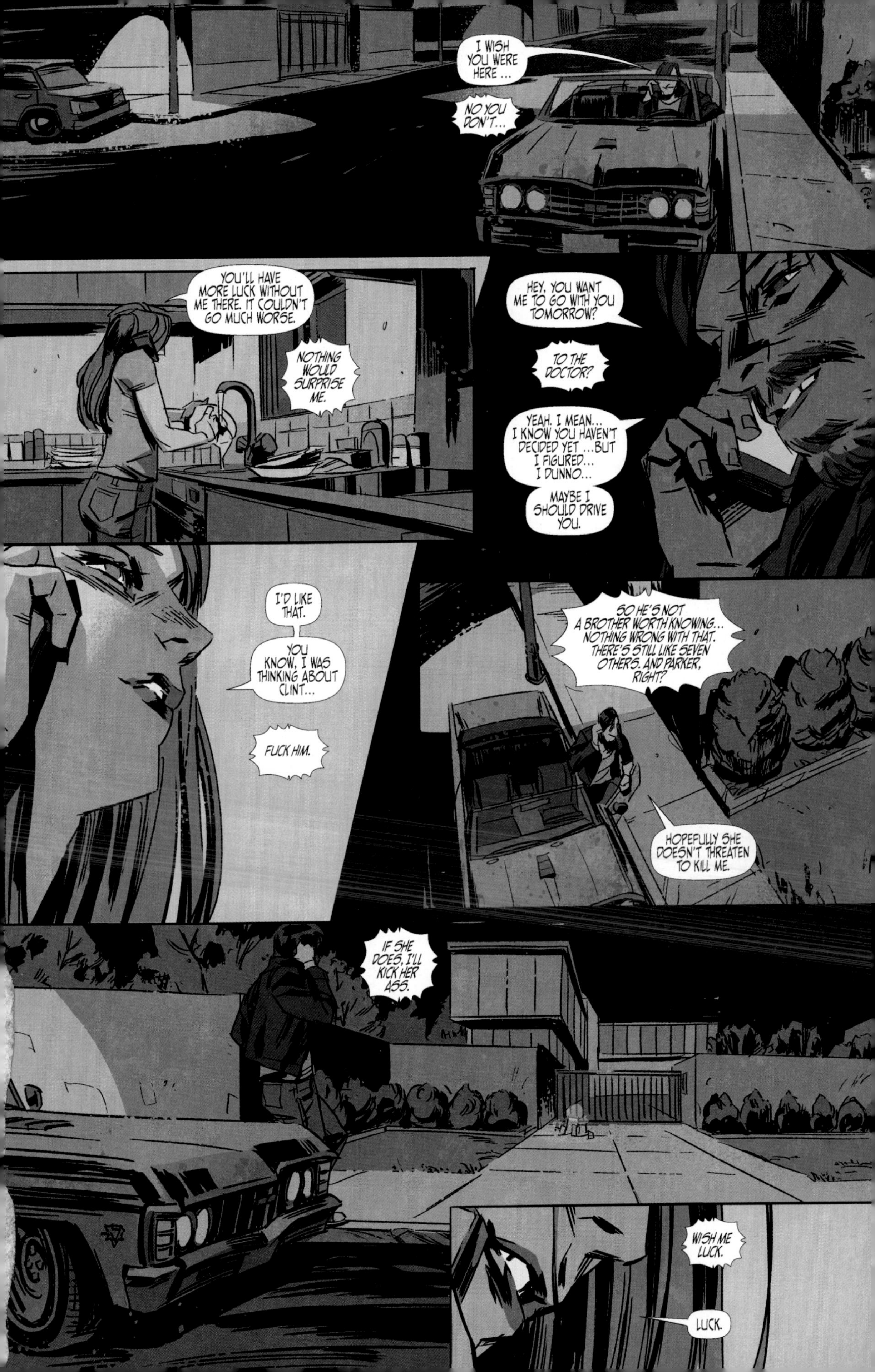
I WISH YOU WERE HERE ...
NO YOU DON'T...
YOU'LL HAVE MORE LUCK WITHOUT ME THERE. IT COULDN'T GO MUCH WORSE.
NOTHING WOULD SURPRISE ME.
HEY, YOU WANT ME TO GO WITH YOU TOMORROW?
TO THE DOCTOR?
YEAH. I MEAN... I KNOW YOU HAVEN'T DECIDED YET ...BUT I FIGURED... I DUNNO...
MAYBE I SHOULD DRIVE YOU.
I'D LIKE THAT.
YOU KNOW, I WAS THINKING ABOUT CLINT...
FUCK HIM.
SO HE'S NOT A BROTHER WORTH KNOWING... NOTHING WRONG WITH THAT. THERE'S STILL LIKE SEVEN OTHERS. AND PARKER, RIGHT?
HOPEFULLY SHE DOESN'T THREATEN TO KILL ME.
IF SHE DOES, I'LL KICK HER ASS.
WISH ME LUCK.
LUCK.

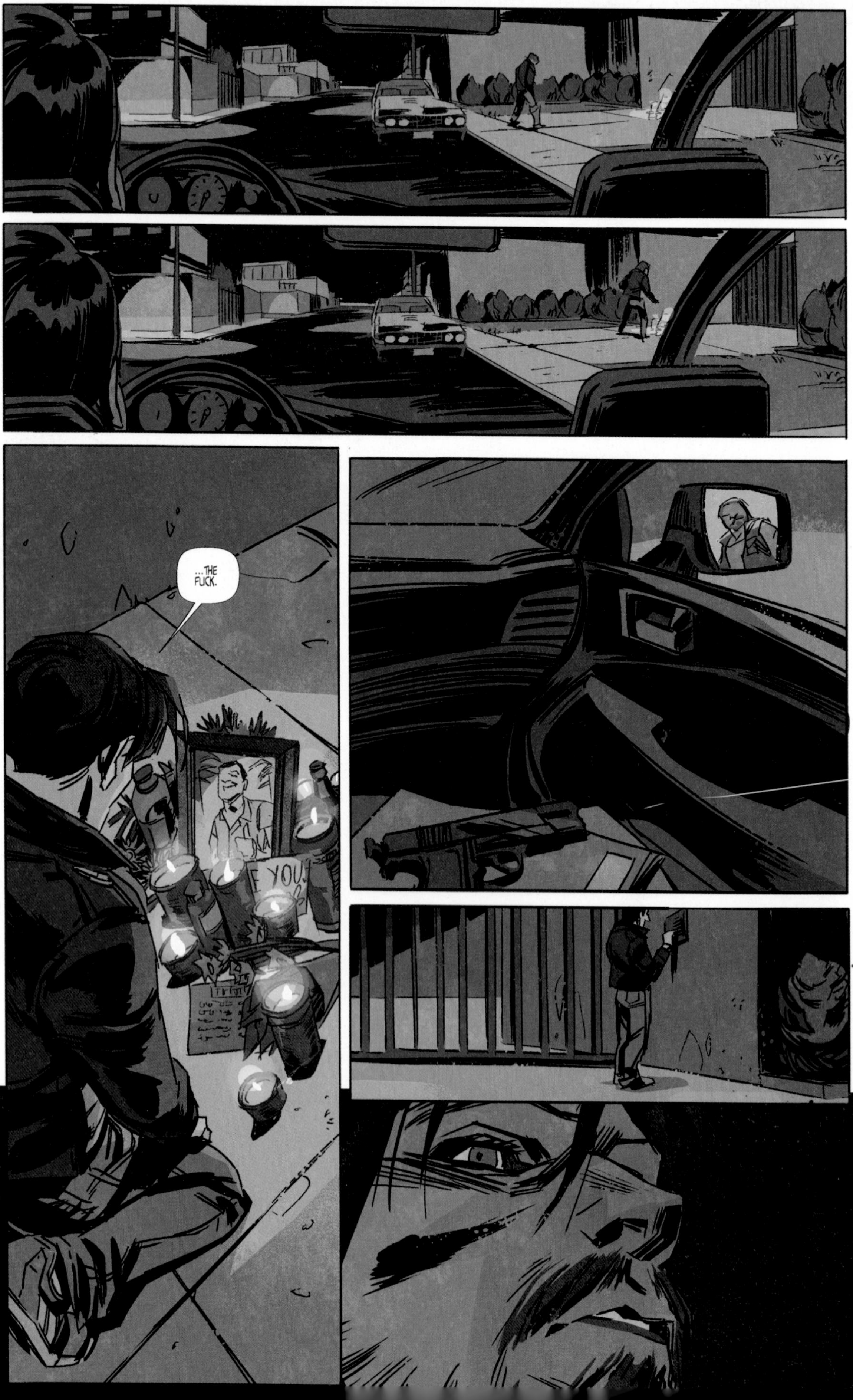
...THE FUCK.

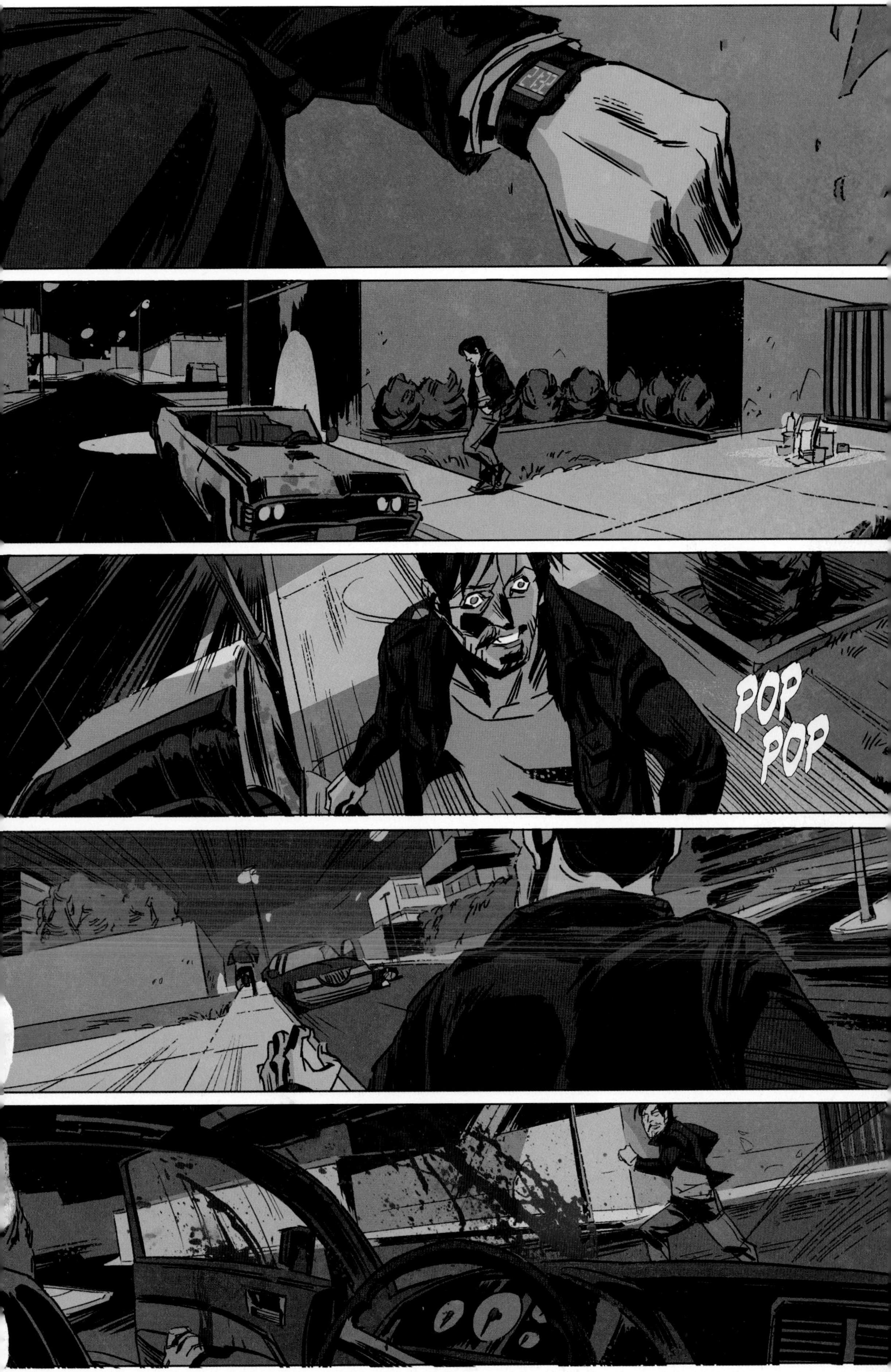
POP
POP

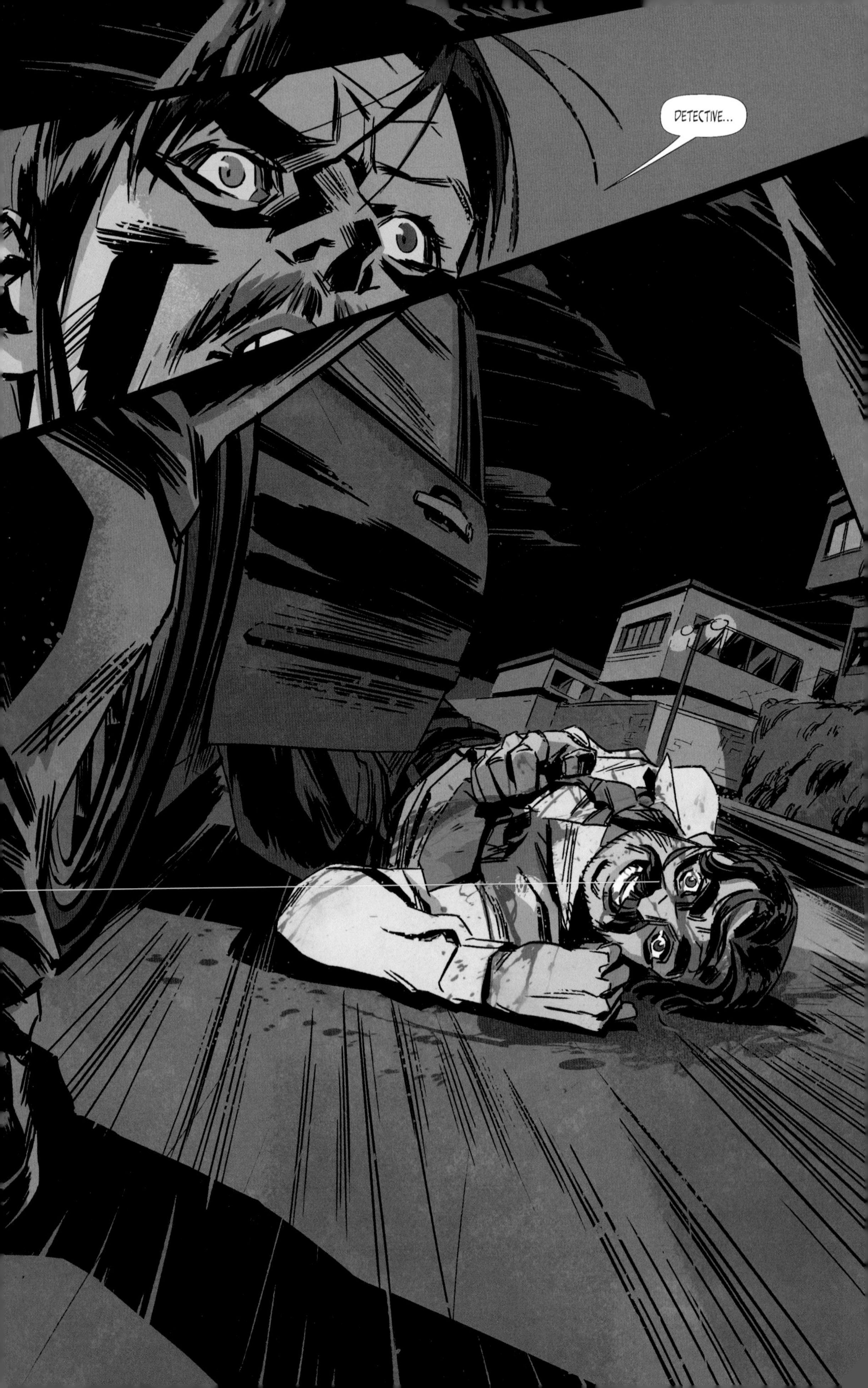
DETECTIVE...

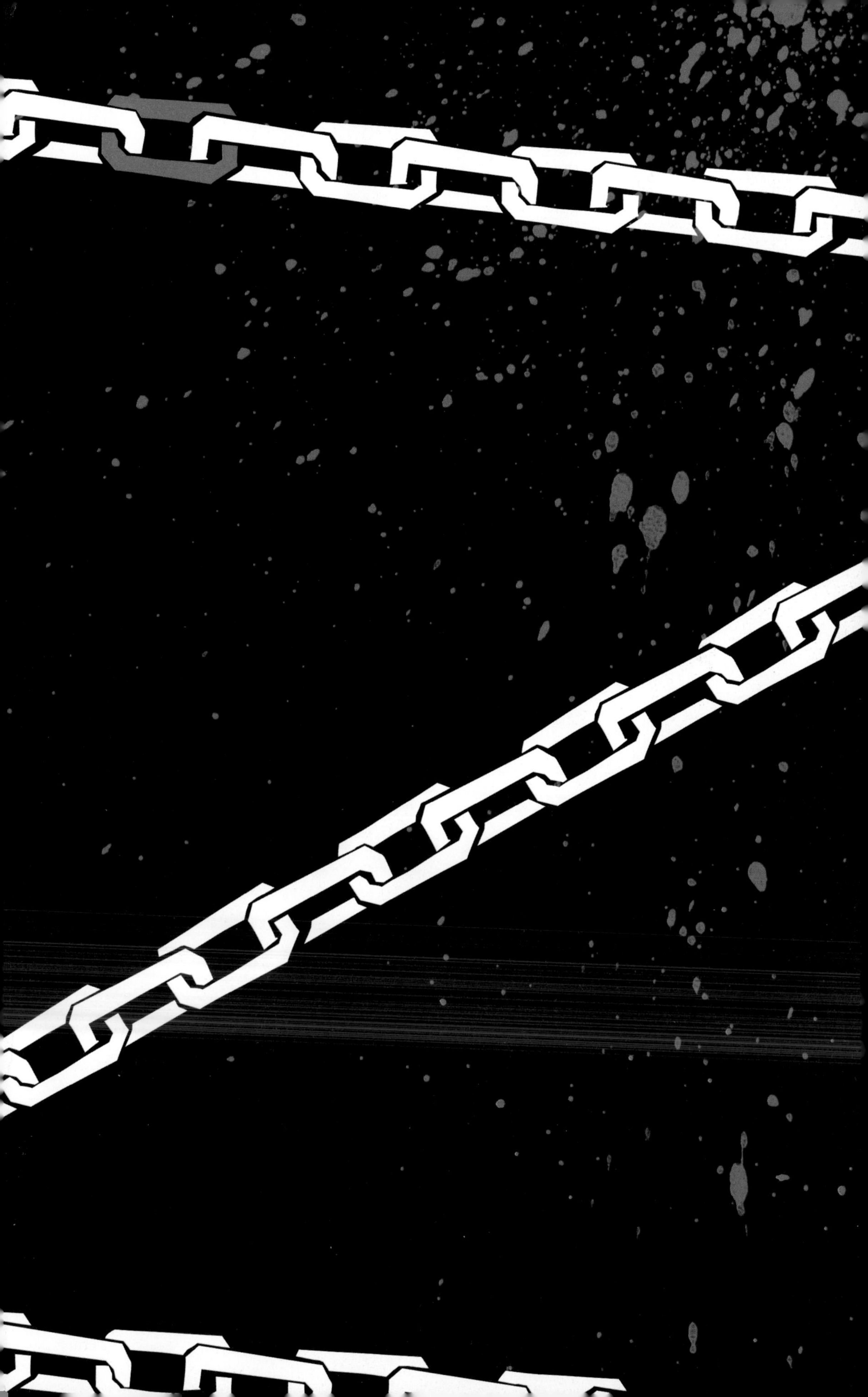

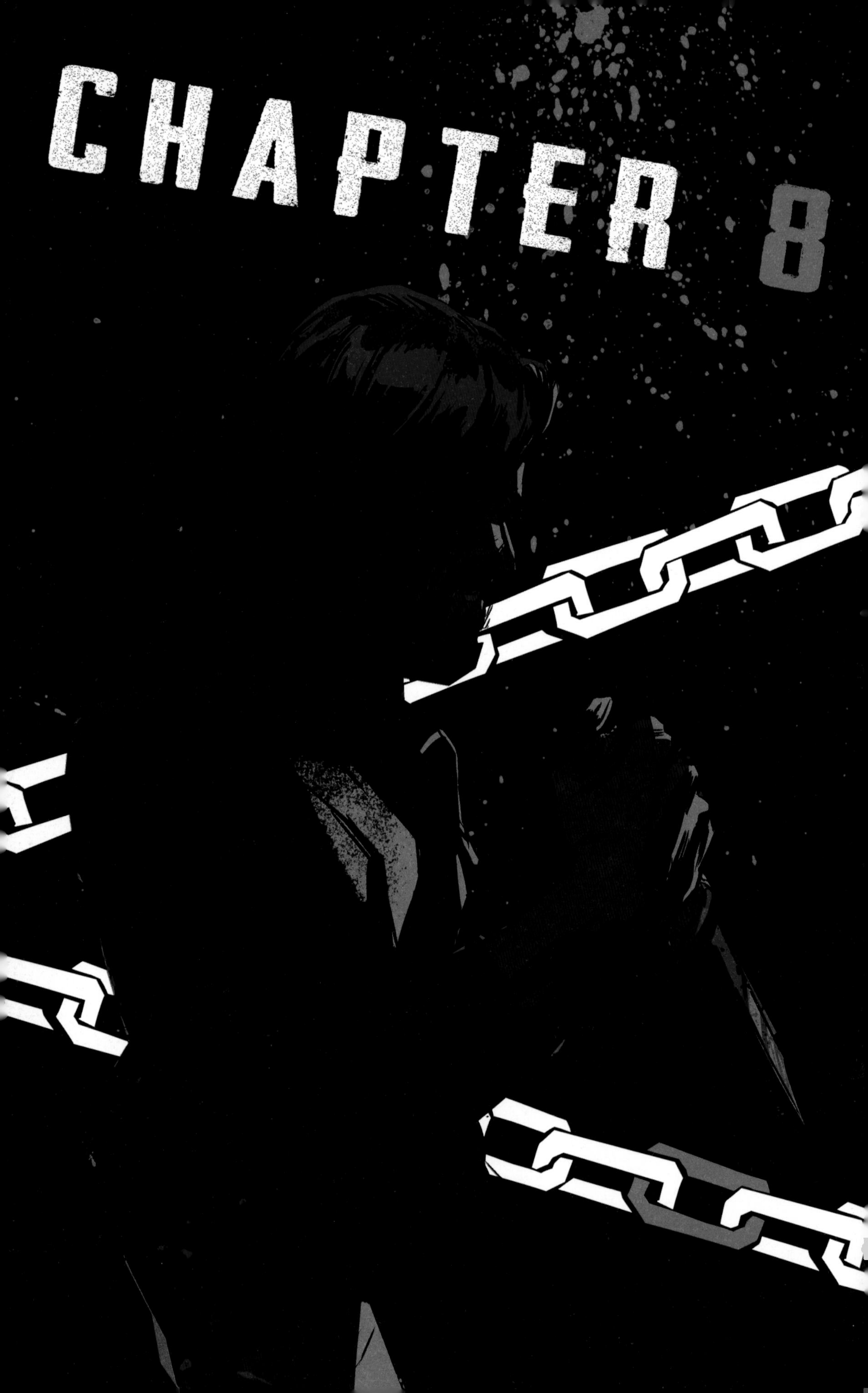
CHAPTER 8

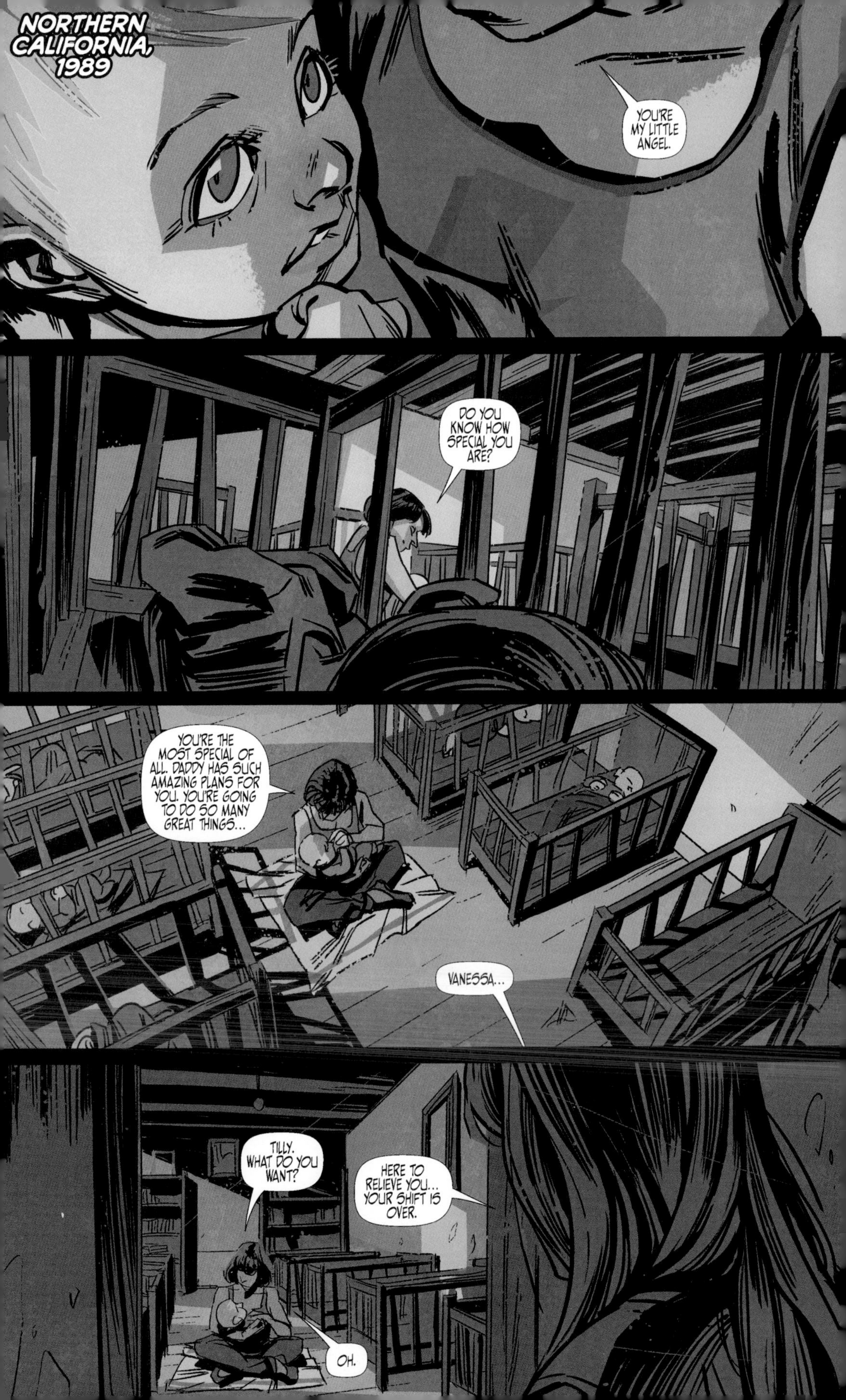
NORTHERN CALIFORNIA, 1989
YOU'RE MY LITTLE ANGEL.
DO YOU KNOW HOW SPECIAL YOU ARE?
YOU'RE THE MOST SPECIAL OF ALL. DADDY HAS SUCH AMAZING PLANS FOR YOU. YOU'RE GOING TO DO SO MANY GREAT THINGS...
VANESSA...
TILLY. WHAT DO YOU WANT?
HERE TO RELIEVE YOU... YOUR SHIFT IS OVER.
OH.

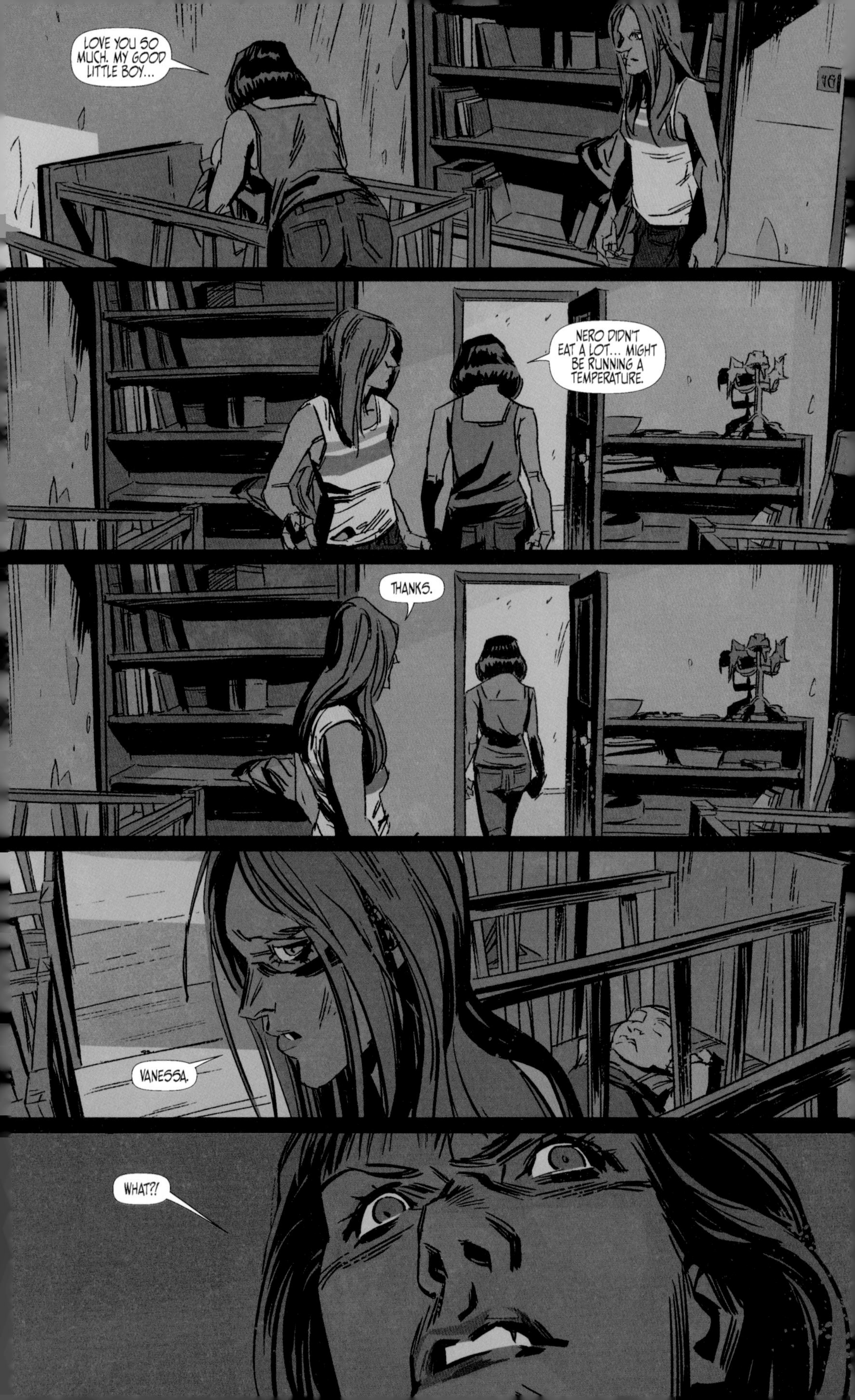
LOVE YOU SO MUCH. MY GOOD LITTLE BOY...
NERO DIDN'T EAT A LOT... MIGHT BE RUNNING A TEMPERATURE.
THANKS.
VANESSA.
WHAT?!

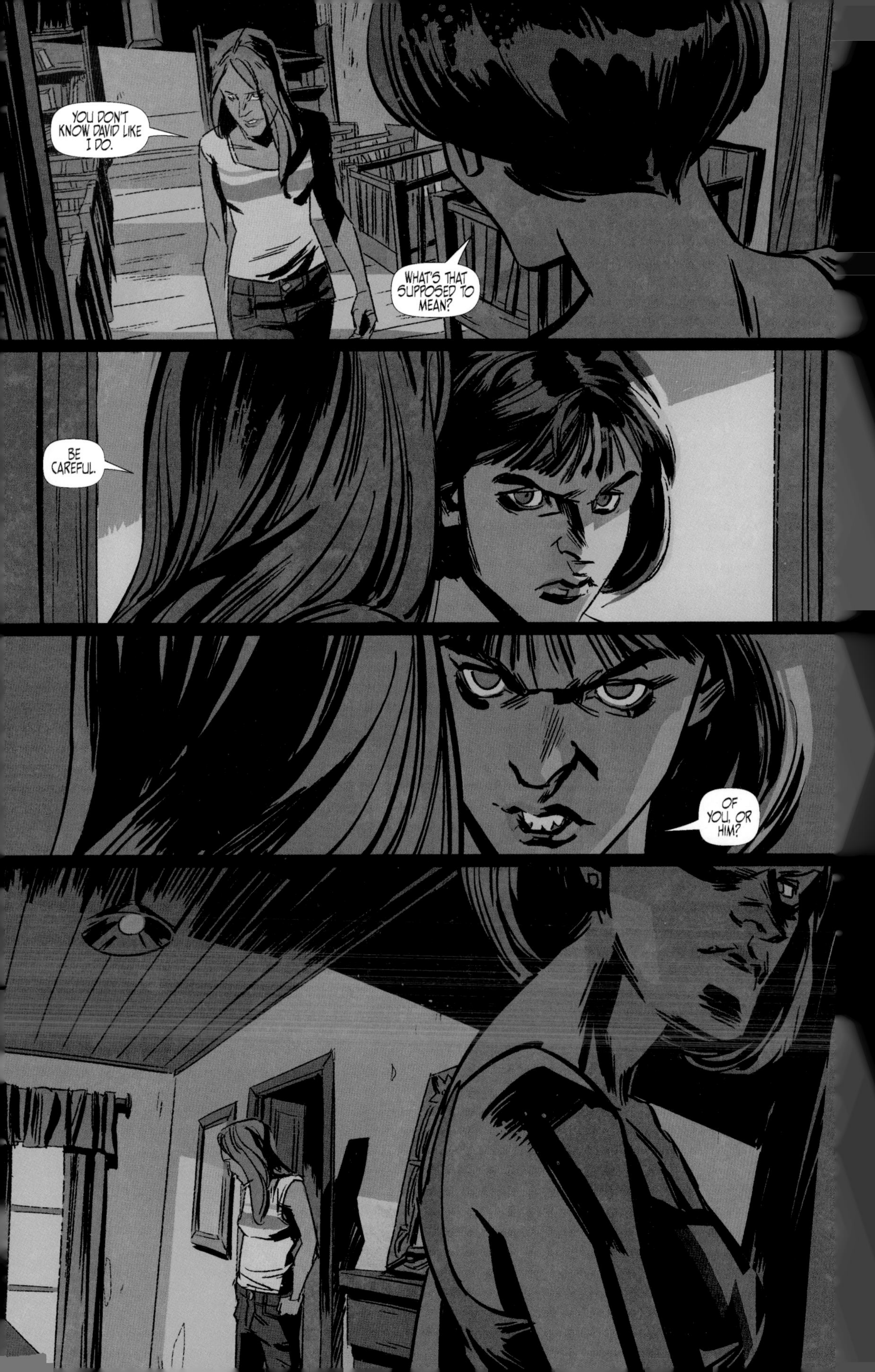
YOU DON'T KNOW DAVID LIKE I DO.
WHAT'S THAT SUPPOSED TO MEAN?
BE CAREFUL.
OF YOU, OR HIM?

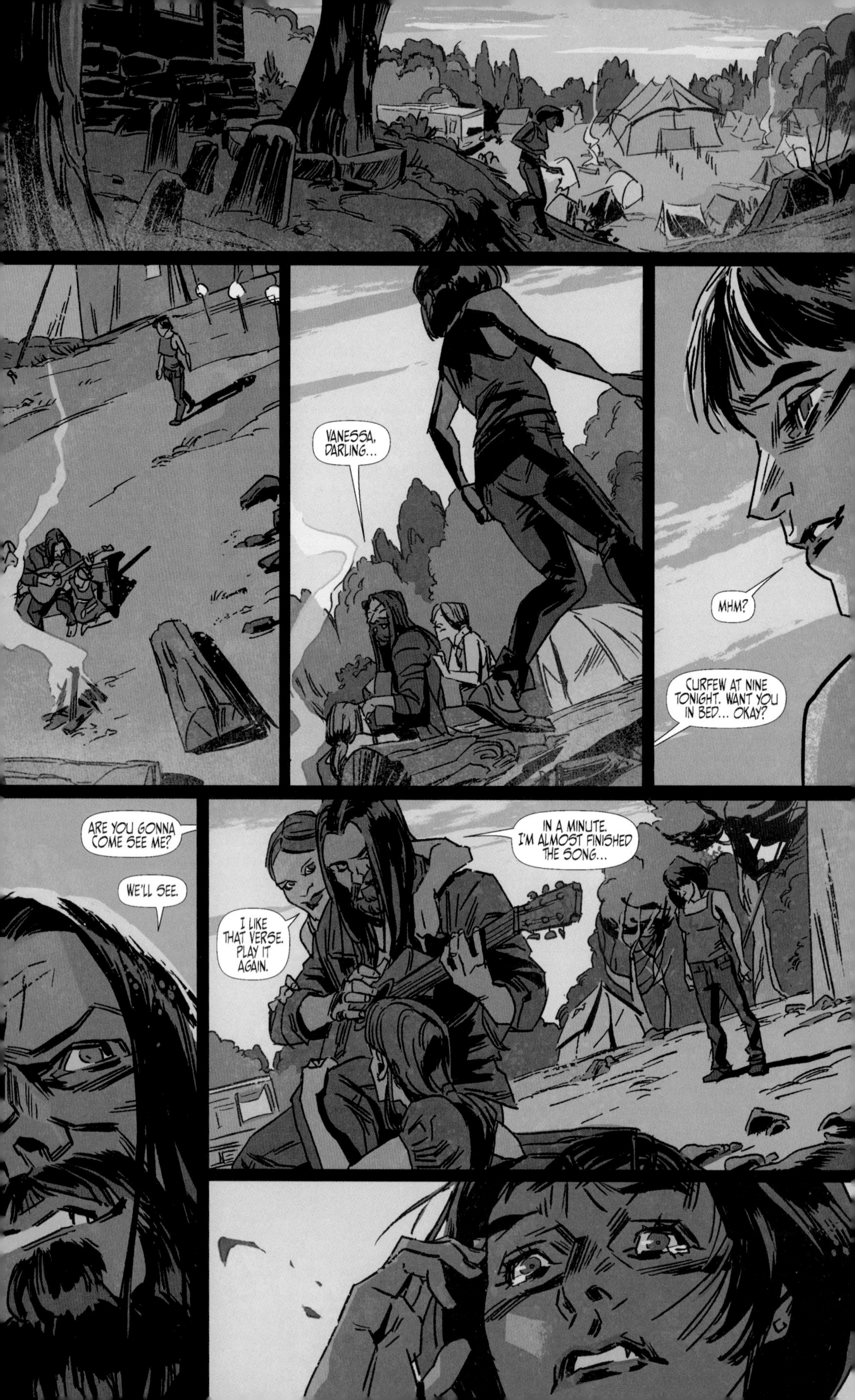
VANESSA, DARLING...
MHM?
CURFEW AT NINE TONIGHT. WANT YOU IN BED... OKAY?
ARE YOU GONNA COME SEE ME?
WE'LL SEE.
IN A MINUTE. I'M ALMOST FINISHED THE SONG...
I LIKE THAT VERSE. PLAY IT AGAIN.

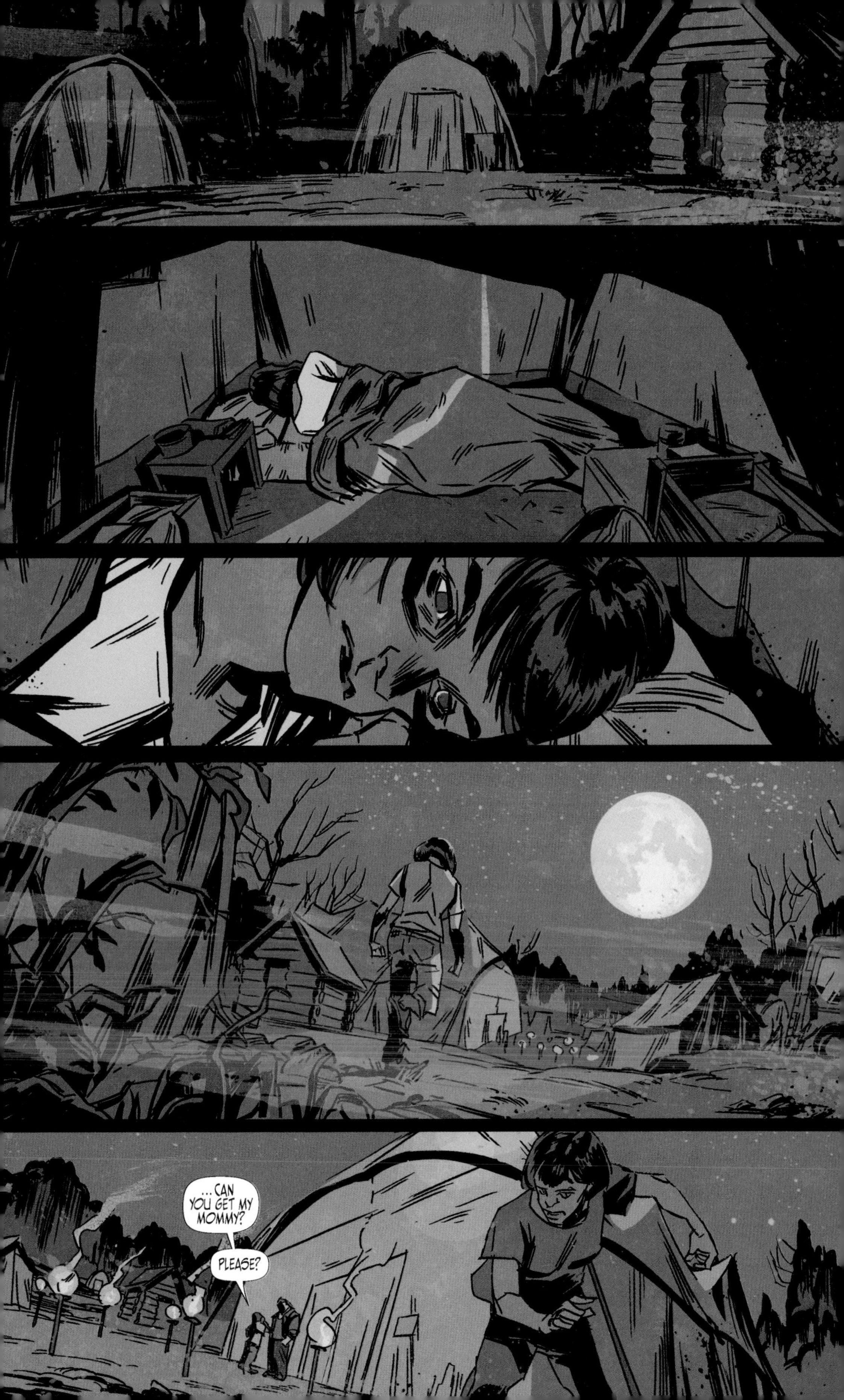
...CAN YOU GET MY MOMMY?
PLEASE?

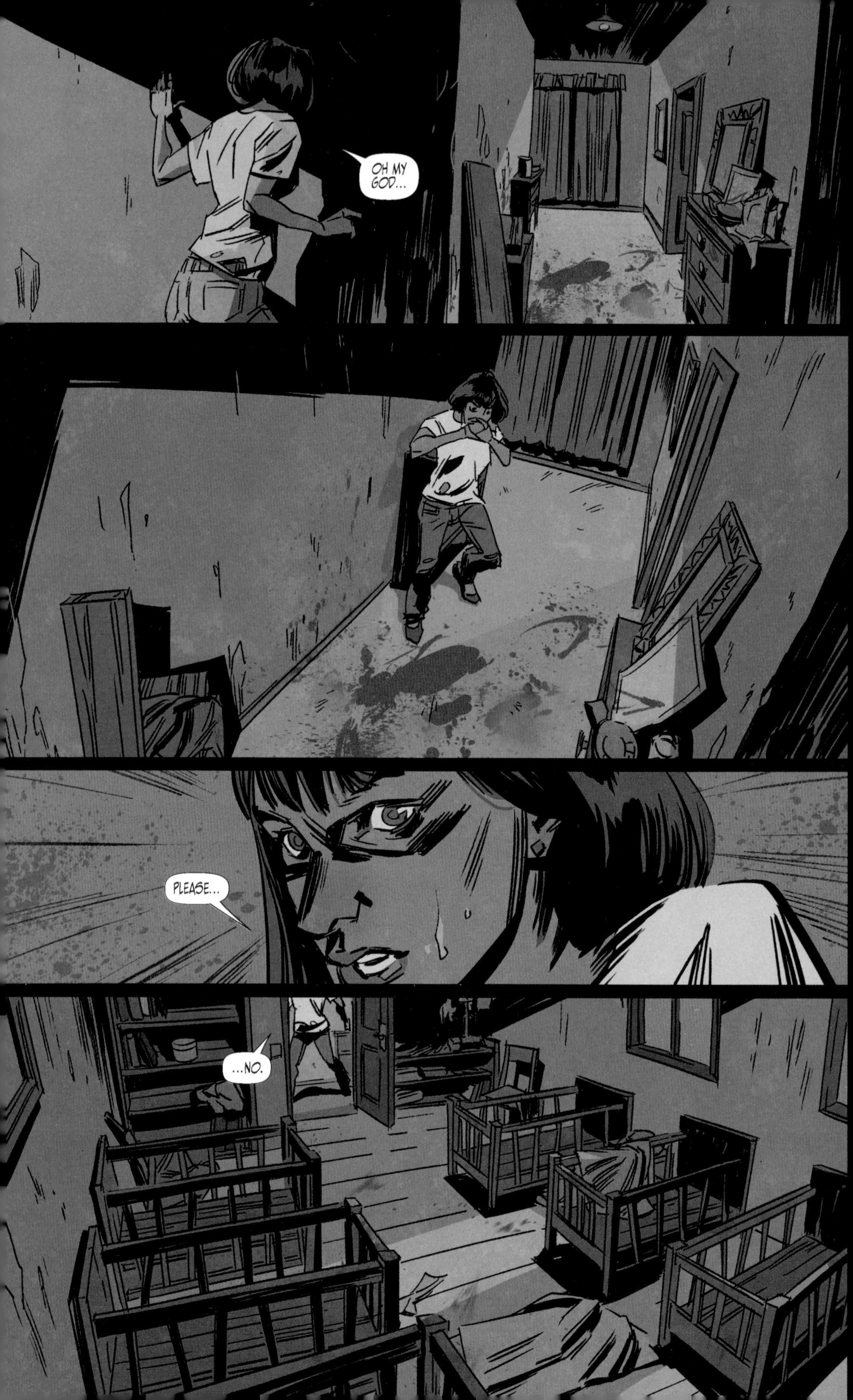
OH MY GOD...
PLEASE...
...NO.

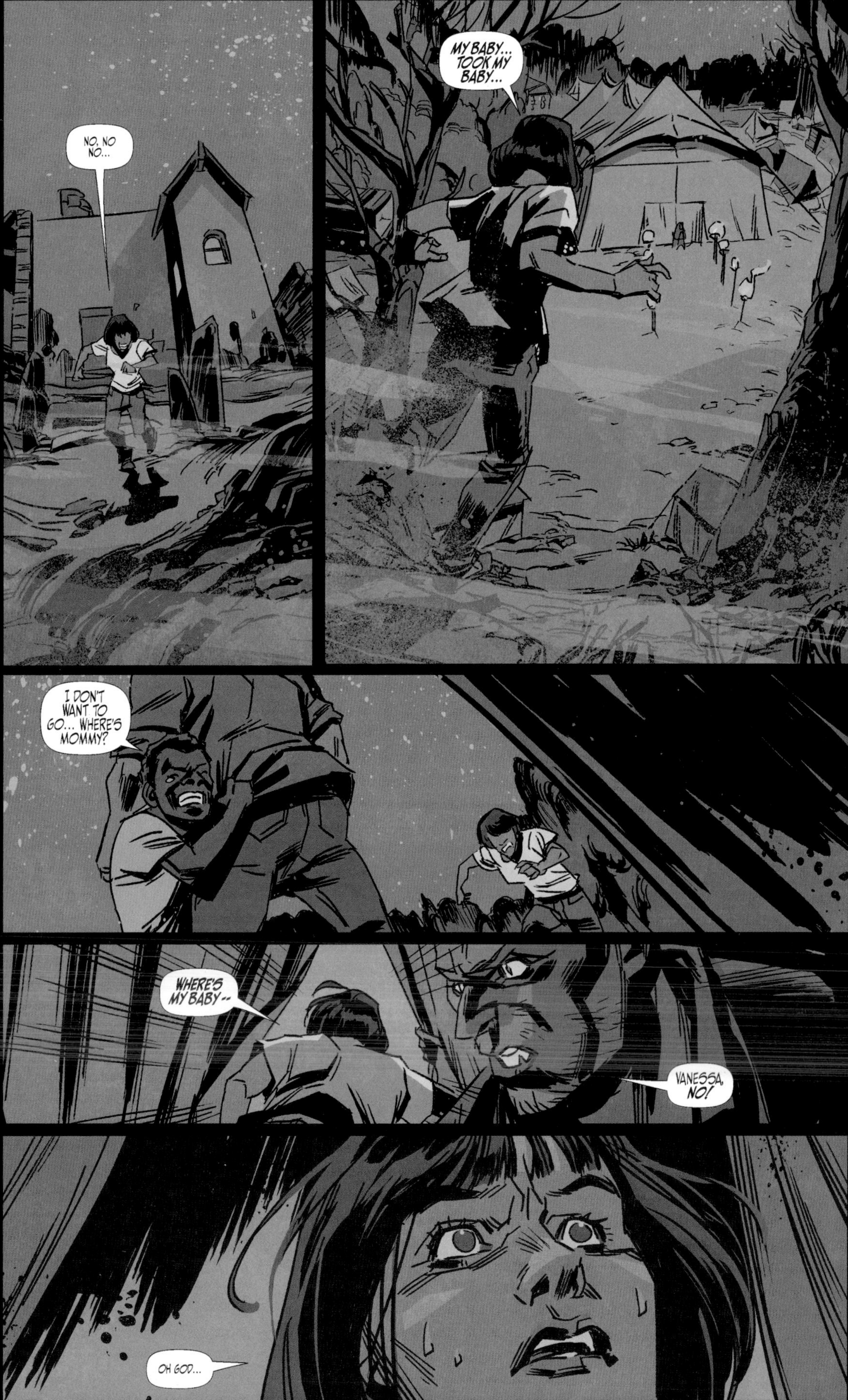
NO, NO
NO...
MY BABY...
TOOK MY
BABY...
I DON'T
WANT TO
GO... WHERE'S
MOMMY?
WHERE'S
MY BABY--
VANESSA,
NO!
OH GOD...

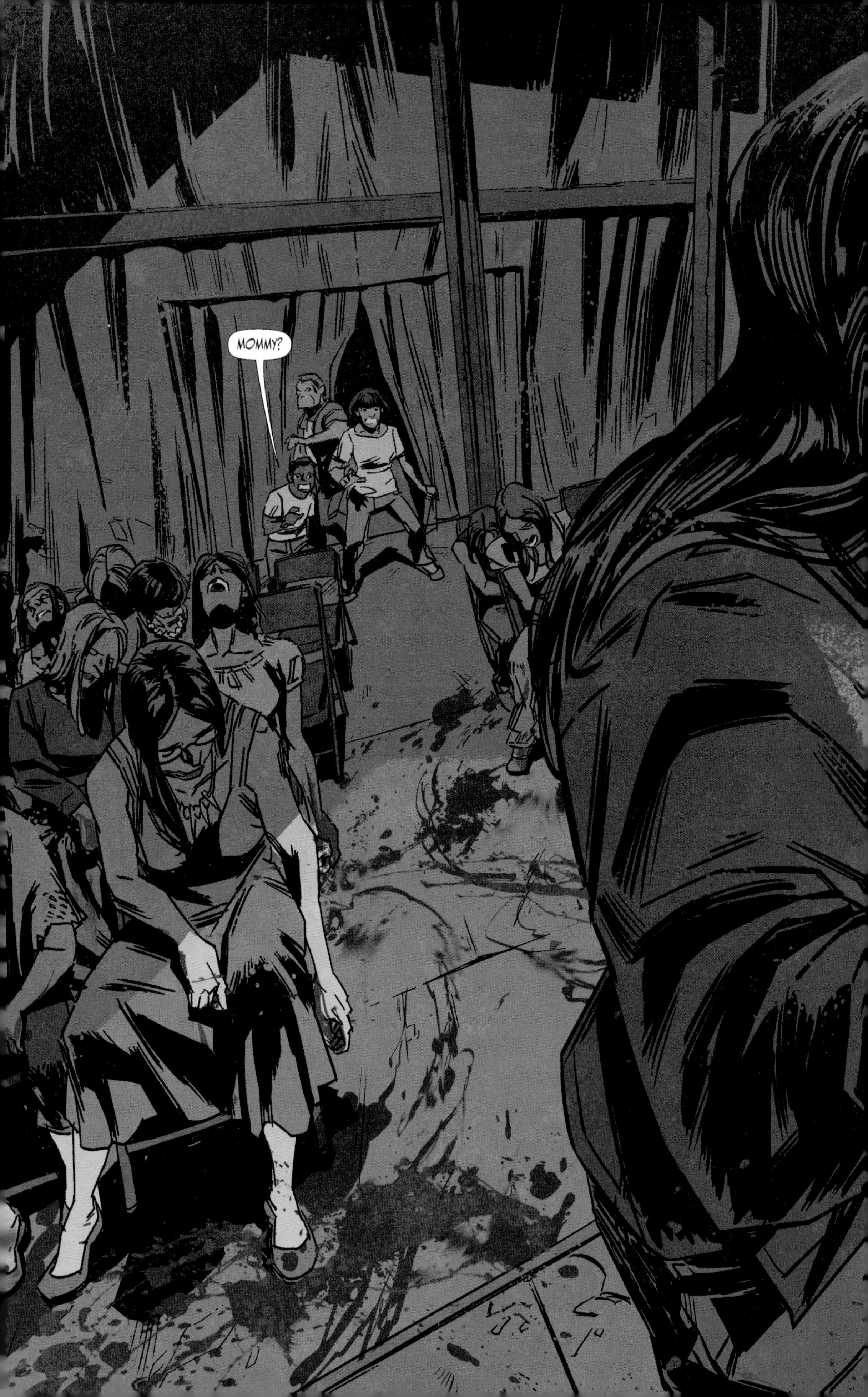
MOMMY?

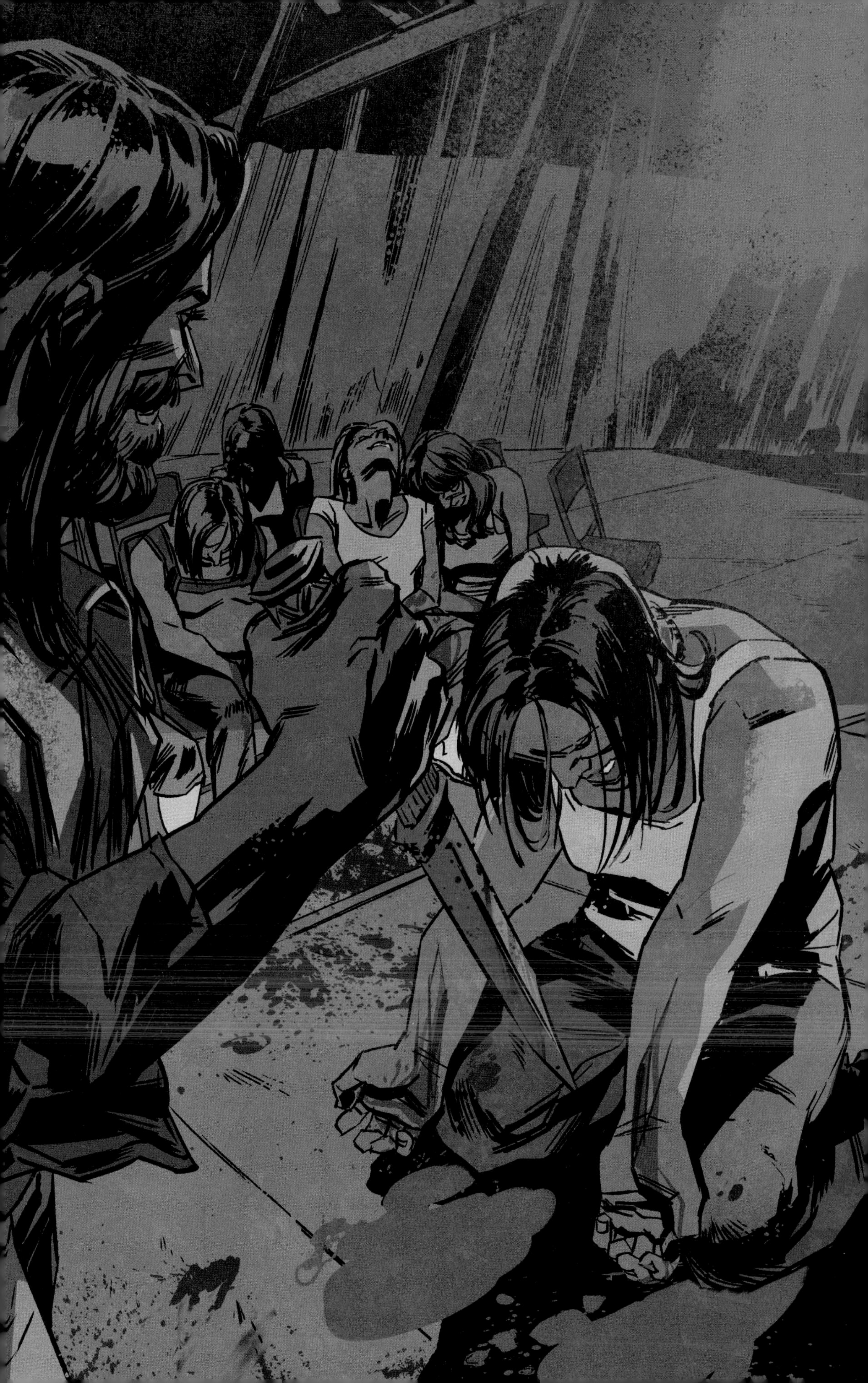

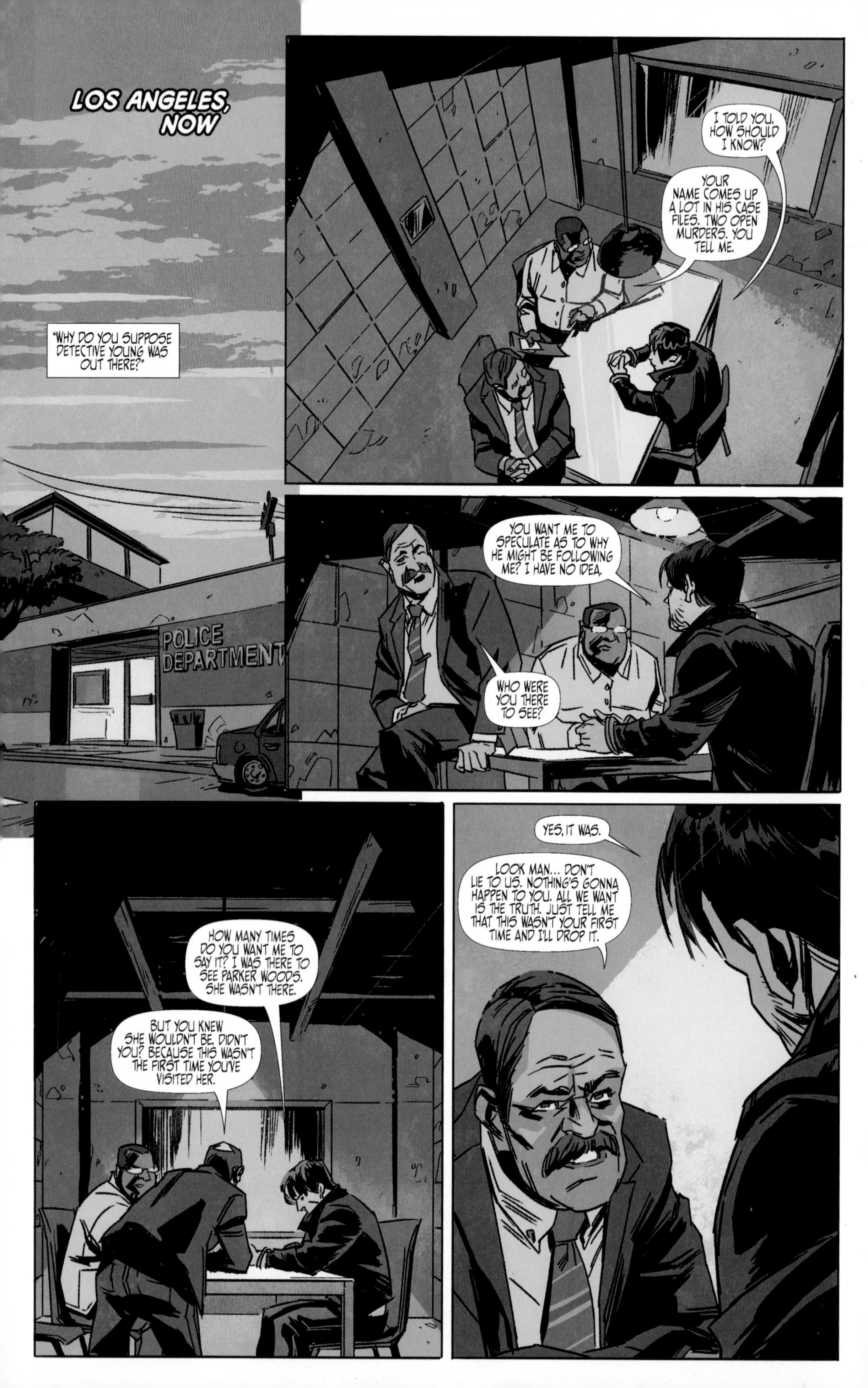
LOS ANGELES, NOW
I TOLD YOU. HOW SHOULD I KNOW?
YOUR NAME COMES UP A LOT IN HIS CASE FILES. TWO OPEN MURDERS. YOU TELL ME.
"WHY DO YOU SUPPOSE DETECTIVE YOUNG WAS OUT THERE?"
YOU WANT ME TO SPECULATE AS TO WHY HE MIGHT BE FOLLOWING ME? I HAVE NO IDEA.
WHO WERE YOU THERE TO SEE?
POLICE DEPARTMENT
HOW MANY TIMES DO YOU WANT ME TO SAY IT? I WAS THERE TO SEE PARKER WOODS. SHE WASN'T THERE.
BUT YOU KNEW SHE WOULDN'T BE, DIDN'T YOU? BECAUSE THIS WASN'T THE FIRST TIME YOU'VE VISITED HER.
YES, IT WAS.
LOOK MAN... DON'T LIE TO US. NOTHING'S GONNA HAPPEN TO YOU. ALL WE WANT IS THE TRUTH. JUST TELL ME THAT THIS WASN'T YOUR FIRST TIME AND I'LL DROP IT.

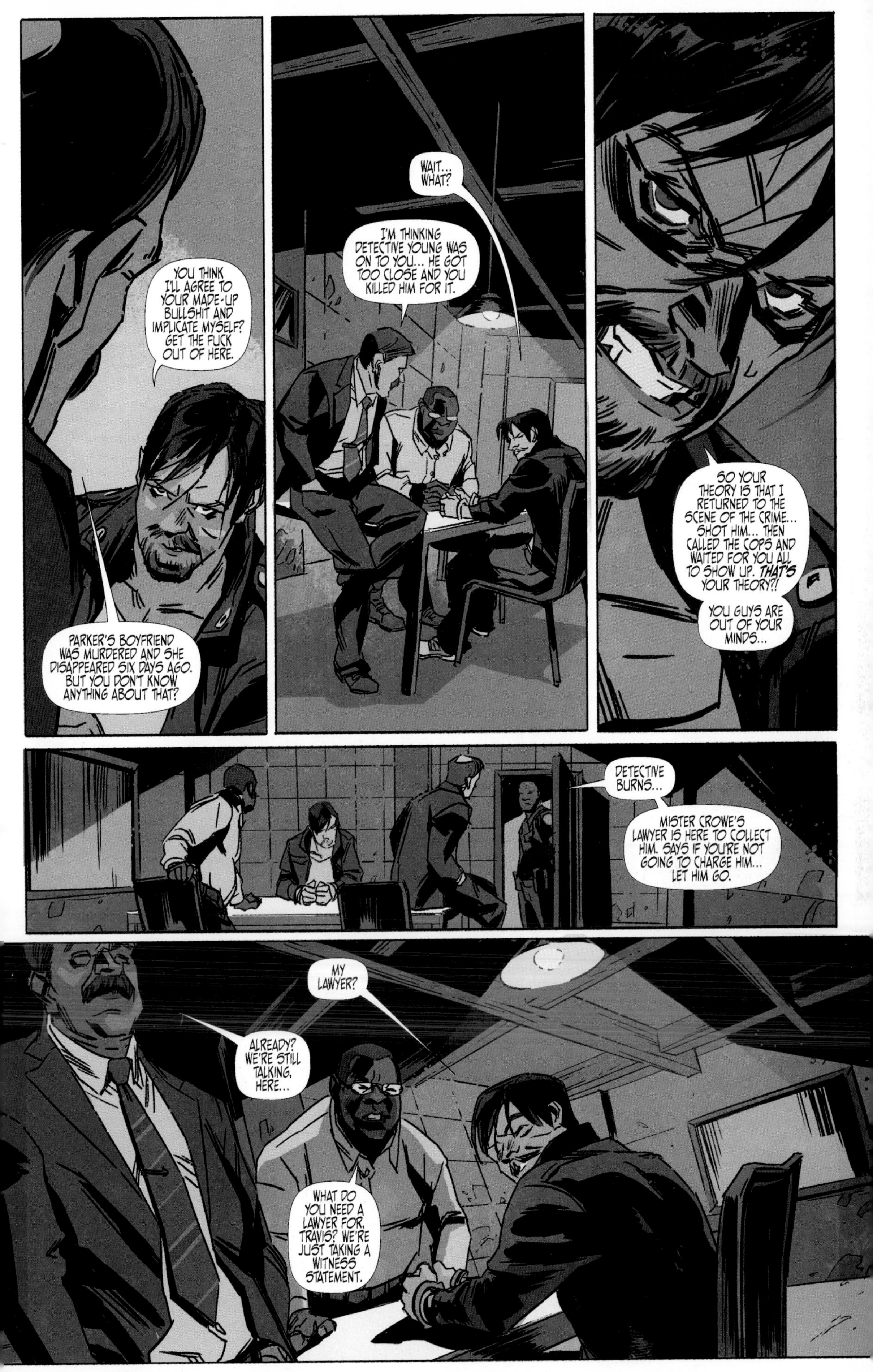

YOU THINK I'LL AGREE TO YOUR MADE-UP BULLSHIT AND IMPLICATE MYSELF? GET THE FUCK OUT OF HERE.
PARKER'S BOYFRIEND WAS MURDERED AND SHE DISAPPEARED SIX DAYS AGO. BUT YOU DON'T KNOW ANYTHING ABOUT THAT?
WAIT... WHAT?
I'M THINKING DETECTIVE YOUNG WAS ON TO YOU... HE GOT TOO CLOSE AND YOU KILLED HIM FOR IT.
SO YOUR THEORY IS THAT I RETURNED TO THE SCENE OF THE CRIME... SHOT HIM... THEN CALLED THE COPS AND WAITED FOR YOU ALL TO SHOW UP. THAT'S YOUR THEORY?!
YOU GUYS ARE OUT OF YOUR MINDS...
DETECTIVE BURNS...
MISTER CROWE'S LAWYER IS HERE TO COLLECT HIM. SAYS IF YOU'RE NOT GOING TO CHARGE HIM... LET HIM GO.
MY LAWYER?
ALREADY? WE'RE STILL TALKING, HERE...
WHAT DO YOU NEED A LAWYER FOR, TRAVIS? WE'RE JUST TAKING A WITNESS STATEMENT.

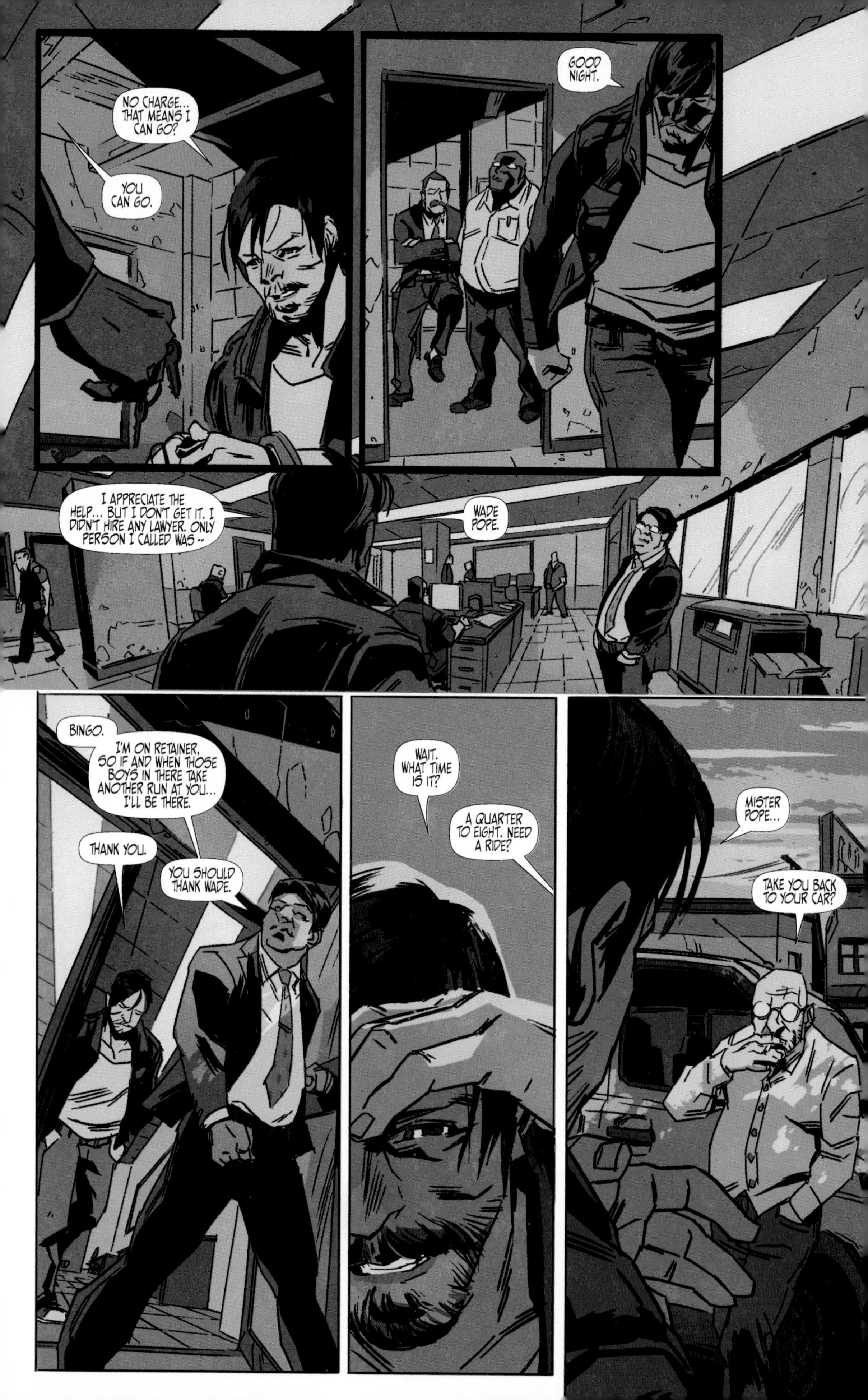

NO CHARGE... THAT MEANS I CAN GO?
YOU CAN GO.
GOOD NIGHT.
I APPRECIATE THE HELP... BUT I DON'T GET IT. I DIDN'T HIRE ANY LAWYER. ONLY PERSON I CALLED WAS --
WADE POPE.
BINGO.
I'M ON RETAINER, SO IF AND WHEN THOSE BOYS IN THERE TAKE ANOTHER RUN AT YOU... I'LL BE THERE.
THANK YOU.
YOU SHOULD THANK WADE.
WAIT. WHAT TIME IS IT?
A QUARTER TO EIGHT. NEED A RIDE?
MISTER POPE...
TAKE YOU BACK TO YOUR CAR?

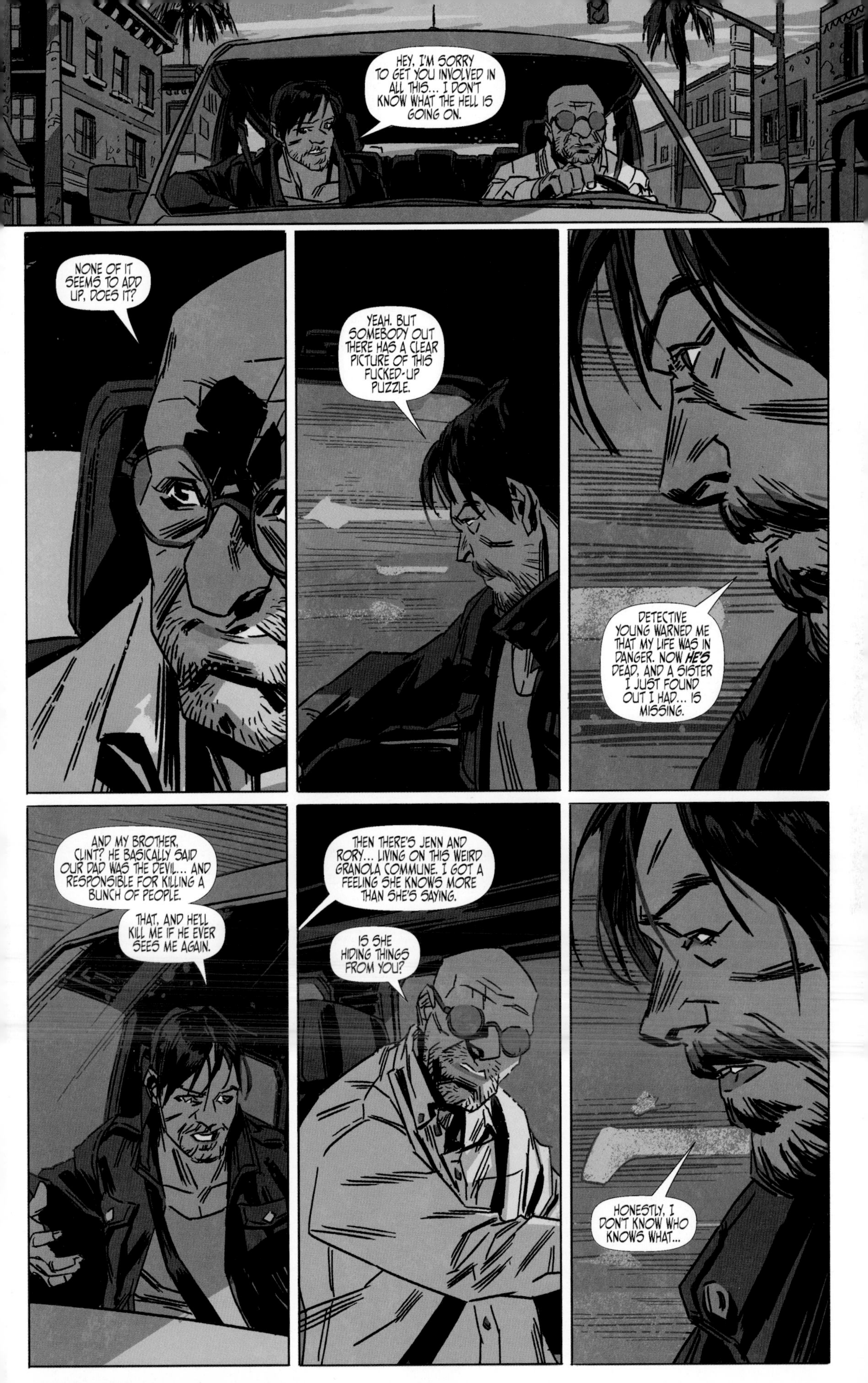
HEY, I'M SORRY TO GET YOU INVOLVED IN ALL THIS... I DON'T KNOW WHAT THE HELL IS GOING ON.
NONE OF IT SEEMS TO ADD UP, DOES IT?
YEAH. BUT SOMEBODY OUT THERE HAS A CLEAR PICTURE OF THIS FUCKED-UP PUZZLE.
DETECTIVE YOUNG WARNED ME THAT MY LIFE WAS IN DANGER. NOW *HE'S* DEAD, AND A SISTER I JUST FOUND OUT I HAD... IS MISSING.
AND MY BROTHER, CLINT? HE BASICALLY SAID OUR DAD WAS THE DEVIL... AND RESPONSIBLE FOR KILLING A BUNCH OF PEOPLE.
THAT, AND HE'LL KILL ME IF HE EVER SEES ME AGAIN.
THEN THERE'S JENN AND RORY... LIVING ON THIS WEIRD GRANOLA COMMUNE. I GOT A FEELING SHE KNOWS MORE THAN SHE'S SAYING.
IS SHE HIDING THINGS FROM YOU?
HONESTLY, I DON'T KNOW WHO KNOWS WHAT...

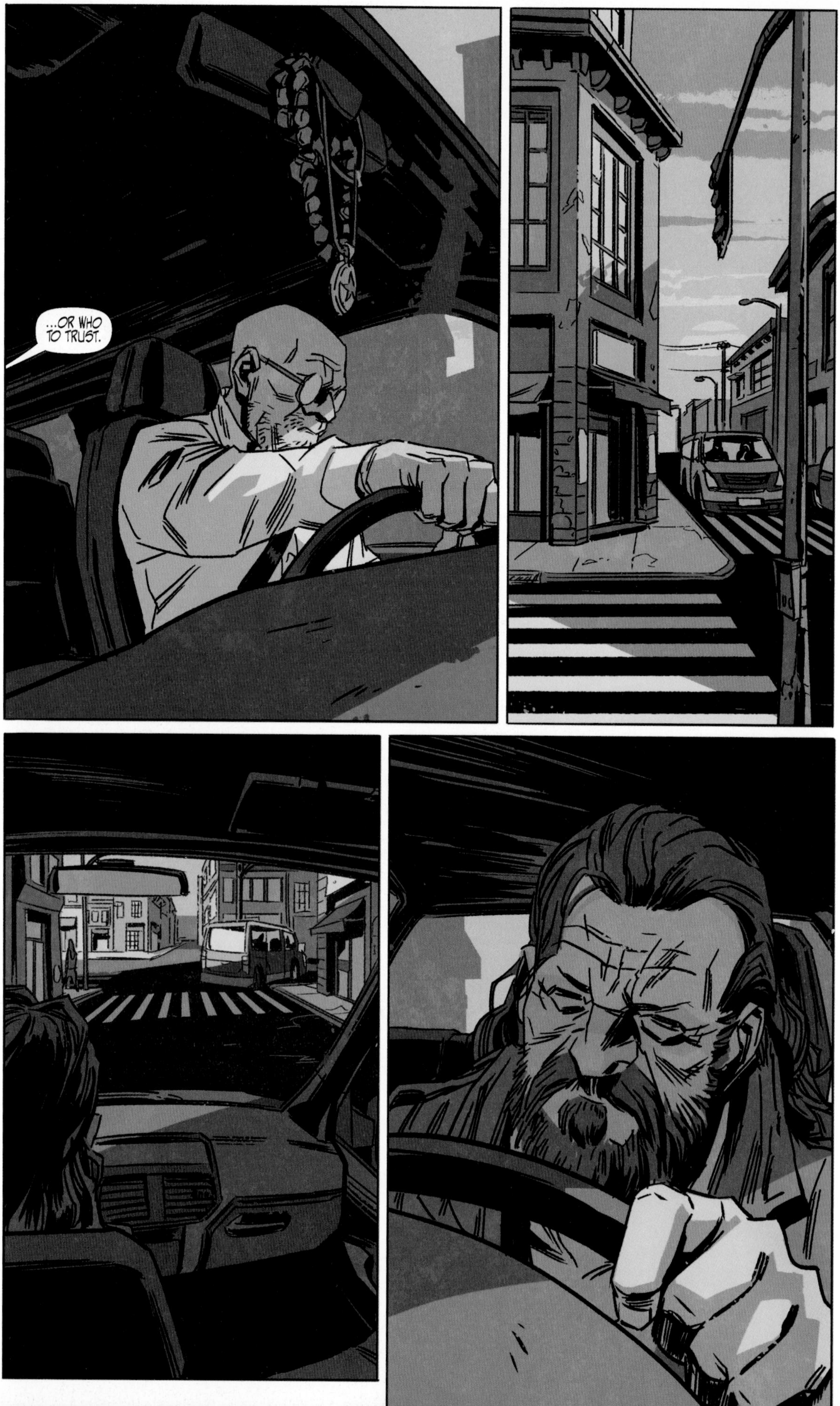
...OR WHO TO TRUST.

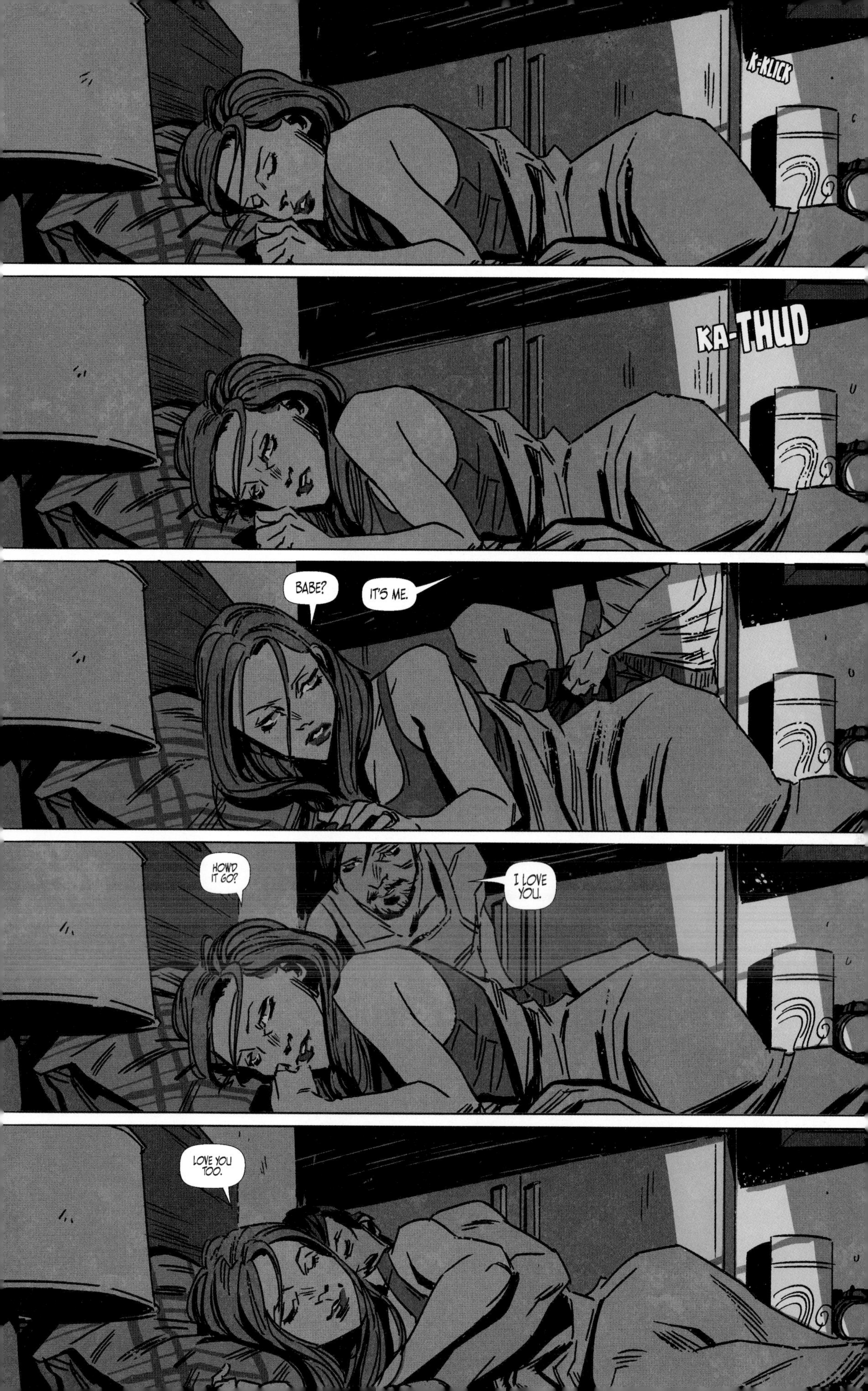
K-KLICK
KA-THUD
BABE?
IT'S ME.
HOW'D IT GO?
I LOVE YOU.
LOVE YOU TOO.

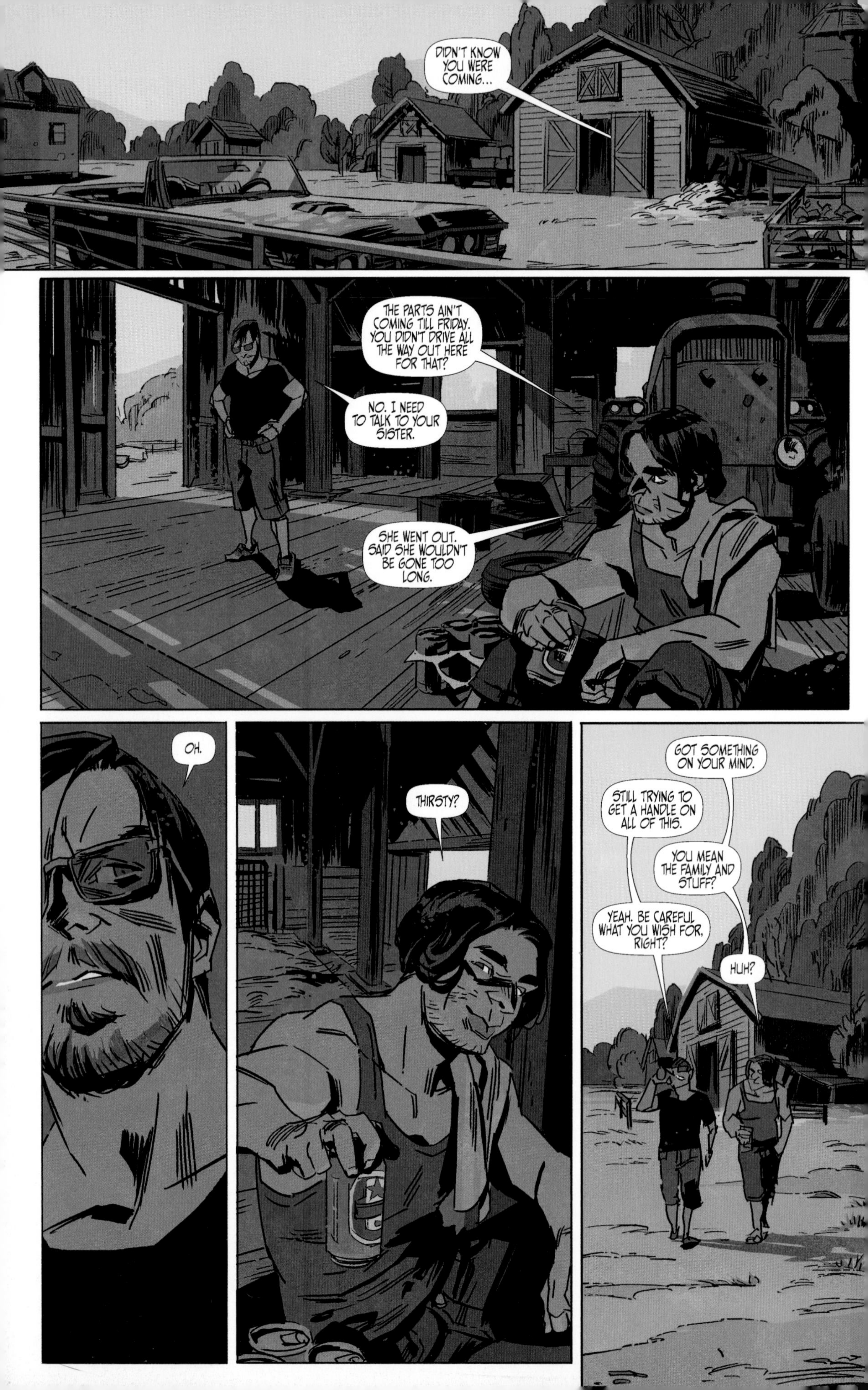
DIDN'T KNOW YOU WERE COMING...
THE PARTS AIN'T COMING TILL FRIDAY. YOU DIDN'T DRIVE ALL THE WAY OUT HERE FOR THAT?
NO. I NEED TO TALK TO YOUR SISTER.
SHE WENT OUT. SAID SHE WOULDN'T BE GONE TOO LONG.
OH.
THIRSTY?
GOT SOMETHING ON YOUR MIND.
STILL TRYING TO GET A HANDLE ON ALL OF THIS.
YOU MEAN THE FAMILY AND STUFF?
YEAH. BE CAREFUL WHAT YOU WISH FOR, RIGHT?
HUH?

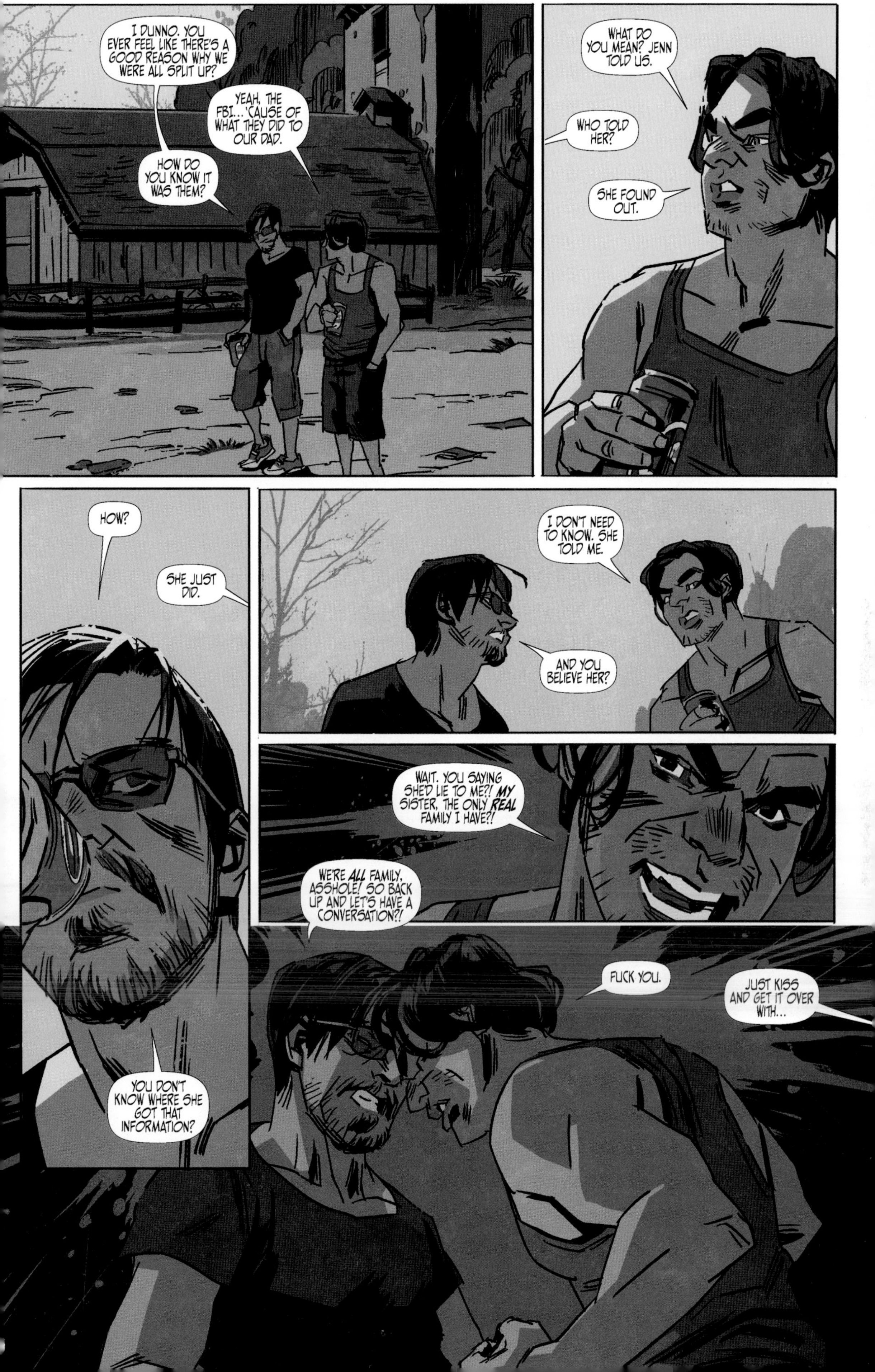
I DUNNO. YOU EVER FEEL LIKE THERE'S A GOOD REASON WHY WE WERE ALL SPLIT UP?
YEAH, THE FBI... 'CAUSE OF WHAT THEY DID TO OUR DAD.
HOW DO YOU KNOW IT WAS THEM?
WHAT DO YOU MEAN? JENN TOLD US.
WHO TOLD HER?
SHE FOUND OUT.
HOW?
SHE JUST DID.
YOU DON'T KNOW WHERE SHE GOT THAT INFORMATION?
I DON'T NEED TO KNOW. SHE TOLD ME.
AND YOU BELIEVE HER?
WAIT. YOU SAYING SHE'D LIE TO ME?! MY SISTER, THE ONLY REAL FAMILY I HAVE?!
WE'RE ALL FAMILY, ASSHOLE! SO BACK UP AND LET'S HAVE A CONVERSATION?!
FUCK YOU.
JUST KISS AND GET IT OVER WITH...

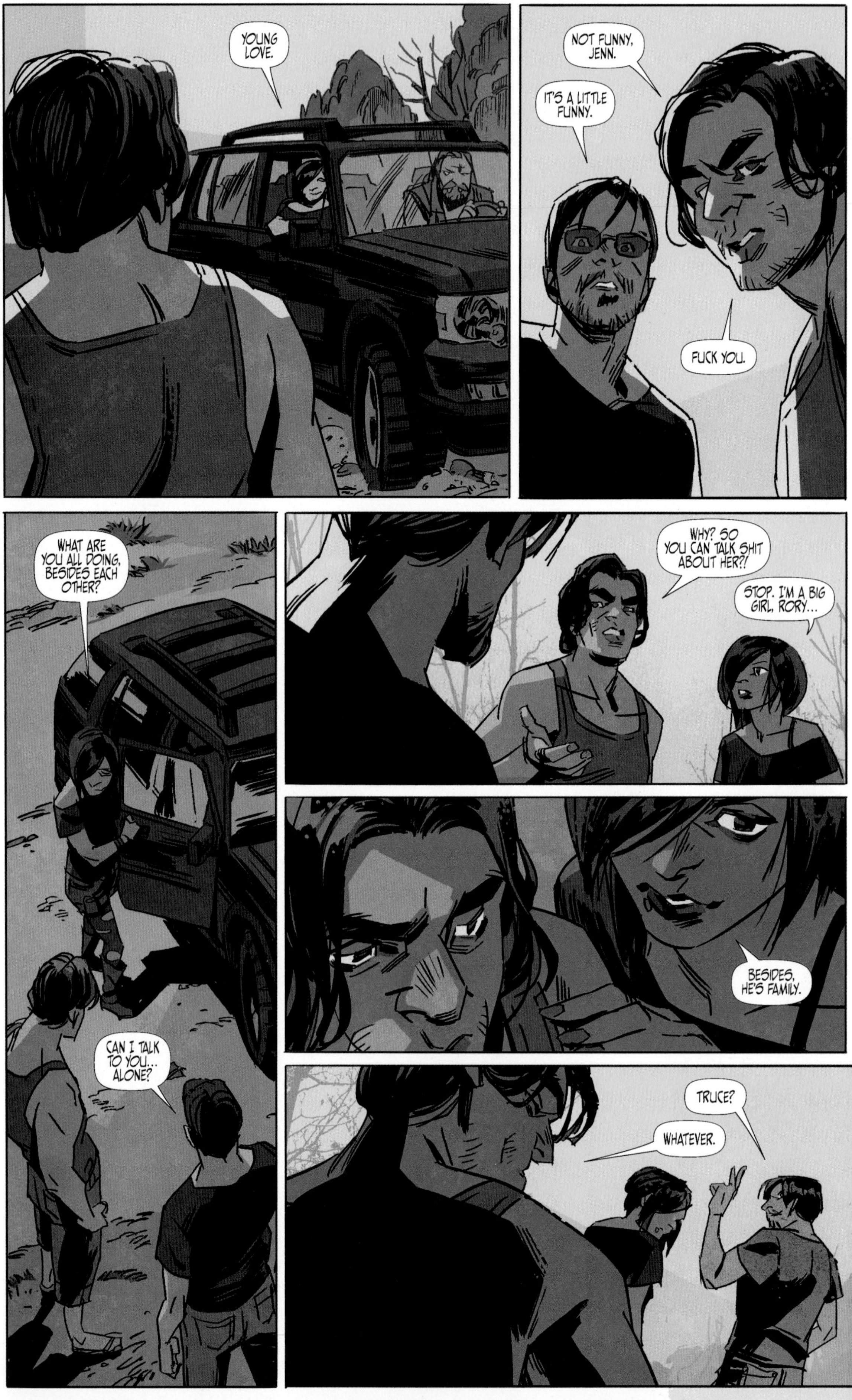
YOUNG LOVE.
NOT FUNNY, JENN.
IT'S A LITTLE FUNNY.
FUCK YOU.
WHAT ARE YOU ALL DOING, BESIDES EACH OTHER?
CAN I TALK TO YOU... ALONE?
WHY? SO YOU CAN TALK SHIT ABOUT HER?!
STOP. I'M A BIG GIRL, RORY...
BESIDES, HE'S FAMILY.
TRUCE?
WHATEVER.

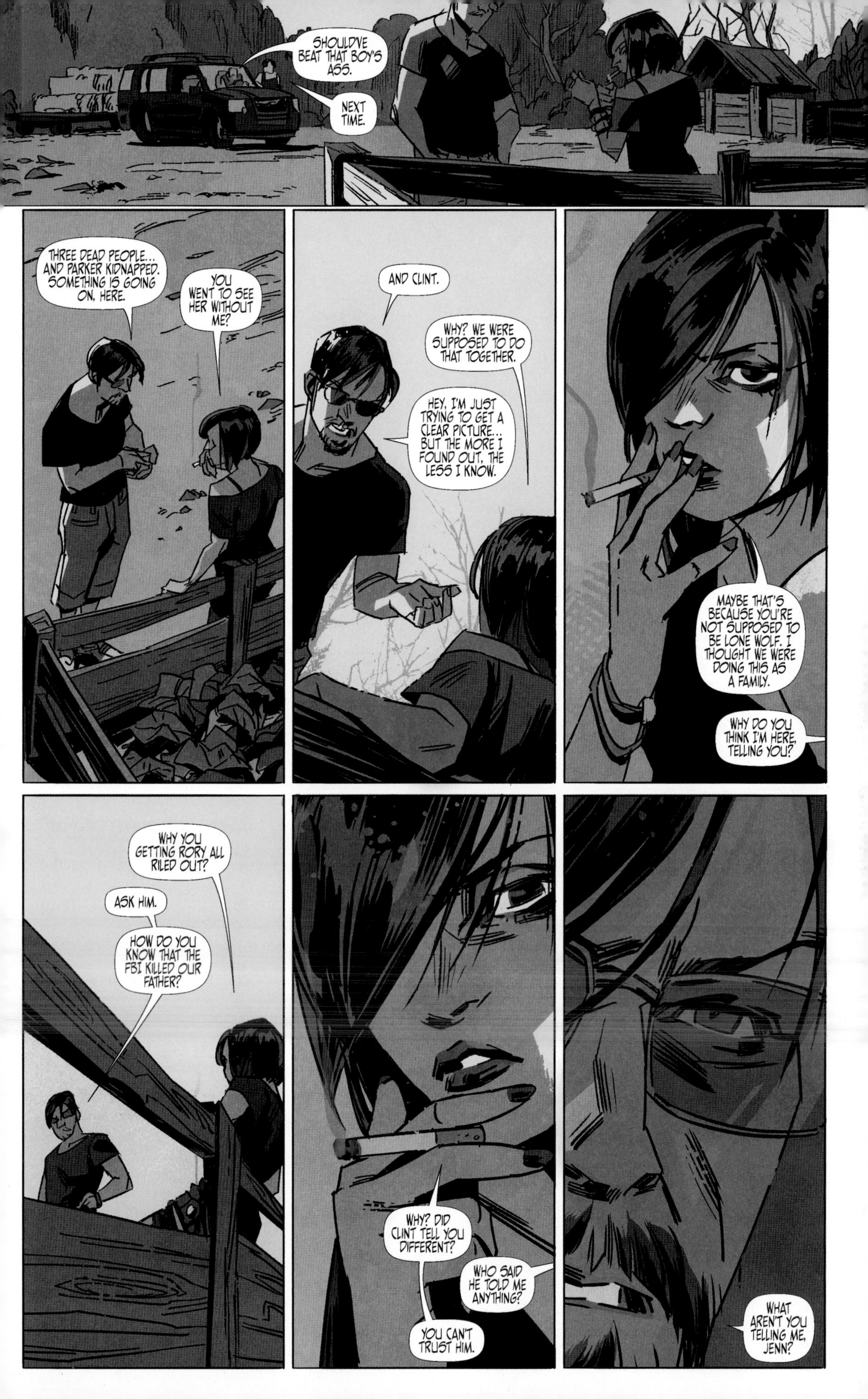
SHOULD'VE BEAT THAT BOY'S ASS.
NEXT TIME.
THREE DEAD PEOPLE... AND PARKER KIDNAPPED. SOMETHING IS GOING ON, HERE.
YOU WENT TO SEE HER WITHOUT ME?
AND CLINT.
WHY? WE WERE SUPPOSED TO DO THAT TOGETHER.
HEY, I'M JUST TRYING TO GET A CLEAR PICTURE... BUT THE MORE I FOUND OUT, THE LESS I KNOW.
MAYBE THAT'S BECAUSE YOU'RE NOT SUPPOSED TO BE LONE WOLF. I THOUGHT WE WERE DOING THIS AS A FAMILY.
WHY DO YOU THINK I'M HERE, TELLING YOU?
WHY YOU GETTING RORY ALL RILED OUT?
ASK HIM.
HOW DO YOU KNOW THAT THE FBI KILLED OUR FATHER?
WHY? DID CLINT TELL YOU DIFFERENT?
WHO SAID HE TOLD ME ANYTHING?
YOU CAN'T TRUST HIM.
WHAT AREN'T YOU TELLING ME, JENN?

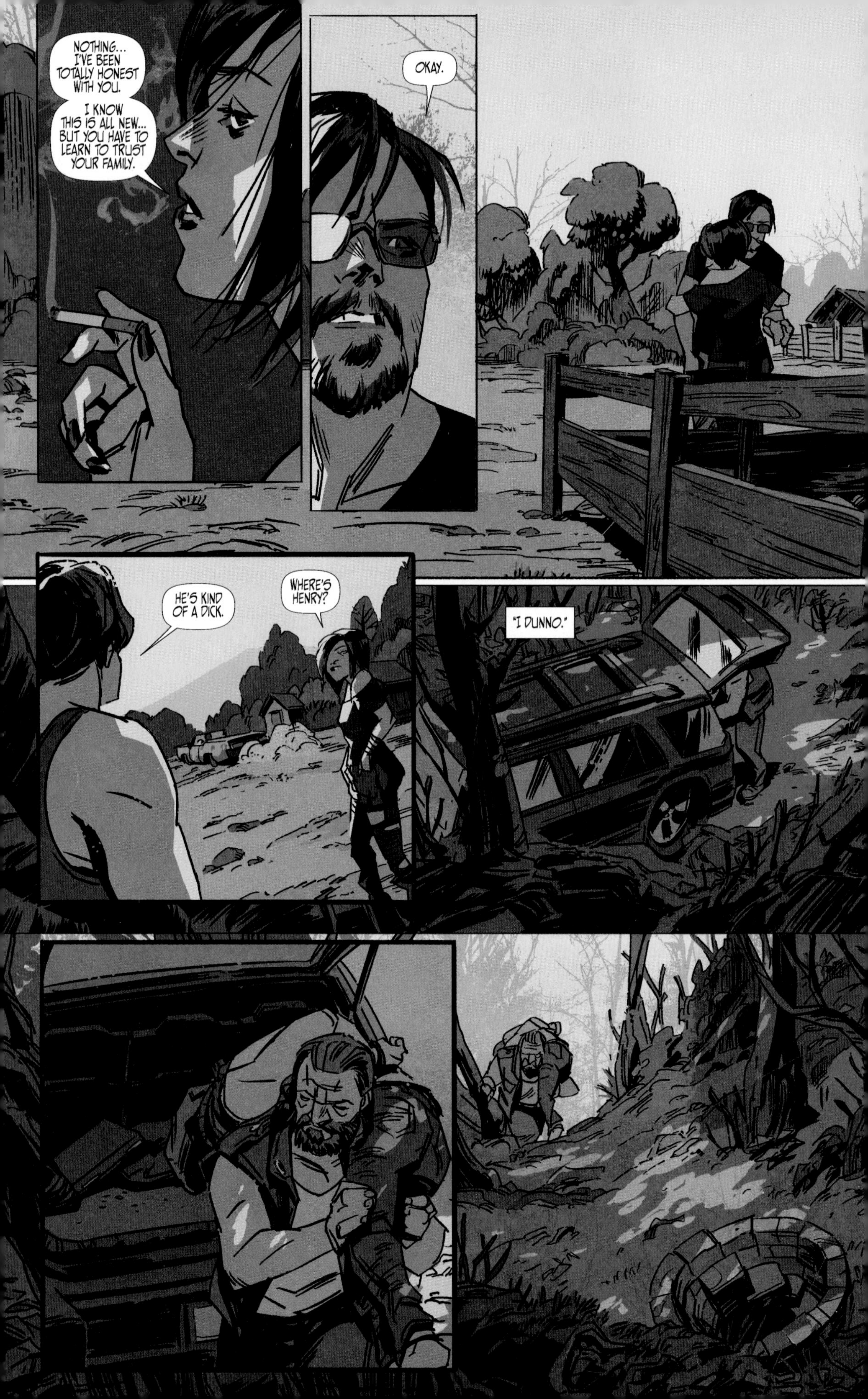
NOTHING... I'VE BEEN TOTALLY HONEST WITH YOU.
I KNOW THIS IS ALL NEW... BUT YOU HAVE TO LEARN TO TRUST YOUR FAMILY.
OKAY.
HE'S KIND OF A DICK.
WHERE'S HENRY?
"I DUNNO."

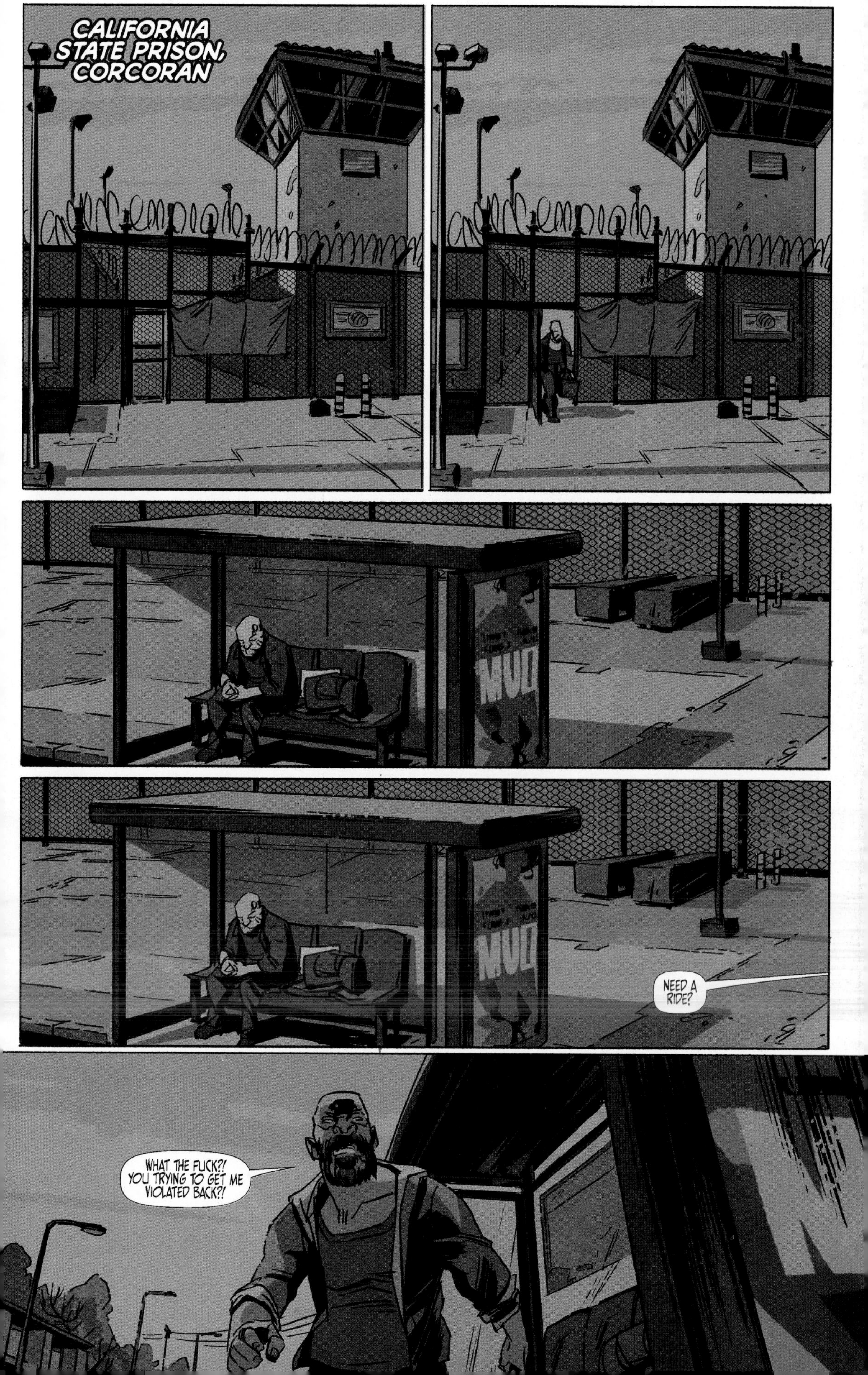
CALIFORNIA STATE PRISON, CORCORAN
MUD
NEED A RIDE?
WHAT THE FUCK?! YOU TRYING TO GET ME VIOLATED BACK?!

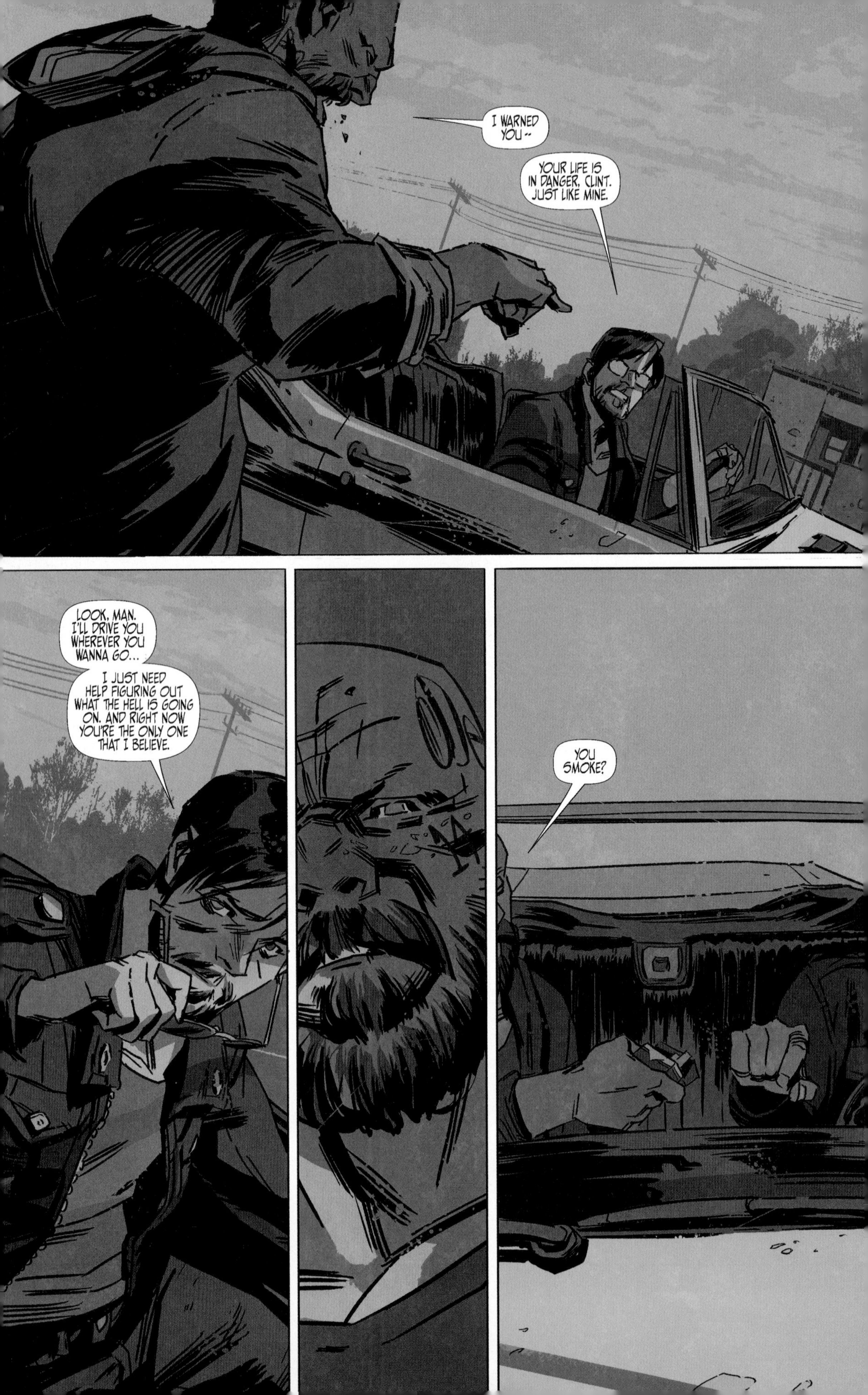
I WARNED YOU --
YOUR LIFE IS IN DANGER, CLINT. JUST LIKE MINE.
LOOK, MAN. I'LL DRIVE YOU WHEREVER YOU WANNA GO...
I JUST NEED HELP FIGURING OUT WHAT THE HELL IS GOING ON. AND RIGHT NOW YOU'RE THE ONLY ONE THAT I BELIEVE.
YOU SMOKE?

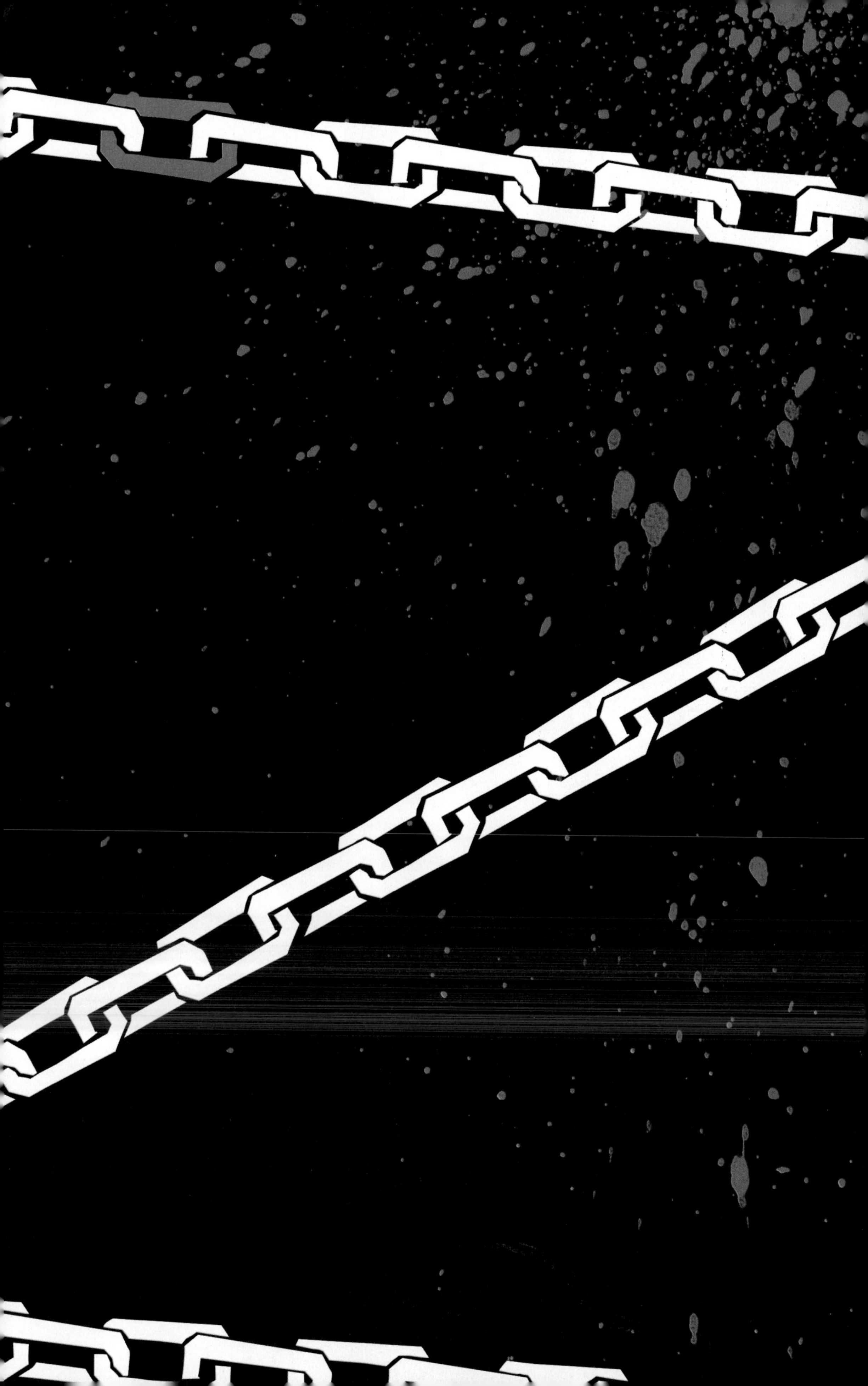

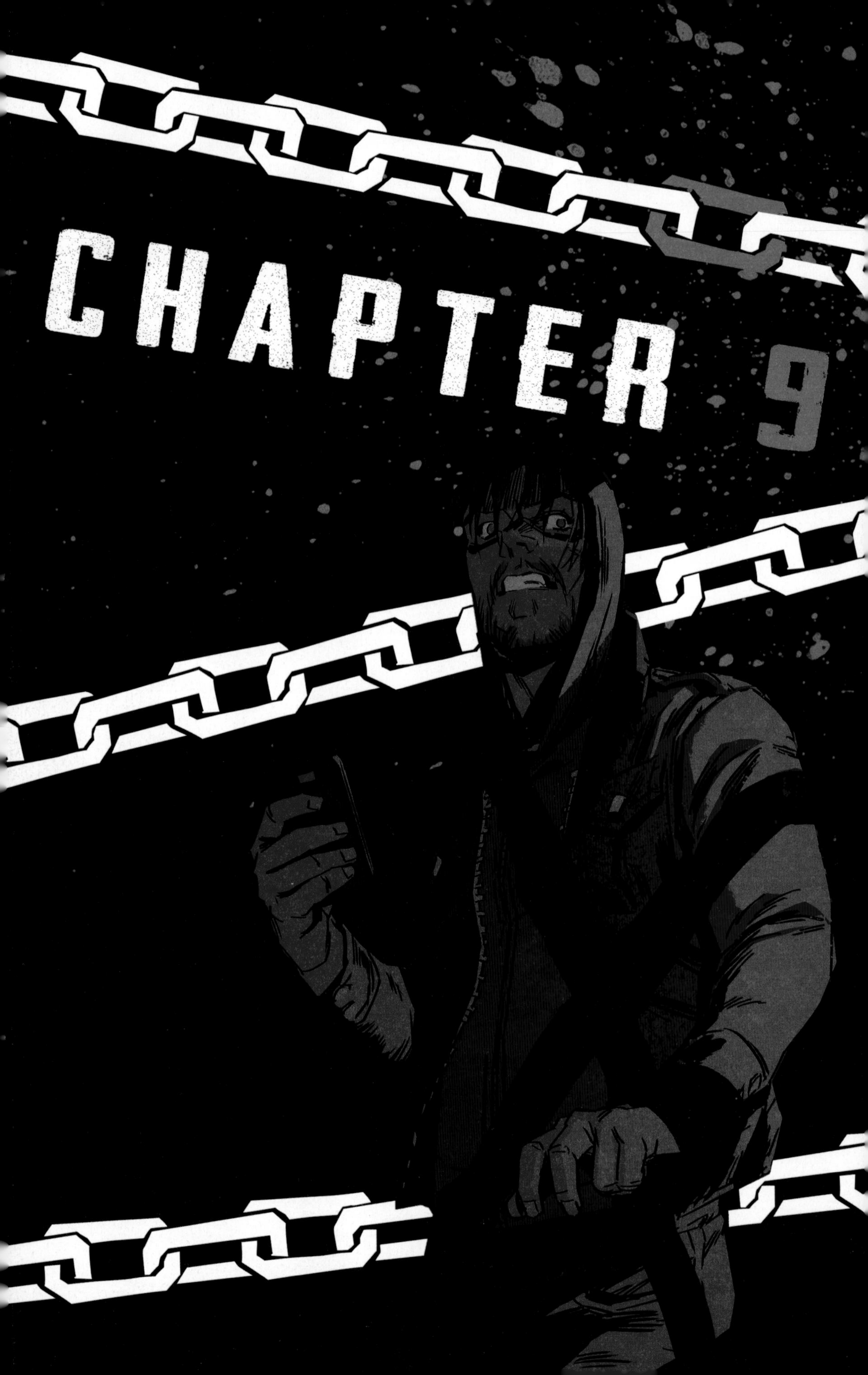
CHAPTER 9

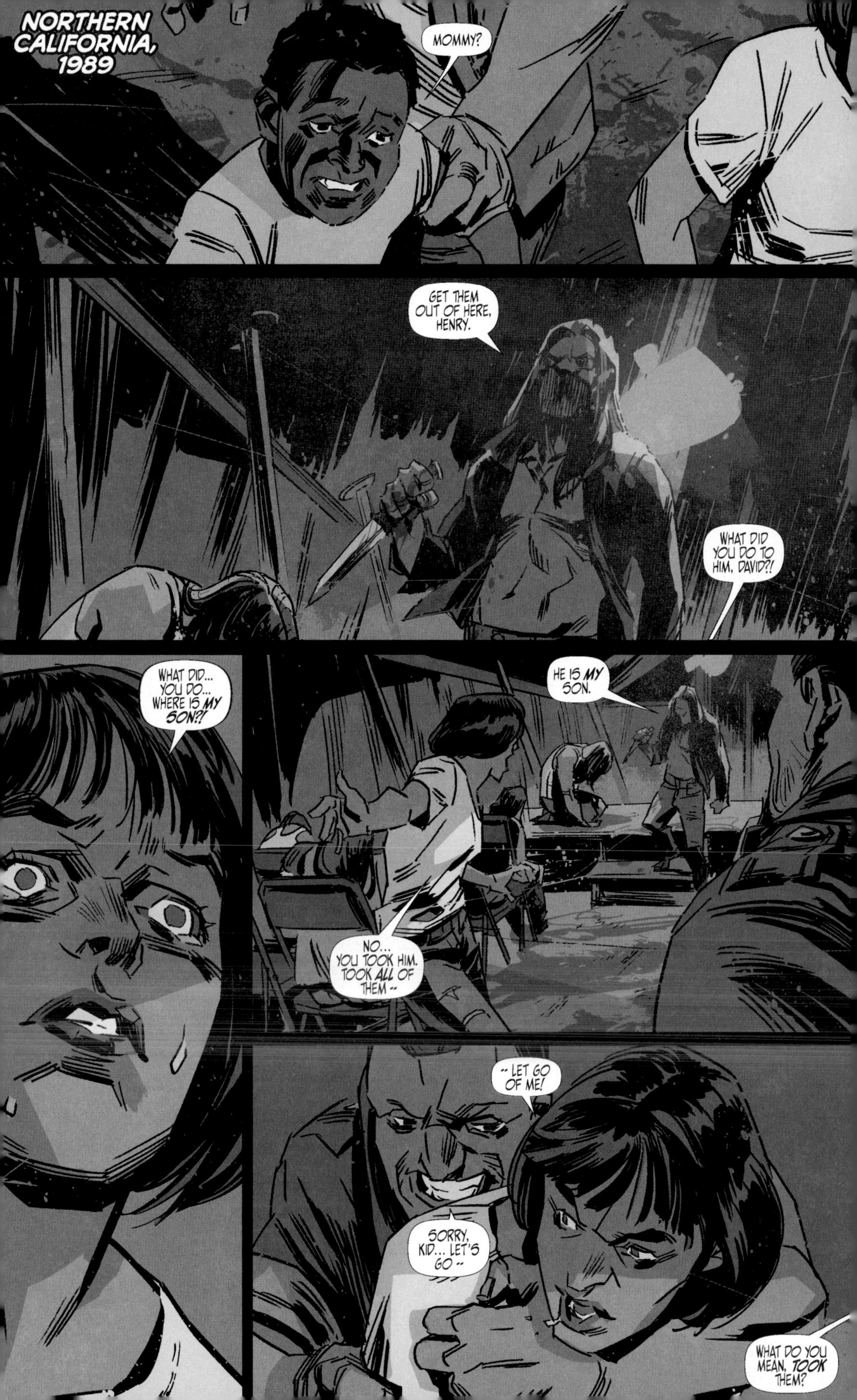
NORTHERN CALIFORNIA, 1989
MOMMY?
GET THEM OUT OF HERE, HENRY.
WHAT DID YOU DO TO HIM, DAVID?!
WHAT DID... YOU DO... WHERE IS MY SON?!
HE IS MY SON.
NO... YOU TOOK HIM. TOOK ALL OF THEM --
-- LET GO OF ME!
SORRY, KID... LET'S GO --
WHAT DO YOU MEAN, TOOK THEM?

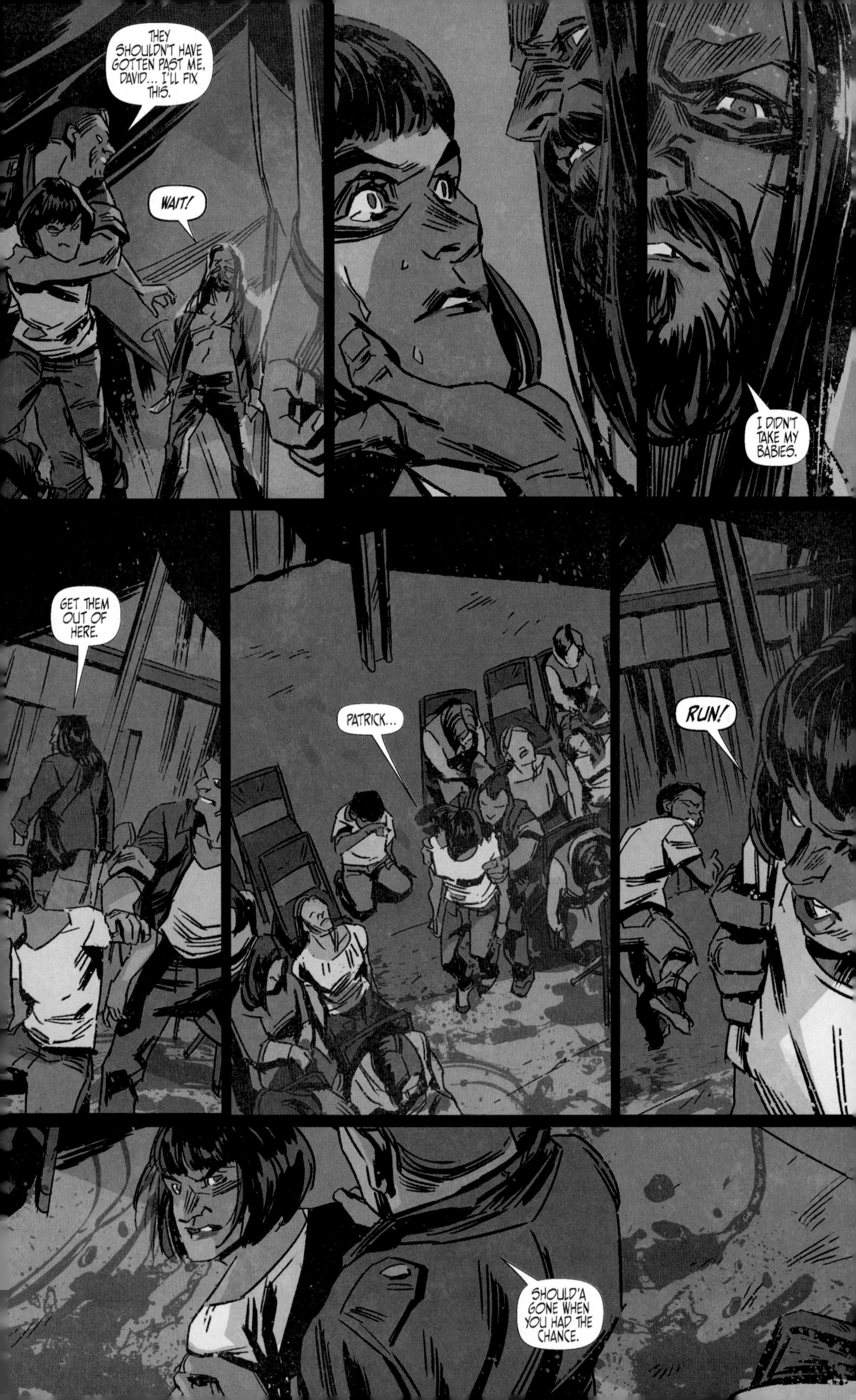
THEY SHOULDN'T HAVE GOTTEN PAST ME, DAVID... I'LL FIX THIS.
WAIT!
I DIDN'T TAKE MY BABIES.
GET THEM OUT OF HERE.
PATRICK...
RUN!
SHOULD'A GONE WHEN YOU HAD THE CHANCE.

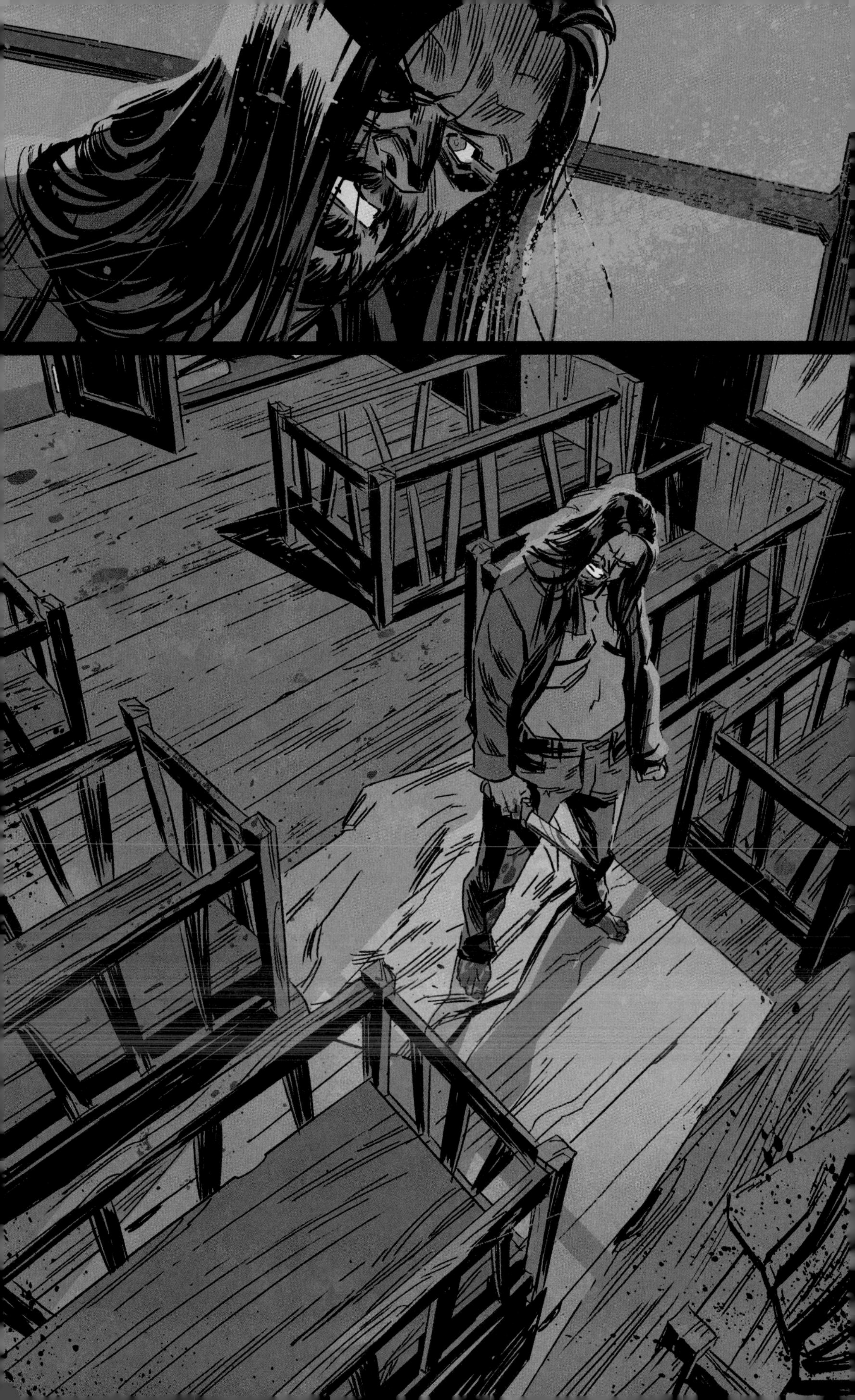

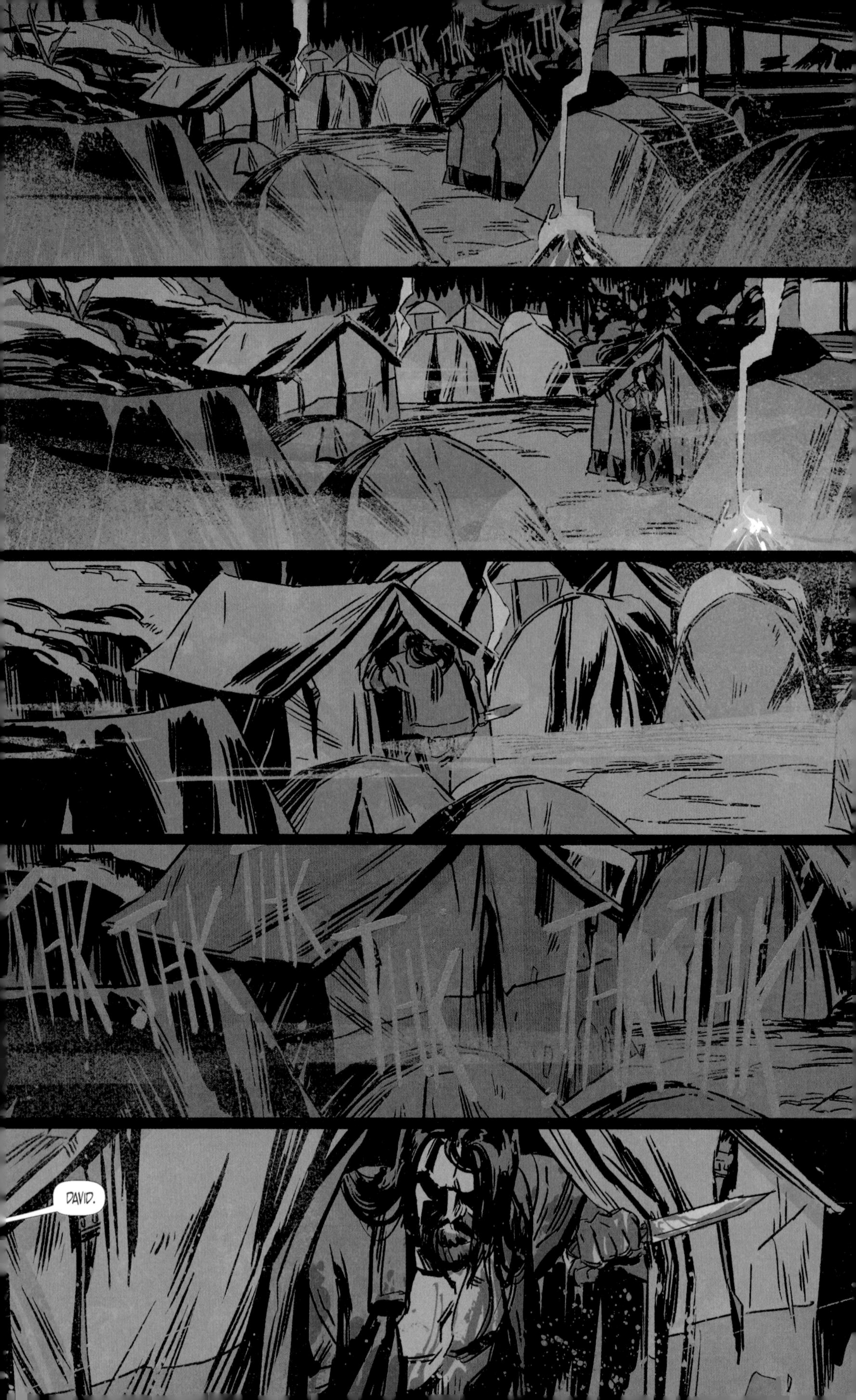
THK THK THK THK
THK THK THK THK THK THK
DAVID.

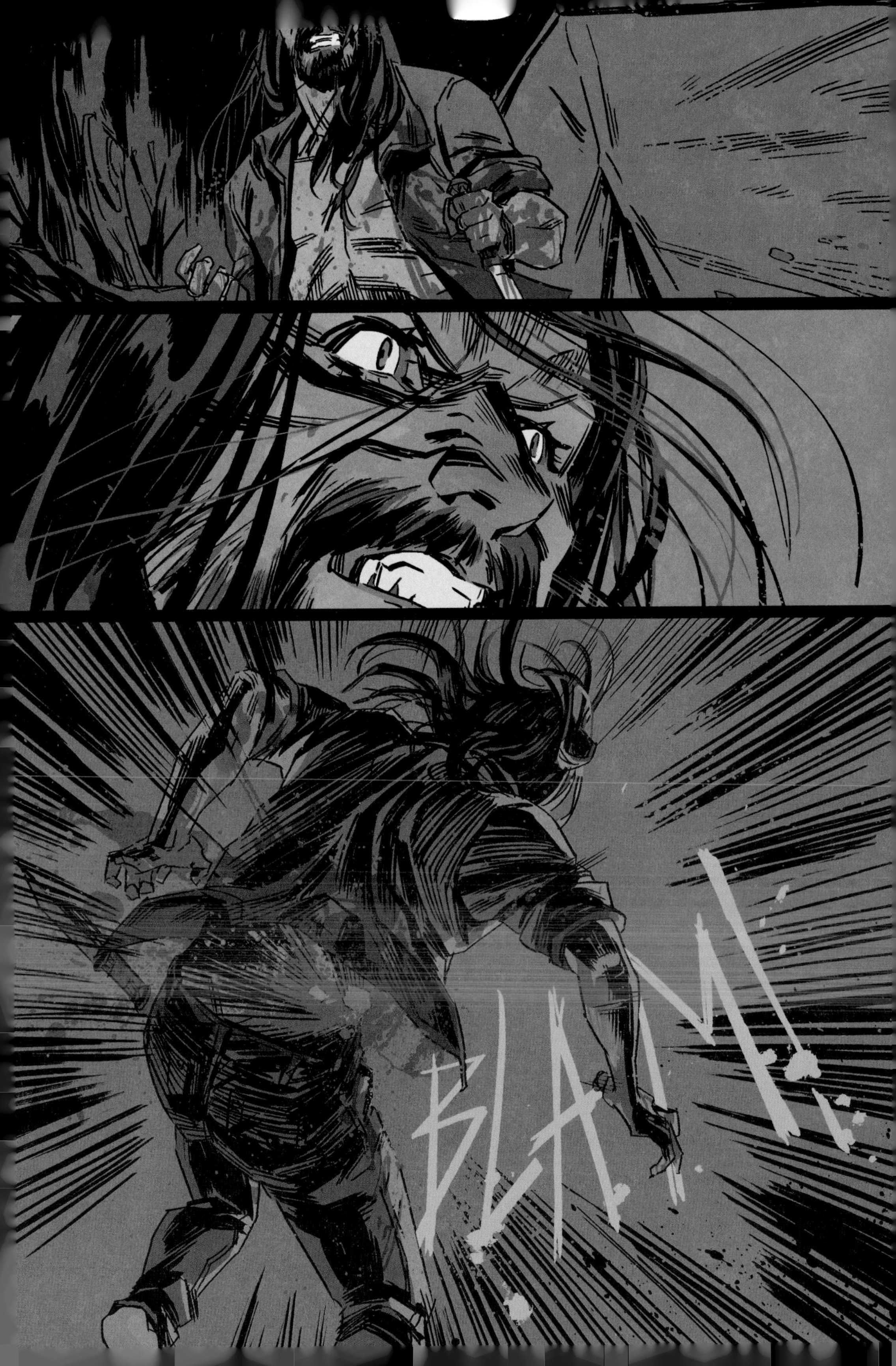
BLAM!!

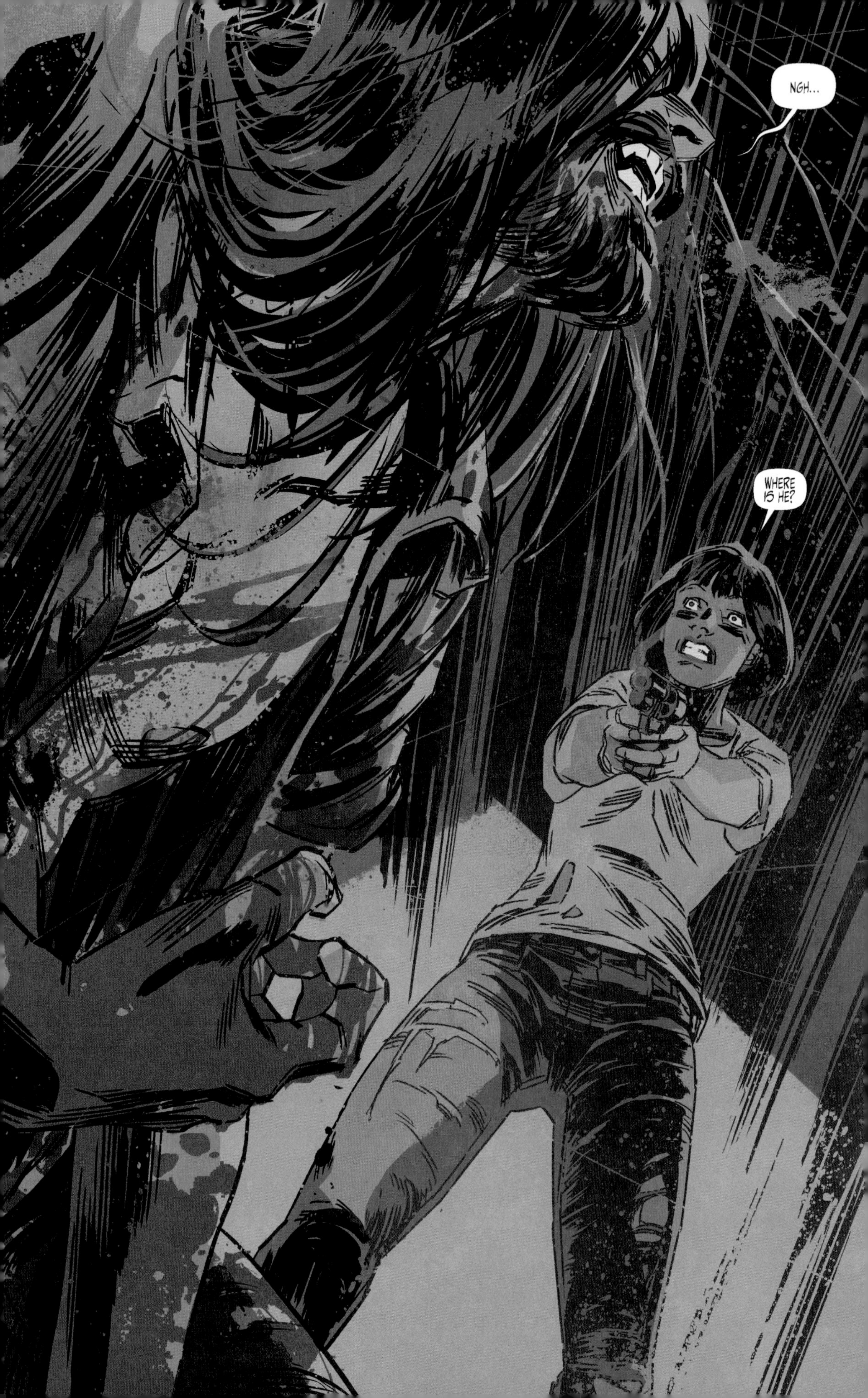
NGH...
WHERE IS HE?

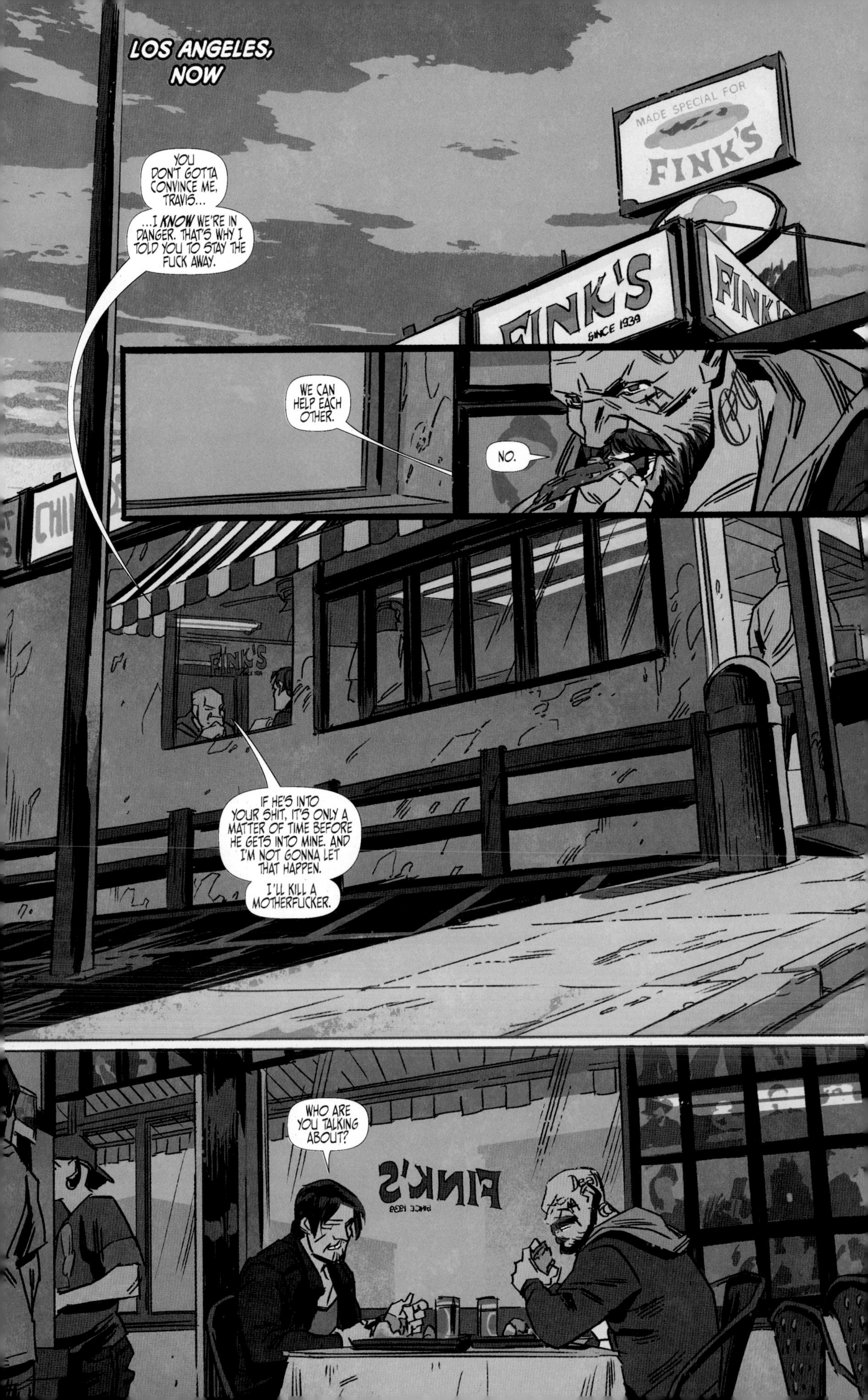
LOS ANGELES, NOW
MADE SPECIAL FOR FINK'S
FINK'S SINCE 1939
YOU DON'T GOTTA CONVINCE ME, TRAVIS...
...I KNOW WE'RE IN DANGER. THAT'S WHY I TOLD YOU TO STAY THE FUCK AWAY.
WE CAN HELP EACH OTHER.
NO.
IF HE'S INTO YOUR SHIT, IT'S ONLY A MATTER OF TIME BEFORE HE GETS INTO MINE. AND I'M NOT GONNA LET THAT HAPPEN.
I'LL KILL A MOTHERFUCKER.
WHO ARE YOU TALKING ABOUT?

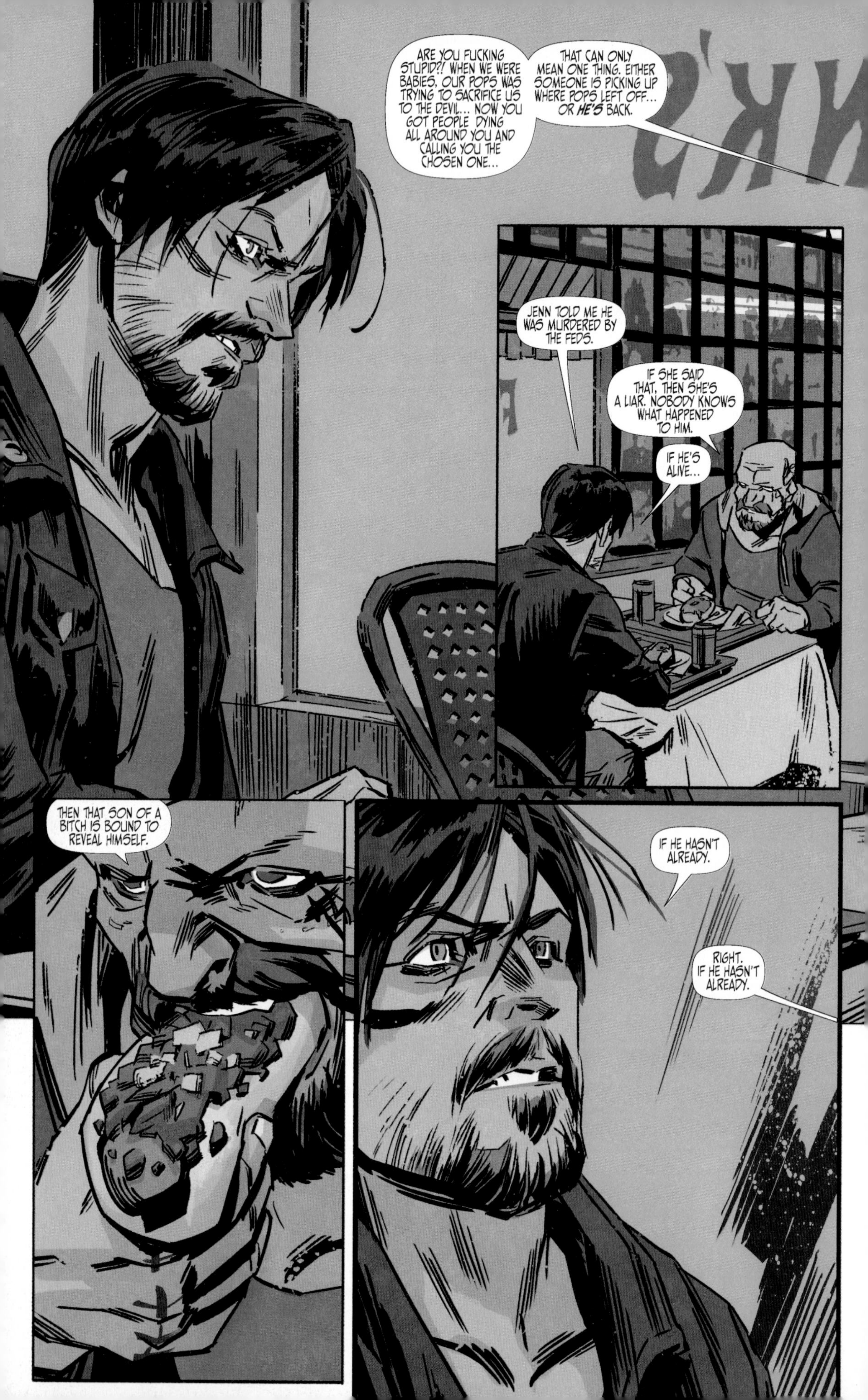
ARE YOU FUCKING STUPID?! WHEN WE WERE BABIES, OUR POPS WAS TRYING TO SACRIFICE US TO THE DEVIL... NOW YOU GOT PEOPLE DYING ALL AROUND YOU AND CALLING YOU THE CHOSEN ONE...
THAT CAN ONLY MEAN ONE THING. EITHER SOMEONE IS PICKING UP WHERE POPS LEFT OFF... OR HE'S BACK.
JENN TOLD ME HE WAS MURDERED BY THE FEDS.
IF SHE SAID THAT, THEN SHE'S A LIAR. NOBODY KNOWS WHAT HAPPENED TO HIM.
IF HE'S ALIVE...
THEN THAT SON OF A BITCH IS BOUND TO REVEAL HIMSELF.
IF HE HASN'T ALREADY.
RIGHT. IF HE HASN'T ALREADY.

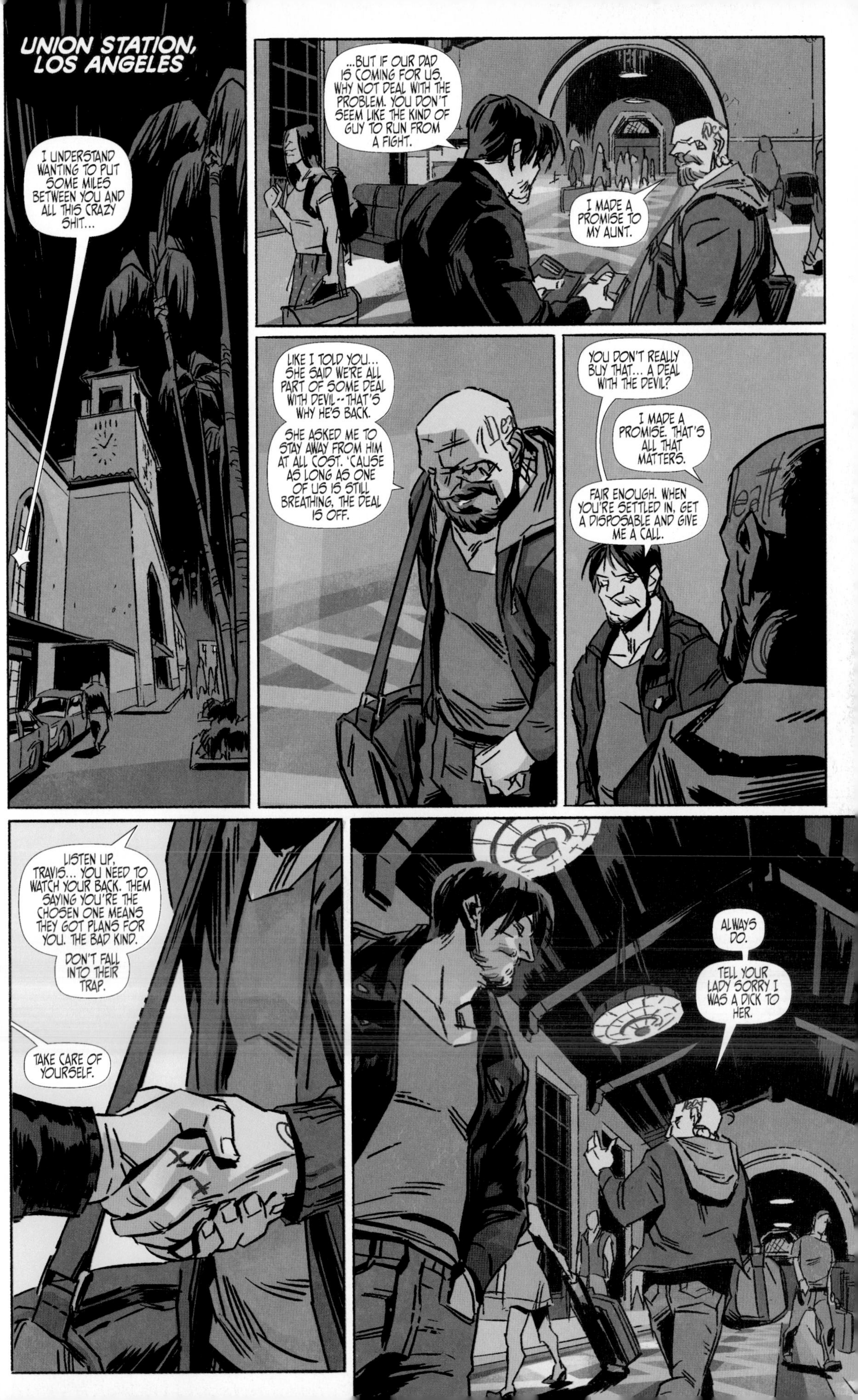
UNION STATION, LOS ANGELES
I UNDERSTAND WANTING TO PUT SOME MILES BETWEEN YOU AND ALL THIS CRAZY SHIT...
...BUT IF OUR DAD IS COMING FOR US, WHY NOT DEAL WITH THE PROBLEM. YOU DON'T SEEM LIKE THE KIND OF GUY TO RUN FROM A FIGHT.
I MADE A PROMISE TO MY AUNT.
LIKE I TOLD YOU... SHE SAID WE'RE ALL PART OF SOME DEAL WITH DEVIL--THAT'S WHY HE'S BACK.
SHE ASKED ME TO STAY AWAY FROM HIM AT ALL COST. 'CAUSE AS LONG AS ONE OF US IS STILL BREATHING, THE DEAL IS OFF.
YOU DON'T REALLY BUY THAT... A DEAL WITH THE DEVIL?
I MADE A PROMISE. THAT'S ALL THAT MATTERS.
FAIR ENOUGH. WHEN YOU'RE SETTLED IN, GET A DISPOSABLE AND GIVE ME A CALL.
LISTEN UP, TRAVIS... YOU NEED TO WATCH YOUR BACK. THEM SAYING YOU'RE THE CHOSEN ONE MEANS THEY GOT PLANS FOR YOU. THE BAD KIND.
DON'T FALL INTO THEIR TRAP.
TAKE CARE OF YOURSELF.
ALWAYS DO.
TELL YOUR LADY SORRY I WAS A DICK TO HER.

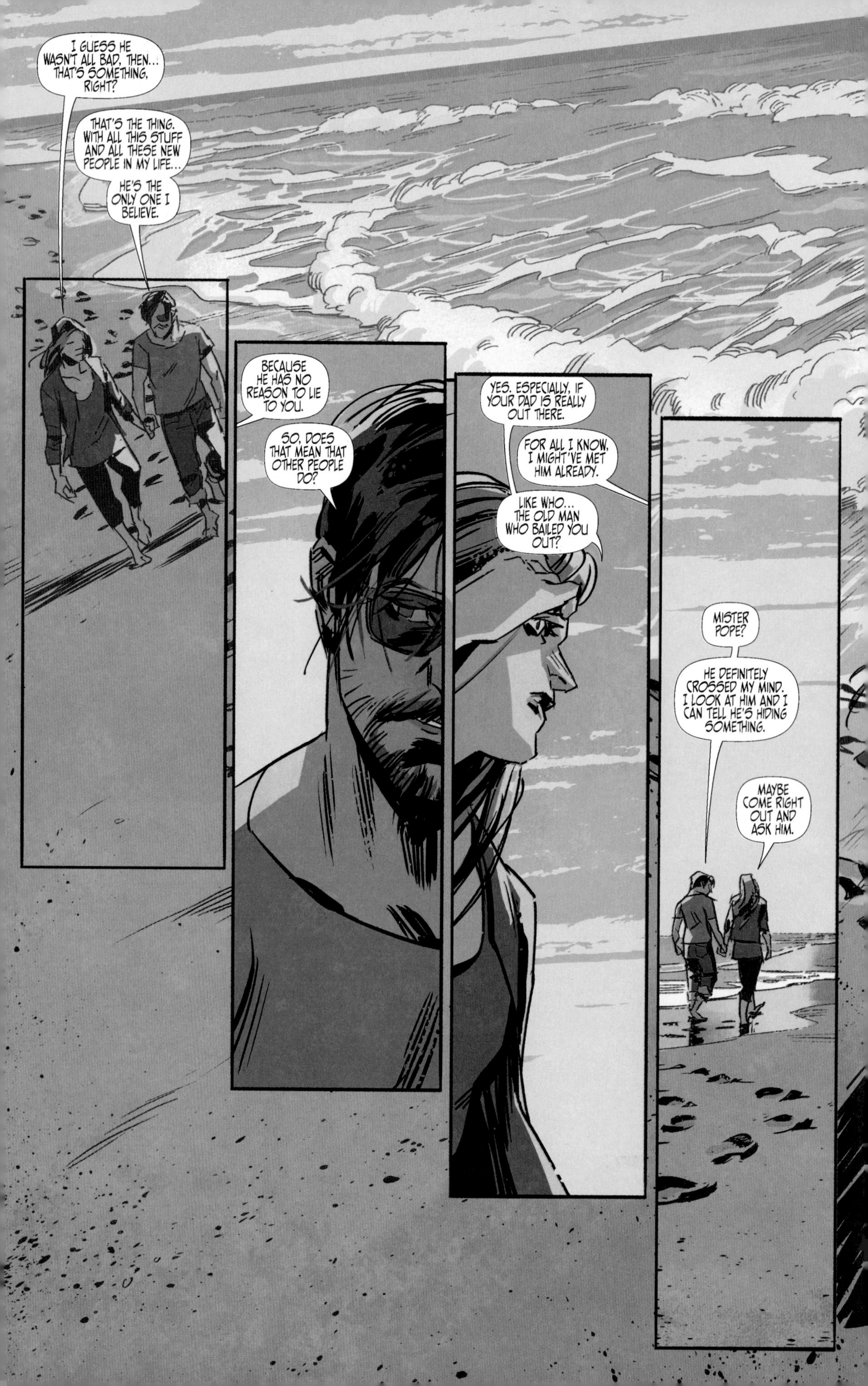
I GUESS HE WASN'T ALL BAD, THEN... THAT'S SOMETHING, RIGHT?
THAT'S THE THING. WITH ALL THIS STUFF AND ALL THESE NEW PEOPLE IN MY LIFE...
HE'S THE ONLY ONE I BELIEVE.
BECAUSE HE HAS NO REASON TO LIE TO YOU.
SO, DOES THAT MEAN THAT OTHER PEOPLE DO?
YES. ESPECIALLY, IF YOUR DAD IS REALLY OUT THERE.
FOR ALL I KNOW, I MIGHT'VE MET HIM ALREADY.
LIKE WHO... THE OLD MAN WHO BAILED YOU OUT?
MISTER POPE?
HE DEFINITELY CROSSED MY MIND. I LOOK AT HIM AND I CAN TELL HE'S HIDING SOMETHING.
MAYBE COME RIGHT OUT AND ASK HIM.

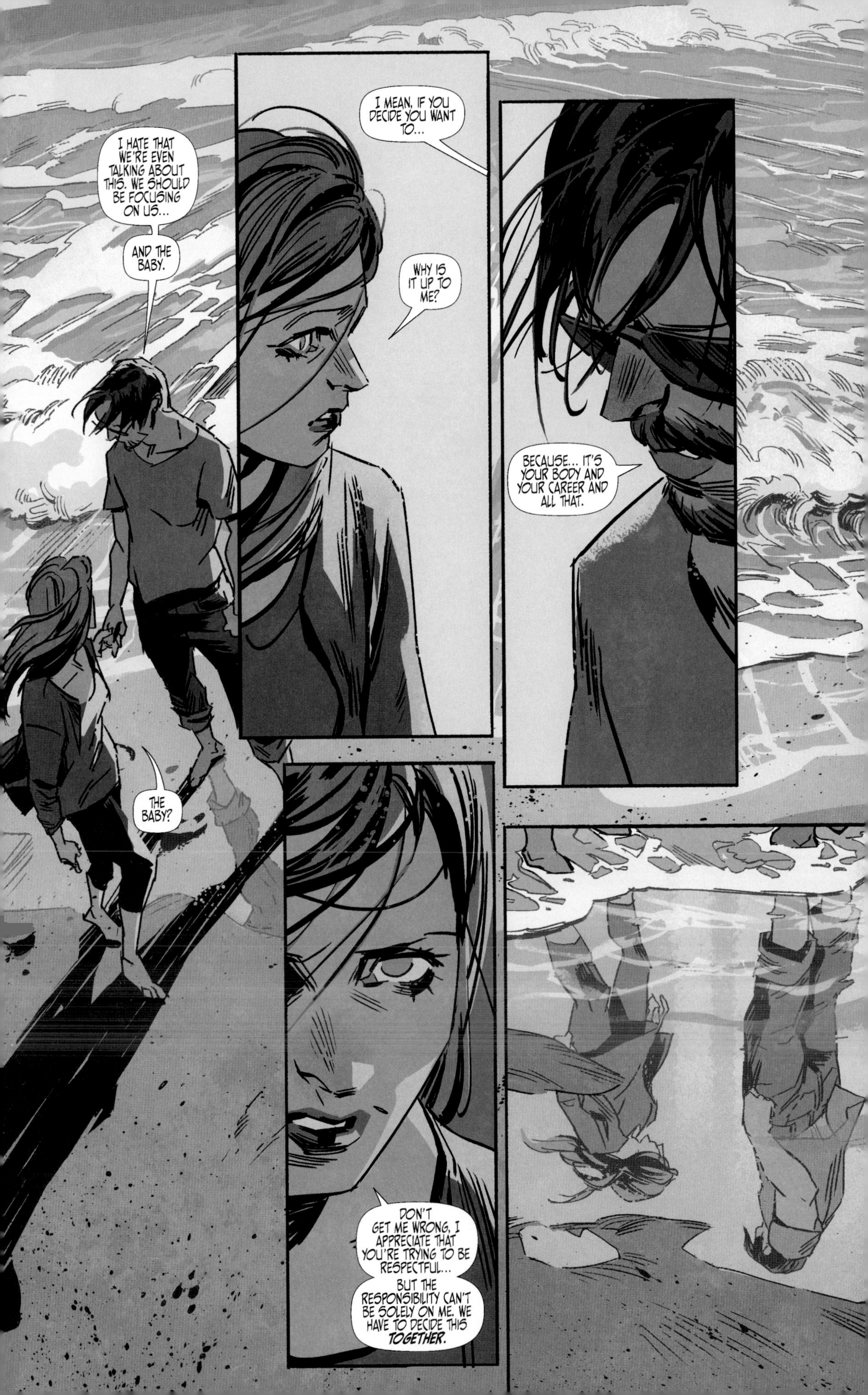
I HATE THAT WE'RE EVEN TALKING ABOUT THIS. WE SHOULD BE FOCUSING ON US...
AND THE BABY.
I MEAN, IF YOU DECIDE YOU WANT TO...
WHY IS IT UP TO ME?
BECAUSE... IT'S YOUR BODY AND YOUR CAREER AND ALL THAT.
THE BABY?
DON'T GET ME WRONG, I APPRECIATE THAT YOU'RE TRYING TO BE RESPECTFUL...
BUT THE RESPONSIBILITY CAN'T BE SOLELY ON ME. WE HAVE TO DECIDE THIS *TOGETHER*.

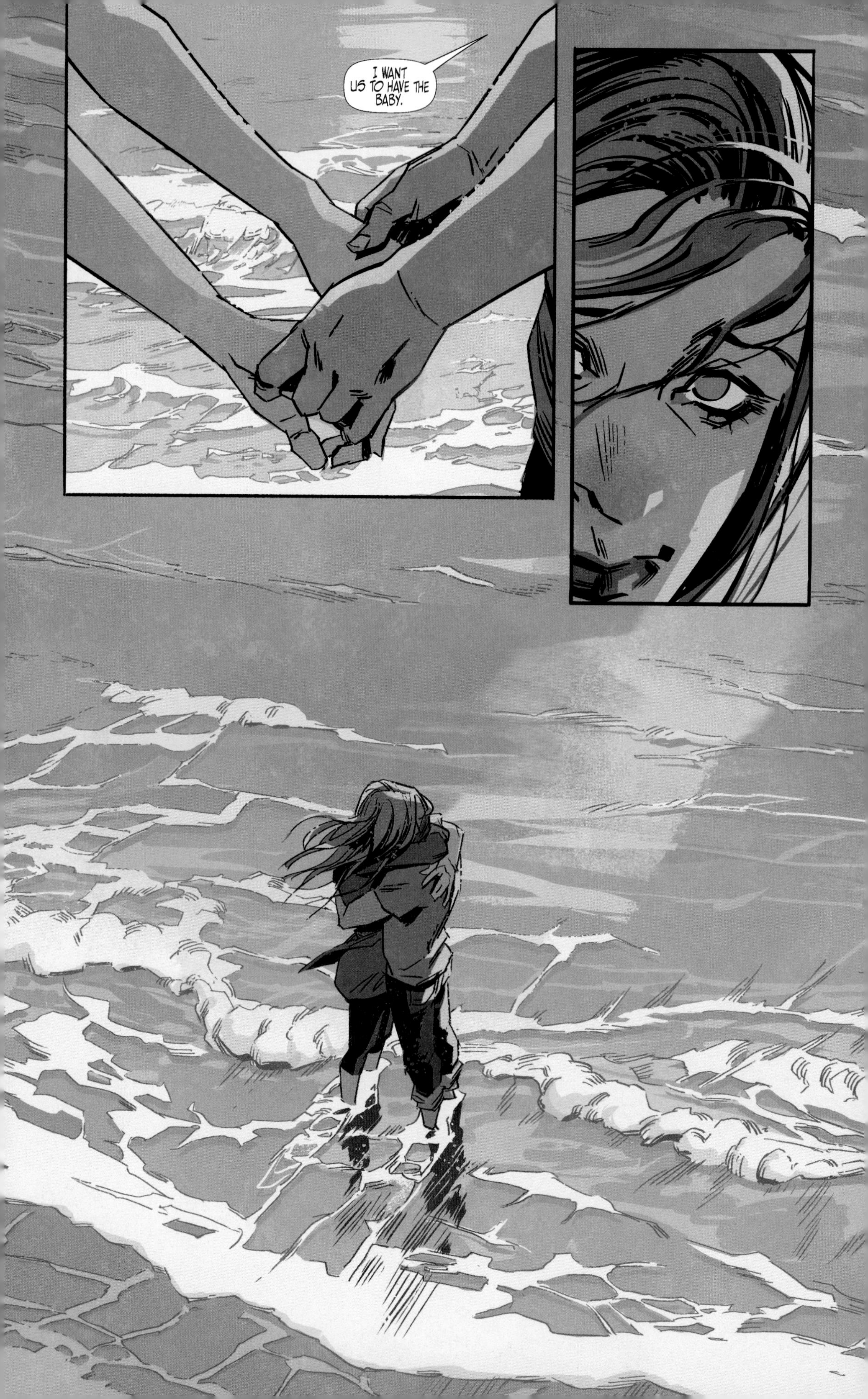
I WANT US TO HAVE THE BABY.

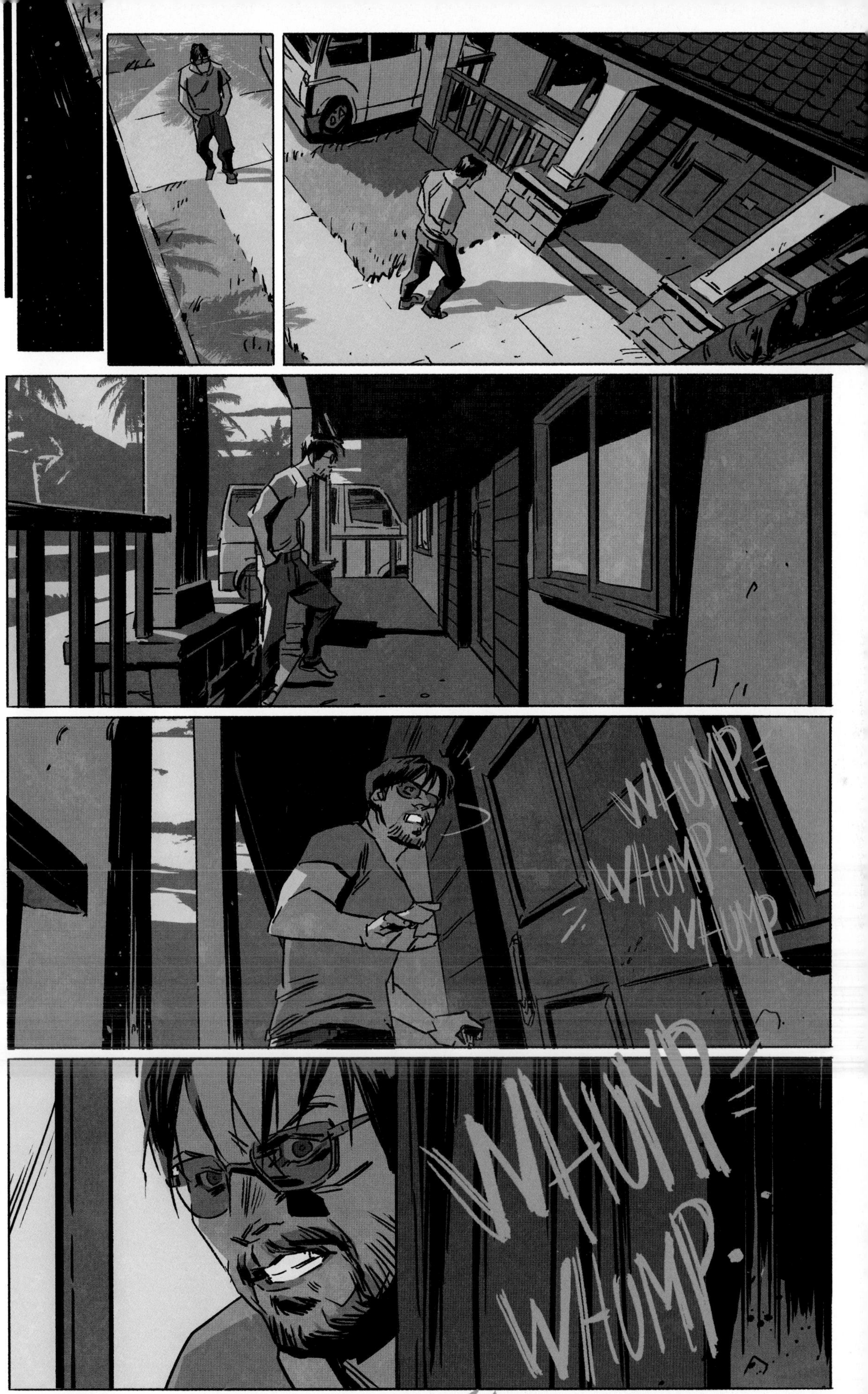
WHUMP!
WHUMP.
WHUMP
WHUMP!
WHUMP.

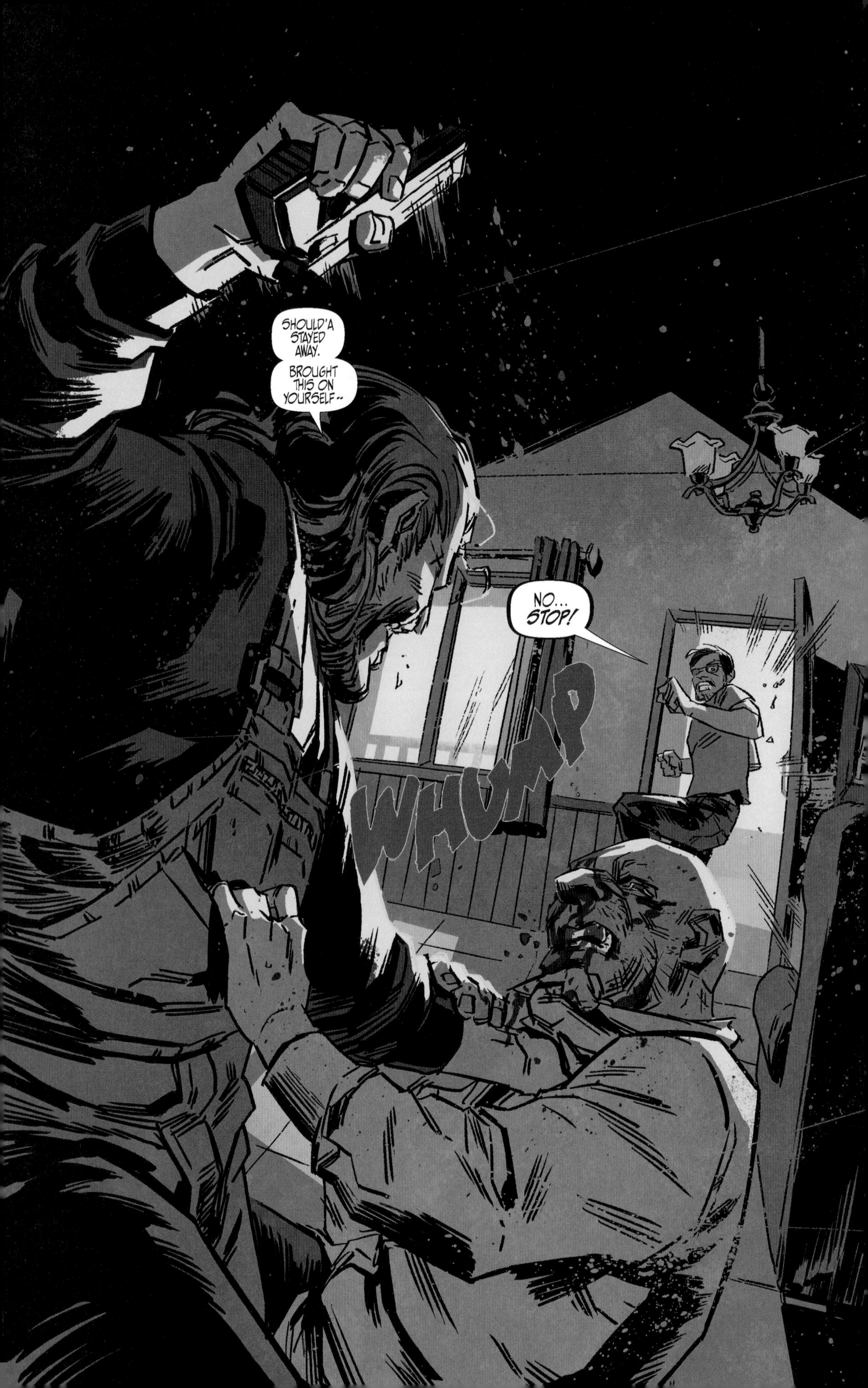
SHOULD'A STAYED AWAY.
BROUGHT THIS ON YOURSELF--
NO... STOP!
WHUMP

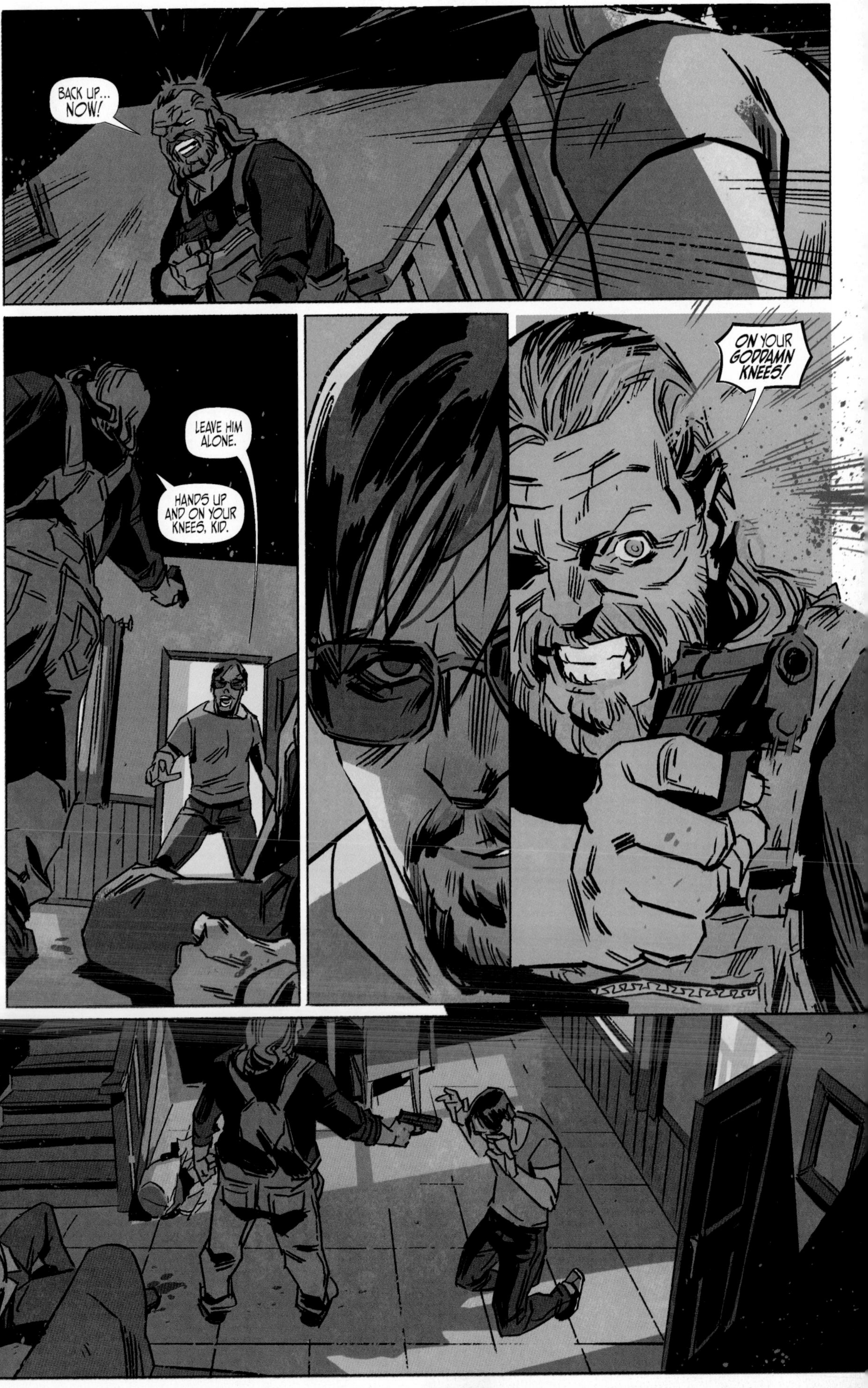
BACK UP... NOW!
LEAVE HIM ALONE.
HANDS UP AND ON YOUR KNEES, KID.
ON YOUR GODDAMN KNEES!

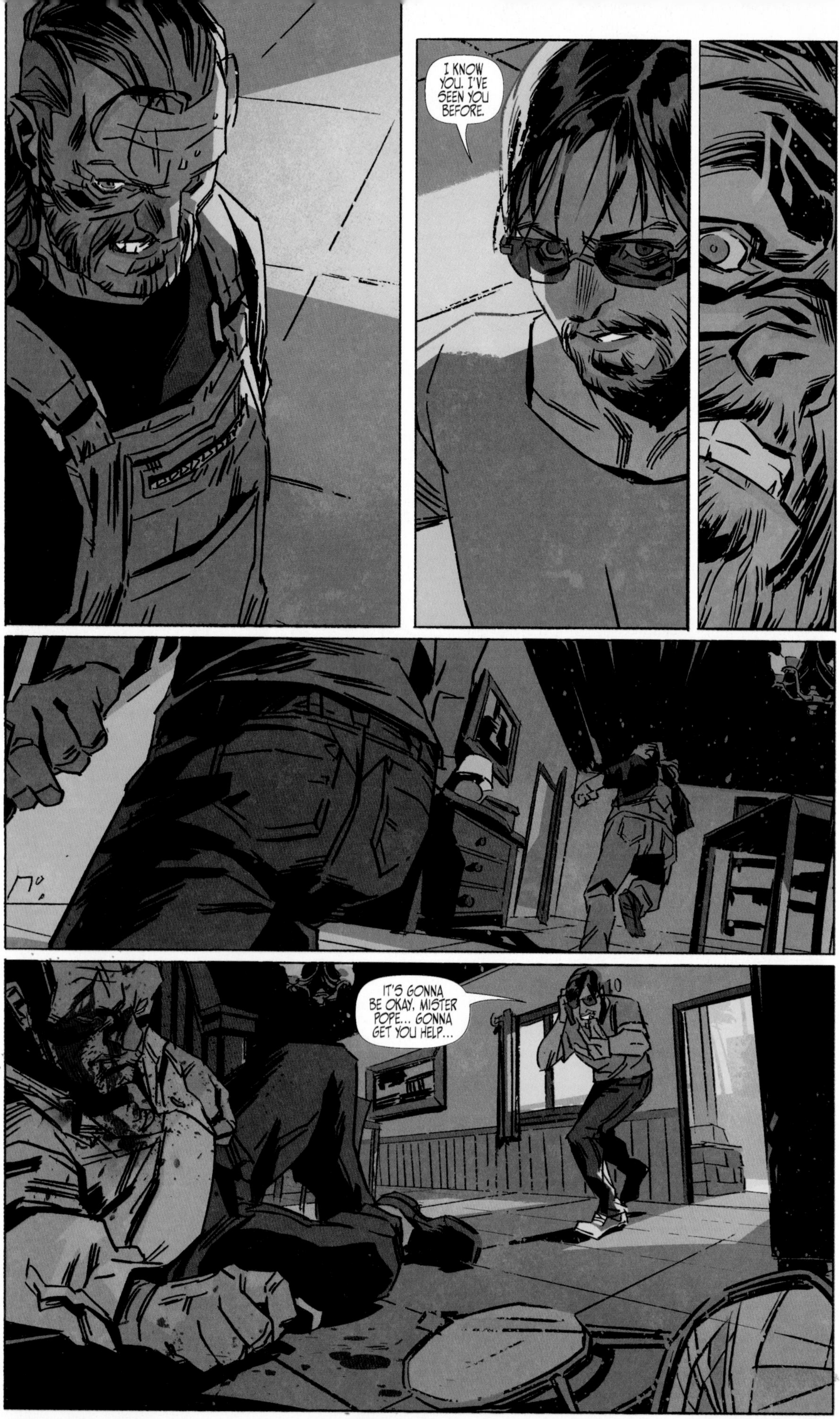
I KNOW YOU. I'VE SEEN YOU BEFORE.
IT'S GONNA BE OKAY, MISTER POPE... GONNA GET YOU HELP...

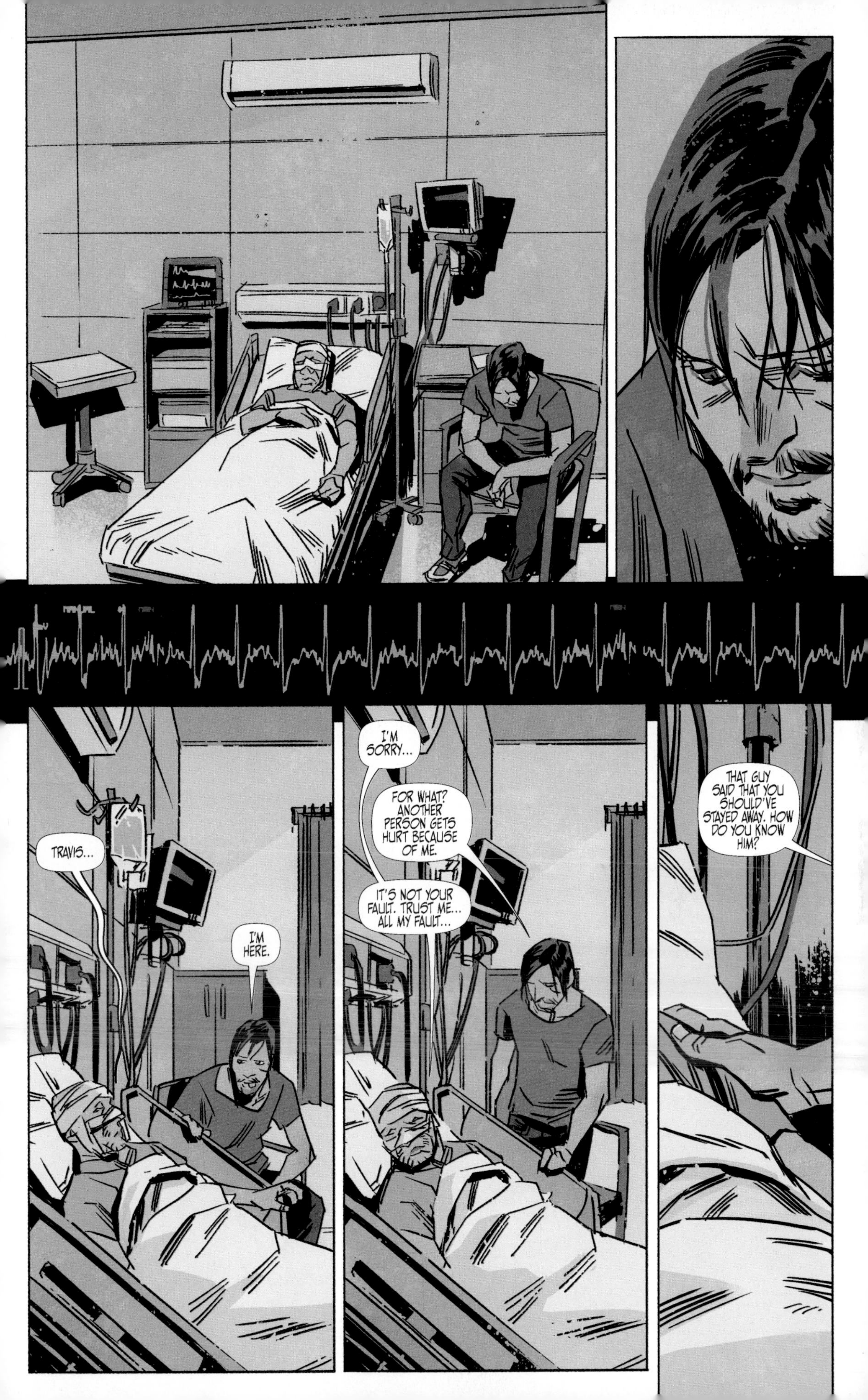
TRAVIS...
I'M HERE.
I'M SORRY...
FOR WHAT? ANOTHER PERSON GETS HURT BECAUSE OF ME.
IT'S NOT YOUR FAULT. TRUST ME... ALL MY FAULT...
THAT GUY SAID THAT YOU SHOULD'VE STAYED AWAY. HOW DO YOU KNOW HIM?

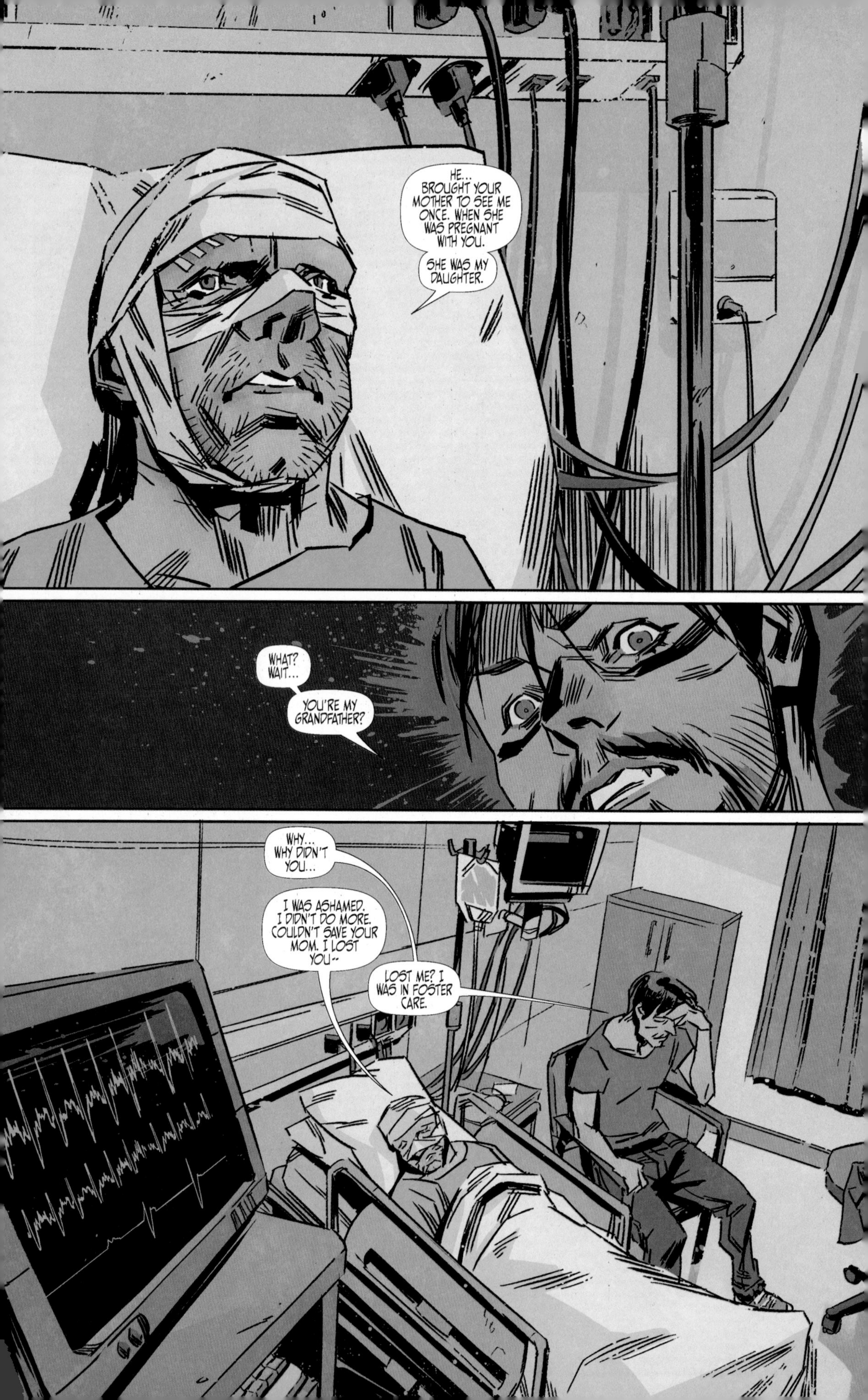
HE... BROUGHT YOUR MOTHER TO SEE ME ONCE. WHEN SHE WAS PREGNANT WITH YOU.
SHE WAS MY DAUGHTER.
WHAT? WAIT...
YOU'RE MY GRANDFATHER?
WHY... WHY DIDN'T YOU...
I WAS ASHAMED. I DIDN'T DO MORE. COULDN'T SAVE YOUR MOM. I LOST YOU--
LOST ME? I WAS IN FOSTER CARE.

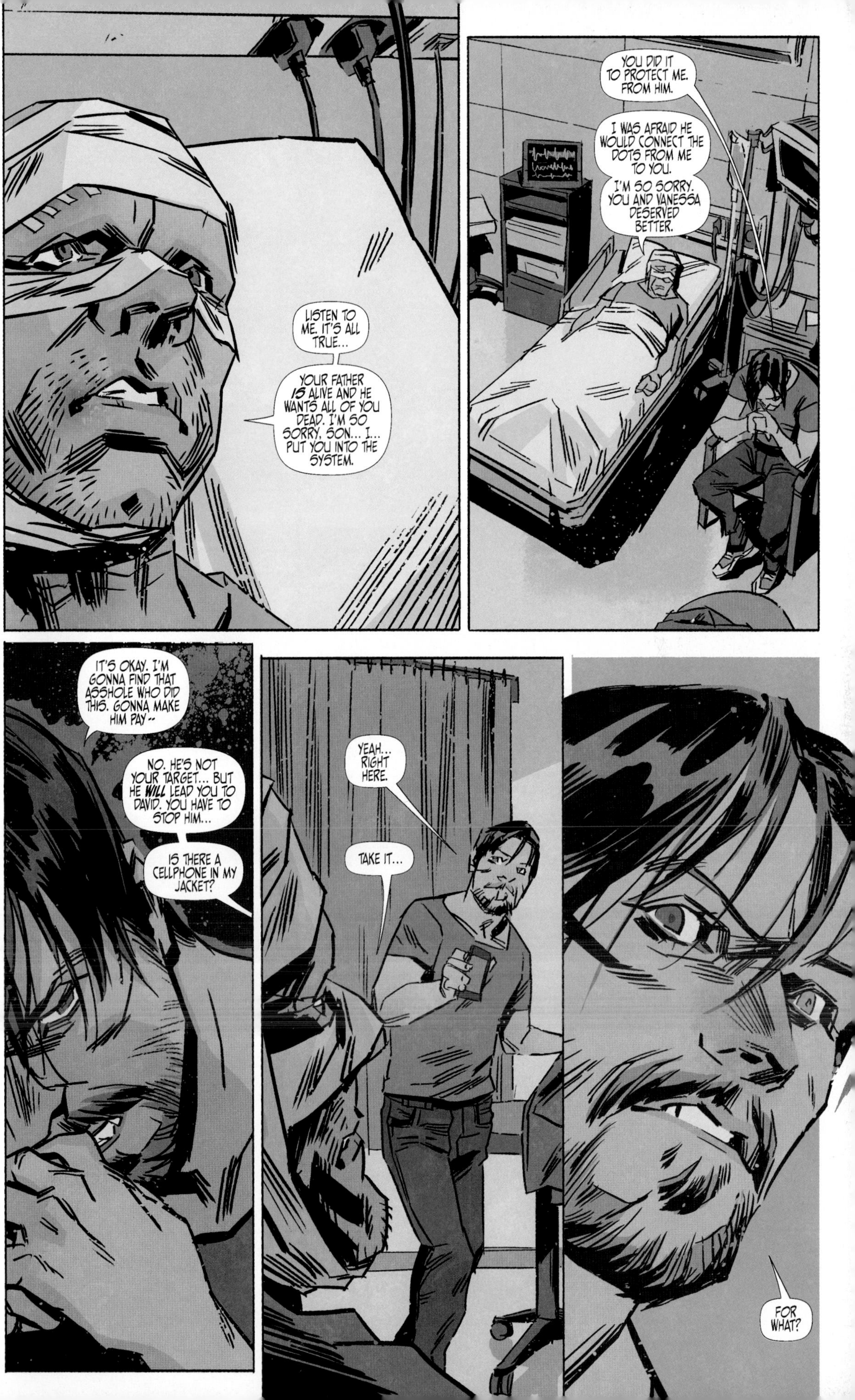
LISTEN TO ME. IT'S ALL TRUE...
YOUR FATHER *IS* ALIVE AND HE WANTS ALL OF YOU DEAD. I'M SO SORRY, SON... I... PUT YOU INTO THE SYSTEM.
YOU DID IT TO PROTECT ME. FROM HIM.
I WAS AFRAID HE WOULD CONNECT THE DOTS FROM ME TO YOU.
I'M SO SORRY. YOU AND VANESSA DESERVED BETTER.
IT'S OKAY. I'M GONNA FIND THAT ASSHOLE WHO DID THIS. GONNA MAKE HIM PAY--
NO. HE'S NOT YOUR TARGET... BUT HE *WILL* LEAD YOU TO DAVID. YOU HAVE TO STOP HIM...
IS THERE A CELLPHONE IN MY JACKET?
YEAH... RIGHT HERE.
TAKE IT...
FOR WHAT?

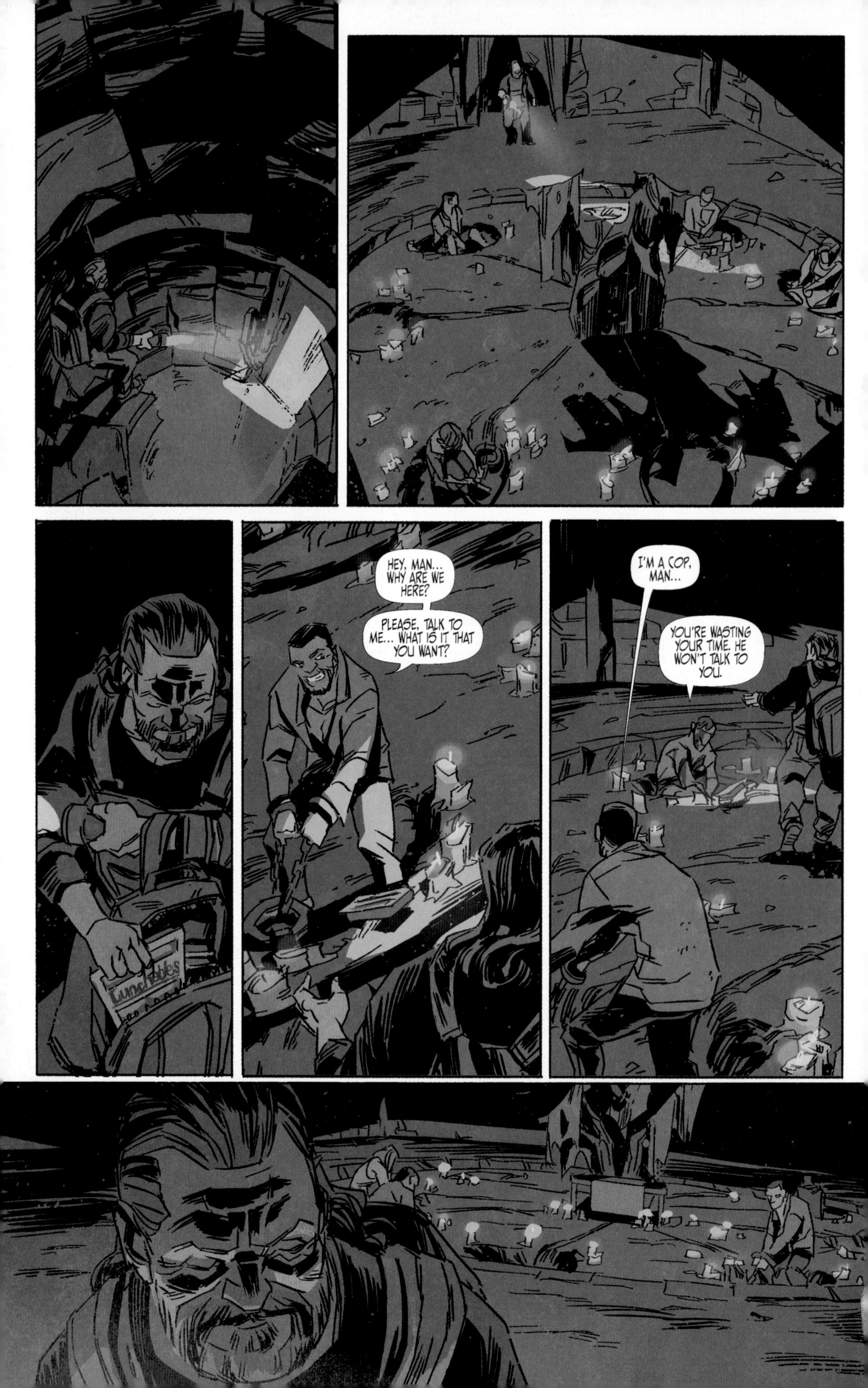

Lunchables
HEY, MAN... WHY ARE WE HERE?
PLEASE. TALK TO ME... WHAT IS IT THAT YOU WANT?
I'M A COP, MAN...
YOU'RE WASTING YOUR TIME. HE WON'T TALK TO YOU.

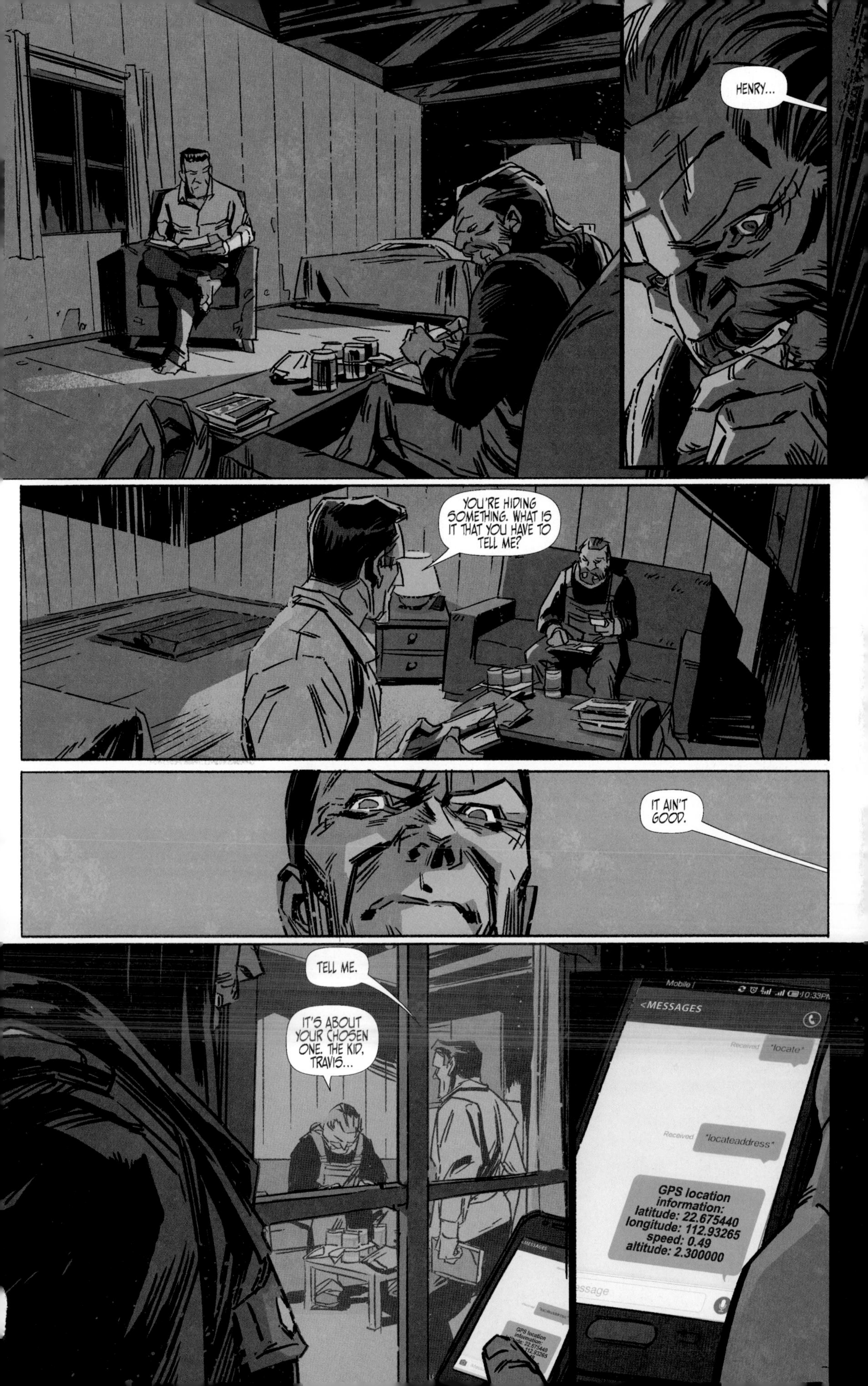

HENRY...
YOU'RE HIDING SOMETHING. WHAT IS IT THAT YOU HAVE TO TELL ME?
IT AIN'T GOOD.
TELL ME.
IT'S ABOUT YOUR CHOSEN ONE. THE KID, TRAVIS...
Mobile
<MESSAGES
Received *locate*
Received *locateaddress*
GPS location information:
latitude: 22.675440
longitude: 112.93265
speed: 0.49
altitude: 2.300000

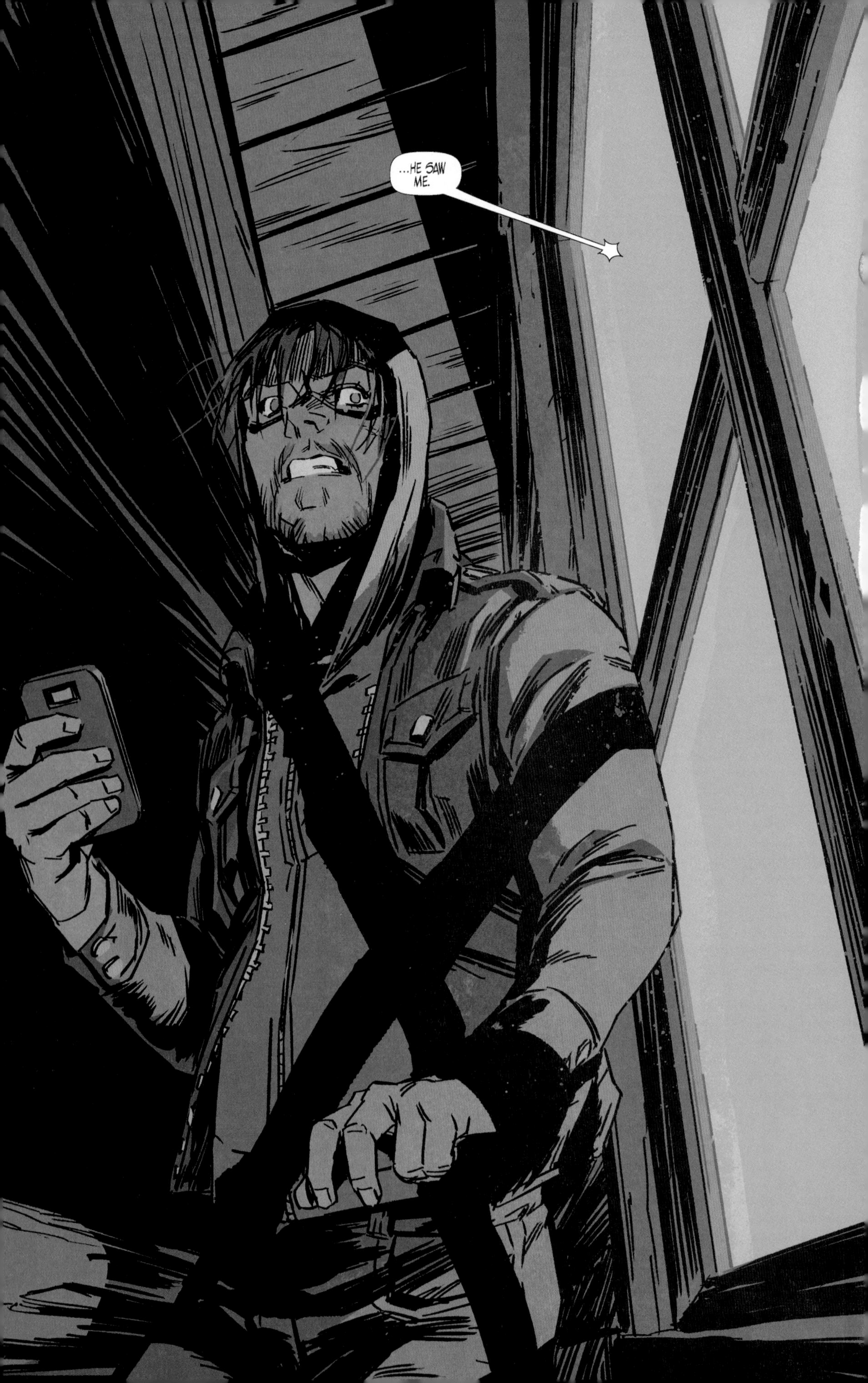
...HE SAW ME.

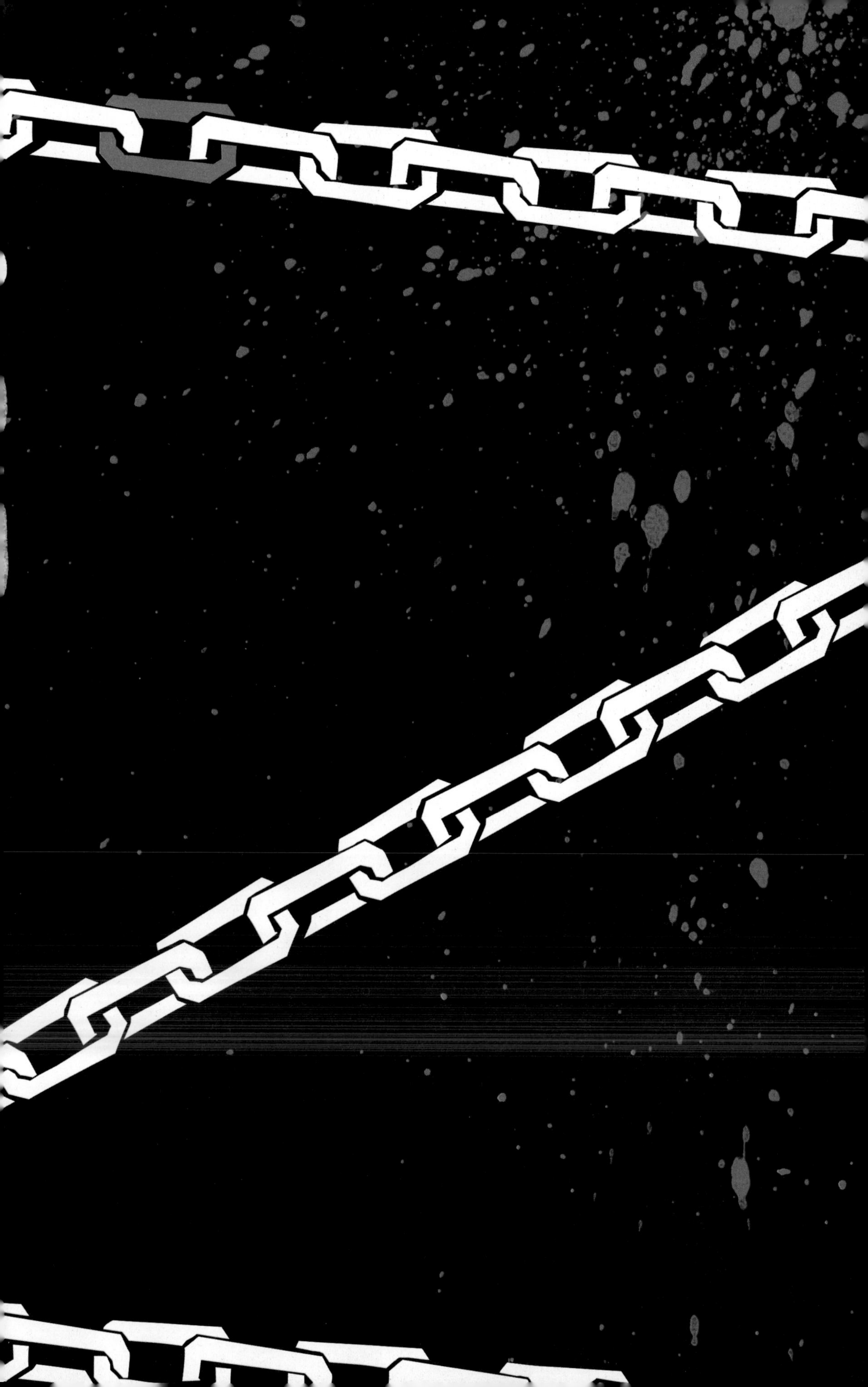

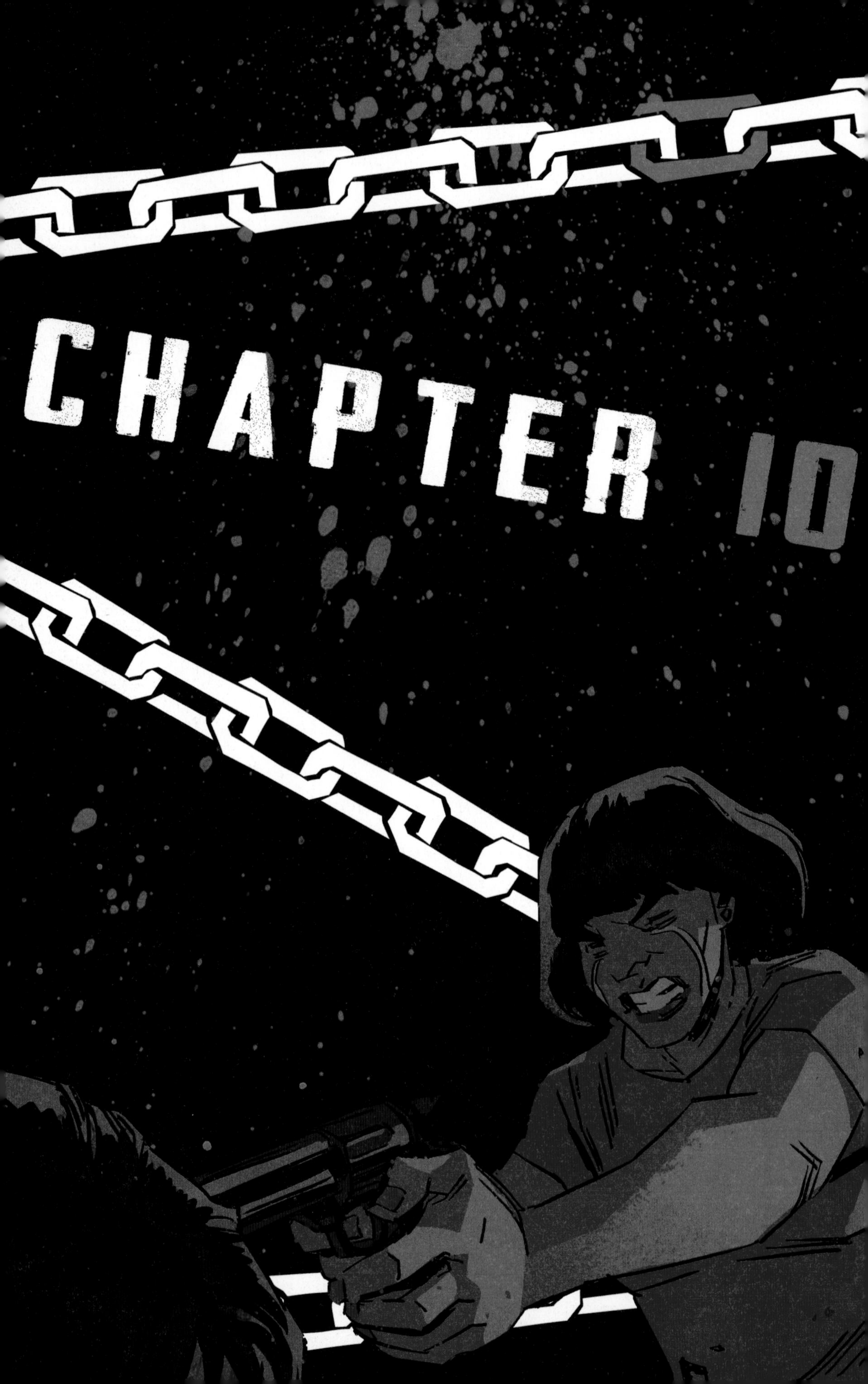
CHAPTER 10

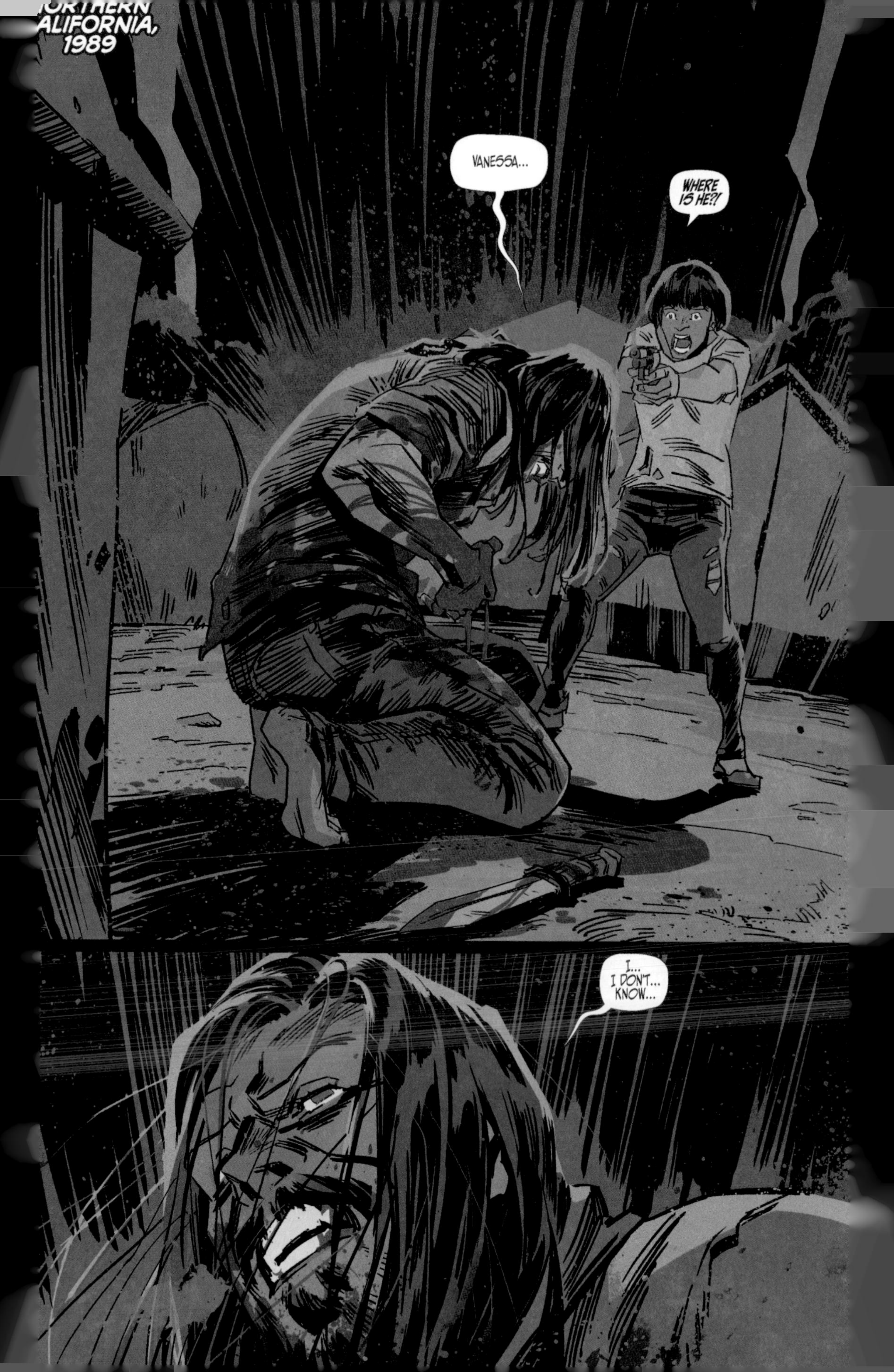
ORTHERN ALIFORNIA, 1989
VANESSA...
WHERE IS HE?!
I... I DON'T... KNOW...

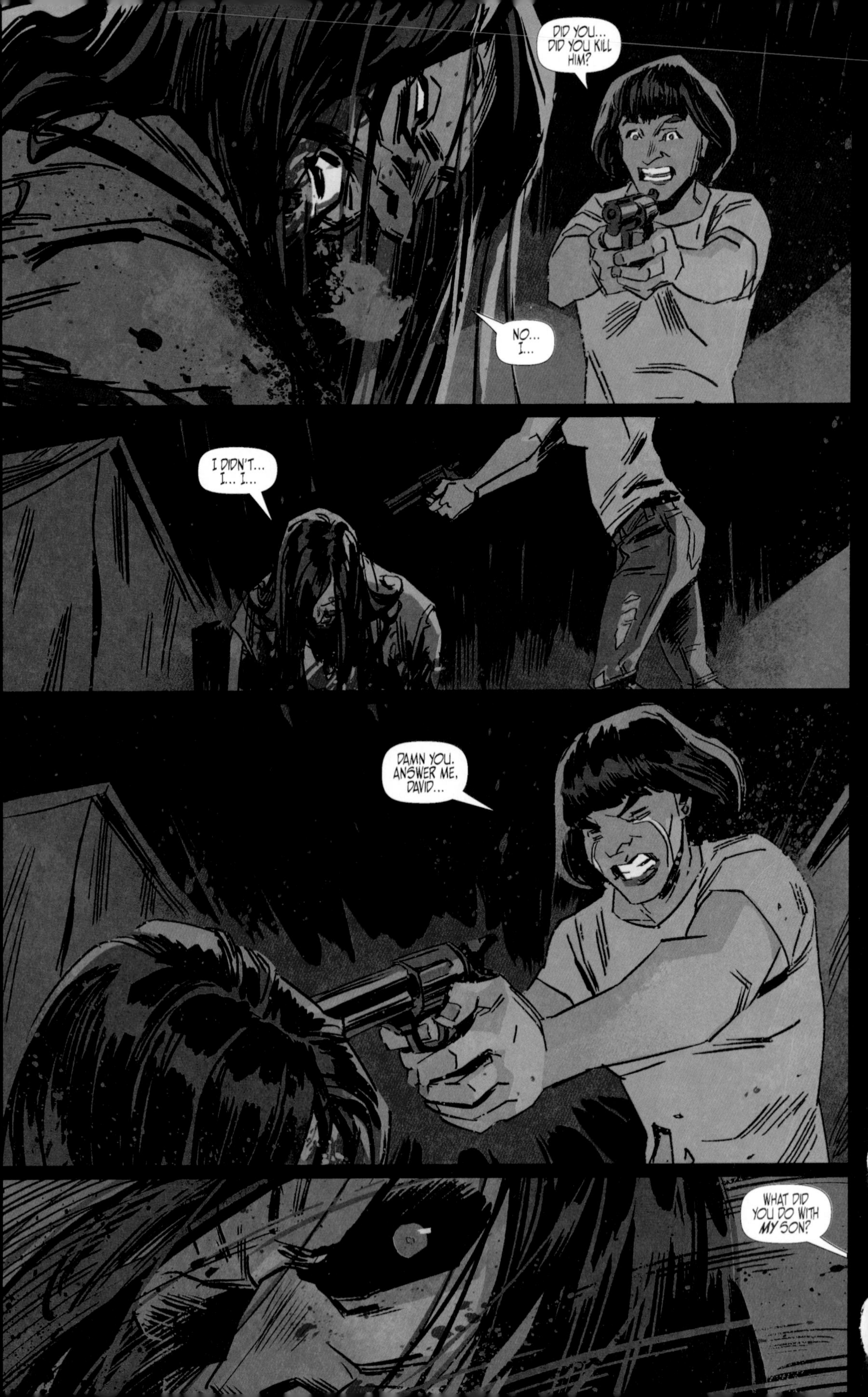
DID YOU... DID YOU KILL HIM?
NO... I...
I DIDN'T... I... I...
DAMN YOU. ANSWER ME, DAVID...
WHAT DID YOU DO WITH *MY* SON?

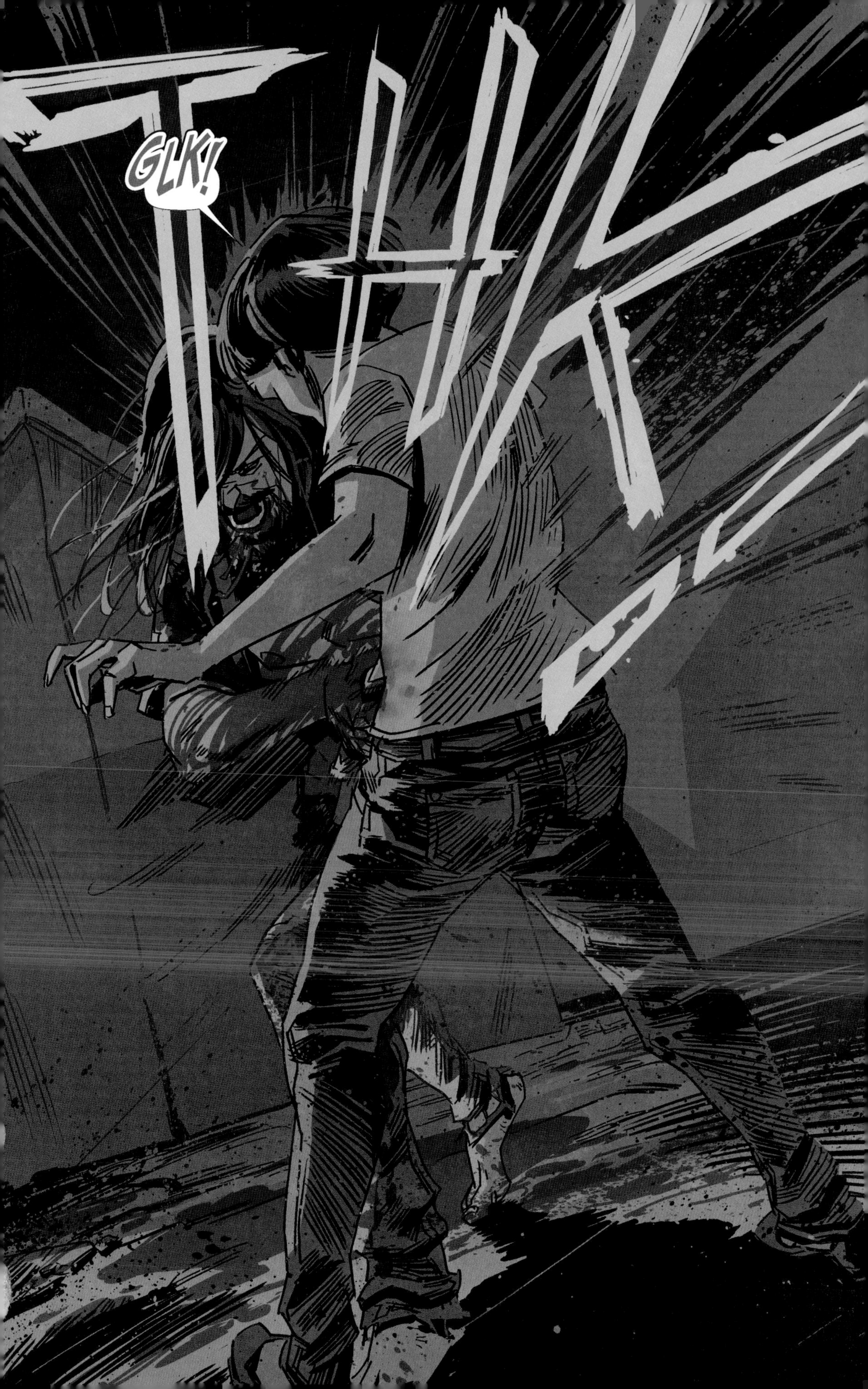
GLK!

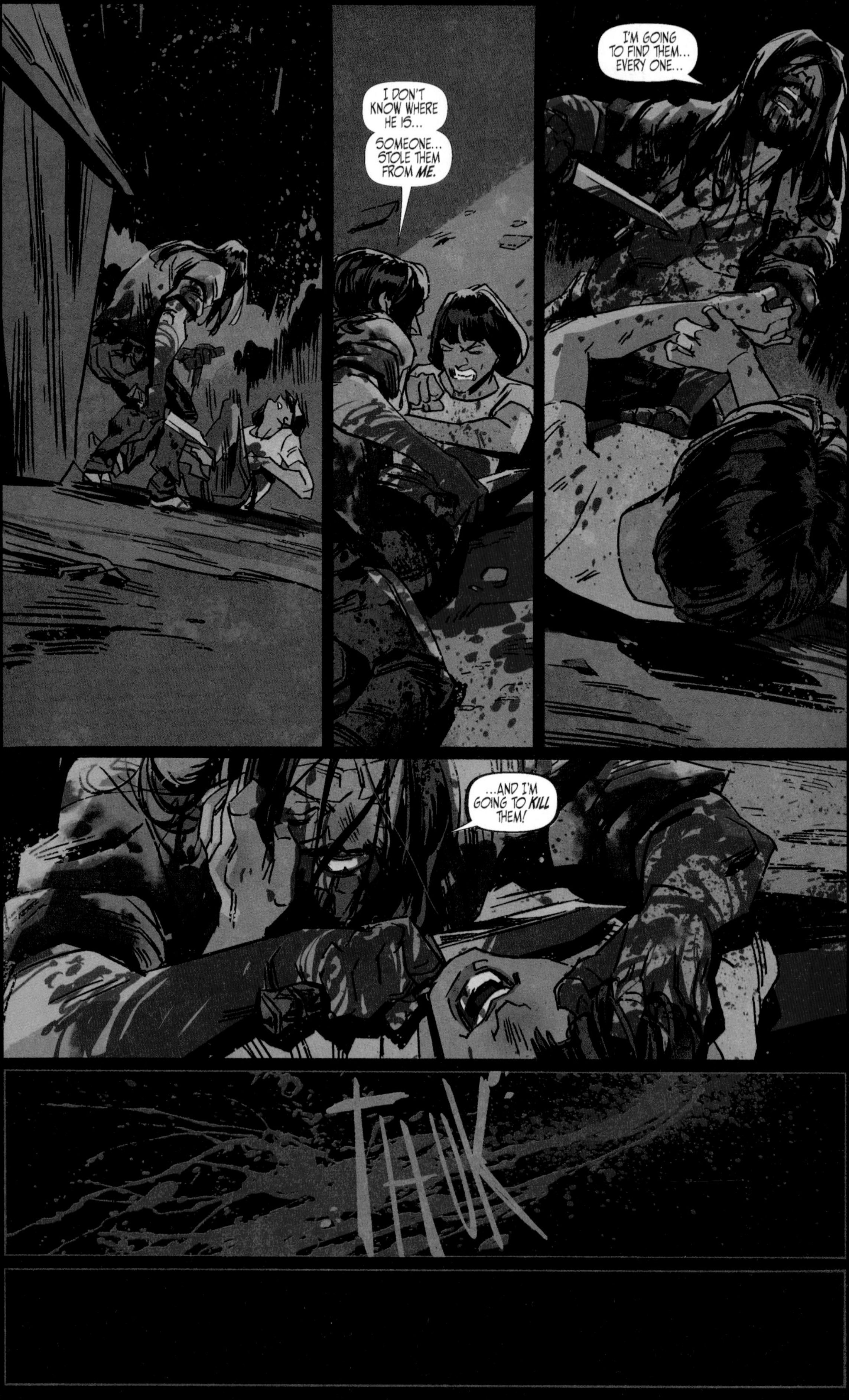
I DON'T KNOW WHERE HE IS...
SOMEONE... STOLE THEM FROM ME.
I'M GOING TO FIND THEM... EVERY ONE...
...AND I'M GOING TO KILL THEM!
THUK

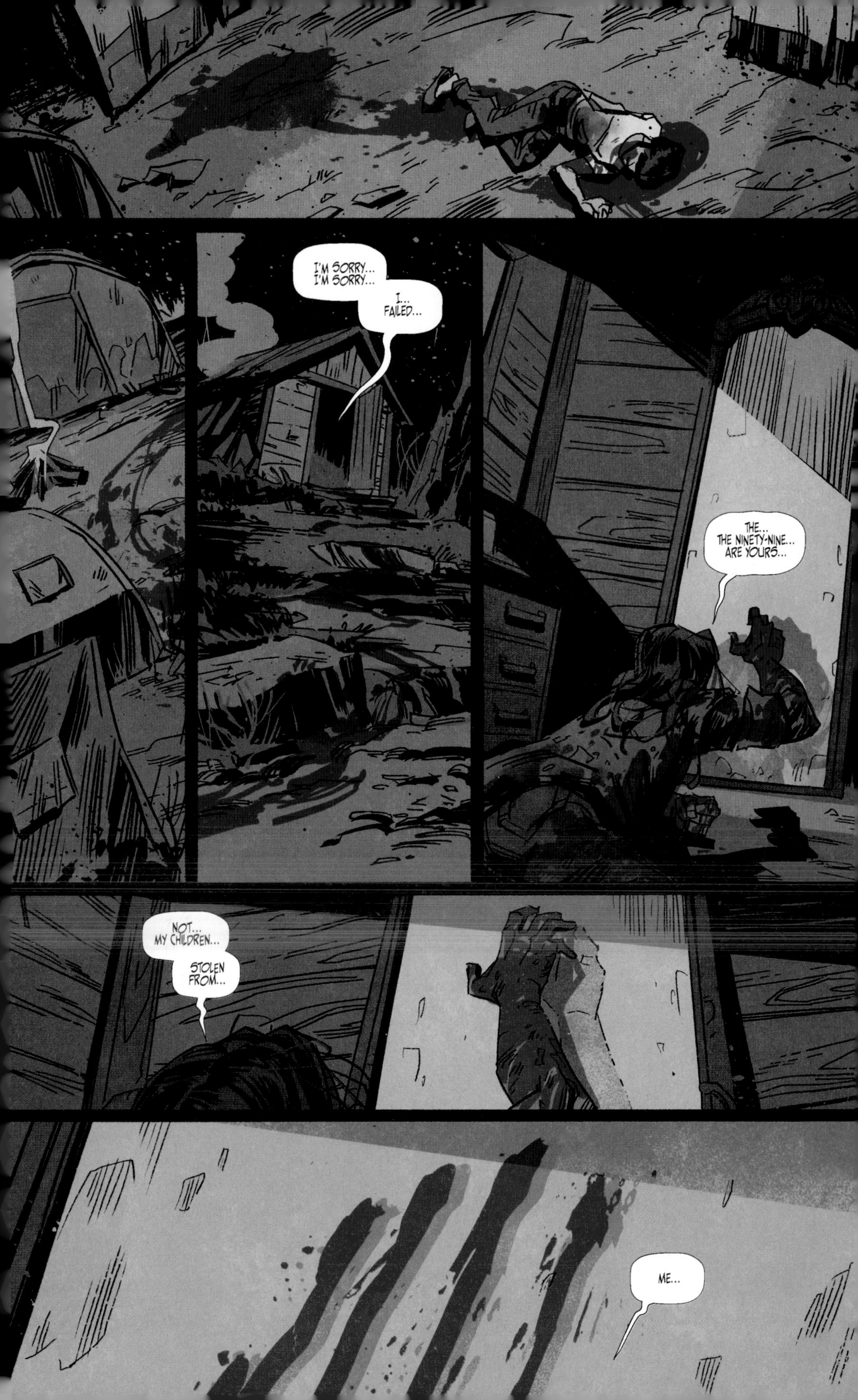
I'M SORRY... I'M SORRY...
I... FAILED...
THE... THE NINETY-NINE... ARE YOURS...
NOT... MY CHILDREN...
STOLEN FROM...
ME...

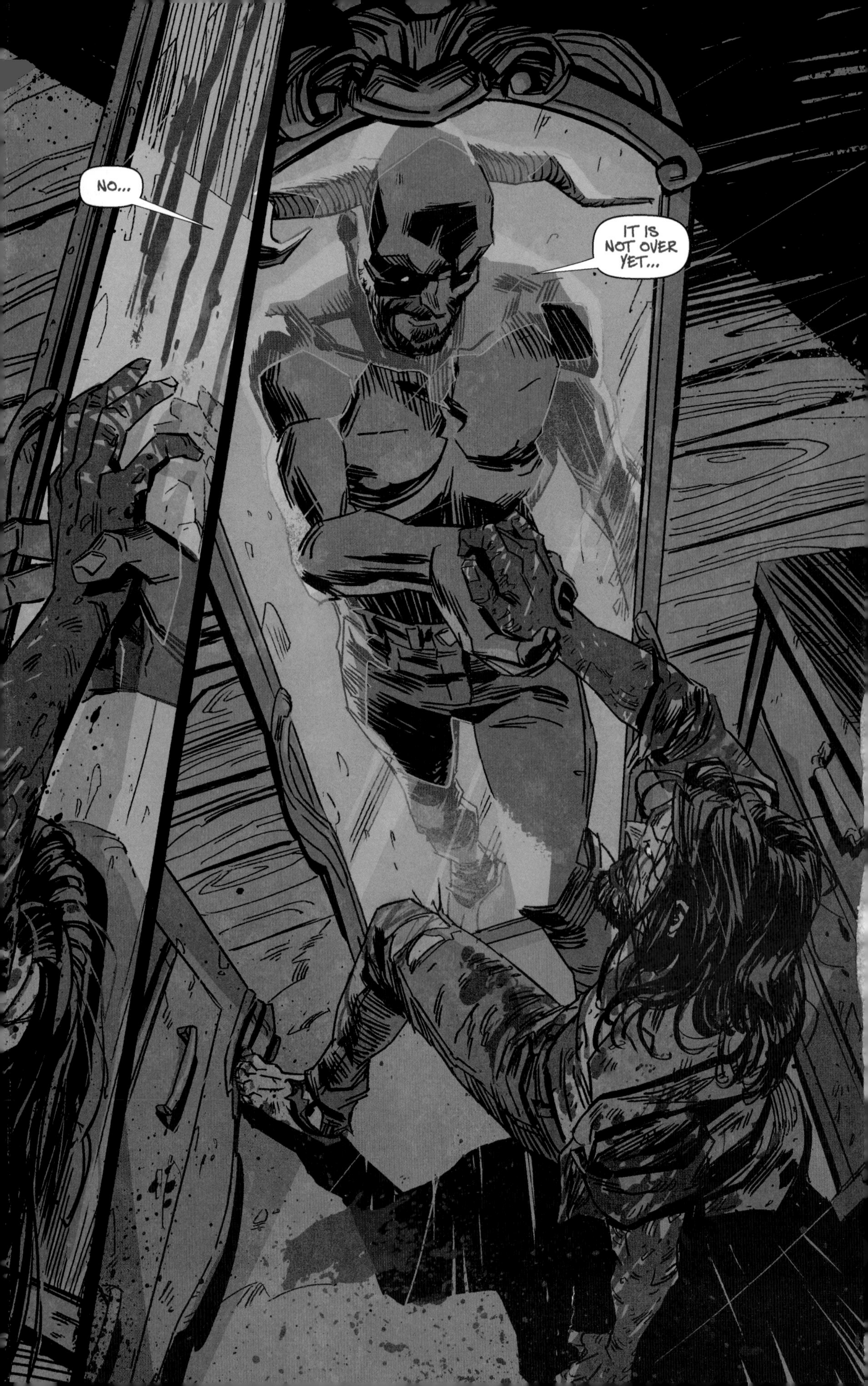
NO...
IT IS NOT OVER YET...

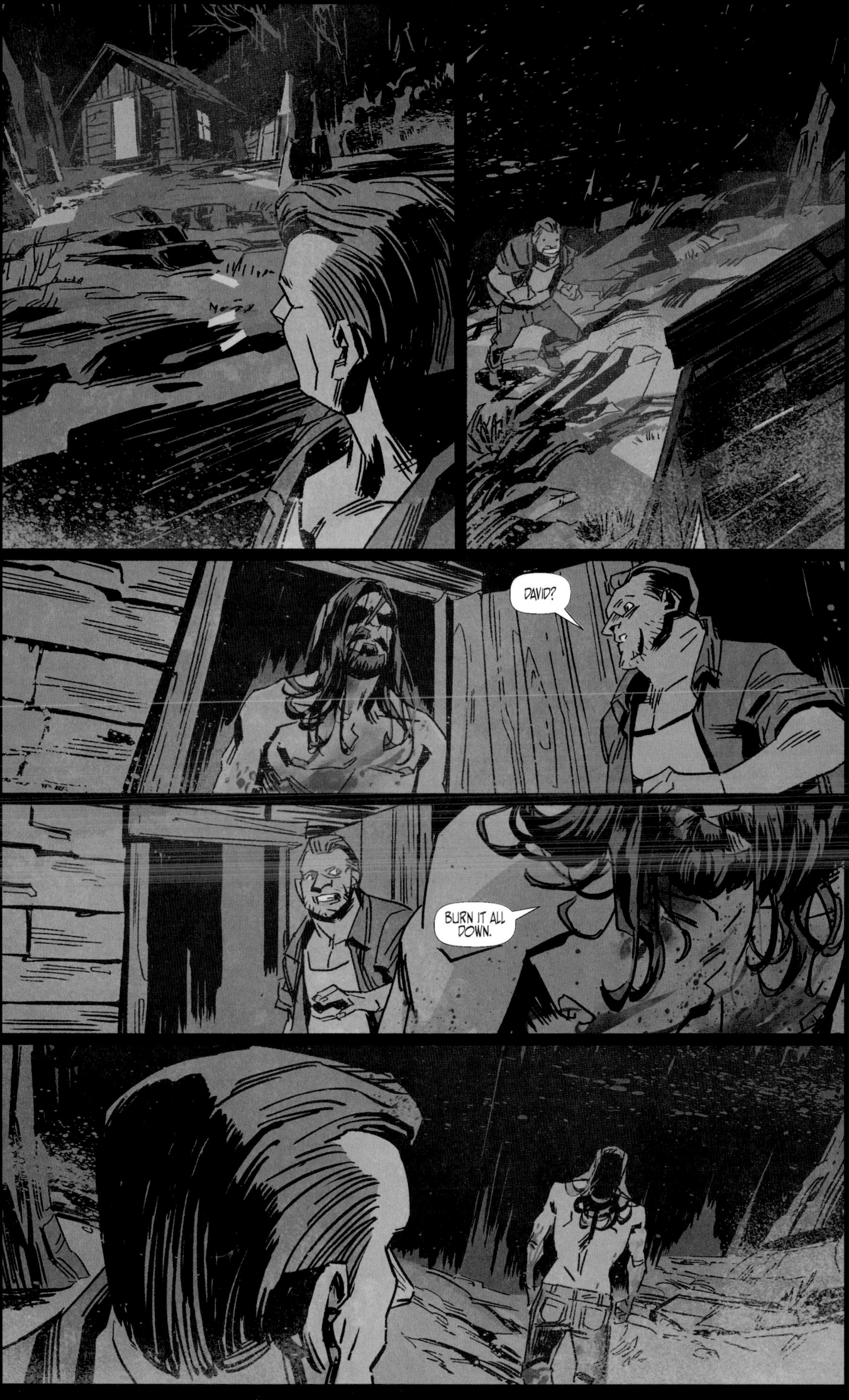
DAVID?
BURN IT ALL DOWN.

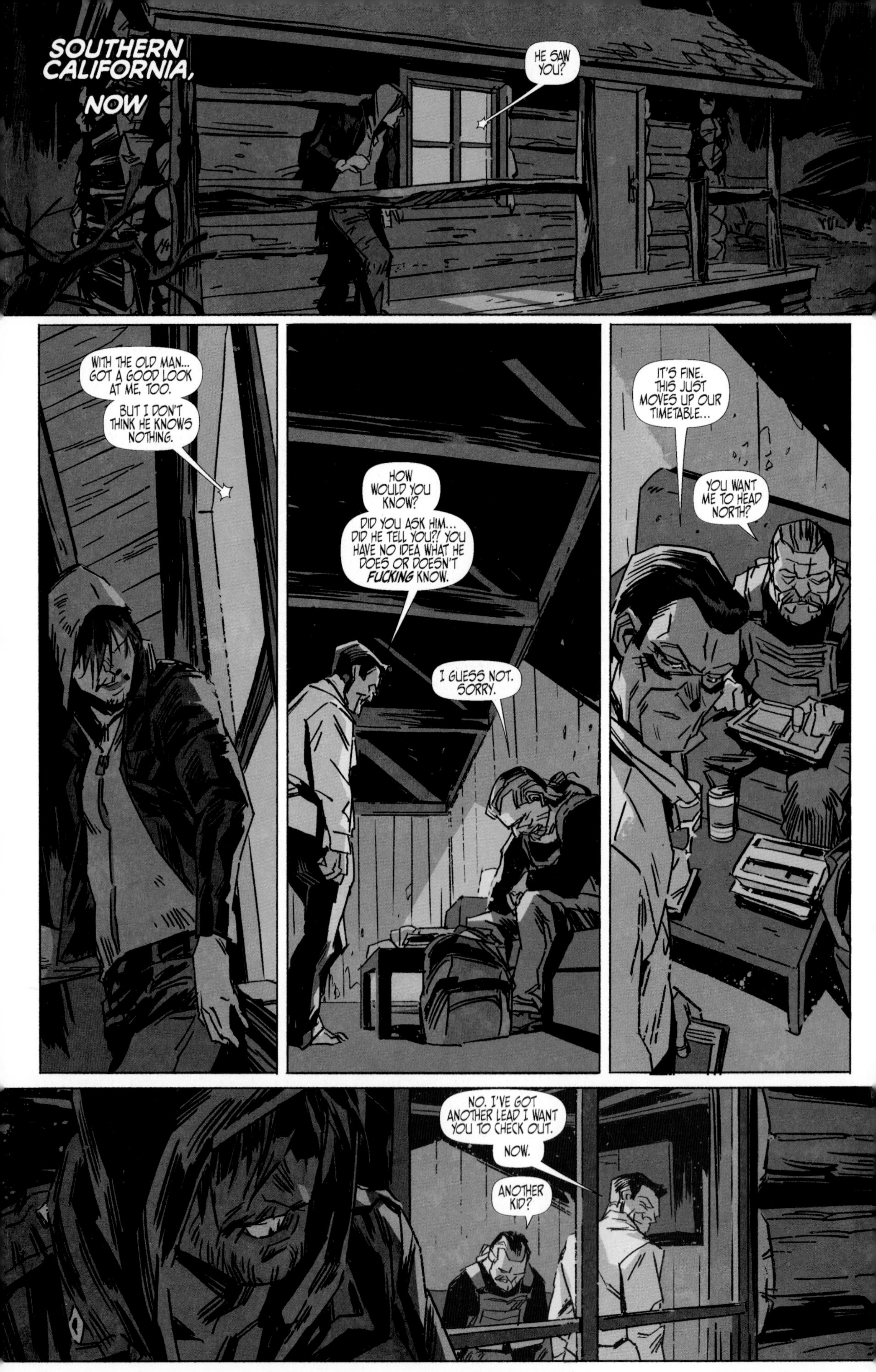
SOUTHERN CALIFORNIA, NOW
HE SAW YOU?
WITH THE OLD MAN... GOT A GOOD LOOK AT ME, TOO.
BUT I DON'T THINK HE KNOWS NOTHING.
HOW WOULD YOU KNOW?
DID YOU ASK HIM... DID HE TELL YOU?! YOU HAVE NO IDEA WHAT HE DOES OR DOESN'T FUCKING KNOW.
I GUESS NOT. SORRY.
IT'S FINE. THIS JUST MOVES UP OUR TIMETABLE...
YOU WANT ME TO HEAD NORTH?
NO. I'VE GOT ANOTHER LEAD I WANT YOU TO CHECK OUT.
NOW.
ANOTHER KID?

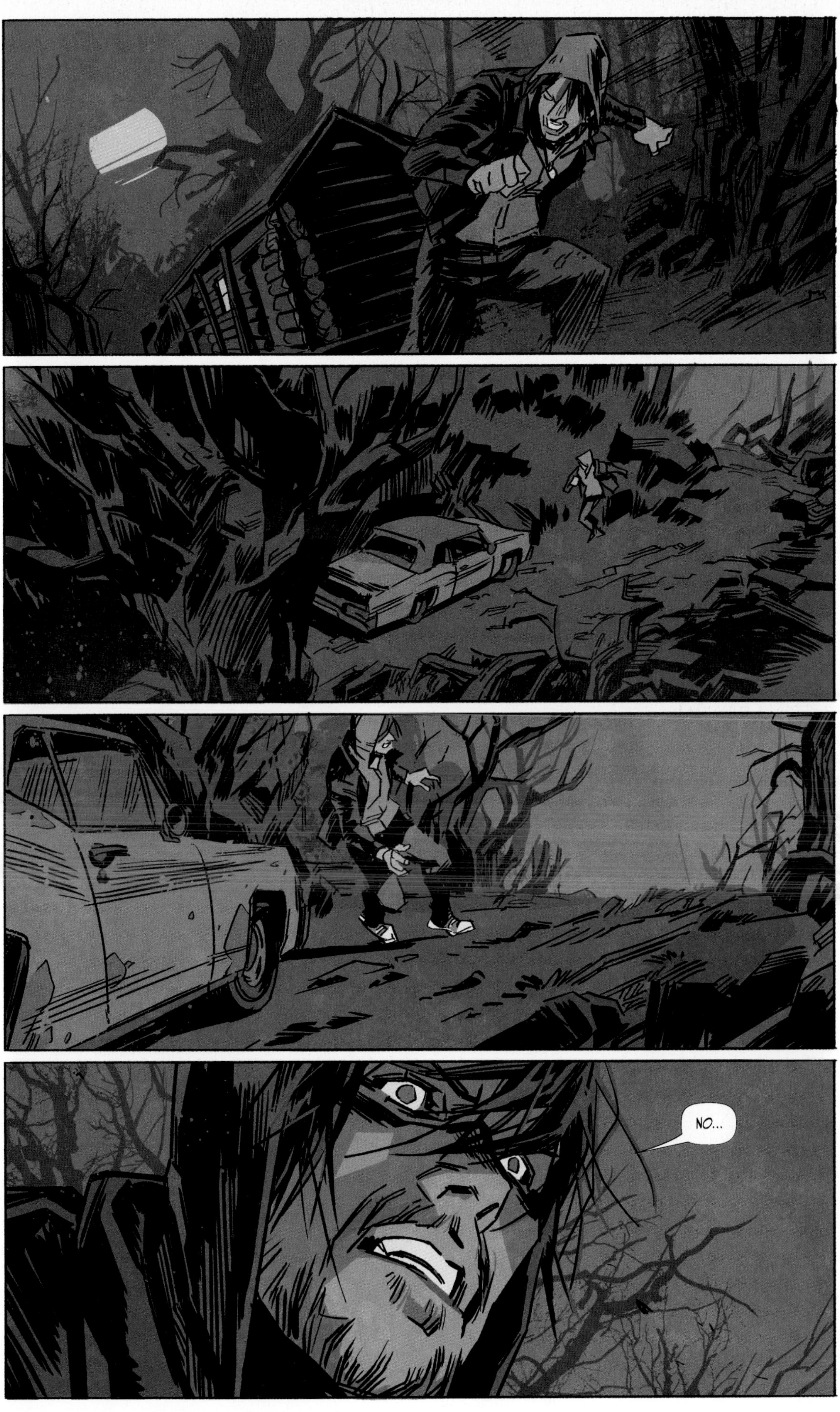
NO...

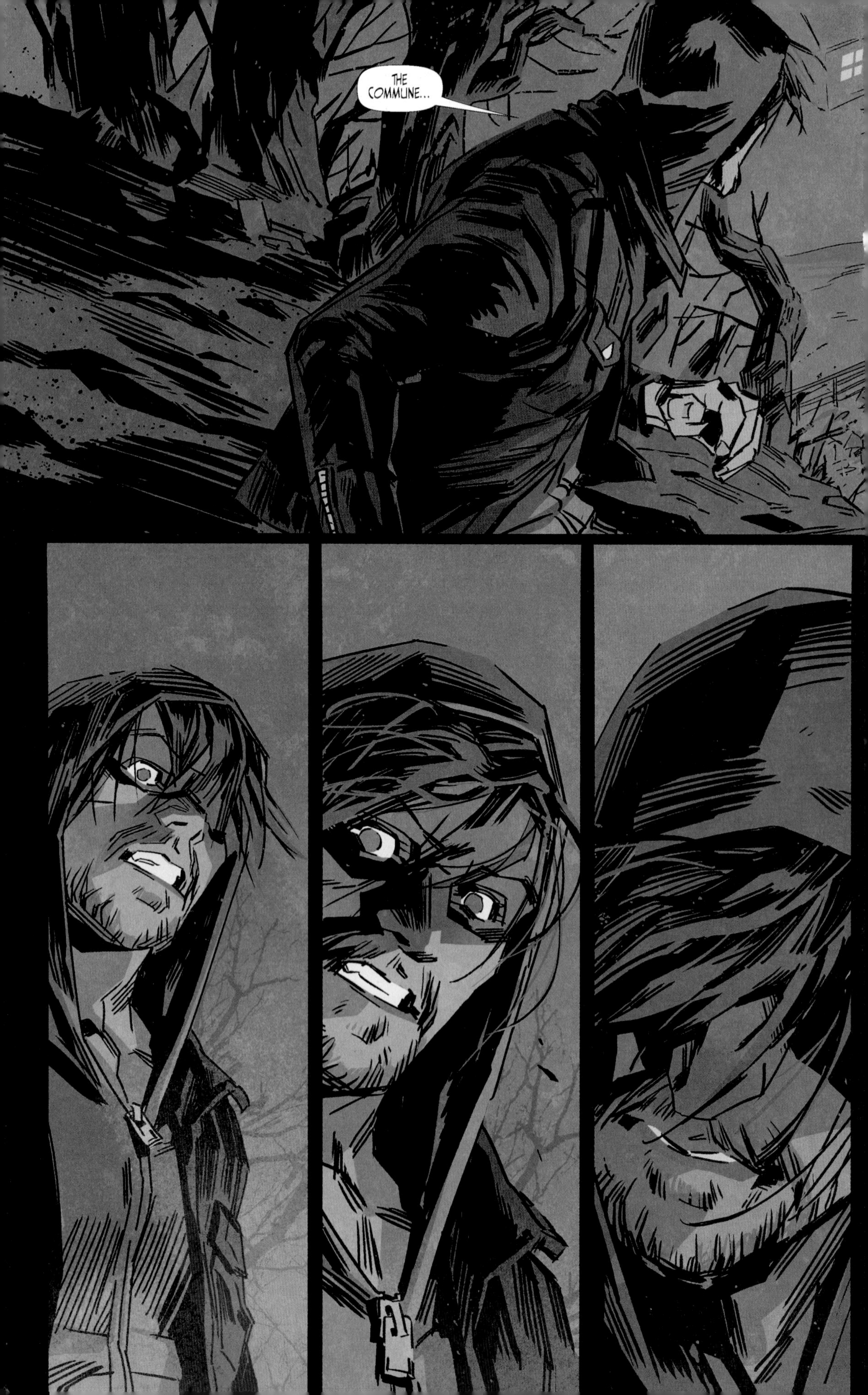
THE COMMUNE...

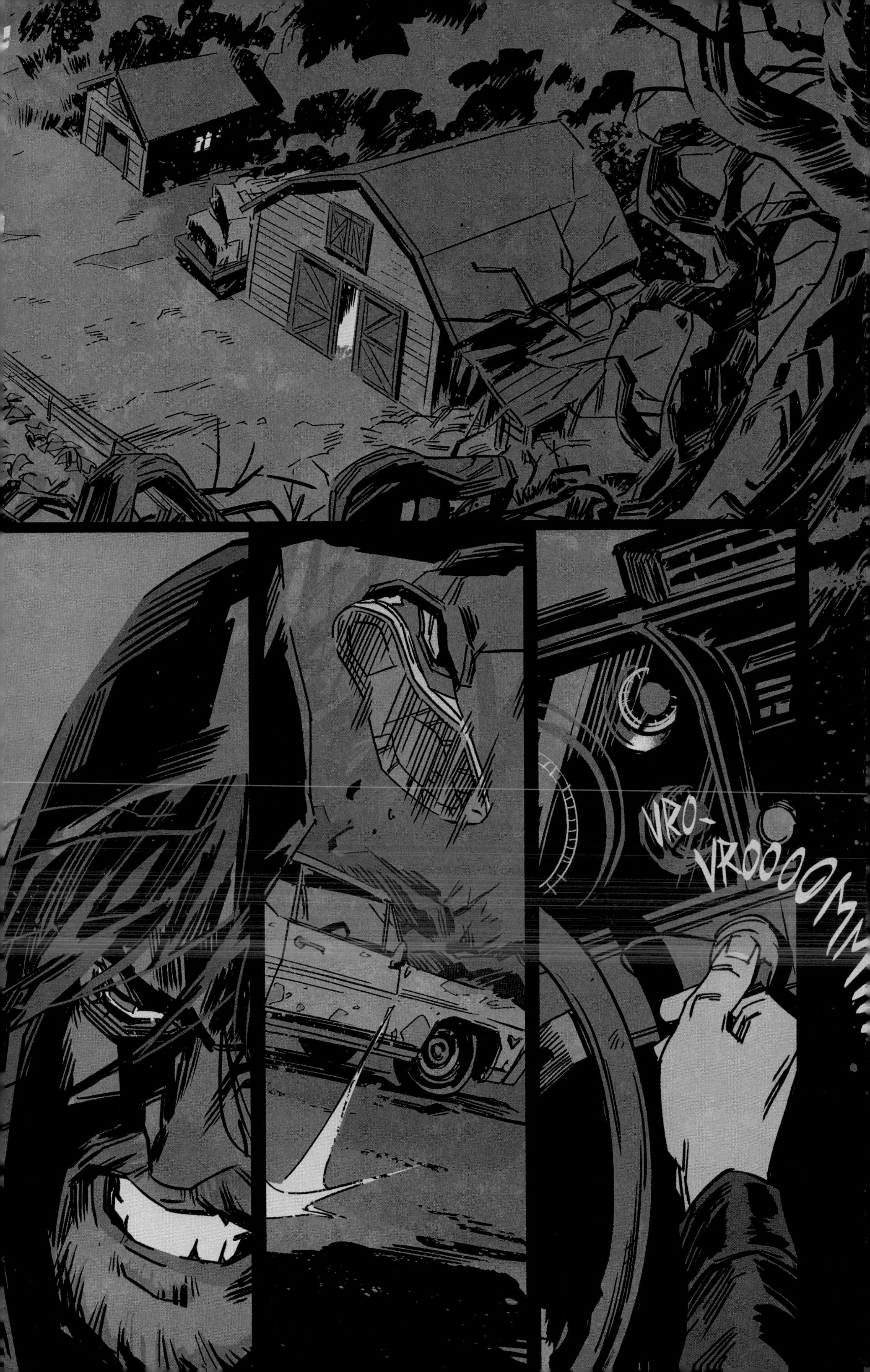
VRO-
VROOOOMMM

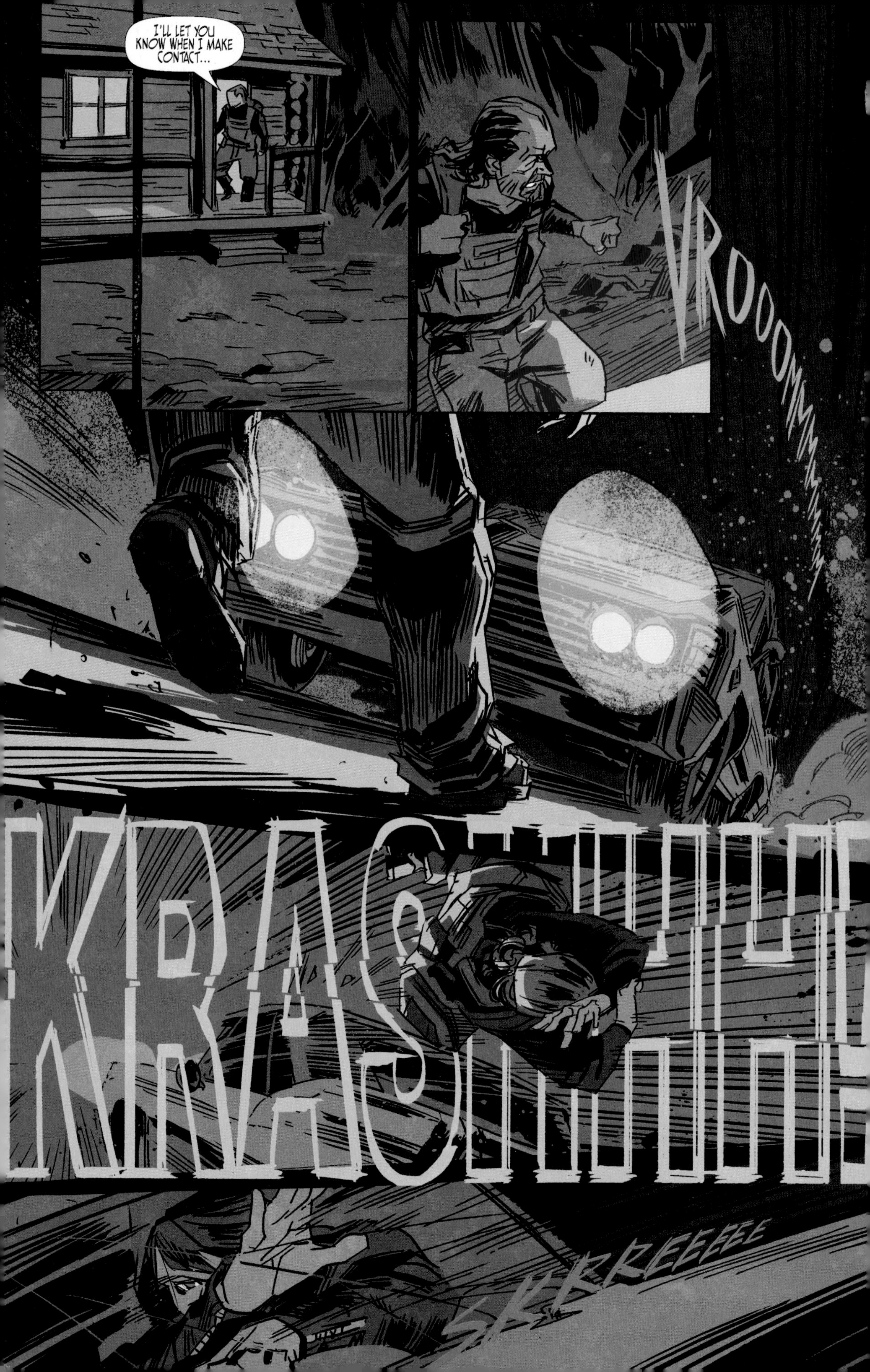

I'LL LET YOU KNOW WHEN I MAKE CONTACT...
VROOOMMMMM
KRASSHHHH!
SKKRREEEEE

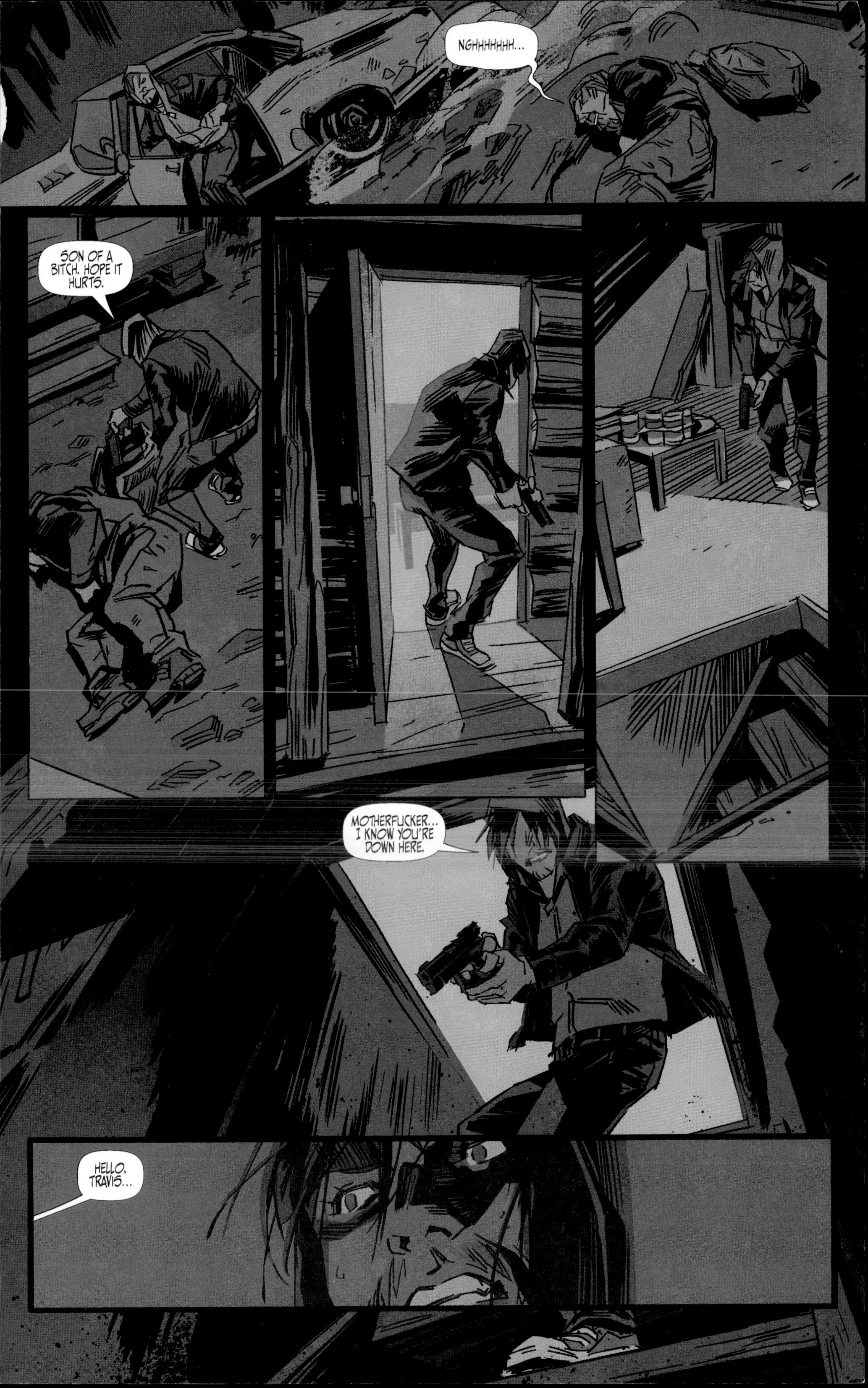
NGHHHHHHH...
SON OF A BITCH. HOPE IT HURTS.
MOTHERFUCKER... I KNOW YOU'RE DOWN HERE.
HELLO, TRAVIS...

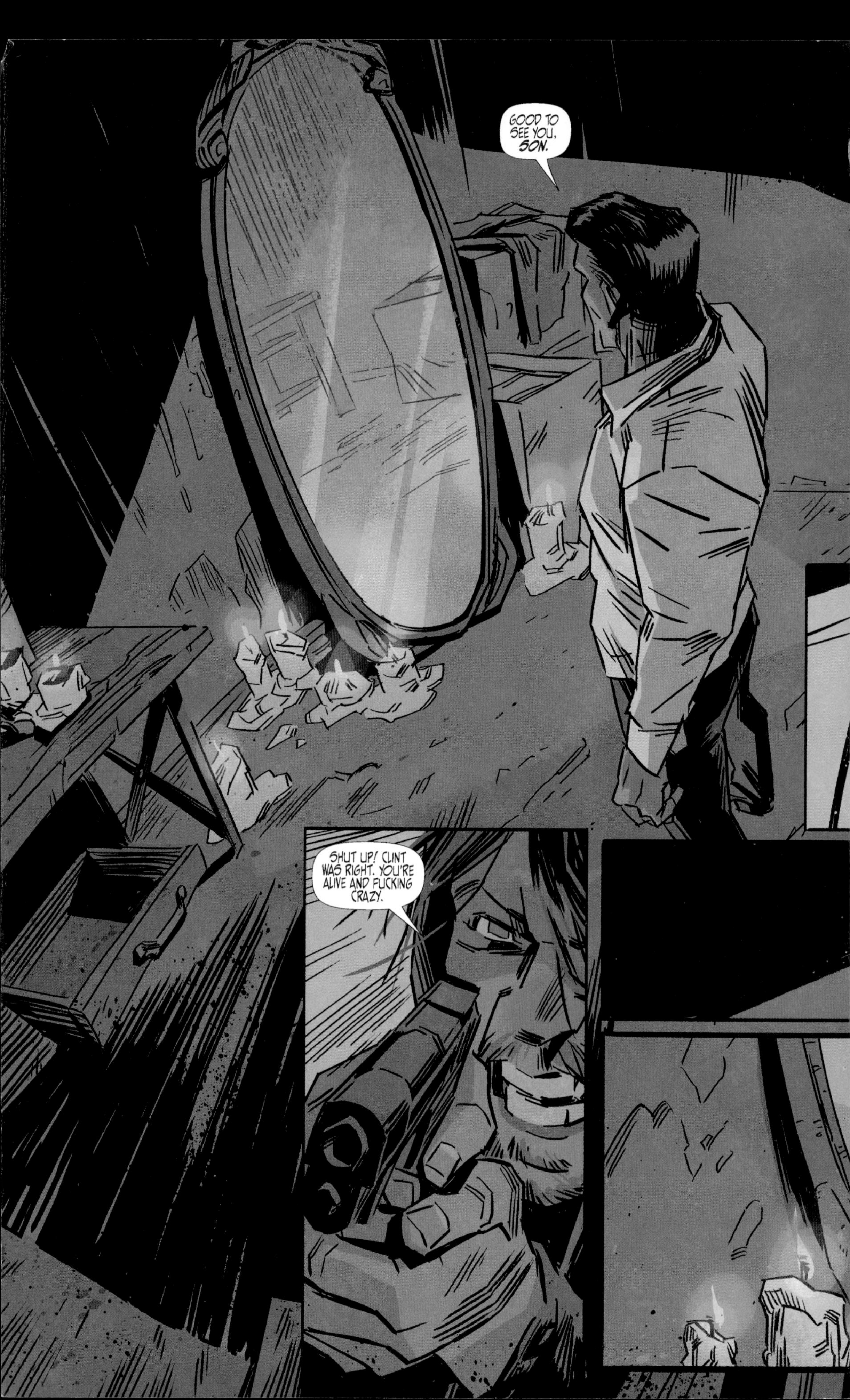
GOOD TO SEE YOU, SON.
SHUT UP! CLINT WAS RIGHT. YOU'RE ALIVE AND FUCKING CRAZY.

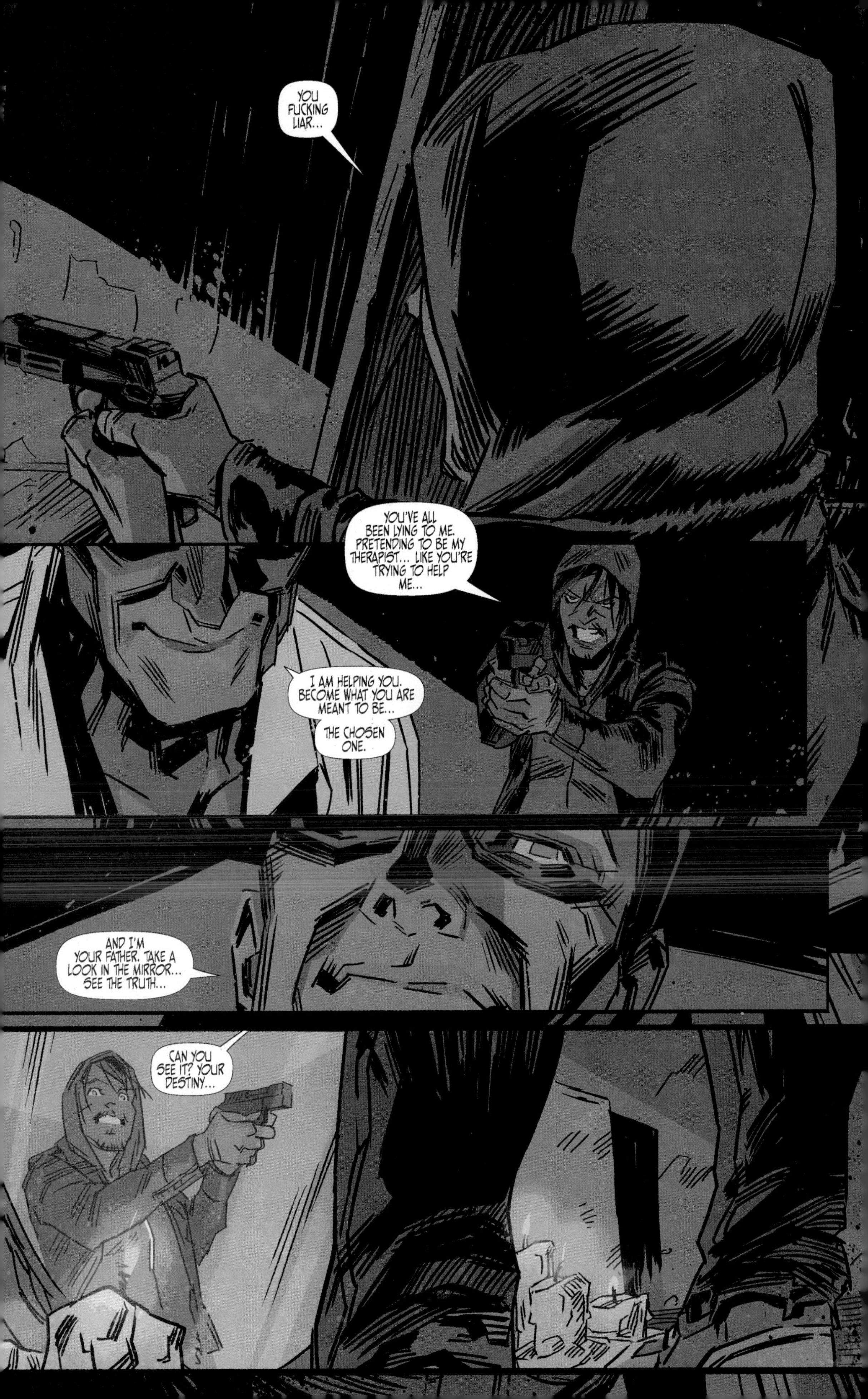
YOU FUCKING LIAR...
YOU'VE ALL BEEN LYING TO ME. PRETENDING TO BE MY THERAPIST... LIKE YOU'RE TRYING TO HELP ME...
I AM HELPING YOU. BECOME WHAT YOU ARE MEANT TO BE...
THE CHOSEN ONE.
AND I'M YOUR FATHER. TAKE A LOOK IN THE MIRROR... SEE THE TRUTH...
CAN YOU SEE IT? YOUR DESTINY...

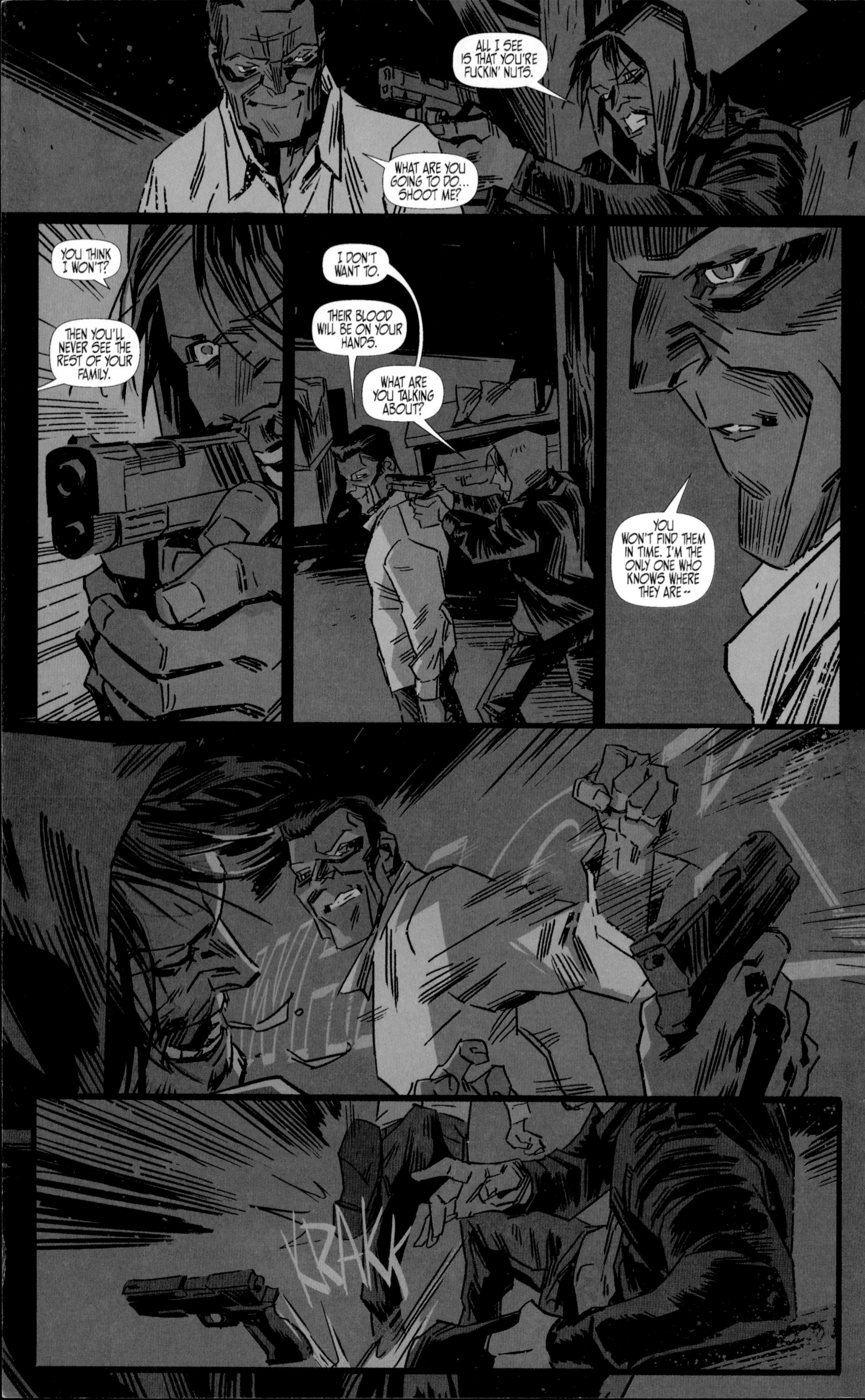
ALL I SEE IS THAT YOU'RE FUCKIN' NUTS.
WHAT ARE YOU GOING TO DO... SHOOT ME?
YOU THINK I WON'T?
THEN YOU'LL NEVER SEE THE REST OF YOUR FAMILY.
I DON'T WANT TO.
THEIR BLOOD WILL BE ON YOUR HANDS.
WHAT ARE YOU TALKING ABOUT?
YOU WON'T FIND THEM IN TIME. I'M THE ONLY ONE WHO KNOWS WHERE THEY ARE--
KRAKK

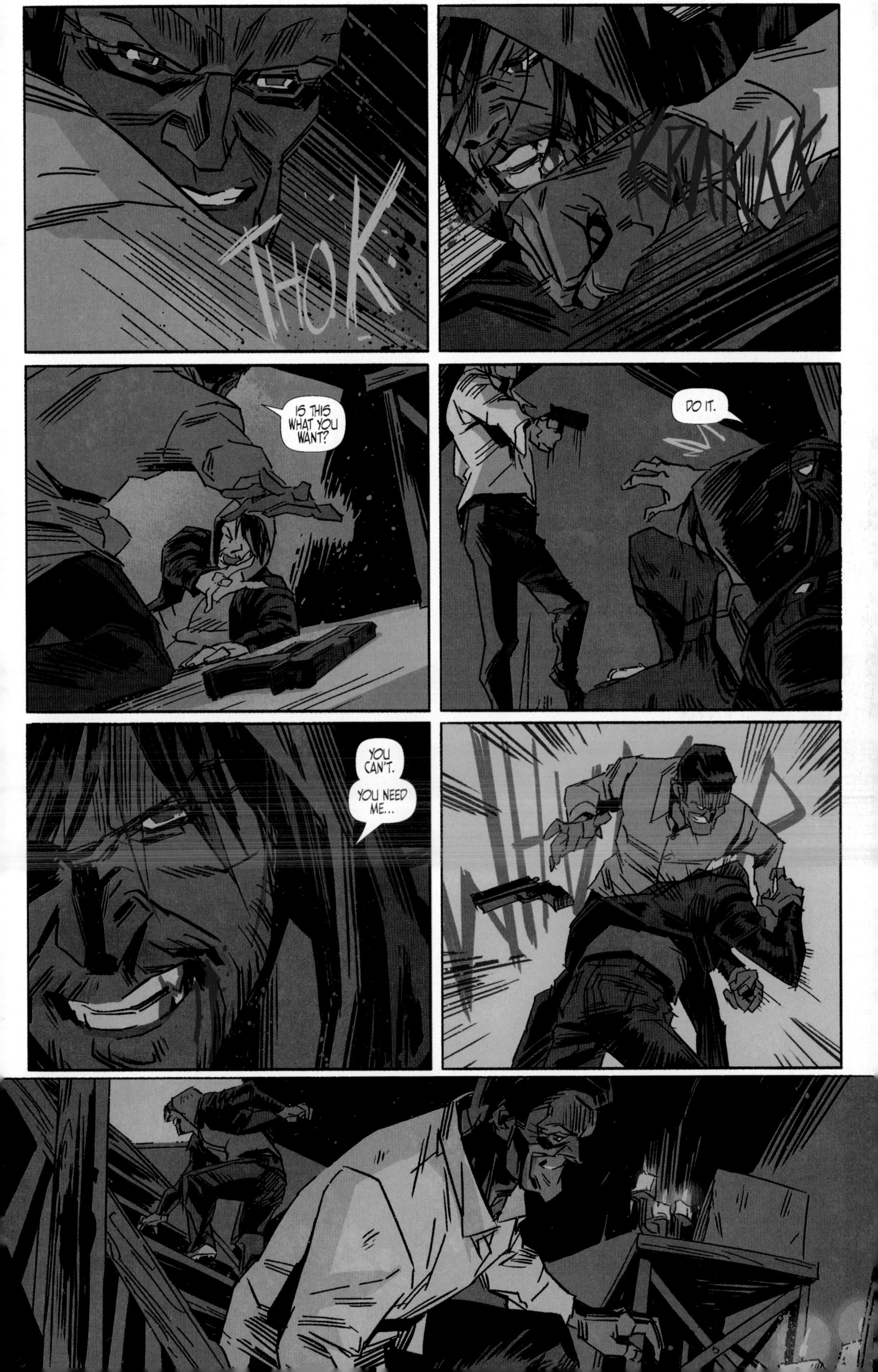
THOK
KRAKKK
IS THIS WHAT YOU WANT?
DO IT.
YOU CAN'T.
YOU NEED ME...

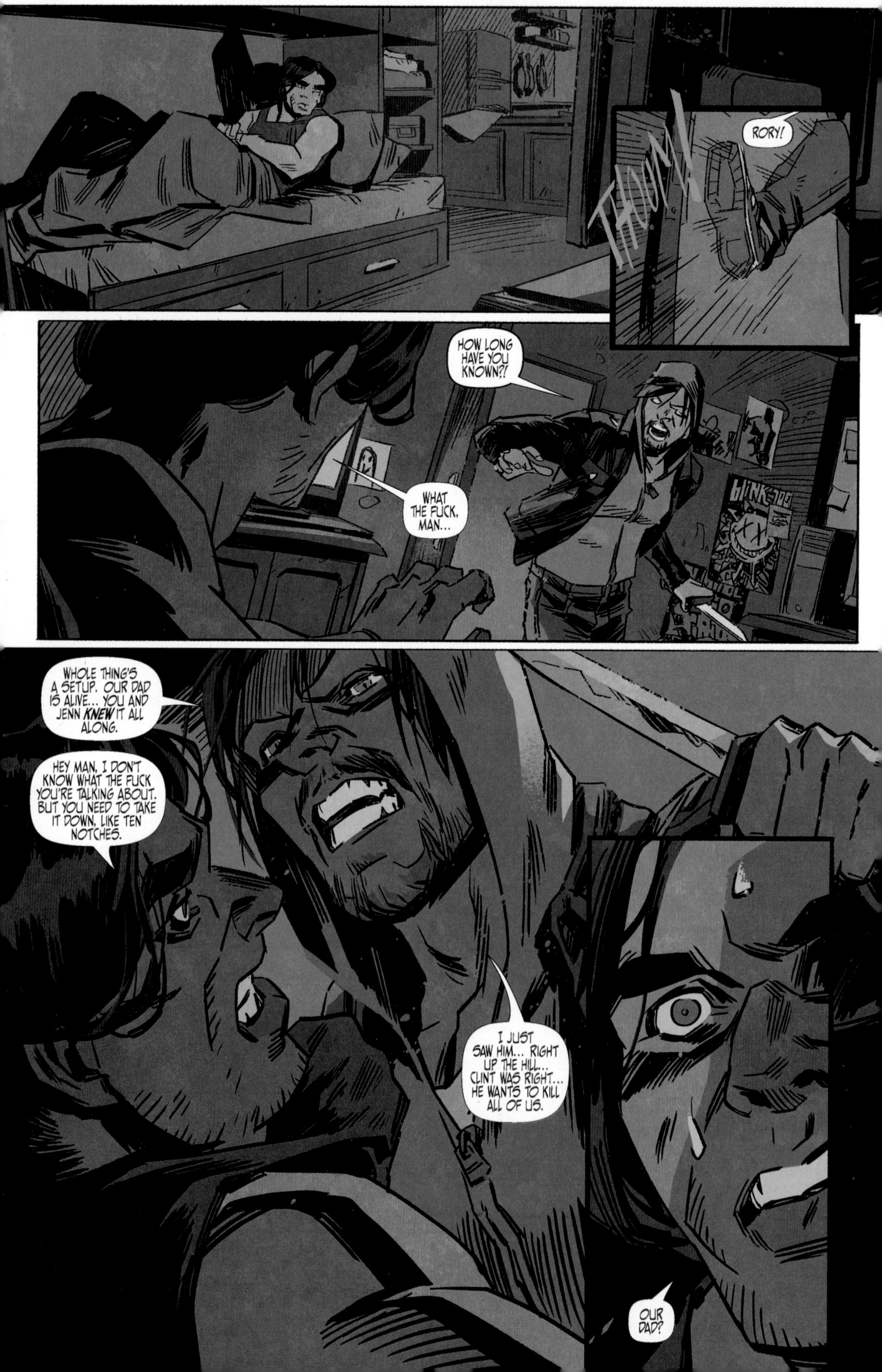
THUMM!
RORY!
HOW LONG HAVE YOU KNOWN?!
WHAT THE FUCK, MAN...
WHOLE THING'S A SETUP. OUR DAD IS ALIVE... YOU AND JENN *KNEW* IT ALL ALONG.
HEY MAN, I DON'T KNOW WHAT THE FUCK YOU'RE TALKING ABOUT. BUT YOU NEED TO TAKE IT DOWN, LIKE TEN NOTCHES.
I JUST SAW HIM... RIGHT UP THE HILL... CLINT WAS RIGHT... HE WANTS TO KILL ALL OF US.
OUR DAD?

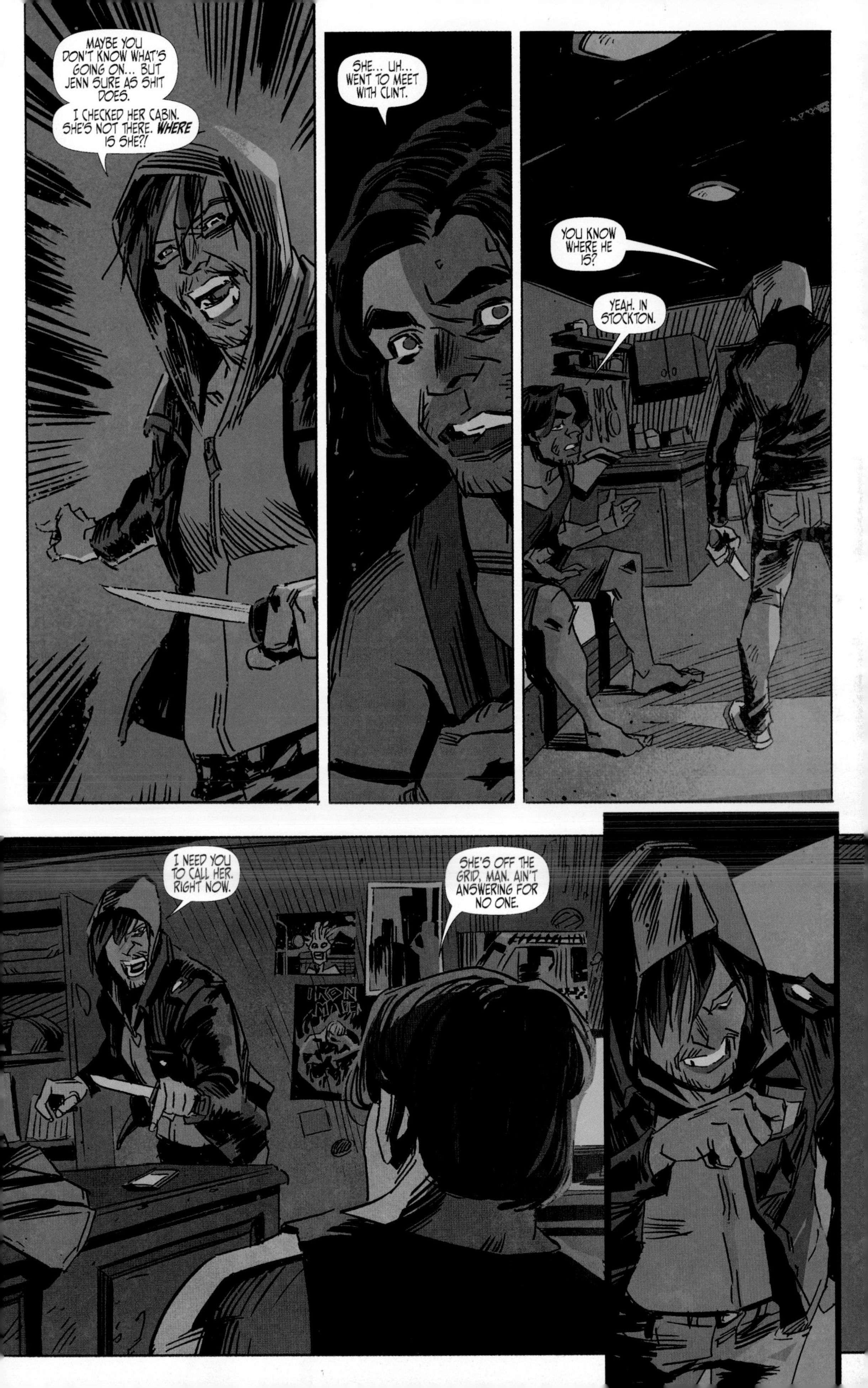
MAYBE YOU DON'T KNOW WHAT'S GOING ON... BUT JENN SURE AS SHIT DOES.
I CHECKED HER CABIN. SHE'S NOT THERE. *WHERE* IS SHE?!
SHE... UH... WENT TO MEET WITH CLINT.
YOU KNOW WHERE HE IS?
YEAH. IN STOCKTON.
I NEED YOU TO CALL HER. RIGHT NOW.
SHE'S OFF THE GRID, MAN. AIN'T ANSWERING FOR NO ONE.
IRON MAIDEN

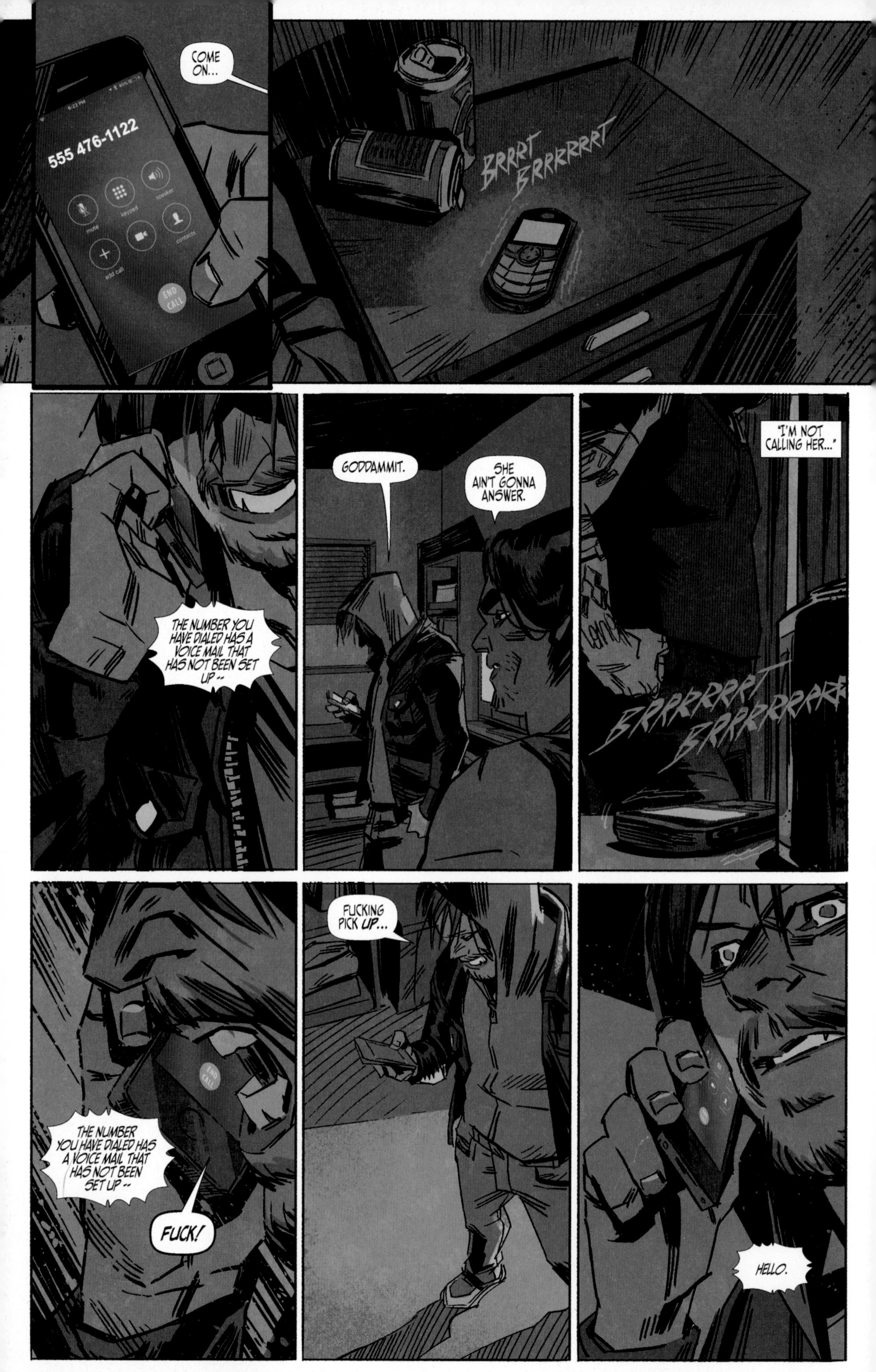
555 476-1122
mute
keypad
speaker
add call
contacts
END CALL
COME ON...
BRRRT BRRRRRRT
THE NUMBER YOU HAVE DIALED HAS A VOICE MAIL THAT HAS NOT BEEN SET UP --
GODDAMMIT.
SHE AIN'T GONNA ANSWER.
"I'M NOT CALLING HER..."
BRRRRRRRT BRRRRRRRRR
END CALL
THE NUMBER YOU HAVE DIALED HAS A VOICE MAIL THAT HAS NOT BEEN SET UP --
FUCK!
FUCKING PICK UP...
HELLO.

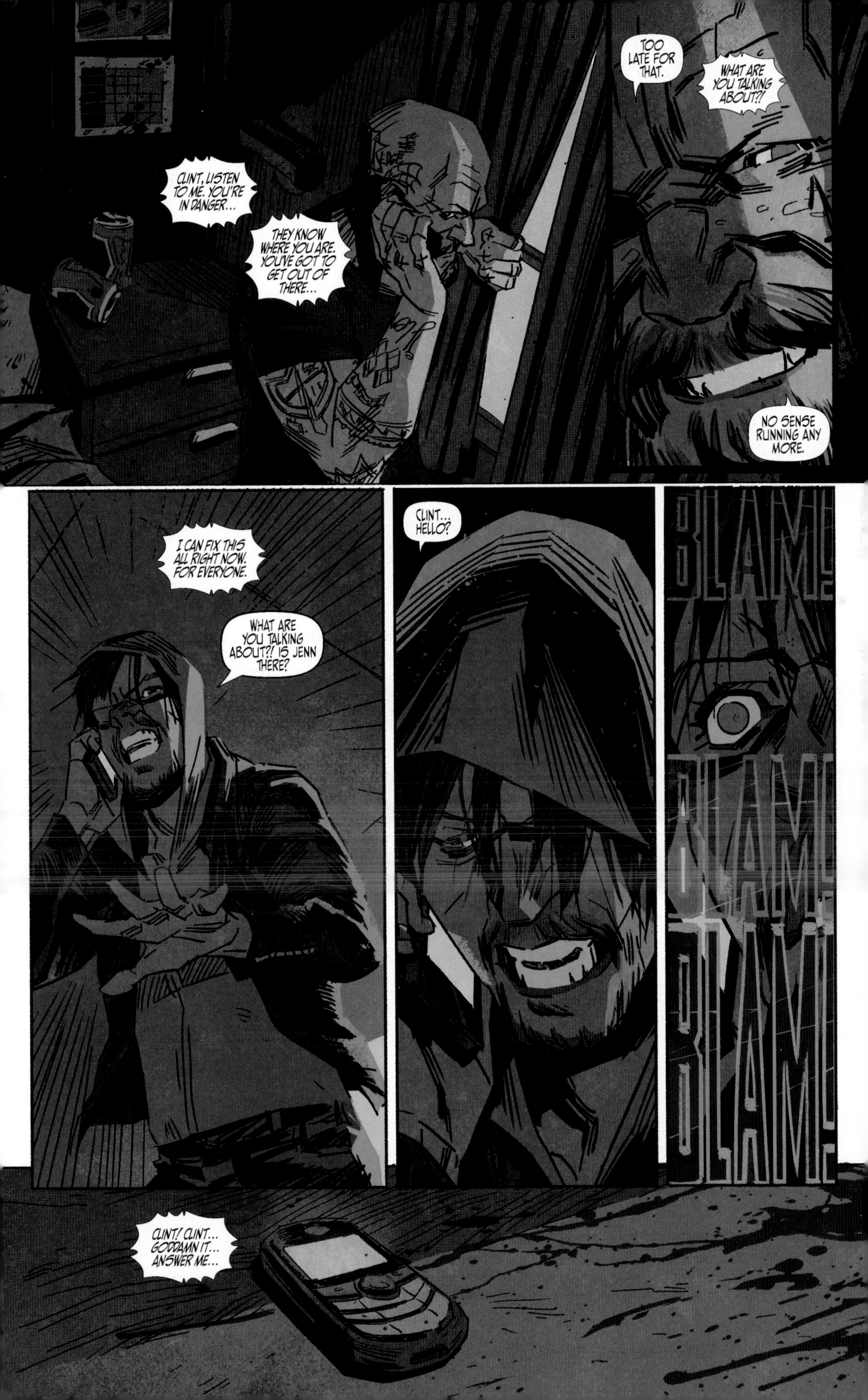
CLINT, LISTEN TO ME. YOU'RE IN DANGER...
THEY KNOW WHERE YOU ARE. YOU'VE GOT TO GET OUT OF THERE...
TOO LATE FOR THAT.
WHAT ARE YOU TALKING ABOUT?!
NO SENSE RUNNING ANY MORE.
I CAN FIX THIS ALL RIGHT NOW. FOR EVERYONE.
WHAT ARE YOU TALKING ABOUT?! IS JENN THERE?
CLINT... HELLO?
BLAM!
BLAM!
BLAM!
BLAM!
BLAM!
CLINT! CLINT... GODDAMN IT... ANSWER ME...

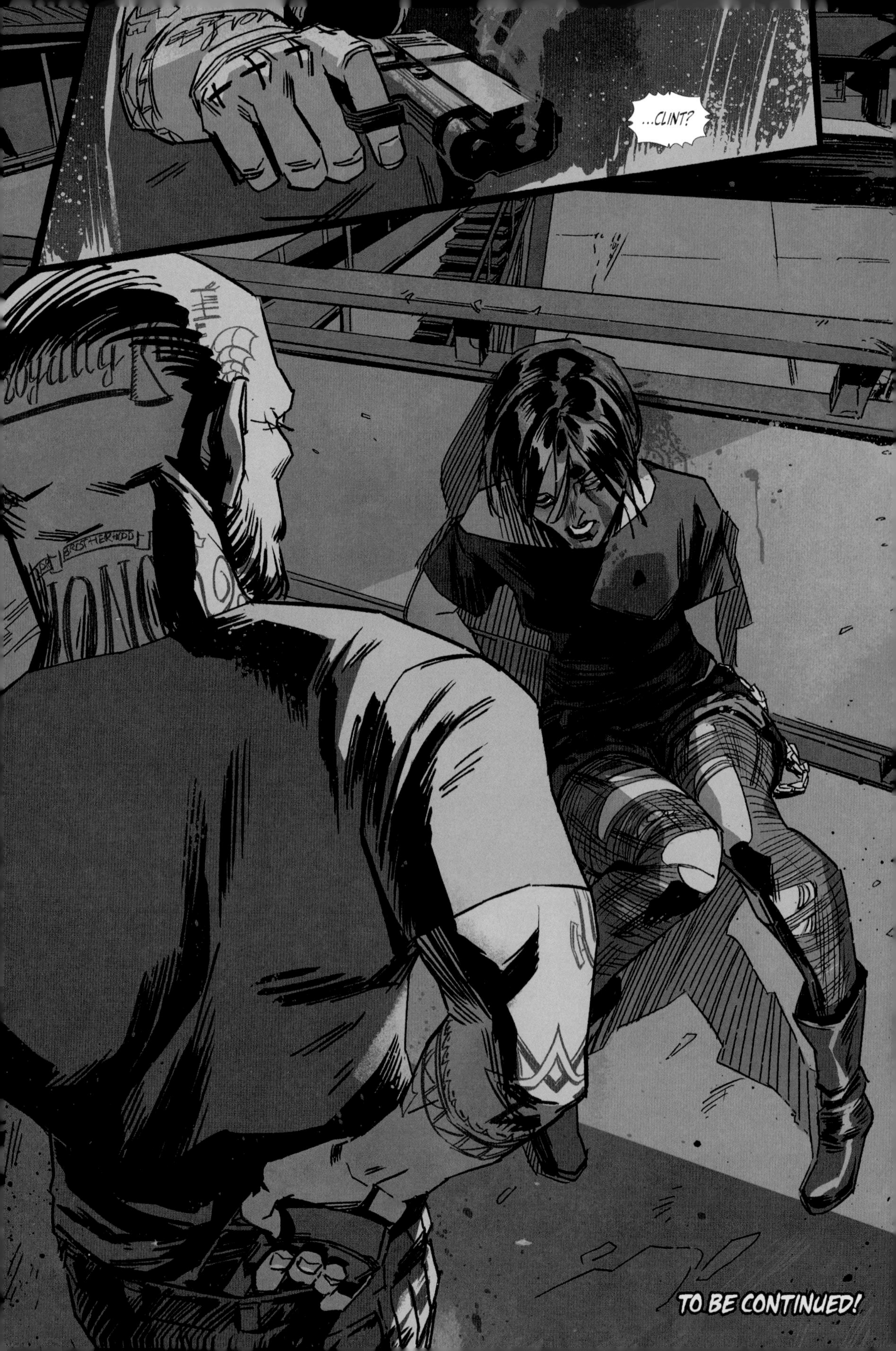
...CLINT?
TO BE CONTINUED!

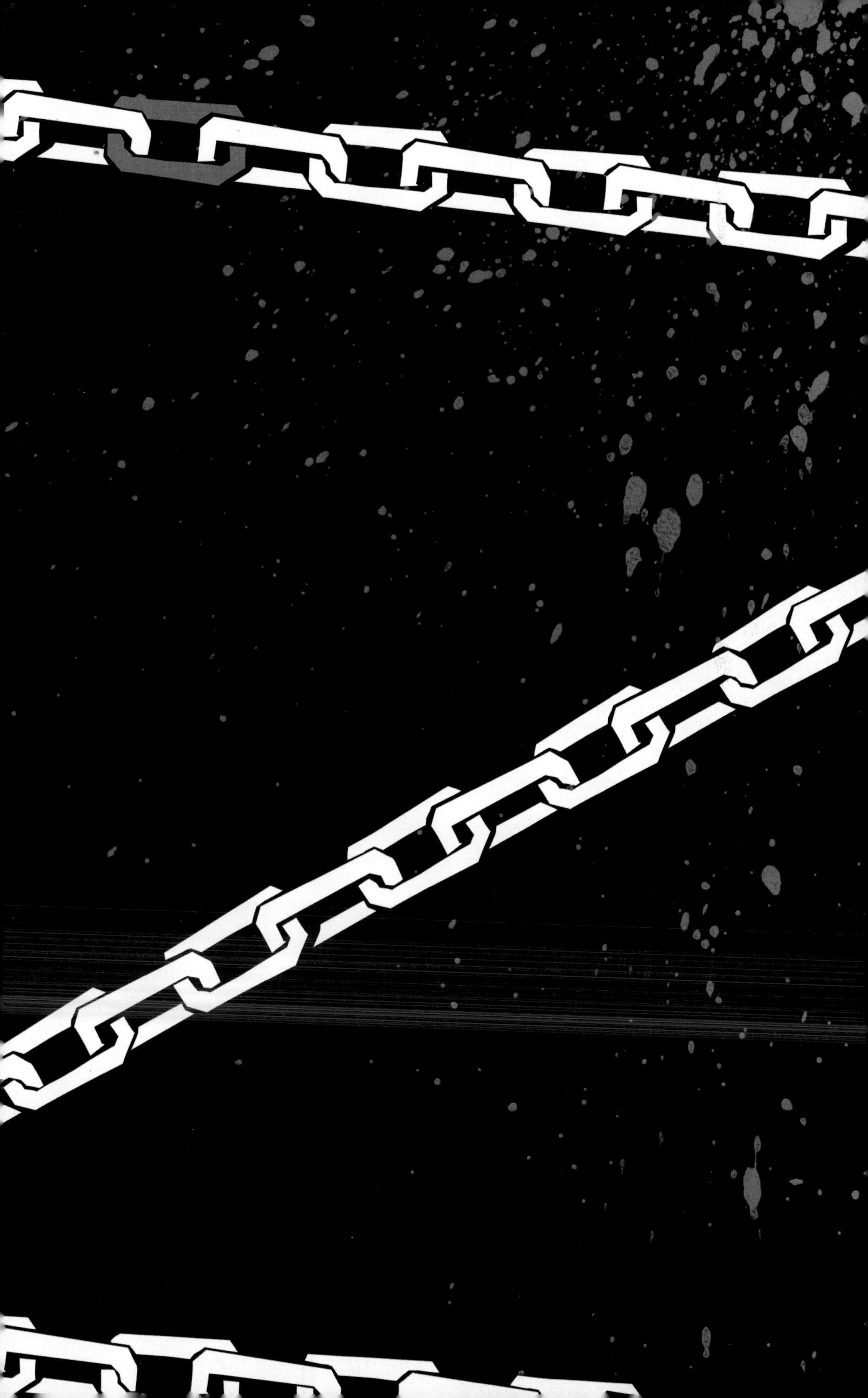

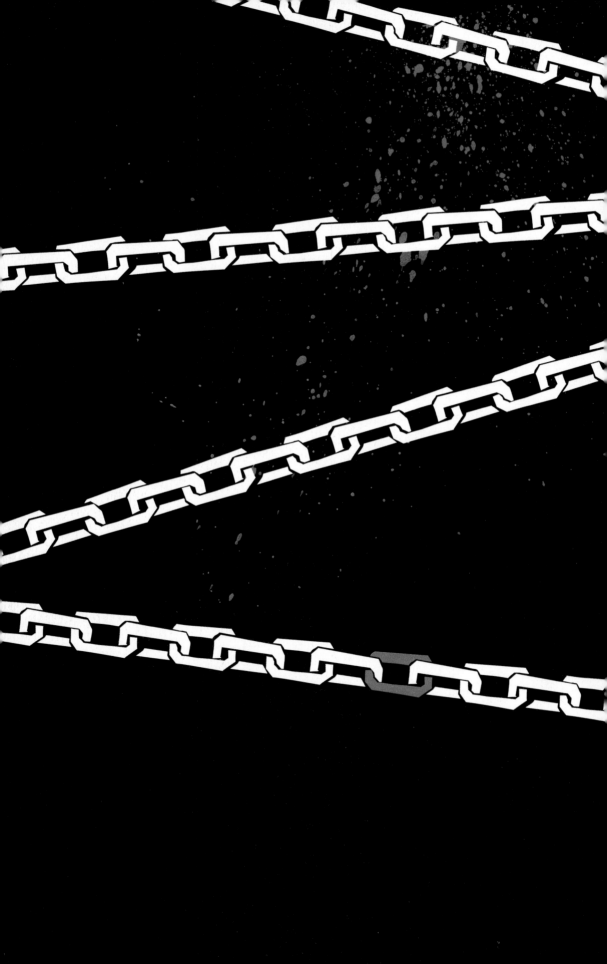

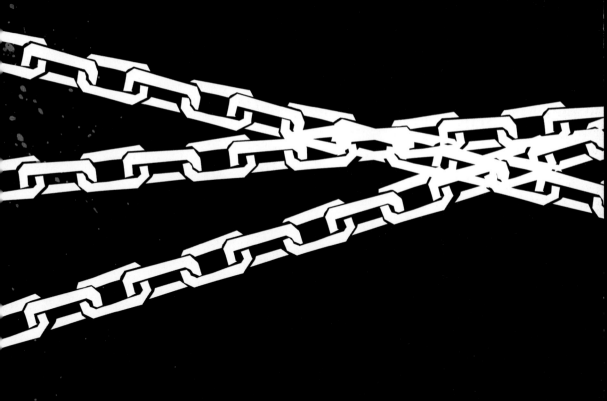

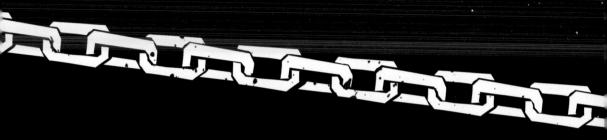

COVER
GALLERY

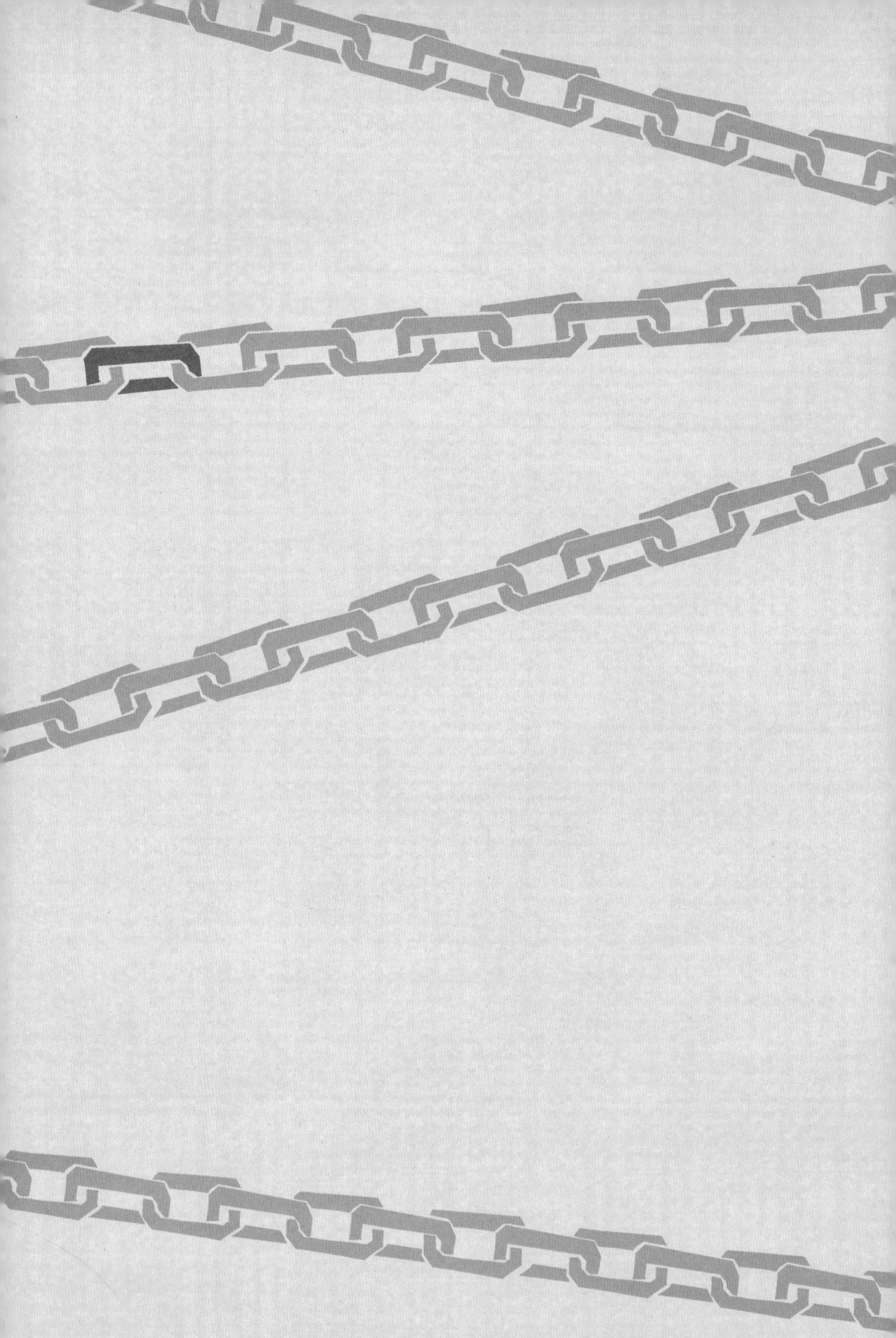

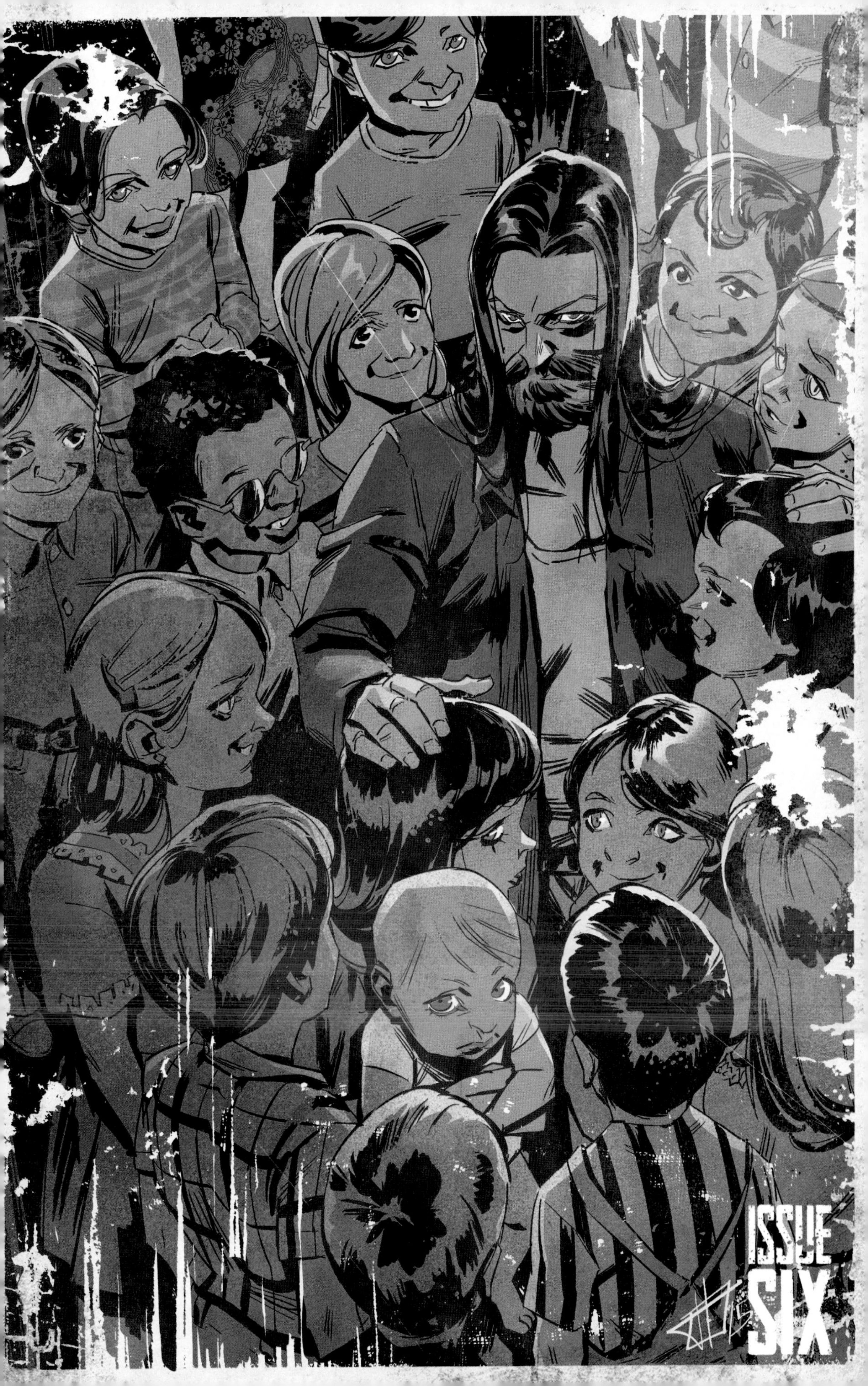
ISSUE
SIX

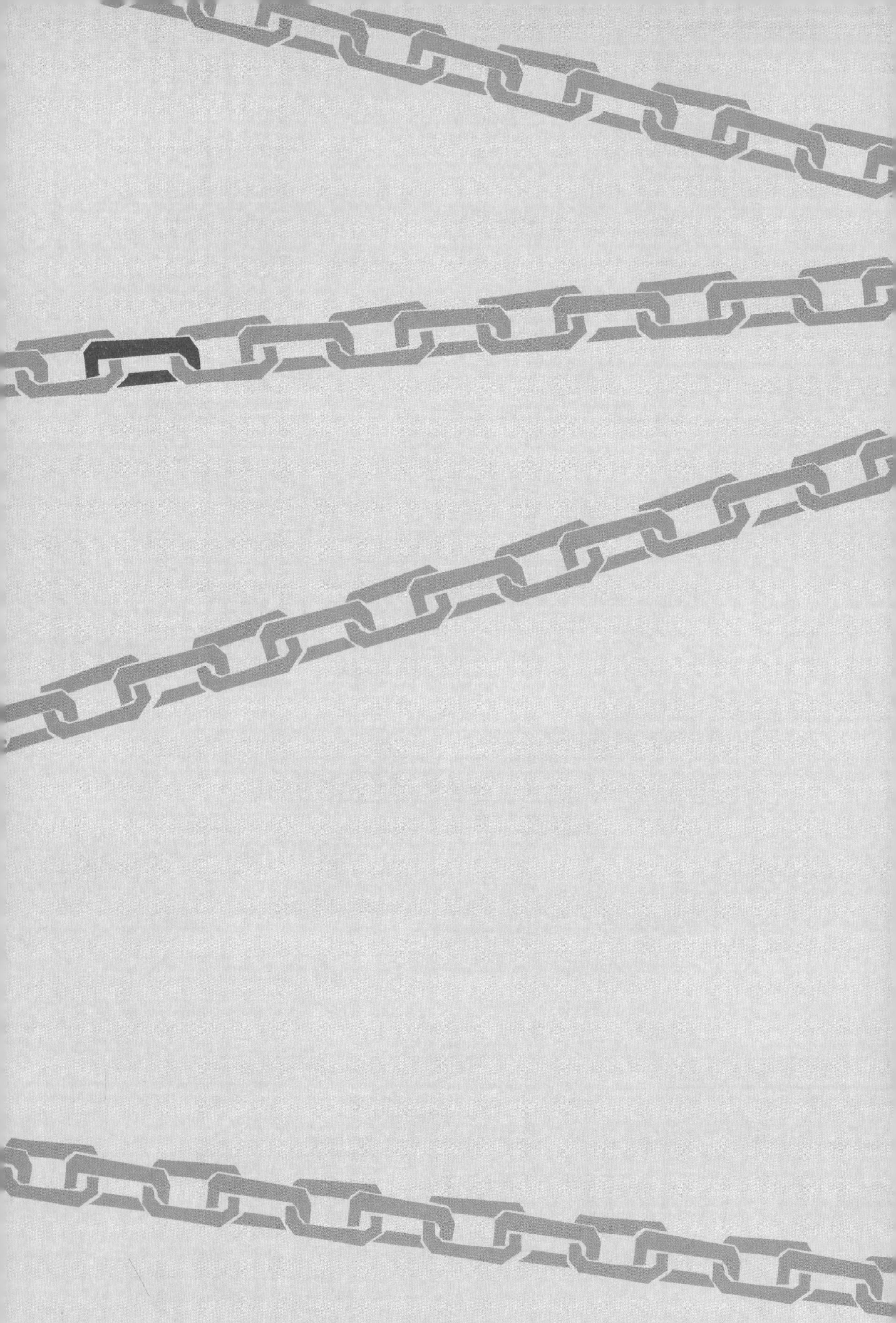

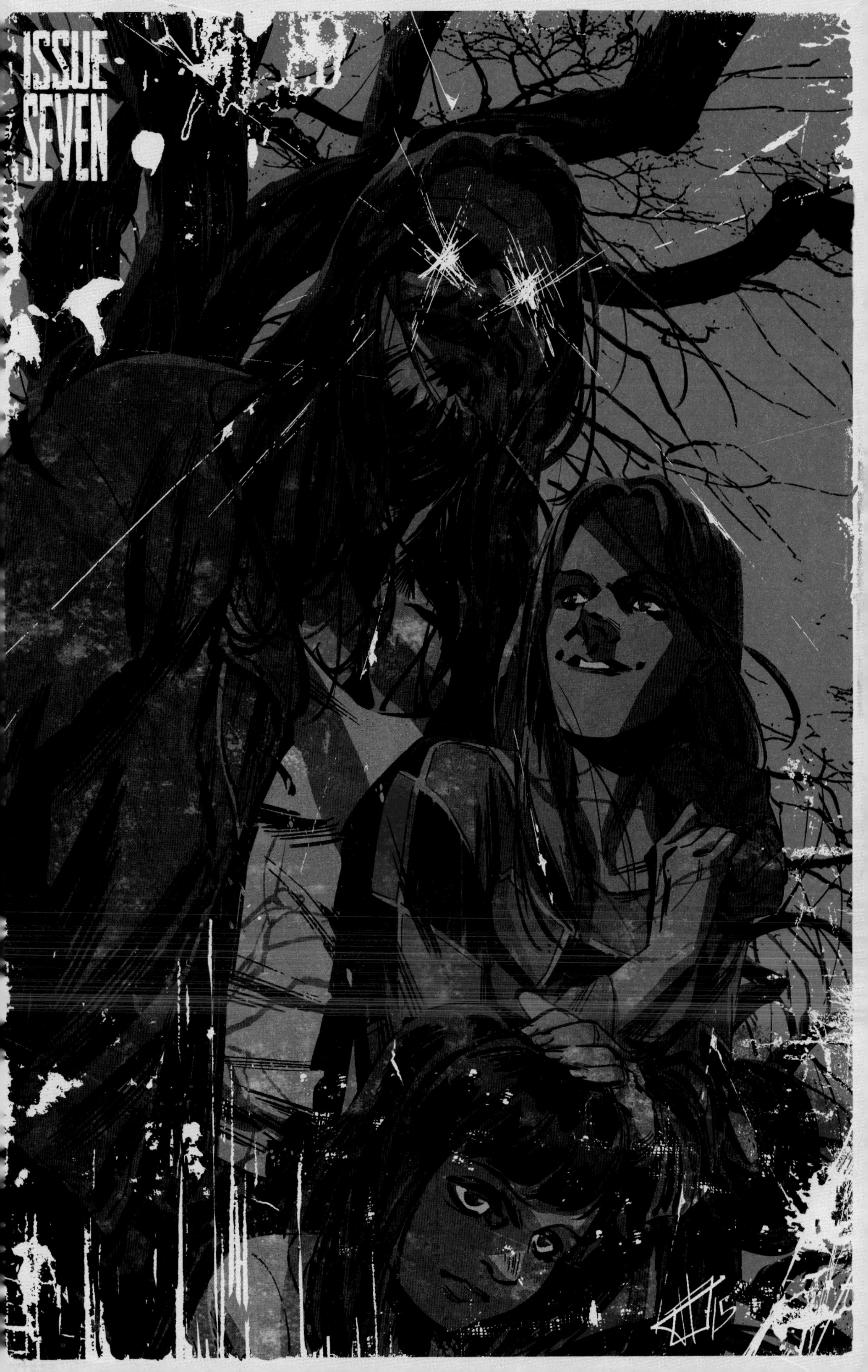
ISSUE
SEVEN

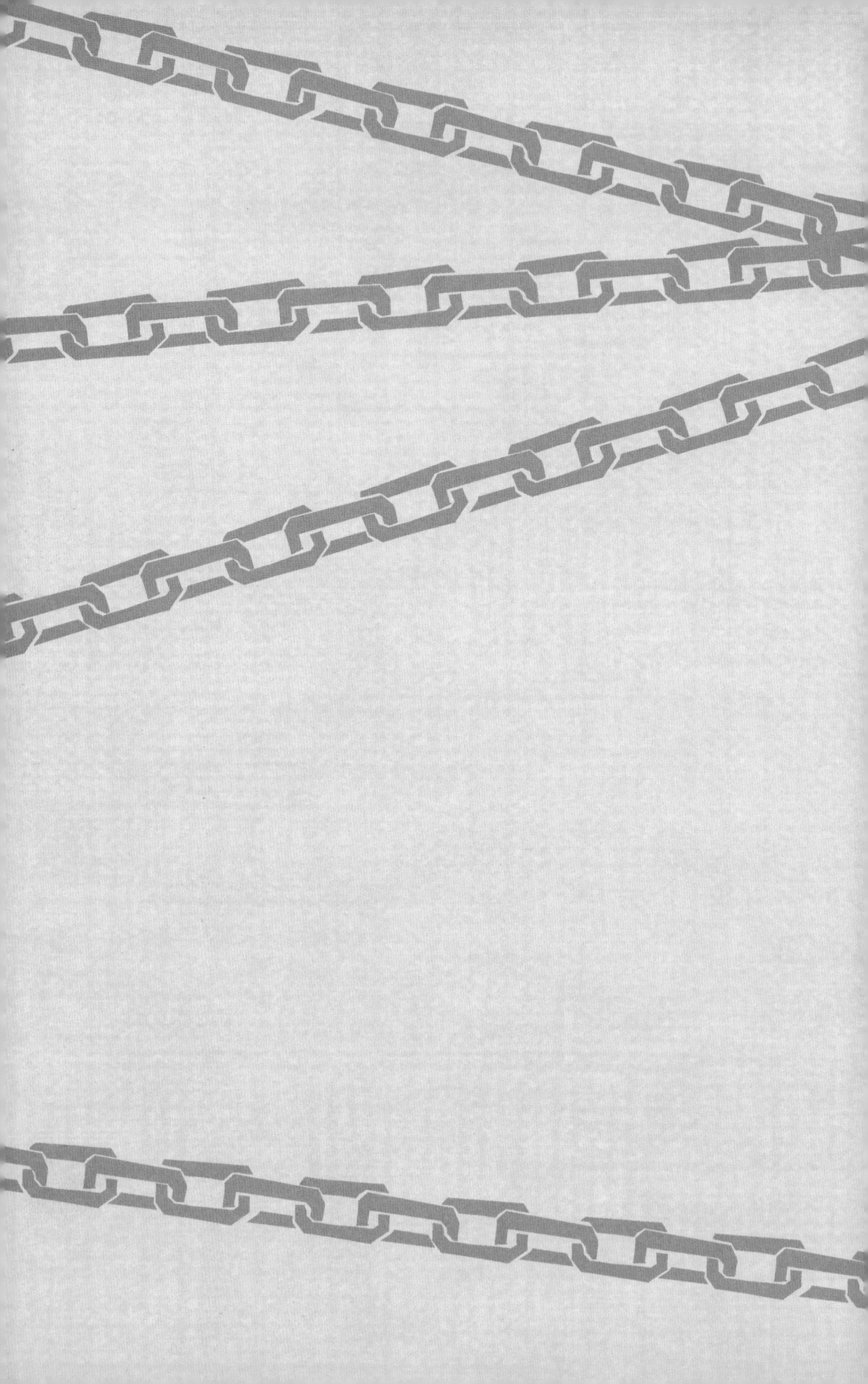

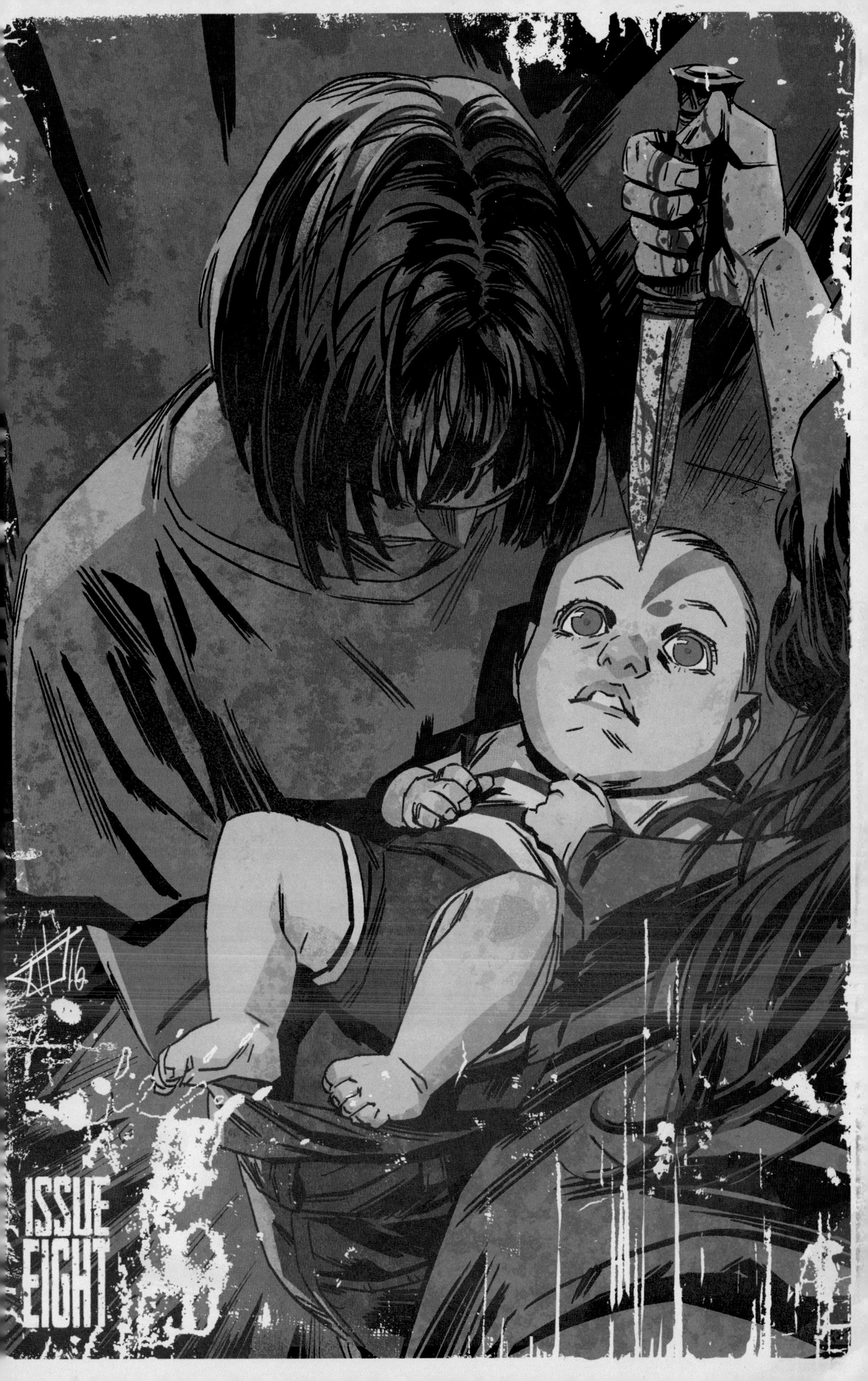
ISSUE
EIGHT

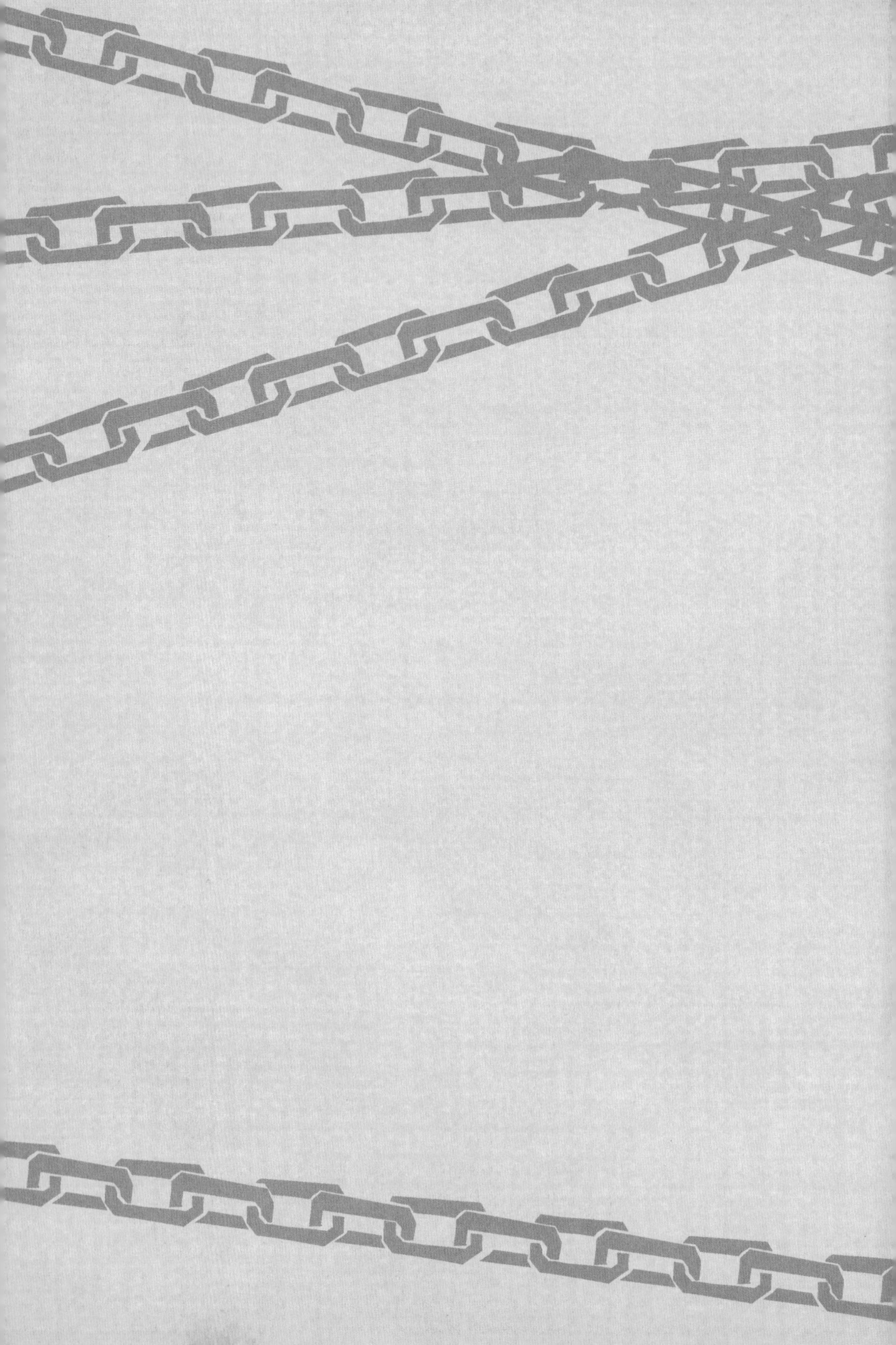

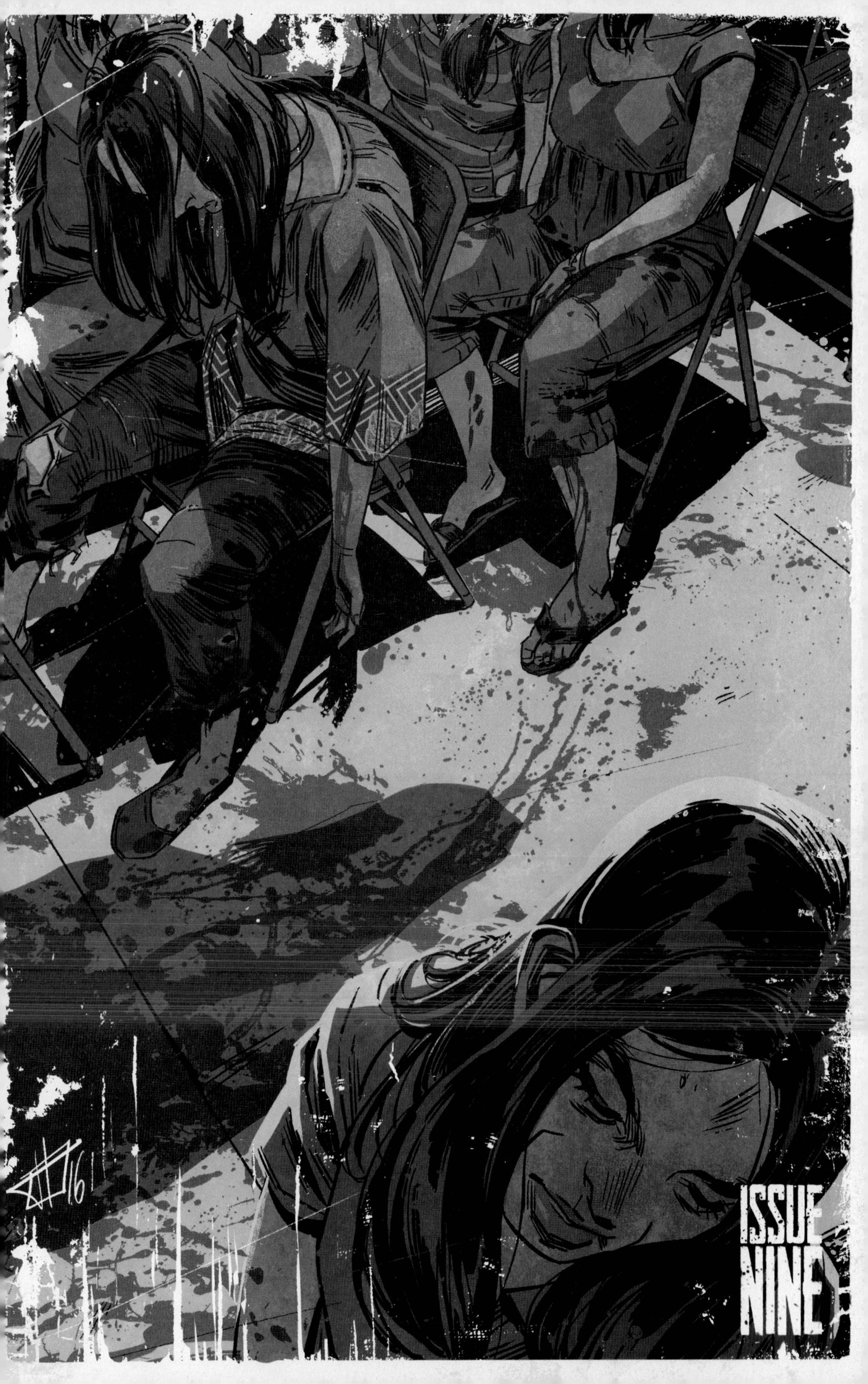
ISSUE
NINE

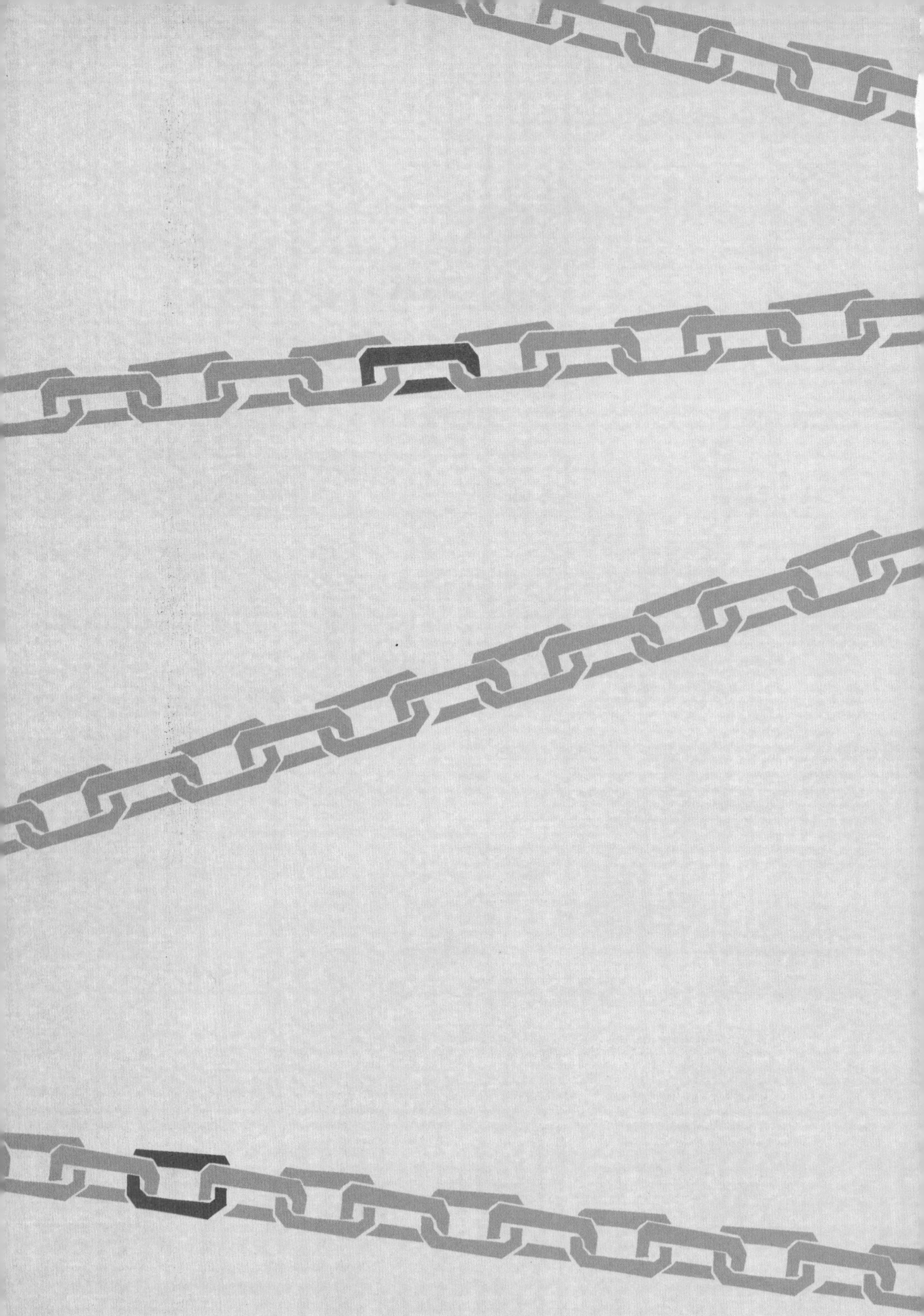

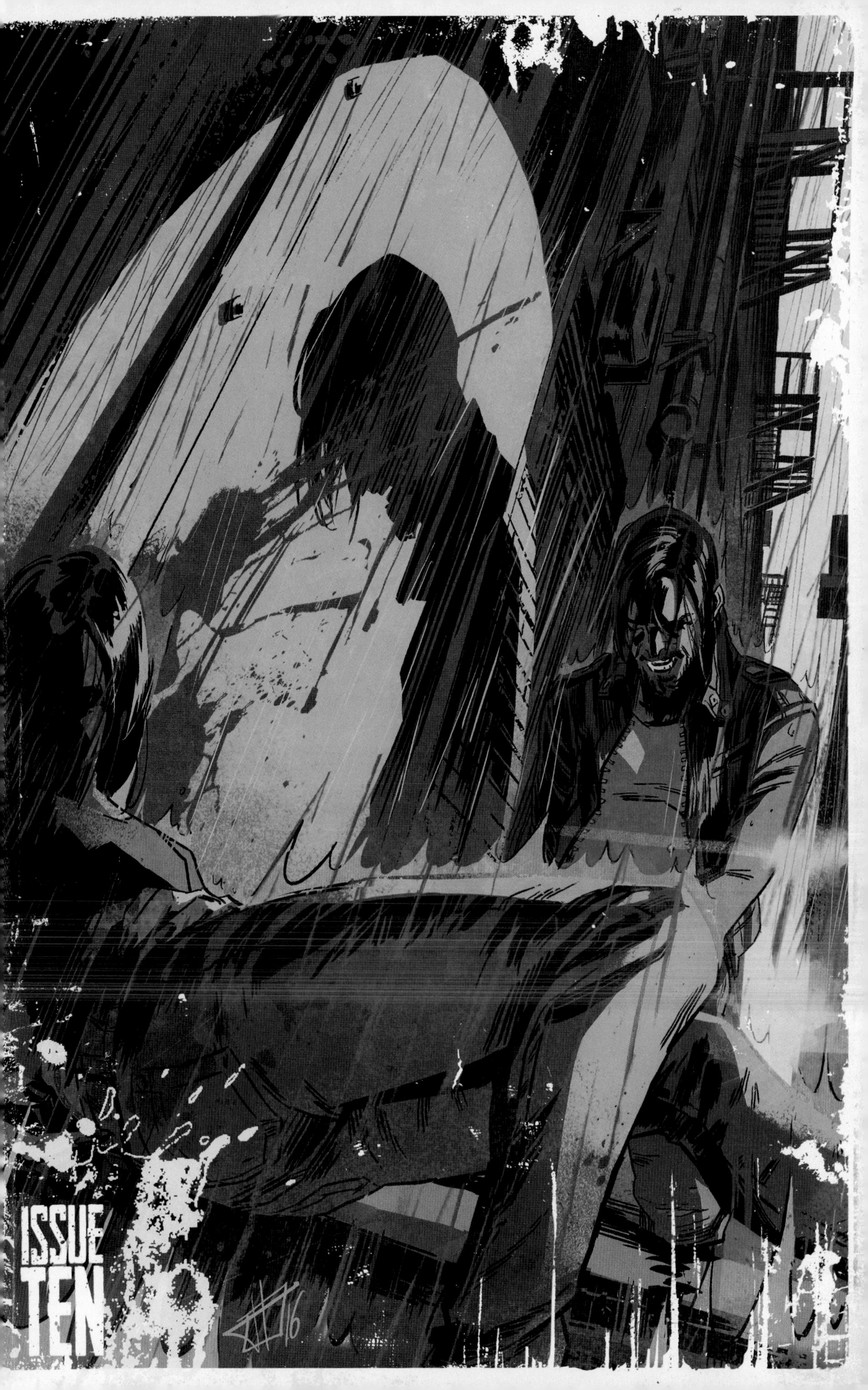
ISSUE
TEN

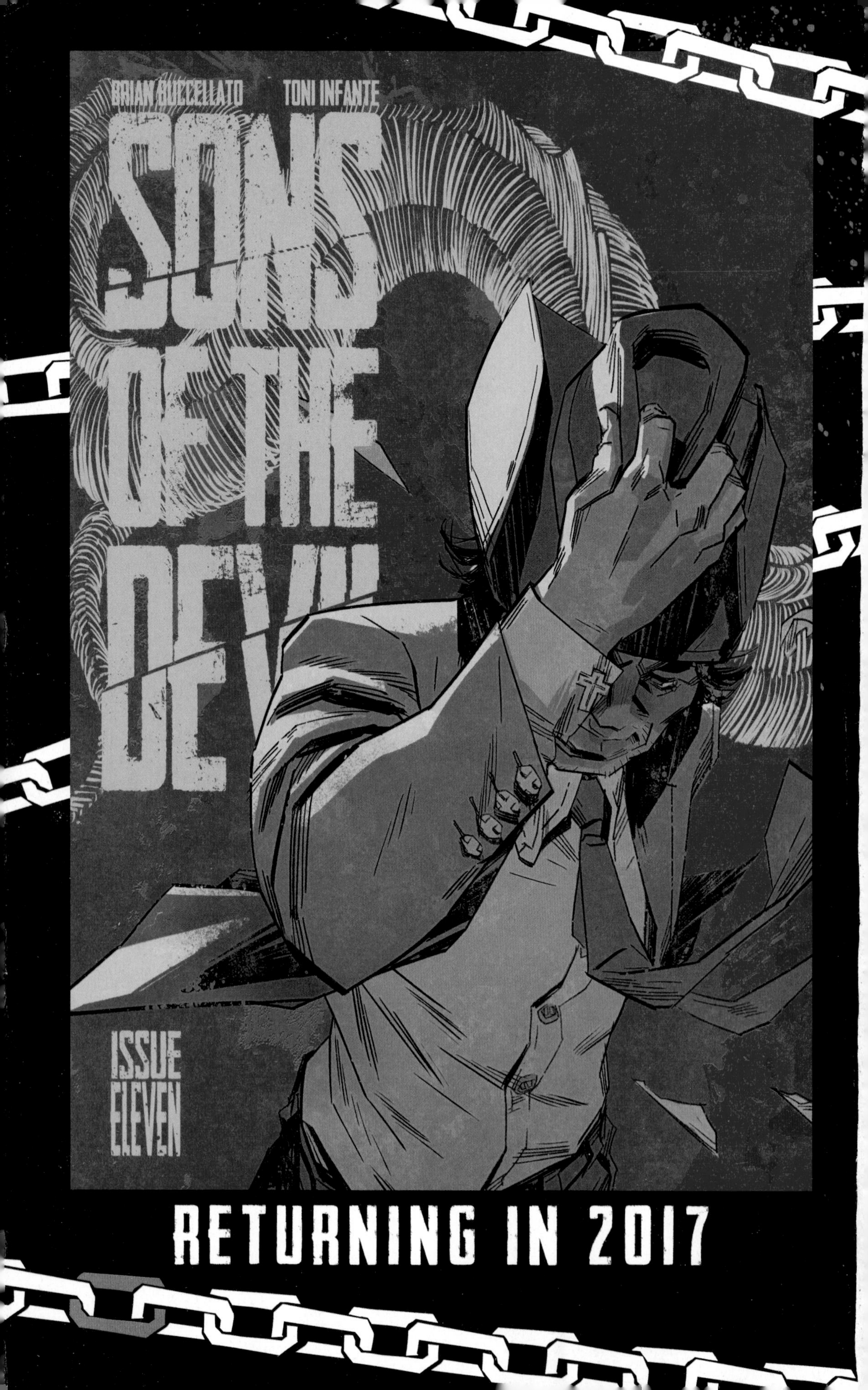
BRIAN BUCCELLATO
TONI INFANTE
SONS OF THE DEVIL
ISSUE ELEVEN
RETURNING IN 2017